"*The Baker's Man* is a charming recipe of magic, romance, friendship, and the importance of staying true to yourself."

—Heather Webber, *USA TODAY* bestselling author of *Midnight at the Blackbird Café*

"Combine four parts love, two parts excitement, a dash of humor, and a pinch of magic and you have Jennifer Moorman's delightful *The Baker's Man*. Moorman's sweet, heartfelt confection will please anyone looking for a charming, witty, utterly delectable read!"

—Lauren K. Denton, *USA TODAY* bestselling author of *The Hideaway* and *A Place to Land*

"In the world of magical realism, Jennifer Moorman is an important new voice. She is a sensitive, engaging, quirky, and soulful storyteller. Her characters speak their truths only to inspire us, the reader, to embrace and respect our own true gifts. As a lifelong fan of Alice Hoffman, I am adding Jennifer to a short list of writers who can carry the torch forward to a new generation."

—Jane Ubell-Meyer, *Founder of Bedside Reading*

"*The Necessity of Lavender Tea* is a sweet, magical coming-of-age tale about the best and hardest parts of love and friendship and family."

—Amy Impellizzeri, *Award-winning Author of Lemongrass Hope and I Know How This Ends*

A SLICE OF COURAGE QUICHE

A SLICE OF COURAGE QUICHE

A NOVEL

JENNIFER MOORMAN

Full Moon Press

A Slice of Courage Quiche

Published by Full Moon Press.

Epigraph courtesy of John O'Donohue, *To Bless the Space Between Us* (New York: Doubleday, 2008), 35.

Quote on page 290 courtesy of Sir Arthur Conan Doyle, "His Last Bow: An Epilogue of Sherlock Holmes" in *His Last Bow: Some Later Reminiscences of Sherlock Holmes* (Project Gutenberg, 2000), 23, eBook.

Quote on page 304 courtesy of Robert Burns, "To a Mouse on Turning Her Up in Her Nest with the Plough, November, 1785," in *Poems and Songs of Robert Burns* (Project Gutenberg, 2005), 1279, eBook.

Library of Congress Cataloging-in-Publication Data is on file.

ISBN 978-1-7347395-0-3 (paperback) | ISBN 978-1-7347395-3-4 (eBook)

Printed in the United States of America

23 24 25 26 27 FMP 5 4 3 2 1

To you who have held on to a dream even when others didn't understand, even when they said it couldn't be done, and still you persevered, you beautiful, brave soul

Blessed be the longing that brought you here
And quickens your soul with wonder.

May you have the courage to listen to the voice of desire
That disturbs you when you have settled for something safe.

May you have the wisdom to enter generously into your own unease

To discover the new direction your longing wants you to take.

—John O'Donohue

CHAPTER 1

WAFFLES AND CANE SYRUP

EVERY RESIDENT IN MYSTIC WATER, GEORGIA, SUFFERED beneath a relentless humidity uncommon for an April spring. Townsfolk complained and decided it must be July. Even the post office snatched three months off the wall calendar, swearing the town had somehow leaped into the blazing melt of summer.

Air-conditioning units shuddered and spluttered, ice melted in freezers, and parents dressed their children in snorkels and goggles, sending them off to school looking like lost travelers, saying the air was more water than oxygen.

Young's General Store sold out of handheld fans, even the atrocious psychedelic ones that people swore they wouldn't be caught dead using. Ladies flapped their fans so wildly to get relief that dogwood blooms ripped from their branches, and Mystic Water looked like a town trapped in a snow globe full of swirling white petals.

People started praying for rain just to ease the swelter. The air was so wet that mold grew on moving car tires. The books in Mystic Water's library swelled on their shelves and dropped like mayflies, littering the hallways and spilling down the stairs. Little Johnny Stone nearly broke his leg trying to kick down the elementary school's flagpole. He said he wanted to poke a hole in the sky to let out the water.

Within a week, townsfolk began boycotting clothing. They didn't want to go outside in anything more than a bathing suit, which made for awkward grocery-store conversations. Nobody knew exactly where to look when Ned Lincoln wore his Speedo to the council meeting. Two days later, the sky burst open like a slit in a water balloon. Rain fell in fast gray sheets, and the storm didn't stop for twenty-six hours, forty-four minutes, and two seconds.

Sunday mornings were Tessa Andrews's favorite. She drank mocha-flavored instant coffee and devoured a cheesy romance novel in bed until her stomach growled. Then she pulled on her most comfortable clothes and drove across the bridge to Scrambled, Mystic Water's diner serving breakfast from five in the morning until three in the afternoon. Nothing bad ever happened to Tessa on Sunday mornings. Not until the Sunday morning the rain stopped.

Tessa woke to a chorus of ducks quacking and a persistent bullfrog croaking out a bass line. *Why do they sound so loud?* she wondered. She opened her eyes and stared into the two shiny black eyes of a portly, knobby bullfrog sitting beside her on the bed. Its wide mouth seemed to be grinning at her. It opened its gaping maw and croaked a good morning. Tessa inhaled so sharply that all the air in the room funneled toward her, bringing the bullfrog so close that she could smell its pond-water breath. She screamed, sat up like someone who'd been jolted by lightning, and jerked the covers toward her chin. The sudden tautness of the duvet launched the bullfrog into the air as though it had been bounced from a trampoline. It sailed through the spinning blades of the ceiling fan, croaking a question, and landed with a splash into the water surrounding her bed.

Tessa's eyes widened like chocolate malt balls. At least two feet of muddy water swirled in from the hallway and into her bedroom, soaking the edges of her once-white duvet, now spotted with pond scum. A family of colorful wood ducks circled around the bedroom, trying to find ways onto the dry land of her bed. For an entire minute, all Tessa could do was stare. A bottle of lotion floated past as though it were a pink rose-scented boat, carrying three ladybug passengers on a voyage. Waterlogged daisies in an overturned vase drifted into a wall, one red flip-flop bobbed out her bedroom door, and the SOLO cup she'd used as a wine glass the night before rocked back and forth like a buoy.

Shock held her immobile for a few seconds, and then she flipped back the covers. Her beautiful condo was drowning. She tested the water with a big toe. It was the same temperature as Jordan Pond in the summer. Tessa inhaled a deep breath, gathering her courage. Then she slipped off the bed into the murk. The wave created by her movements caused two gray tennis shoes to surf out of her closet and crash into her legs.

She waded through the water, picking up sopping-wet items and cradling them in her arms as she moved down the short hallway into the combination living room, dining room, and kitchen. The front door was a victim of the rising water. The door had bulged and cracked away from its frame, allowing gallons of water to fill her home. The coffee table knocked into her knee as it floated in the living room. She glanced down and saw that her cell phone and notebook were still on the table. She'd missed fifteen calls. Tessa unloaded the wet items in her arms onto the floating table and grabbed her phone. She scrolled through the missed calls from clients, her mama, and Lily Connelly, her best friend.

Tessa dialed Lily's number. Before she could say a word, Lily launched into a conversation. "Where have you been?" Lily demanded. "I've been calling for hours. Jakob told me he saw on the seven o'clock morning news that Jordan Pond rose ten feet overnight and that all of Oak Bend is flooded. And I asked him, 'Why does Oak Bend sound so familiar?' You know how distracted I've been lately, and he said, 'Doesn't Tessa live in Oak Bend right off the pond?' And I freaked out. I've been calling and calling—"

Tessa released a pitiful sob. She yanked open her front door the rest of the way and more water flowed in. She couldn't distinguish Jordan Pond from her front porch or front yard or even fifty yards in any direction. She was now living in the pond. Something scaly and quick flitted past her bare leg, and she screamed into the phone, dancing around like a drunken ballerina.

Lily shouted, "Tessa! What is going on?"

Tessa pressed herself against the nearest wall and stared at the murky water. She blubbered, "There are ducks in my bedroom. I slept with a bullfrog."

"You slept with who? Don't tell me you let Petey sweet talk you into staying over last night. You know he's totally wrong for you. Weren't you just telling me that he bored you to death? Those were your exact words. 'He bores me to death, Lily. I fell asleep the other day during a conversation—'"

"Lily!" Tessa said. "My condo . . . it's under water."

"Are you serious?" Lily asked.

Tessa nodded even though she knew Lily couldn't see her head bobbing or the tears rolling down her cheeks. "I'm standing in the living room in my pajamas, and I think there are fish in the kitchen. You remember in the sixth grade when Bobby Fletcher told everybody there were gators living in Jordan Pond? You think he was lying, don't you?" She felt a full-blown panic attack building inside her, and she struggled to maintain control of it.

"Tessa, you hold on, okay? I'll be right there."

By the time Tessa heard Lily's voice calling out to her, she had packed a couple of small bags with clothes and miscellaneous personal items she didn't want to leave unattended in her wrecked condo. She had also changed into a pair of shorts and a gray Eeyore T-shirt. When Tessa sloshed toward the front door, she saw Lily sitting in a rowboat wearing a bright-orange life jacket that clashed horribly with the pale-pink shirt she wore. Her long, curly blond hair was pulled into a loose bun on the top of her head. A white-haired older man sat at the stern. The rowboat floated outside her condo where there used to be a sidewalk and the azaleas she'd planted. She thought, *Don't park there. You'll*

kill the bushes. Which were drowning at least five feet under the water. A laughing sob bubbled up her throat.

She and Lily locked eyes, and her bottom lip trembled. Lily reached out to her. "Be careful." Lily took the bags from Tessa. "We've seen all sorts of debris floating on top of the water. There's no telling what's underneath."

Underneath? Like my condo, my car, my life.

The man handed Tessa a life jacket and said, "I know it's not that deep here, but it's a lot deeper in other places. Better safe than sorry."

Tessa nodded, slipped the jacket that smelled like last year's mildew over her head, and secured it around her chest and waist. He motioned for her to approach him at the rear of the boat, and while keeping the weight in the boat balanced, he pulled Tessa over the stern.

Tessa slid into the boat like an uncoordinated baby seal, belly first with arms trapped beneath her body weight. She flopped onto her back and stared up at the man with his head haloed by white marshmallow clouds drifting across a faded blue sky.

"Thank you," she said as he pulled her into a sitting position. She crawled over a bench seat toward Lily and sat. Then she exhaled, trying hard not to start crying again. She tugged off her pink rain boots and dangled them over the side of the boat as water poured out. Then she wrangled them back on her wet feet.

"This is Harold Spencer," Lily said. "He's one of the men who volunteered to help those who are stranded today." Lily lifted her oar and paddled in rhythm with Harold.

Tessa hugged her arms around her middle even though the rising sun warmed her cheeks. Soggy air clung to her skin like heated syrup. "How's the rest of town? Are there a lot of people who need help?"

"Yes, ma'am," Harold said. "Most of the people in the low-lying areas are either under a good bit of water or the roads around them are flooded. Anybody stuck in a flooded home has been pulled out now, though. The other men have motorboats much faster than Bessie here," he said, patting the edge of the rowboat. "And they picked up people a lot quicker. Mrs. Connelly here flagged me down as my grandson Adam and I were rowing Mrs. Jolene Evans to her niece Bonni on Walnut Street. Adam stayed behind to make sure she got there safely."

Tessa nodded. "That's nice of y'all." She looked at Lily. "I haven't called Mama yet. You think she's having a conniption about now?"

"I called her. She *was* having a conniption and wanted to know why you didn't call her first. I told her it's because Jakob and I live closer."

"Did she buy that?" Tessa felt too frayed at the edges to try and soothe her mama's worries effectively.

"Sure," Lily said. "She was just relieved you were okay. She'd already talked to your neighbor, John somebody, a little bit ago, and he said the whole bottom floor of the building was under water. She didn't know why you didn't call anyone sooner. What took you so long?"

Tessa stared at an armada of clear plastic bowls with blue lids floating past. A spring wreath decorated with pastel-colored plastic eggs and tied with a soggy blue ribbon weaved in and out of the current that pulled everything downhill, back toward the epicenter of the pond. "I went to bed late." Leaning over she whispered, "After two glasses of wine." Lily nodded her understanding. "Thanks for coming to get me." She swiped at tears, feeling the puffiness of her cheeks. "Where am I going to live?"

"Hey now," Lily said, pausing in her rowing and sliding closer to Tessa. She looped her arm around Tessa's shoulders. "It'll dry up, and we'll get in and assess the damage. Then we'll see if we can fix it. You can stay with us if you can tolerate a two-year-old holy terror, and you know your mama will take you in." Lily squeezed Tessa's shoulder. "It's not as bad as it seems right now."

"It seems awful," Tessa said. A toothbrush sailed past on miniature rapids.

"Wanna grab breakfast at the diner? Isn't that your usual routine?" Lily asked.

"Is it even open?" Tessa tucked her short brown hair behind her ears.

"It is. I drove past it on my way to you. Downtown is dry. How about a huge stack of waffles smothered in cane syrup?"

"You think they'll let me eat inside? I smell like a river rat."

"You've smelled worse. Remember when you were on that boiled cabbage kick? Dang, you reeked for days." Lily nudged her elbow into Tessa's side.

Tessa couldn't help but chuckle. She *had* stunk. Nobody liked the smell of cabbage sweating out of the pores, not even the one sweating. "I think I might need biscuits and gravy too. For comfort, you know."

Lily grinned and lifted her oar. "Mr. Spencer, will you please row two damsels in distress who are in desperate need of Southern cooking toward downtown? We would be much obliged for your kindness," she said, laying her Southern accent on thick.

Mr. Spencer chuckled as he smiled and changed directions, pointing the bow toward Scrambled.

CHAPTER 2

HOMESTYLE BISCUITS AND COMFORT GRAVY

Tessa thanked Mr. Spencer again as she climbed out of his boat onto dry land, which was still five blocks from downtown. She slung her purse and a bag over her shoulder while Lily grabbed Tessa's other bags, and they walked the remaining way to Scrambled. People milled about everywhere, emerging from shops and fluttering around street corners like butterflies released from cages. Kids, unable to absorb the immensity of a disaster the way adults did, leaped into water puddles hugging the curbs.

For a moment Tessa wished she could slip back in time and join them in their carefree existence. Their giggles traveled up the sidewalks and pressed against her chest, warming her, comforting her in a way that made a voice in her head say, *It's all going to be okay.* Tessa adjusted the bag on her shoulder and exhaled. Sunshine peeked around billowy clouds. A bluebird swooped down, chirping madly, as if calling to his family and telling them the worst had passed. Tessa wondered, *Had it? Had the worst passed?*

As they approached the diner, Tessa looked up at the familiar sign bolted to the new building—two cartoonish eggs sat in a brilliant-blue bowl with the word *Scrambled* arcing over them. For more than fifty years, another building, Bea's Bakery, had stood in its place. Tessa felt the familiar ache of loss, followed by a longing for pastries and chocolates that could soothe her worries. In a freak fire, the bakery had burned to the ground two and a half years ago, nearly suffocating her, Lily, and their best friend and owner of Bea's Bakery, Anna O'Brien. Their lives had been saved but not the bakery or the building.

Anna had rebuilt a structure on the lot, but she had moved her bakery and taken her sweets to Wildehaven Beach, Georgia, a seaside town less than two hours away on the Atlantic Ocean. Anna sold the new building, housing the diner and the apartment above it, to Harry and Cecilia Borelli. Scrambled didn't replace what the town of Mystic Water lost in the fire, but it soothed the townsfolk in a new way, wrapping the people in the toasty comfort of biscuits and gravy or folding confidence into basil, goat cheese, and tomato omelets.

Scrambled was nestled in between the brick building of Lily's clothing boutique and the hardware store with its window decal peeling at the edges. A Radio Flyer red wagon, holding a teddy bear wearing a hard hat, was parked in the window.

A sodden garden smeared dirt across the diner's front patio, and the garden trailing along the side of the building looked as though angry fists had pummeled the earth. Many of the plantings slid from their positions or lay beaten against the saturated soil.

Before Tessa even reached the door, she could see and hear the crowd of people in the diner. Many looked just like her—wide-eyed, lost, and seeking relief.

Lily opened the door and ushered Tessa inside. The air inside reminded Tessa of the Sunday mornings of her childhood. She recalled images of her family crammed into the breakfast nook while they dragged pancakes through syrup. Tessa imagined browned link sausages lined up on paper towels and her mama scolding her daddy when he ate one after another without stopping, not even to breathe. But this morning, foreign smells infiltrated the room. The stink of exhaustion, floodwater, and rubber boots mingled with the aromas of coffee and bacon.

Sapphire-blue vinyl booths lined the walls, and tables holding two or four chairs were scattered across the middle of the room. Colorful canvases, created by a local artist, decorated the walls. Small white placards hung beneath the artwork and displayed the artist's name and her prices. Tessa's pink rain boots squeaked against the tile floor as she and Lily weaved their way through the crowded room to an empty booth. Within a minute the usual waitress, Laney Tucker, strolled over. Her wavy strawberry-blond hair was a mess of curls pulled back from her face in a loose ponytail. She dropped two laminated menus on the table.

"Welcome to the madhouse," Laney said. "You girls okay?" She gave Lily and Tessa a once-over. "From the looks of *you*, I'd say no," she said to Tessa.

"My condo is under water. Lily rescued me in a rowboat," Tessa said, trying to stop her bottom lip from quivering.

"Oh, sweetie, I'm sorry. You've got the same story as more than half of the people sitting in here right now. Most are sure their homes are ruined." Laney shook her head and sighed. "You got a place to go?" Laney's honey-brown eyes were full of compassion.

"Mama's or Lily's," Tessa said as she cleared her throat, dislodging the sorrow trapped there.

"Well, I don't have much, but you let me know if you need anything. We have a twin bed in Bert's room if you need to use it. He'd love to have company to build new block cities with," she said with a grin. "He would think he'd won the jackpot having an assistant builder."

"Thanks, Laney. I appreciate the offer."

Laney reached over and gave Tessa's hand a squeeze. "Drinks are on the house today. The kitchen is about fifteen minutes behind schedule, as you can imagine. Want your usual?"

"We're going all out today, Laney," Lily said. "Bring us two orders of waffles with heaps of butter and a stack of bacon and two orders of biscuits with extra gravy, please. And probably a wheelbarrow to roll us outta here when we're done."

"And two pairs of sweatpants?" Laney asked with a smile.

Lily chuckled and said, "I like the way you think."

Tessa dragged her last piece of biscuit round and round her plate like a buttermilk race car zipping through gravy. She popped it into her mouth as she eyed the half-eaten waffle on the plate in the middle of the table. She pointed at it with her fork.

"If I eat the rest of that, I will probably explode."

"I actually thought you might explode two biscuits ago," Lily said. "Especially after that fourth cup of coffee, which, by the way, has given you an eye twitch."

Tessa reached up and rubbed her left eye just as her cell phone began to ring. She dug her hand into her purse, grabbing a pack of tissues, a tube of ChapStick, and a notebook before locating her cell. "It's Mama," she sighed as she answered the call. "Hey—"

"Tessa Marie Andrews, I have been calling you *for hours*. Are you okay?"

"Yes, ma'am, I'm alive—"

"Are you still at the condo?" her mama interrupted. "Lily called to tell me you were okay. Thank goodness someone had the good sense to tell me *something*. I've been pacing around here, making your dad crazy, haven't I, Clayton?"

Tessa heard her daddy's rumbly voice in the background. "Mama, I'm okay . . . I think. But we're not at the condo anymore. I'm at Scrambled with Lily—"

"We've heard horror stories about the condition of the homes around Jordan Pond. How's the condo? Is it okay?"

"No, ma'am." She exhaled. "The place is a disaster."

Tessa described the state of her flooded condo and choked down more tears. Somehow talking to her mama made her feel vulnerable and childlike. By the end of the conversation, she dabbed at her eyes with a napkin. When Tessa ended the call, she asked Lily, "Do you mind dropping me off at their house?"

Before Lily could answer, Tessa's phone rang again. This time it was their best friend, Anna, calling from Wildehaven Beach. Anna had just seen the news about Jordan Pond, and knowing Tessa lived on the water, she wanted to know if she and Eli needed to come to Mystic Water to help. Tessa didn't know exactly what she needed at the moment—other than a good cry—but she promised Anna she'd call back when she was settled in at her parents' house. Tessa dropped the phone back into her purse.

She pulled out her notebook. These days Tessa kept meticulously numbered lists to ensure she didn't make bad decisions. The lists kept her life under control, because in the past, Tessa's impulsive decisions resulted in more heartache than she wanted to admit. Two and a half years ago, after falling—even briefly—for Anna's now boyfriend and being one of the main catalysts that caused Bea's Bakery to burn down, Tessa no longer trusted her own judgment. When making big decisions—or any decisions these days—Tessa preferred to have at least three people agree on a correct course of action before she took it.

Tessa started a new page with the heading *What should I do?* Then she wrote the numbers one through five down the left side of the page. She looked up at Lily. "What should I do?"

"Don't eat that waffle. I just washed my hair, and I don't want you exploding all over me."

Tessa groaned, but beside the number one she wrote, *Don't finish waffle.*

Cecilia Borelli walked over to the table and motioned for Lily to scoot over. In her late fifties, Cecilia still wore her black hair in a wavy, shoulder-length style. She and her husband, Harry, had moved to Mystic Water two years ago from New Jersey to escape the brutal winters. But they couldn't decide where to start their new life, and Cecilia swore she and Harry had blindfolded themselves and thrown a dart at a map on the wall. The green dart had lodged itself into Mystic Water, Georgia. The two of them had been a great fit right away. With Cecilia's business acumen and baking skills combined with Harry's cooking talents, Scrambled had prospered and become a staple in Mystic Water.

True to her Italian American upbringing, Cecilia never let anyone leave without ample amounts of food and hugs. She placed a plastic-wrapped quiche on the table. Then she reached over and patted Tessa's hand. "Laney told me your place is flooded. Where are you going to stay?"

"My parents' house."

Cecilia frowned. "You're too old to move back in with your parents. My boys were out at eighteen."

"I don't plan to move home permanently," Tessa said, feeling defensive. It wasn't as though she was returning home because she'd run out of money. "As soon as the water recedes, I'm going to see what can be repaired at the condo."

"People are saying it's going to take a couple of weeks before proper repairs can be made to the places that are salvageable," Cecilia said. "And I heard the houses around Jordan Pond are anything *but* salvageable." She pushed the quiche toward Tessa and dropped a pair of keys on the table. She pointed toward the ceiling. "Why don't you move into the apartment upstairs, free of charge. It's completely furnished, and no one is using it. It's tough to move back in with your parents. Believe me, I know. After Paul was born, Harry and I moved in with his mother for a few months, and we nearly killed each other—his mother and me. It's not easy going home after you've been out on your own."

Tessa glanced at the apartment keys, and her defenses relaxed. "Oh, Mrs. Borelli, that's very generous, but I couldn't impose."

"If I offer it, it's not imposing. Take it. It's sitting empty."

Tessa looked at Lily for support. Lily shrugged.

"I appreciate it, but I'll be fine at my folks' place."

Cecilia's dark eyebrows rose on her forehead. "There are many degrees of *fine*. Let me know if you change your mind. Take this quiche with you. It's basil and Italian sausage with a butter crust."

"Thank you. I love this one," Tessa said, curling her hands gently around the quiche.

"I know you do," Cecilia said. She tapped her burgundy fingernails on the table in a wave of clicks. Then she looked at Lily. "How's that beautiful baby girl?"

Lily smiled. "A two-and-a-half-year-old princess with a wild streak."

Cecilia laughed. "She's spirited all right. Bring her by to see me soon. Tell her I'll make her cake-batter pancakes."

Lily clicked her tongue. "You spoil her."

"I hope so." Cecilia glanced toward the kitchen. "Back to work for me. Tessa, tell your mother I said hello." She pocketed the apartment keys.

"Yes, ma'am." Tessa watched Cecilia walk away, and once she was safely tucked into the kitchen, Tessa asked, "Would you take the offer?"

"Do you really want to live with your parents for weeks?"

Tessa exhaled. "No, but . . . maybe repairs to my condo won't take as long as they usually do in disaster situations."

"Tessa, I love you, and I'm going to be honest with you."

Tessa slumped against the booth. "When are you ever not?"

"You swam out of your front door this morning. You told your mama it was ruined. Your car is currently under water up to the roof. It's going to be a while before you can put your life back in order."

Beside the number two in her notebook, Tessa scribbled,

Move home for weeks? Then she drew a frowny face.

Lily dropped enough money on the table to pay for the bill and to leave a generous tip for Laney, who had been moving around the diner nonstop since they'd arrived. She hefted Tessa's bags from the seat. Tessa closed her notebook and dropped it into her purse. She slid out of the booth and glanced toward the ceiling, wondering what it would be like to live above a diner.

"You think the apartment perpetually smells like bacon grease?" Tessa asked.

"Let's hope for biscuits," Lily said with a smile. "But if not, at least the carnivores in town would be uncontrollably attracted to your bacon scent." Lily laughed when Tessa glared at her.

"Are you talking about men or dogs?" Tessa grumbled.

Lily snickered. "Based on your track record, is there a difference?"

Tessa snorted and followed Lily out of the diner.

CHAPTER 3

GOOD-FOR-YOU GARDEN OMELET

AFTER TOSSING AND TURNING MOST OF THE NIGHT, TESSA WOKE before the sun rose. She lay in her childhood twin bed, one foot sticking out from beneath the fluffy comforter stitched with pink roses. She stared at the ceiling fan going round and round. Anxiety gained momentum inside her like a steam locomotive chuffing and increasing its power. She thought of her wrecked condo, of the furniture she'd so carefully chosen, of the stench of pond water tainting everything.

She rolled out of bed and padded into the hallway of her parents' ranch-style home. Her daddy's snores growled, signaling she had a few more minutes of time alone. Tessa searched through one of the bags she'd dragged from her condo and pulled out a water-stained romance novel. The swooning, buxom brunette clutched a muscled Native American as though she would die without him. *Maybe her condo flooded too*, Tessa thought. She could go for some clutching herself.

She started a pot of Maxwell House coffee that she hoped wouldn't wake her mama too soon and curled onto the sun-porch's patchwork couch. She lazily flipped through the book until she found one of the good parts. She tried to read and relax her mind, but not even the desperate love and breathy sighs held her focus. Nothing pulled her mind away from chiseling at the same question over and over again: *What am I going to do?*

Tessa poured coffee into a handmade pottery mug detailed with swaths of lavender pigment and a kiln-fired glossy finish. She stared out the kitchen window and allowed herself a few minutes to feel an aching sense of loss over losing her condo. By the time she'd finished her second cup, her mama was awake, and Tessa made sure the tears were gone.

"You're making a plan, aren't you?" her mama, Carolyn, asked from the kitchen table, where she sat with a mug of steaming coffee and the lifestyle section of the *Mystic Water Gazette.*

Tessa opened the dishwasher and put her mug on the top rack. "The plan for today is not to have a panic attack."

"I'm serious," Carolyn said. "You need to know what you're going to do. Have you called the man who runs the homeowners' association for your building yet? Have you filed a claim with insurance for the condo and your car?"

"Mama, it's six thirty in the morning," she said. "I'll call the HOA guy at a decent hour, and I'll contact the insurance company as soon as I get to work. Speaking of working, I should probably get going. The office is probably flooded with calls." Then she snorted a sad laugh. "Flooded. Pun *not* intended."

Carolyn side-eyed her and stirred more sugar into her coffee. "Now, don't mope around all day feeling sorry for yourself. Lots of people are in worse states than you."

Tessa huffed. "I don't have a car or a place to live."

"You have your health."

"Not my *mental* health," Tessa mumbled.

"Don't sass me."

Tessa's shoulders sagged as she exhaled. "I know you're right. It could be worse, and I'm grateful for a place to stay."

"Don't forget to take your things with you."

Tessa blinked at her mama. "What do you mean?"

"You know your dad and I are leaving town. We've committed to house swap with that couple from Washington."

The words oozed like cold cane syrup through Tessa's brain. "Huh?"

"The house swap," Carolyn said, enunciating each word clearly. "We won't be back until July."

Brakes squealed in Tessa's head. "Hold up. July? It's April. You can't leave. I don't have a place to live. What am I gonna do?" She swayed on her feet.

"First, you're gonna calm down. Come over here and sit before you fall and crack your head on the tiles."

Tessa slumped into a chair, dropping her head onto her folded arms. "Mama," she whined, her words echoing in the hollow cave created by her body and the table, "can I get *a little* sympathy?"

"A little, yes. But we've had this trip planned for months. We had no way of knowing the town would flood, and it's too late to change our plans. The renters know about the flood, but our house is just fine, and the town is already drying. They'll be here tomorrow afternoon. What about Mrs. Borelli's offer?"

Tessa lifted her head. She'd nearly forgotten. "I should take that?"

Carolyn sipped her coffee. "Do you have *another* plan?" When Tessa shook her head, her mama sighed. "Then, yes, but you need to work on what you're going to do next. You can't mooch off the Borellis indefinitely." Before Tessa could argue that she wasn't planning on *mooching* off anyone, Carolyn continued. "How will you get to work? You know you can borrow the Caddy."

Tessa cringed as she thought about driving the 1979 orange Cadillac Eldorado again. Wasn't it bad enough that she'd had to drive it all through high school while people called it "the Great Pumpkin"? It reeked of headache-inducing, vanilla-scented car air freshener. The air conditioning didn't work, and it was nearly as long as a school bus.

During the hot summer months in Mystic Water, the cracked leather seats could cause second-degree burns on any exposed skin. Tessa remembered many afternoons when she'd climbed out of the car soaked in sweat, with her hair plastered to her neck in sticky strands. She still blamed the car for her lack of high school dates.

"Oh, don't look like you've eaten a sour grape," Carolyn scolded. "A car is a car, and right now, you don't have one."

Less than an hour later, Tessa borrowed the Great Pumpkin with a reluctance she hadn't felt since high school. But her mama was right. A hideous operational car was better than a sleek sunken one. She parked downtown in front of Andrews Real Estate, a company her mama started more than thirty years ago. She checked voice messages first. A slew of clients—buyers, sellers, and renters—inquired about the current state of Mystic Water after the worst flood the town had seen in at least sixty years. A few sellers wanted to know if their closings would still happen, others wanted to discuss property values, some renters were stranded with nowhere to go because their properties were underwater just like Tessa's, and the final message was from a cryptic out-of-towner who left her number and asked for a return call with no explanation. Tessa jotted her number on a sticky note before going through a mental list of whom she needed to call first, starting with her own insurance company to start filing claims for flood damage.

By early afternoon Tessa felt like she'd called nearly everyone in town, including the president of the HOA for her condo building, to ascertain accurate and up-to-date details on Mystic Water. She'd unfolded a map of Mystic Water on her desk and outlined the seriously affected areas with a blue highlighter. Her condo was contained within a blue boundary of devastation.

Staring at the map, self-pity surged through Tessa. Her grandma Mildred would have said this was a sign. "A sign of what?" Tessa would ask. She could almost hear her grandma's slow, gravelly voice replying, "A sign that your life is a garbage heap of mistakes and poor choices." Grandma Mildred hadn't been known for her encouraging pep talks. "Cantankerous" was a more accurate description.

Tessa called and updated her clients before finally dialing the number she'd scrawled on the sticky note. Trudy Steele, who had a voice as brittle as hundred-year-old parchment paper, announced her name instead of giving a proper hello. She explained that she had inherited a local home in Mystic Water; however, she lived across the country in San Jose and had no desire to keep the property.

As Tessa wrote down the address, her hand faltered. A bumblebee knocked against the office window three times before it flew away. "That's Honeysuckle Hollow," she said. "It's one of the oldest historical homes in Mystic Water." Mrs. Steele remained unimpressed. When she told Tessa her desired selling price, Tessa gasped. "The square footage alone demands more than that. You're basically giving it away at that price."

Mrs. Steele scoffed into the phone and said, "That house has never meant anything to me. I'd burn it down if that weren't illegal. There's probably nothing but cobwebs, termites, and ill will holding that place together. They can bulldoze it and turn it into a gas station for all I care. I overnighted the keys to your office today. You should have them tomorrow."

The phone burned against Tessa's ear, and she pulled it away from her face. Mrs. Steele's anger radiated like summer heat on asphalt, but Tessa felt indignant on behalf of the people who had made Honeysuckle Hollow their home for more than one hundred years.

She knew the last local owner, Dr. Matthias Hamilton, had died two years ago, and he'd been the third-generation owner. Dr. Hamilton hadn't lived in the house himself, but he'd rented it out for weddings and social events. Tessa had never understood why he hadn't wanted to live in his family's house, but he'd taken care of it just the same.

Dr. Hamilton had been a quiet, kind man. He treated the prize-winning damask roses in the front yard like children and gave cuttings to anyone who walked by. He dug a winding river through the backyard garden and filled it with koi, naming each fish after a famous fictional character. Tessa remembered a fat albino koi named Captain Ahab and a skinny golden koi named Dorian Gray that liked to stare at its reflection in the mirrored rocks lining the bottom of the riverbed. Even thinking of bulldozing over Honeysuckle Hollow's backyard made Tessa's chest constrict.

Tessa assured Mrs. Steele she would properly assess the house once she received the keys, and then she'd get back to her regarding the listing. It had been years since Tessa had seen the inside of Honeysuckle Hollow, but from driving by the property recently, she knew the front yard had fallen into disrepair in the last couple of years. The backyard would likely be overgrown, but burning down the historical home was ridiculous and cruel.

After replying to a few dozen emails, Tessa walked to Scrambled, which was up the block and around the corner from her office. There were a handful of afternoon diners, so Tessa settled into a two-top table by the front windows and ordered a garden omelet with a strawberry lemonade. All through the meal, Tessa's mind wandered between her condo drowning a couple of miles away and Honeysuckle Hollow sitting abandoned on Dogwood Lane. She'd attended a garden party there years ago when Dr. Hamilton was still alive. Her vague memory recalled the scent of rosemary, which was probably growing untamed in the backyard, infusing the air with its woodsy scent. She thought about blooms of lavender waving in the spring wind. Had the rainstorms flooded the backyard river? Were any koi still alive? She forked the last bit of tomato and basil into her mouth just as Cecilia bustled out of the kitchen.

"Changed your mind?" Cecilia asked. "Harry told me you called." She dropped a set of keys on the tabletop.

"I want to pay rent," Tessa said. "I wouldn't feel right living here for free."

"Don't be silly," Cecilia said. "It's a favor for one of my favorite customers. Go get settled in, and Harry and I will bring you food to stock your refrigerator. No arguments," she added when Tessa opened her mouth to object to more handouts.

"At least let me help you in some way," Tessa said. "Isn't there anything I can do to say thank you?"

Cecilia tapped a burgundy fingernail against her lips. "Help me tonight with the garden. The rain nearly destroyed my plants. I could use another pair of hands."

Tessa's mouth turned down. "I'm not sure that's a good idea. I kill plants."

"On purpose?"

"No." Tessa released a laugh. "They just don't seem to thrive in my care. And by *thrive*, I mean *live*."

Cecilia smiled. "You've never had a good teacher. My garden is hardy. It survived the storms, so I think it can handle you."

After grabbing her bags from the Great Pumpkin, Tessa hiked the stairs to the apartment above the diner and fished the keys out of her pocket. The apartment smelled like just-out-of-the-oven cinnamon rolls and sticky, sweet cream-cheese icing. Tessa inhaled deeply and dropped her bags beside the L-shaped tan couch. She spun in a complete circle on the walnut hardwood, scanning the living room and attached kitchen. Tessa had imagined the Borellis would have decorated the apartment to suit their more mature, traditional tastes, but the space was modern and trendy with a touch of masculinity.

The living room walls were painted in an earth tone resembling the color of the pages in an old paperback novel. Splashes of sage green complemented the neutral marble countertops and dark cabinets. A large map of the world pasted to a corkboard hung on one long wall. Tessa stepped toward it. Silver pushpins were scattered across the continents. She bounced her fingertips along their trail as though connecting the dots of someone's life, each silver circle a place visited by an unknown traveler. A red heart-shaped pushpin had been pressed into the spot marking Mystic Water, Georgia. A gemstone globe sat on a shelf of built-in bookshelves lined with classic novels and travel magazines. She glanced toward the bedroom.

Afternoon sunlight filtered through the gossamer curtains, dusting golden stripes across the ivory duvet. Tessa dropped her laptop bag on the bed. Dark walnut furniture anchored a soft wool rug to the polished hardwood. A framed photograph of Harry, Cecilia, and two handsome young men sat on the dresser. She lifted it and smoothed her thumb over the glass, thinking the men must be their sons, Paul and Eddie. Tessa could see the resemblance, and the oldest son, Paul, stared out at her with his blue eyes crinkling at the corners, as if he had a joke he couldn't wait to tell her. She felt a fluttering in her stomach and returned the photograph to its spot.

One of the few pairs of shoes that Tessa salvaged from her condo had been her ratty gray tennis shoes left over from her high school days. Her mama had insisted she throw them away years ago, but Tessa had kept them for no other reason except they reminded her of the day she'd sat on the bleachers during after-school football practice. She'd worn her new gray tennis shoes while pretending to take pictures for the school paper, but she was secretly photographing only Jeremiah Lee, the kicker.

During that particularly windy practice, a strong gust shoved the kicked ball out of its perfect line and rocketed it toward Tessa on the bleachers. Her face had been glued to the camera, so she hadn't seen the projectile heading for her. Jeremiah's football missile nailed her in the side of the head, knocking her backward off the bleacher. Tessa had been stunned, folded like a human taco between two rows, with her legs sticking into the air like cattails in a pond and her arms splayed at her sides. The camera bounced several feet away.

She blinked up to see Jeremiah leaning over her, asking if she was okay while he searched her face with his brown eyes. He clutched one lucky gray tennis shoe in his hand, reached for her opposite hand, and tugged her into an upright position. Then he sat down beside her, so close that she felt the heat radiating through his sweaty practice gear. Tessa remembered nodding and smiling and telling him she was fine, even though she had to reach up several times to make sure her head hadn't cracked in half. Jeremiah's relief showed in his smile, which showcased his slightly crooked bottom teeth and off-center grin. She'd fallen in love with that smile. Jeremiah chucked her in the shoulder with his fist and ran back to practice, cradling the football in his arm. It was the first time he noticed her, and she gave full credit to the new shoes.

Sometimes she still slipped them on and remembered a seventeen-year-old Jeremiah smiling down at her. In those day-dreams she pretended she hadn't been knocked goofy by his football and wasn't lying wedged between the bleachers. Instead, she imagined they were lying in the grass behind the football field, and Jeremiah was grinning at her like a boy in love.

Tessa blinked down at the worn-out shoes with fraying laces and thought maybe there was still a little bit of luck left in them. They'd survived the flood. As she rounded the corner of the building, heading toward the front door of the diner, she stopped beside a red geranium in a terracotta pot that had fallen from its perch. The cracked pot exposed the geranium's roots and spilled its dirt. The kelly-green leaves thumped against her shoe in the breeze. Tessa leaned down and scooped the dirt into a neater pile, covering the vulnerable roots. The soil tingled against her skin as she brushed the dirt from her fingers.

"Harry has gone to fetch a new pot for that one," Cecilia said. "He'll repot it before he preps for tomorrow morning's breakfast rush."

She handed Tessa a trowel and led her around the side of the building. Wind blew up the alley, rustling through basil leaves, stalks of rosemary, and tomato vines. Tessa closed her eyes and inhaled, breathing in the scent of an Italian pizzeria. The sight of the pummeled garden pulled a sigh from Cecilia. Some plants had fallen over, others had been beaten into the mud, and still others suffered broken stalks, scattering pieces of themselves across the alley.

Cecilia fisted her hands on her hips and shook her head. "Looks like a slush of mud pies and weeds. That storm uprooted more than half of my garden." She pointed at a tangle of green spear-shaped leaves with long tendrils wrapping themselves around one another in a complicated knot. "Start there with the mint. See if the buried pot is still intact. I can't have the mint taking over the garden, and believe me, it will if we're not careful. Mint is a traveling plant."

Tessa knelt and used her trowel to poke around in the dirt.

Every time her hands or arms struck the mint, the plant released the fresh scent of Christmas and hot tea into the air. She inhaled, and the clutter in her head began to clear. Soon Tessa heard metal striking stone. She scraped away the dirt until she saw the sienna-brown edges of the buried pot. Tessa slid her hand around the stone vessel, her fingers finding a crack that splintered through the pot. "Feels broken."

"Go ahead and dig it out," Cecilia said. "I think I have another pot around back."

Tessa worked on unearthing the mint pot, and when she was finished, she fetched the new container for Cecilia. Once the mint was repotted, Cecilia gave Tessa one task after another. They worked their way down the garden for nearly an hour. Tessa's worries and anxieties about her present situation lessened as she worked. For the first time in a couple of days, she felt the tension between her shoulder blades release a little. While Tessa patted the soil around a patch of thyme, Cecilia disrupted the stillness.

"Why did you choose to work in real estate?" Cecilia asked as she tucked dirt around the base of a rosemary bush.

Tessa pushed off her knees and balanced on her toes. She scooped a handful of soil with one hand and sprinkled it into her open palm, mimicking an hourglass counting time. The wet earth spread warmth from her fingers, up her arms, and into her chest. "It's what I knew. My mama put me to work young, doing odd jobs at the real estate office for her. Filing, answering the phone, sorting through the mail. I followed her everywhere, to houses, rentals, and plots of land, and I learned a lot. It seemed natural for me to keep doing it, even after college. I also enjoyed it."

"What did you study in college?" Cecilia asked.

"Business major," she said. "Pretty boring stuff. I did minor in architecture, though, because I've always been interested in it." A strong breeze, smelling of cloves, rushed down the alley and tangled Tessa's hair in her face. She spit strands of hair from her mouth and shoved it out of her eyes. "If I'd have known how much I'd love studying architecture, I might have majored in it instead. Maybe gone on to receive a master's degree."

Cecilia scraped her trowel through the dirt in an absent-minded way, making parallel lines in the earth. "Why didn't you?"

"Get a master's?" Tessa asked. "I guess I never had the drive needed to be an architect. I would have enjoyed learning more, but I love it here. I liked being at the office with Mama before she retired. I like helping people find their homes. It's a rewarding job, and real estate is what I know. It was a safe and sensible choice, coming home and taking over the family business."

"As if children ever do what is safe and sensible," Cecilia said with a small smile. "Children do what they want, regardless of what parents say."

The air swirled with bristling energy, and the soil beneath Tessa's hands warmed by degrees. She pulled her hands away from the earth. The plants around Cecilia shivered.

Tessa cleared her throat. "Like your sons?"

"Not Eddie. He's always been sensible and taken the safest route, even when he was a child. He calls me every week. We see him at holidays." Cecilia stood and brushed dirt from the knees of her gardening khakis.

"But not Paul?"

Cecilia exhaled a sigh, and basil leaves fluttered. "Paul never did anything the easy or sensible way. He has a master's degree, and what does he do with it? Nothing. He gives up a successful job so that he can travel all over the globe writing travel stories."

Tessa thought of the map in the apartment. "The pushpins on the map . . . those are where Paul has been?"

"Harry's doing," Cecilia said with a dismissive wave. "He's proud of his adventurer."

"And you're not?" Tessa stood and brushed her hands against her pants.

Cecilia shrugged and deadheaded a fennel flower. "It's not that I'm not proud. I worry. I'm his mother. Do you know what becomes of an old adventurer who travels the world alone, never settling down, never having a family?"

A dandelion pod released its feathery seeds into the windy air. A dozen mini puffs of escaping wishes danced around her before being swept down the alley. "He sits around telling great stories?"

"And who does he share these great stories with when he is all alone?" she asked. "I don't want him to grow old without anyone, but more than that, I'd like to see him. It's been five years. It might as well be a lifetime." She walked up the alley toward the front of the diner.

Tessa knew the conversation was finished. Plants seemed to lean away from Cecilia as she passed, pushing against one another for comfort. Tessa reached out and pressed a sage leaf between two fingers, releasing the oils onto her skin. She sighed and wished for a man she'd never met to come to Mystic Water.

CHAPTER 4

MINT TEA AND CARAMEL CREAMS

TESSA BALANCED A POT OF MINT ON HER HIP WHILE SHE wiggled the key into the apartment lock. Cecilia had given Tessa the herb and insisted she take care of it. She worried about the repercussions if she were unable to keep the plant alive. Finding herself wilting beneath the look she'd seen on Cecilia's face a time or two sent a shudder down her spine. Mr. Borelli stood behind Tessa on the landing as she pushed open the door.

"You know y'all didn't have to do this," Tessa said. "You've done enough already, letting me stay here for free. Y'all didn't have to make food for me. I can cook."

Mr. Borelli smiled and carried two bags full of fresh food into the kitchen, pushing the door closed with his foot. "That's not how Lily tells it. Seems I remember a story about a turkey catching fire in the oven and a casserole dish exploding on the stove. Last Thanksgiving, was it?" He grinned to show he was teasing.

Tessa groaned and shook her head. "Lord have mercy, they're never going to let me forget that."

"Or cook Thanksgiving dinner again, I suspect." Mr. Borelli unloaded the bags and began sorting foods in the refrigerator.

Tessa noticed a wooden plant stand in the living room, so she situated the mint on it and scooted the stand near the bookshelf and window. "Mr. Borelli, you don't have to put away the groceries too," she said as she opened the living room window. A breeze slipped in and tickled magazine pages, causing them to flutter and whisper. She listened for a moment and then returned to the kitchen.

"Call me Harry, and I don't mind helping. Neither one of us do. There are a lot of people in a bad way right now, and we'd like to help any way we can. You've been supporting us since we opened, and we appreciate that," he said. "Besides, helping you keeps me out of Cece's way a bit longer. She's in a mood."

Tessa bit her bottom lip. "I think that's my fault."

"You can't take the blame for Paul," Harry said. A scent of cloves blew through the open window. Tessa breathed it in.

"How did you know her mood was because of him?" Tessa stacked fresh tomatoes in a colander on the countertop.

"No one else makes her want to whip up a batch of strawberry pancakes and French toast made with challah bread," Harry said. When Tessa's forehead wrinkled, he added, "Those were Paul's favorites as a little boy."

Tessa leaned her hip against the counter and crossed her arms over her chest. "And eating it makes her feel closer to him?"

Harry closed the refrigerator and tucked the canvas bags beneath his arm. "I think she's hoping that one of these days he'll smell them and come home."

"Would he think of this as home? You've only been here a couple of years. He didn't grow up in Mystic Water."

Harry smiled. "Home is where your heart is, where you feel comfortable, safe, and loved. But I think Paul has forgotten that having somewhere to come home to can be a good thing. One of these days, he'll remember."

"He'll smell those pancakes and come here," Tessa said, trying to encourage Harry.

He nodded. "I sure hope so."

Tessa followed his gaze toward the wall map. "How do you keep track of where he's been?"

Harry walked toward the map and smashed his thumb against the red heart-shaped pushpin, securing it deeper into the corkboard. "Postcards mostly. It's difficult to call when you're in the jungle in Malaysia or backpacking through the Andes. I keep hoping he'll bring me chocolate from the Alps." He nodded toward the mint plant. "Make sure it gets plenty of water. And Cecilia packed you a bowl of home fries from today's batch. They're in the refrigerator. You let us know if you need anything else. Make yourself at home."

"Thanks again, Mr. Borelli—Harry," Tessa corrected. "I really appreciate it."

Harry showed himself out, and Tessa stared at the wall map before poking the mint plant with her finger. "Don't die."

Tessa stepped out onto the front stoop, and a tornado of warm wind swirled around her, tossing her brown hair into her eyes. She tucked strands behind her ears and hoped the winds didn't mean bad weather was returning. Once she locked the apartment, she headed down Main Street toward Sweet Stop, the candy shop. The early evening wind whipped down the sidewalk, causing Tessa to duck her head and keep her eyes to the pavement. An absurd childhood saying popped into her head—step on a crack, you break your mama's back—and she wondered why kids came up with such macabre ideas. Still, Tessa was careful to avoid the cracks, and she glanced up now and again to locate the pink-and-white striped awning.

The closer she got to Sweet Stop, the stronger the smell of sugar became. When she pushed open the door, the shop looked filled with a fine dusting of pink, sugary sparkles floating through the air. The rows and shelves of glass jars filled to bursting with candies mesmerized Tessa. Sweet Stop was a wonderland of color and memories, taking Tessa back to her childhood. She couldn't stop the smile that stretched across her face. She could almost hear Lily's and Anna's little-girl laughter echo down an aisle, and she imagined their huddled shadows ghosting around the end of a row, disappearing behind a jar of red-rope licorice.

Gummy bears pressed their sticky paws against a short, fat jar, asking to be freed. Red Hots sizzled beside a jar full of Skittles that created a jumbled rainbow. Tessa strolled up an aisle, smiling at Ring Pops with sugar diamonds the size of a child's palm. Lily and Tessa had loved pretending they wore engagement rings, while Anna pretended to hock her blue diamond for a ticket to the ocean. Pop Rocks were arranged by color, and Tessa brushed her fingers over packets of Big League Chew. She had almost choked on the sticky strands of grape gum after being dared to chew the whole pack at once. Back then, Tessa was too afraid not to fit in to say no to a stupid idea. And no one could turn away from a double-dog dare.

Two teenage girls passed her and went straight for the chocolate section. They leaned toward each other and snickered, sharing secrets and laughing in a way only young girls can. When Tessa found the aisle with caramel creams, she noticed an elderly woman scooping Bonomo strawberry taffy into a pink candy-shop bag. Tessa grabbed a bag from the nearest shelf and flipped open the lid on the caramel creams. She scooped in the candy until the bag was three-quarters full, then she folded down the top. When she finished, Tessa was startled to find the elderly woman standing beside her, staring up at Tessa with raven-black eyes.

"Eaten anything from the garden yet?" the woman asked, her high cheekbones becoming more prominent when she smiled. Her skin was the color of chai with cream, smooth and rich.

Her voice reminded Tessa of a young girl's. It was as though her body had grown old without her knowledge. Her clothes were a rainbow of colors, causing her to look like a Bohemian traveler. Her silver-streaked dark hair was partially covered by a multicolored striped scarf. A fuchsia blouse peeked out from beneath her black vest, and a patchwork skirt swung loosely around her small frame. She smelled like lavender and pine needles. A memory surfaced in the back of Tessa's mind.

"Crazy Kate?" Tessa asked before she could stop herself.

Kate Muir lived in a cottage at the southernmost tip of town near a curve in the Red River. A thick grove of knobby trees hid the cottage from the road, and children had been warned to stay away from Crazy Kate's house, which meant that nearly every kid in town had been dared to creep through the forest in the hope of catching a glimpse of the town eccentric. What made Kate Muir crazy was watery knowledge; rumor was that she was older than everyone else in town and had lived in Mystic Water before time began.

When they were eight years old, Lily and Anna had dared Tessa to sneak up to the cottage and bring something back as evidence of her success. Tessa sneaked through the trees with her heart pounding so fiercely in her chest that she felt her pulse in her tongue. She imagined her mama finding out and banishing her to her room without phone privileges for all time. The thick canopy transformed sunlight into a dreamy green haze that glowed against Tessa's skin.

As she neared the cottage, Tessa heard the river bubbling over rocks. Wind chimes made from miscellaneous homemade materials hung from branches. Cobalt-blue glass bottles sprouted from a crape myrtle like magical extensions. The wind blew, and the forest filled with ghostly voices and sounds like those made by a child's music box. Suncatchers dangling from low branches reflected the sunlight, sending dancing, vibrant colors across the damp earth and across Tessa's clothes.

She lost track of time staring at the changing colors and listening to the eerie music. Then the front door of the cottage opened, and Crazy Kate stepped out. Her hair was jet black, braided in a long plait that fell down her back. Crazy Kate sniffed the air, turned her head, and looked straight at Tessa. In a panic, Tessa reached out, snatched the nearest suncatcher, and ran for her life.

Crazy Kate's voice fractured Tessa's memories and brought her back to the present. "I said, have you eaten from the garden?"

"I'm sorry?" Tessa asked, stepping backward, feeling like her eight-year-old self in the woods.

Crazy Kate stepped toward Tessa, holding her bag of candy against her chest. "The garden. I saw you working with Cecilia Borelli tonight. I noticed she gave you a plant."

"Oh," Tessa said and tried to smile. "You mean at the diner?

Yes, ma'am. The storm made a mess of Mrs. Borelli's garden, and I was helping her repair what we could. She uses the herbs and vegetables from the garden in her cooking."

"Well?" Crazy Kate asked. She nodded her head as if coaxing Tessa to say more.

Tessa frowned. "Well what?"

Crazy Kate's exhalation sounded annoyed. "The plant, child! Have you used it in your cooking yet?" She gazed at Tessa in a way that made Tessa glance around the shop for an escape route.

"Sort of," Tessa said. "I don't really cook, but she gave me mint, so I made tea."

Crazy Kate's dark eyes widened, and she bounced on her toes. The pink candy bag crinkled in her tightening grip. She smiled, and Tessa was caught off guard by Crazy Kate's unexpected beauty.

"And what happened?" Crazy Kate asked.

"I drank it, and I should be going. Have a good night." Tessa tried to walk past her, but Crazy Kate grabbed her arm with surprising strength.

"You have to tell me what happened to you after you drank it," Crazy Kate said.

"I don't mean to be impolite, but this conversation is a little weird, and I'm not sure what you're asking."

Crazy Kate tightened her grip. "That land around the diner is special. You, of all people, should know that. Tell me what happened to you tonight after you drank the tea."

Tessa pried Crazy Kate's fingers from her arm. She lowered her voice and whispered, "I'm going to apologize ahead of time for disrespecting an elder, but you're crazy."

"And you're a thief," Crazy Kate whispered in return. "We're all imperfect, thankfully."

Tessa's mouth dropped open.

"That was my favorite suncatcher, and you were, what? Eight? Awful young to be a delinquent," Crazy Kate said. "When the lavender and rosemary in the garden are mature, I'll need dried lavender and Cecilia's rosemary tea. My memory is giving me a bit of trouble these days, and I could use a boost. You can bottle the rosemary tea and bag up the lavender. Bring it to my house. It won't make up for what you stole, but it's a start."

Crazy Kate patted Tessa on the arm and smiled. Mischief crackled from her fingers and prickled Tessa's skin.

"Go on, child," Crazy Kate said with a sparkle in her eyes. "Sprinkle some thyme from the garden into your potatoes, and tell me you don't know the rain is coming before everyone else." She spun on her tiny feet and headed for the cash register.

Once Tessa was back inside the apartment, she walked over to the pot of mint tea she'd brewed. She scooped out the few leaves stuck to the bottom of her empty mug. Pressing the wet leaves between her fingers, she closed her eyes and focused on how the mint made her feel. Her fingers felt slimy and cold, and she opened her eyes and rolled them.

"Really, Tessa?" she asked herself. "You're listening to Crazy Kate?"

Tessa poured herself another mug of mint tea and microwaved it until steam swirled from the top. She dropped the pink bag of caramel creams on the coffee table. Then she grabbed one of the travel magazines from the bookshelf and tucked herself into the couch. She squished herself into the corner cushions, held her mug in both hands, and propped the magazine across her thighs. As Tessa sipped and lazily flipped through the pages, she occasionally reached over and pulled a piece of candy from her bag. She was halfway through the first magazine before she stopped on a four-page article about the breathtaking landscape of New Zealand and its inhabitants, the Māori, written by Paul Borelli.

Tessa read straight through his article, and by the end of it, she wanted to go there immediately. In fact, she wished she had been there *with* him. Paul wrote like a storyteller, pulling in his readers like a man weaving a tale around a campfire.

She tossed the magazine onto the coffee table and grabbed more from the bookshelves. Just as she assumed, the magazines all contained Paul's articles, probably Harry's doing again. Tessa drank three more glasses of tea while she traveled across the world with Paul and his bewitching words. She fell asleep dreaming of trekking through the Amazon jungle, championing for rain forest protection, eating her fill of mangoes and passion fruit, and sharing a tent with a handsome explorer.

CHAPTER 5

Deconstructed Breakfast Burrito

THE NEXT MORNING TESSA WOKE TO THE SOUND OF HER CELL phone ringing at 6:00 a.m. She tried to roll toward her nightstand where she kept her phone charging, but instead, she rolled into a couch cushion. She stared for a few seconds at the tan fabric one inch from her face before she remembered she was in the apartment above the diner. Tessa flipped over and reached for her phone on the coffee table, which was papered with magazines and caramel cream wrappers.

She checked the number; it was the president of her building's HOA. "Good morning, Mr. Fleming. Tell me you have good news."

"I have a mix of news," he said.

"Good news first," Tessa said, sitting up on the couch and

stretching her neck. She raked her fingers through her hair.

"The water has started to recede," Mr. Fleming said. "You can come on back and see the place for yourself. Salvage what you can."

Tessa's heart squeezed. "*Salvage* sounds disheartening."

Mr. Fleming cleared his throat. "If you've already contacted your insurance company, you might alert them that they can send out someone to assess the property. Most of the residents didn't have flood insurance, and the government didn't register this event as a FEMA disaster, so no grants are available. Did you have flood insurance?"

Tessa rubbed her eyes. "No. Why would we have? Mystic Water hasn't flooded in more than fifty years."

Mr. Fleming cleared his throat. "Doesn't mean your insurance won't pay *something.* A developer stopped by this morning, Tessa. He's interested in buying up this whole place—all the units, even the undamaged ones—and remodeling the building in the next year or so. He's offering residents very high prices, especially considering the extreme damage. It's a good deal. For all of us."

Tessa stood. "I don't think I'm following you. It sounds as though someone has offered to buy our building, and people are selling? But we can repair flood damage."

"I think it's best if you come on down and have a look for yourself. Then you call me back, and we'll talk more," Mr. Fleming said.

Mr. Fleming ended the call, and Tessa stared at the mess of magazines, all open to Paul's articles. She scooped up the candy wrappers and rushed around to clean up the clutter. She returned the magazines to the shelves, which gave her time to think about the conversation with Mr. Fleming. Was the state of most of the condos that devastating? Were the other owners leaving? Couldn't they repair the damage? But how much could anyone repair without insurance help? Even if FEMA grants had been an option, everyone knew they didn't cover nearly enough to return the house to the state it was in before the damage.

Tessa jotted the questions down in her notebook, and then she flipped back to yesterday's unfinished list, which asked *What should I do?* Number one: *Don't finish waffle.* And she hadn't. Number two: *Move home for weeks?* That was a moot point now since her parents had house swapped for months. Tessa drew a line through number two. Beside number three she wrote, *Sell my home?*

"Is it that bad?" Tessa asked. Then she heard Lily's voice in her head reminding Tessa that she swam out of her condo a few days ago.

She glanced at the mint plant on the stand. It had stretched its gangly legs toward the map. A few tendrils were wrapped around silver pushpins in Alaska, Hawaii, and French Polynesia. Traveling around the world seemed glamorous from one perspective, and Tessa had escaped right into Paul's adventures the night before. But the thought of being homeless made her feel as though she'd eaten undercooked scrambled eggs. She skipped coffee, which was, in hindsight, a rotten idea because she would need all the fortification she could get when she drove to her condo.

The closer Tessa got to her condo building and Jordan Pond, the more the air reeked of mildew and decaying, sodden leaves. Miscellaneous items, stolen by the floodwaters, collected at the sides of the streets and speckled front yards. A three-legged lawn chair lay against the curb, crumpled and muddy. Baby dolls, splattered with pond scum, convened beneath an oak tree. A ruined summer dress and broad-brimmed hat hung from the lowest branches of a Japanese magnolia, looking like a ghost billowing in the breeze.

High-powered, industrial vacuums snaked their long hoses out of homes, sucking the water from the interiors and dumping it into the gutters lining the streets. Hundreds of flood-drying fans filled the air with a constant humming, and the entire town vibrated beneath the noise.

Tessa parked the Great Pumpkin in the lot behind her condo building. There was still a good three inches of stagnant water putrefying in the sun around the edges of the concrete foundation. Tessa kicked off her flats and tugged on her pink rubber boots. The amount of muck and grime covering the walls of the building, covering the abandoned cars, covering *everything*, shocked her, even though she'd seen how flooded it was.

Beneath the mud and debris, only the roof of her car was still its original slate-blue color. The insurance company would probably total her car since the water had risen over the dashboard. With the electronic system, it would cost more to repair than the car was probably worth. They'd scheduled to come out and assess the car this week. Once she had the money, she'd start thinking about what she wanted, but buying a car was further down her to-do list.

Tessa sloshed through the water, squelching as she walked, and when she rounded the corner leading to her ground-floor condo, she gasped. Jordan Pond had receded, but it looked as though it had also tossed out a half-century's worth of gunk and tree branches onto the surrounding areas. Her backyard looked like a combination of Mississippi swamp and garbage pit.

Someone had tried to close her condo door, but the door had swollen like a magazine in a swimming pool, and it refused to shut completely. Tessa leaned into the door, but it didn't budge. After ramming her shoulder against it, it groaned open and sent a low wave of water through the living room.

For a few seconds Tessa couldn't even react. Looking inside her condo felt like looking at a foreign hut she'd never set foot in before. There was no way this place had been her home. Filth covered the furniture, floors, and her personal belongings. Water stains marked the walls three feet high. The sheetrock was destroyed, probably already growing enough mold to call for an evacuation.

She moved through the condo in silence, the sight of each room bringing more tears to her eyes. When she stepped into her bedroom, a fat toad croaked at her from the bed. It stared at her with glassy black eyes. "Have it," she whispered. "It's yours." Then she called Lily.

Tessa hefted another cardboard box from the front stoop of the apartment and carried it inside. The cardboard stunk like spilled beer and pond water. She held it as far from her body as possible without dropping it. Water rushed through the pipes as the faucets in the bathroom turned on. Tessa walked through the bedroom and into the adjoining bathroom.

Lily knelt in front of the garden tub and held a muddy stuffed animal beneath the water. She scrubbed its head and arms with a bar of soap. "I need you to promise you'll never tell Mrs. Borelli we contaminated her bathtub while washing muck out of your stuff," Lily said. "How attached are you to this?" She held up the soiled teddy bear. Its wet fur was matted and pitiful.

Tessa's bottom lip trembled. She'd received that teddy bear as a gift from her grandpa on her sixteenth birthday, but she knew if she opened her mouth to tell Lily, she'd blubber.

But Lily could see Tessa's fragility a mile away. She dropped the bear in the tub and stood, reaching for a mud-stained towel. "Hey, it's okay," she said, pulling Tessa into a hug. "Look at all the stuff we saved." She made a sweeping motion with her arm.

Shoes, picture frames, an assortment of kitchen items, and a few armfuls of books had been salvaged from her ruined condo. They were scattered across the bathroom floor, drying on towels.

"Your clothes are at the cleaners," Lily reminded her. "You'll have a fully functioning wardrobe in a few days. You have a working car, even if it *is* the Great Pumpkin. The Borellis stocked your fridge. And let's not forget you have a perfectly good place to stay."

"You're right." Tessa pulled in a steadying breath. "I *know* you're right. Focus on what I have, not on what I lost. But . . . I can't stay in the Borellis' apartment forever."

"Of course not," Lily said. "But we're not talking about forever. We're talking about right now. And right now you have plenty of people who are making sure you're okay. Let's brew some tea. I have a little bit longer before I need to be back at work, and I think you need a mental break."

Tessa glanced around at the pieces of her life on the bathroom floor before following Lily into the living room. Lily pointed at the mint plant, which stretched long runners in two directions. Half of its green, leafy legs grew toward the open window, and the others reached for the wall map. "What are you feeding that thing?" Lily asked.

"Water," Tessa said.

"I thought mint was a creeper not a climber," Lily said. "Not that I'm a botanist, but Mama loves growing spearmint. Hers looks like bushes. Yours is growing like ivy."

Tessa shrugged. "Mrs. Borelli said her plants are hardy. Maybe this is a special variety of mint." She walked toward the mint and popped off a handful of leaves. Then she patted its head as though it were a pet.

Tessa dropped the leaves into the porcelain teapot on the counter and put the kettle on the stove while Lily washed her hands and made herself a cup of coffee in the Keurig. Lily opened the refrigerator and pulled out a carton of strawberries. Two recipe cards were attached to the front of the container.

Lily eyed the top recipe card and read Cecilia's note: *For when you need comfort.* "Does Mrs. Borelli know what happened the last time you decided to cook?"

Tessa snatched the strawberries from Lily. "It's for *pancakes.*" She plucked the recipe card from the carton and read through the instructions. "This sounds like an easy recipe. No one can destroy pancakes."

Lily reached for a strawberry and bit into it. "Except you."

"Except me." Tessa sighed. "At least the other recipe is for tea. I can't mess up tea, right?"

Lily raised her eyebrows in response. When the kettle whistled, Lily pulled it from the stove. She filled the teapot and watched as mint leaves floated to the top. She leaned over the teapot and inhaled. "I love how refreshing mint smells. It clears my head."

A calming effect settled over Lily's features. Tessa thought of the conversation with Crazy Kate in Sweet Stop. Lily filled a mug with tea for Tessa before grabbing her mug of steaming black coffee.

"Do you think herbs have special powers?" Tessa asked.

Lily sat down across from Tessa at the table. She cupped her mug in both hands. "Like medicinal properties? Sure. There's a ton of proof that supports it."

Tessa fiddled with the hem of her T-shirt. "What about magical properties?"

Lily snorted. "Like what?"

"Like maybe eating an herb, say *thyme* for example, could give you the ability to predict the weather . . . before it happens," Tessa said, feeling stupider with each word she spoke. Why did she care what Crazy Kate thought? If she believed the local nut, Tessa might as well join her at the edge of town.

Lily narrowed her eyes at Tessa, and then she laughed. "What are you going on about? Have you been eating Brian Mumford's brownies? Cause you *know* those aren't 'regular.'" Lily joked. "If an herb could make me predict the weather, then I'd make a bazillion dollars, because even my weather app can't tell a rainy day from a sunny one half the time."

"Forget it," Tessa said, but still she leaned over her mug

of mint tea and inhaled. Her mind cleared instantly; the tense muscles in her shoulders relaxed. She glanced across the room at the wall map as thoughts of traveling swept into her mind. "What are you doing tonight? Do you think Jakob could spare you? We could make the pancake recipe."

"You mean, I could make the recipe while you loiter around in the kitchen?" Lily asked with a smile.

"Basically, yes. I don't feel like being alone tonight, and Mama and Daddy are gone for months. If I hang out with anyone else, I'll have to pretend that I'm not depressed, and I don't have the energy."

"I wish I could, but you know I'm trying to finish up designing that new children's line for my shop. I've promised buyers it will be ready for a show by July. If I don't stay on schedule, I'll never get finished. Tomorrow?" Lily asked.

Tessa slumped a little more in her chair. Her eyes wandered to the wall map again. "Sure. Tomorrow's fine." Her cell phone rang, and she got up, grabbed it off the coffee table, and sent the call to voice mail.

"Your mama?"

Tessa rolled her eyes and groaned. "No, it's Marty."

"Marty the meat guy?"

"Most people call him a butcher," Tessa said, dropping the phone onto the couch. She walked back to the kitchen and sat before propping her elbows on the table and covering her face with her hands.

"I thought you didn't want to go out with him after the group-date disappointment," Lily said.

"I don't. Not really." Tessa lowered her hands and shrugged. "He's not that bad."

Lily chuckled. "Based on your last description of him, I'd

say smelling like raw hamburger meat all the time isn't on your wish list of potential dates."

"Sometimes I get lonely. I don't want to sit at home by myself every night."

"Enjoy being alone while you can," Lily said, blowing across the top of her coffee. "I never have a minute to myself anymore."

"Being *alone* and being *lonely* aren't the same," Tessa said. "You probably don't even remember what it feels like to be lonely." She felt the beginnings of tears, so she cleared her throat and glanced away. What did Lily know about being lonely? She had a warm house to go home to after work, a husband who loved her, and a daughter who wanted to be just like her. Self-pity crept in like a poisonous vapor, swirling around Tessa's kitchen chair, rising higher until it settled over her like a miserable mist, sinking her lower into the chair.

After a few seconds of silence, Lily asked, "What did your mama say about the buyer and your condo?"

Glad for the change of subject, Tessa answered, "She said I should seriously consider it." When Lily looked at her with raised eyebrows, Tessa added, "Actually she said I'd be a fool not to take the offer." She tucked her hair behind her ears. The thought of giving up her condo—her *home*—left her feeling unbalanced. She drank more tea and toyed with the corner of the recipe card.

"I know this stinks to high heaven right now, but you're a realtor," Lily said. "You know better than anyone else how to find the perfect place."

A breeze blew through the window, bringing with it the scent of lavender. Tessa sat up straighter. "Why haven't I thought of that?"

"Because you're not thinking like a realtor. You're thinking like someone who just lost her first home. I know you loved it, but the condo wasn't your forever place." Lily paused only long enough to drink more coffee. "Fortunately for you, a wealthy developer wants to buy the whole place from y'all at a more-than-decent price, and you can put that money toward something new. Think of it as an adventure, and you're the best person to lead this one. You have all the information right in your office. I bet there are at least a dozen places you could start looking at right away."

The tightness in Tessa's chest loosened. "You're right. I'm focusing on the miserable part of this situation."

"In your defense, this situation is exceptionally miserable, but we can turn this around, make this a new opportunity." Lily glanced at the clock on the wall. "I need to get going." She gulped down the rest of her coffee and placed the mug in the sink. "Don't mope around all day, okay? It's going to work out."

"You sound like Mama," Tessa said. "I don't see why no one will let me feel sorry for myself." She allowed a small smile to ghost across her lips.

Lily looked at an invisible watch on her arm and grinned. "You have exactly ten minutes to throw yourself the best pity party ever. Then go to the office and see what's available on the market. I bet there's something that'll catch your eye."

Tessa stood. "Thanks, Lily. I'd be lost without you."

"I bet you say that to all the girls." Lily winked at Tessa. She grabbed her purse and waved as she left.

Tessa picked up her notebook from the coffee table and flipped to the most recent list. Number three asked, *Sell my home?* Beside it, she wrote, *Mama: Yes. Lily: Yes.*

Tessa dug through the containers of food Harry and Cecilia had given her. She pulled out black beans, homemade salsa, diced peppers, and two eggs. Scrambled eggs were one of the only dishes Tessa could cook without burning something or making herself or someone else sick. She cooked the eggs and peppers together and plopped them onto a plate along with the beans and salsa. Then she grabbed an open bag of tortilla chips she'd found in one of the cabinets in her condo. She popped one into her mouth and chewed. Definitely stale, but they were edible, and she dropped a few handfuls onto the plate. Then she sat down at the kitchen table, eating her deconstructed breakfast burrito and drinking mint tea, trying to feel a shred of enthusiasm about the prospect of looking for a new home.

CHAPTER 6

HOPEFUL HASH BROWNS

AFTER FINISHING HER EARLY LUNCH, TESSA WALKED TO HER office. She flipped through the mail, stopping when she held a large mailer sent from Trudy Steele. Tessa ripped open the end of the envelope and tilted it upside down. A set of miscellaneous keys, including a tarnished skeleton key, fell onto her desk. *Honeysuckle Hollow.* A prickle of excitement skittered over her skin. She tabled her curiosity and finished sorting the mail and making phone calls. By midafternoon, she was caught up with her office work, and she'd even printed out house listings to look at for herself. When she left the office, she first met with a client across town, and then afterward, she made the short drive to Honeysuckle Hollow.

Dogwood Lane was at a higher elevation than the rest of Mystic Water, so the flood waters had streamed down the streets toward the lower sections of town, leaving the historic neighborhood with nothing more than soggy grass and patches of muddy yards.

Tessa parked in front of the neglected brick Victorian house. Weeds choked the front lawn. A sea of dandelions bobbed in the breeze, scattering their feathery seeds into the air like spring snowflakes. Irises knifed through the weeds, pushing purple and white buds above the wildness. Snaking vines had taken over the wraparound front porch. Tessa wove her way through the tall grass and weeds, and a cloud of grasshoppers leaped ahead of her like personal escorts leading her toward the door.

She gripped a peeling wooden handrail framing the front stairs, and it snapped outward beneath her weight, breaking away from its mountings. She lost her balance and nearly tumbled sideways off the stairs, but she fell against a column, giving it an awkward bear hug while smashing her face against the wood. When she pushed away from the column, it groaned. She warily glanced up at the roof sheltering the porch. Was there a chance it would collapse on her head? She brushed dingy white paint flecks from her cheek.

The porch boards creaked as she scurried for the front door. The windows lining the front of the house were soiled with two years' worth of inattention. A rotted porch plank had fallen halfway into the dirt crawl space beneath the porch. Tiny animal prints traveled up and down the collapsed board like mud paw stamps. A critter was obviously using the board like a bridge from its lair to the top world.

She pulled the keys from her pocket and realized the skeleton key was the one that would open the antique lock on the front door. She'd never used a real skeleton key before, and for a moment she felt like a heroine in one of her romance novels, about to unearth long-lost secrets.

Electricity tingled through her fingers and up her arm as she turned the key in the lock, causing her breath to catch. Maybe the house was just as excited as she was. Tessa pushed open the door, finding herself in the two-story foyer. Filtered light streamed through the windows, which allowed her to see her way around well enough since the electricity wasn't on. Off to one side of the foyer was a stunning, skillfully crafted wooden staircase. Tessa touched the finial at the base of the railing. No one constructed staircases like this anymore. Even though it was covered in a thick layer of dust and spiders had weaved gossamer tapestries through the spindles, its unmistakable beauty remained apparent. A strong breeze swirled through the house, raced past Tessa, and went out the open front door as though the house was exhaling, thankful for a visitor.

To her right was a dining room with a tray ceiling and a bay window. A long table had been covered with a motley assortment of sheets. To the left was a living room with another bay window and a large cast-iron fireplace. Like the dining room, the furniture had been covered, but Tessa doubted the sheets served as much protection from two years of disuse. The house smelled musty and forgotten, like cardboard boxes in storage.

Tessa marveled at the details and the tile work on the cast-iron fireplace. She crouched in front of it and realized it was a pass-through. She could see a large room on the other side. The hearth was coated with ash, soot, and an unknown substance in a goopy black pile. Remains of a half-burned log sat crumbling on the grate.

"Wow," she said. "This fireplace is a great feature."

She pulled a work notepad and pen out of her purse to make notes but stopped writing when she heard a strange sound, like Styrofoam cups rubbing together. The racket grew steadily louder. Tessa backed away from the fireplace. A whooshing noise barreled down the chimney, and a colony of bats exited through the pass-through fireplace. Tessa screamed and flapped her arms and hands around her head as though her hair were on fire. The bats darted by her face. Rapid wings brushed against her skin, which caused the pitch of her scream to jump to another octave.

Tessa's flailing caused a hefty, rectangular book to fall from the mantel. It slapped the floor, sounding like a gunshot, and dust mushroomed around it. The bats flew straight out the open front door. Tessa screamed for another five seconds. She pressed her hands against her pounding heart and dropped onto the nearest sheet-covered chair. A cloud of dust erupted around her, clinging to her hair and clothes.

When she could breathe normally, she texted Lily: I was attacked by killer bats. I almost died.

Tessa gathered up her notepad and pen, which she'd flung across the room. Then she picked up the fallen book. She brushed her fingertips across the front cover, revealing the words *Guests of Honeysuckle Hollow* embossed in shiny silver letters against navy-blue leather. Tessa returned to the chair and flipped through the pages. Handwritten entries filled the entire book. The first few dated back more than ten years ago.

The first entry read: *Honeysuckle Hollow was the answer to a desperate prayer. After my husband was laid off from the bubble gum factory in Willow Grove, our savings dwindled quickly, and we couldn't afford our rent. Before long, we had nowhere to go. A chance visit to Dr. Hamilton saved us. We've called Honeysuckle Hollow our home (and what a fairy-tale home) for the past month, free of charge, and now with Philip back on his feet again with a great job in Mystic Water, we found a place to rent. This house was a godsend.*

The second guest's handwriting looped across the page in delicate, tightly knit letters: *While traveling south, our youngest son became extremely ill. We were forced to stop in Mystic Water and seek help. Dr. Hamilton was on call at the hospital, and we saw him just in the nick of time. Timmy was so ill that he required hospitalization for two weeks. Rather than letting us pay for a hotel in the nearest town, Dr. Hamilton offered Honeysuckle Hollow to us for no cost. We couldn't believe the generosity. Once Timmy was well enough to leave the hospital, we stayed one more week in Honeysuckle Hollow before returning home. This magic house was such a blessing during our time of need.*

Tessa glanced around the room. She had known that Dr. Hamilton rented the place for parties and special events, but she hadn't known that Honeysuckle Hollow had been a haven for those who were down on their luck and out of options. She inhaled a breath deep enough to expand her chest.

"You deserve to be beautiful again," Tessa said to the house. She closed the book and put it with her purse.

She hesitated before exploring the house any further. What if there were bigger creatures making Honeysuckle Hollow their home? Maybe she should call the exterminator first. But her curiosity had her rising from the chair.

Tessa tiptoed out of the living room and up a short hallway beside the staircase. She walked into the expansive room she had seen through the fireplace opening. The family room opened into a breakfast nook and a spacious kitchen with an island. The island had been added years after the kitchen was created because its cabinetry was a much newer style, probably intended to match the original house. To a trained eye like Tessa's, it was obvious the island wasn't antique.

But the worst addition to the kitchen was the graffiti. The thieves, or perhaps rogue teenage artists, had spray-painted extra-large words in florescent paint. She tilted her head to try and decipher a drawing that stretched from one kitchen wall to the high ceiling. Tessa categorized graffiti as a foreign language. No matter how long she stared at it, the meaning never came to her.

It didn't take long to piece together how the vandals had made it into the house. French doors leading from the breakfast nook opened into the backyard, but one door had busted off its hinges, and every pane of glass in the other door had shattered. Glass littered the floor and crunched beneath Tessa's flats. The appliances were missing, and from the looks of the deep grooves in the hardwood floors, they had been dragged out of the kitchen and through the French doors.

"Such a shame," she said as she passed through the kitchen.

Clusters of mold spotted the window casings, and one window was partially open, allowing wild honeysuckle vines with creamy-yellow and bright-pink blooms to reach inside and tangle around a chair at the kitchen table. Their fragrant blooms waved to Tessa as she passed by.

There was a full downstairs bathroom with a claw-foot tub covered by a filthy shower curtain draped over a circular ring hanging from the ceiling. Tessa grabbed the shower curtain in one hand and stood back as she yanked it open. A mangy calico cat cowered near the tub's drain. Its eyes widened, its back arched, and it hissed at Tessa. She raced out of the bathroom, straight through the kitchen and into the backyard.

The half-acre backyard was wilder than the front. Tessa stopped almost as suddenly as her feet hit the brick patio, skidding to a halt and pitching forward. She glanced over her shoulder to see if the cat had chased her. Nothing stirred in the house. Her cell phone dinged, and she yelped.

Tessa read a text from Lily: Killer bats? Stop eating Brian Mumford's brownies.

Tessa texted: Do cats have rabies? She slid her phone into her back pocket and took in the complete chaos of the yard as her heart rate settled again.

A massive oak tree tossed deep shadows across half of the garden. Weeds mingled with plantings and created a jungle of brambles, thorns, and vibrant, blooming flowers. Pink hydrangea blooms stretched along the shaded areas of the yard. Red roses clustered and twisted into one corner. Honeysuckle vines spread across three-quarters of the fencing, creating a green leafy wall around the perimeter.

A winding, geometrically tiled path disappeared into the overgrowth. Although the untamed plantings seemed to have reclaimed every available space, Tessa saw the curving river through the mess. She judged the safest route and high-stepped through the yard, praying snakes had not made Honeysuckle Hollow their home too. Bats and cats were startling, but snakes elicited another level of freak-out.

Tessa propped her hands on her knees, leaned over, and peered into the murky water. Algae bloomed on every surface beneath the water, creating a green haze, and there appeared to be no water circulation. The pump required electricity, so the river had been stagnant for at least two years. Now it was the perfect breeding ground for mosquitos. Tessa felt a nip on her neck and slapped her hand against it. A fat orange koi with three white spots forming a triangle on its back swam over and lifted its lips to the surface, asking for food.

"Well, hey there, fella," she said. "I can't believe you're still alive. I don't have any food for you. I suppose you're sick of eating algae, huh? I'll see what we can do about fixing the water pump. I bet swimming around in your own—in icky water isn't your idea of paradise."

A brilliant red cardinal landed on a low branch of the oak tree and chirped at her. The spring wind picked up again and brought with it the sweet, spicy scent of cloves and an echoing sound of laughter. *Must be neighborhood kids*, she thought, even though she wasn't sure there *were* any neighborhood kids on Dogwood Lane other than Lily's two-year-old daughter, Rose.

Tessa surveyed the rear facade of Honeysuckle Hollow. The exterior brick of the house had survived the abandonment better than the paint and the wood, but those were easy to repair. She hadn't inspected the second story yet, and she needed to assess its current state before she left.

The staircase creaked like a pair of old man's knees as Tessa ascended it. The upstairs smelled hot and sad, like an old barn left to rot. There were four bedrooms and two full bathrooms upstairs, including the primary room and its adjoining bathroom. At some point in the history of the house, someone installed carpet over the hardwood in the bedrooms. Now the carpets were dingy and stunk of mildew and urine. Tessa tried to breathe only through her mouth, even though Lily once told her that when people breathed through their mouths, it meant they were tasting the smells. Tessa gagged. Nobody wanted to *taste* what she smelled.

With a bit of imagination, Tessa could see how magical the primary bedroom had been. With its high vaulted ceilings in the turret of the house and a bay window stretching across one wall, this space could be a retreat. The middle window of the set had shattered panes. Mold covered the carpet beneath the window, and Tessa knew she would find it damp. She backed out of the room and walked toward a pair of French doors that led to a covered balcony overlooking the backyard. Some of the boards were rotted and one was missing entirely.

Tessa pulled out her notepad, jotted down a few notes about the house, and decided to return to her office. She would call Mrs. Steele and fill her in on the state of the house. Tessa already had ideas about how to bring light and shine back to Honeysuckle Hollow, and she hoped she would be able to encourage Mrs. Steele to repair a few of the minor problems before putting the house on the market. Tessa knew a local contractor who might be willing to lend a hand to repair a home that had helped so many people.

Tessa parked the Great Pumpkin up the street from her office. She grabbed her purse and the house listings she'd tossed into the front seat. Time hadn't allowed her to visit any of the possible houses for her, but she'd get around to viewing them soon. As she walked up the sidewalk, she passed by Scrambled just as Nell Foster exited the building with an armful of to-go bags. Nell's rumpled clothes and frizzy red hair made her look as though she'd had the kind of day that made it easy to forget to brush her teeth or make sure her shoes matched, which was a departure from the flawless law-clerk attire she wore during the week.

Tessa paused. "Hey, Nell. You need a hand getting those to your car?"

Nell glanced up at Tessa and blinked. Her brown eyes seemed to look straight through Tessa, focusing on nothing. Then her bottom lip trembled, and her body sagged forward like an empty paper bag.

Tessa hurried over and grabbed the bags from Nell's arms. "Hey, are you okay?"

Nell's exhausted expression revealed all Tessa needed to know about how *okay* Nell wasn't. Her lips were pinched as though she'd been eating lemons. She wiped at her watery eyes, smearing her eyeliner across her cheeks. She reached up to pull her fingers through her curly hair, but they caught in snares of knotted curls. "I could really use a hot shower or a long soak in a tub or a ticket to Bermuda. Don't suppose you have any of those handy?"

Tessa cradled the bags in her arms and grabbed Nell's shirt-sleeve with her hand. She tugged Nell down the sidewalk to a bench.

Tessa propped the bags beside her on the bench seat. "What's happened?"

Nell released a shaky sigh. She swirled her hands in the air. "Oh, what *hasn't* happened? We lost both our cars and our house and our clothes and our food in the flood, and we moved in with Liam's mama who has a one-bedroom house. *One bedroom*. Can you imagine? Three adults and three children. It's a nightmare. *I'm* a nightmare. Look at me. I look like the hobo version of Raggedy Ann, and the children are practically barefoot and wearing the same clothes they woke up in on Saturday—oh, I've washed them, of course, but it doesn't matter. A few more days like this and they'll probably call me an unfit mother, and they'd be right. I'm unraveling like an old sweater. I yelled at Ava this morning for chewing her cereal too loudly. And the boys, they have so much energy that they're bouncing off the walls. Literally. Liam knows I'm at the end of my short rope, so he's ridden over the ridge to see if he can find us an extended-stay hotel room. I *can't* keep living with his mama in that tiny house." Nell closed her eyes and inhaled a shuddering breath before dropping her head toward her chest and crying.

Tessa put her hand on Nell's arm. Tessa had been throwing a pity party for herself for days, but here in front of her sat a woman who had lost more than Tessa had *and* who had nowhere to go. At least Tessa had the Borellis' apartment to stay in until she found a place. She felt selfish for not giving much thought to what the other townspeople might be going through because of the flood.

The wind swept down the street and ruffled the house listings sticking out of Tessa's purse. She glanced at them and thought of Honeysuckle Hollow and how it had helped people during their times of devastation and need.

"The food smells delicious. Scrambled has the best comfort food," Tessa said.

Nell's smile was tired and slow. "Doesn't it? Cecilia made a special side for me. She called it Hopeful Hash Browns. You think they'll give us hope?" Nell's awkward laugh exposed how silly she thought the question was.

"If you believe they will give you hope, they will. Having

hope is a good thing. Are you driving the food back to Liam's mama's?"

Nell shook her head and pointed toward the downtown park at the end of the street. "The kids are with Liam's mama, probably swinging from the monkey bars and daring each other to jump off the top. I'm bringing the food to them."

"I have an idea," Tess said. "Go eat with them, and when you're finished, see if his mama will watch the kids a little longer, and you come to my office. I'm going to make a few calls to some of the landlords who have rental properties and see if I can find y'all a good deal on temporary housing."

Nell's brown eyes widened. Sunbeams reflected off her pale-pink cheeks. "Can you do that? Do you think you can find us a place in town?"

Tessa nodded. "I do. Come back and see me after you eat."

Nell hugged Tessa spontaneously. "Thank you, thank you. With the kids in school here, it would be so much easier if we could find something in Mystic Water. I wasn't even thinking about renting—well, to be honest, I haven't been thinking coherently at all—but if we could find a place big enough for us . . . Gosh, Tessa, thank you so much. Really, I'm going to cry again."

Tessa patted Nell's arm. "I don't mind helping. It's my job to find homes for people."

Nell stood and struggled in vain to smooth the wrinkles from her clothes. "You're a lifesaver."

Tessa lifted the lunch bags from the bench and passed them to Nell. "I'll see you soon."

Nell hurried down the sidewalk toward the park. Tessa smiled as she walked to her office, thinking, *First, I'll help Nell, and then I'll help Honeysuckle Hollow.* Her smile widened.

CHAPTER 7

HOME FRIES

AS THE SMOKY-ORANGE SUN LOWERED, SWIRLS OF ROSE PINK, pale melon, and gold striped the sky. Tessa closed down her computer at work. After spending an hour with Nell Foster and finding her family temporary housing, Tessa had written down everyone else on Nell's street who needed help too. She'd had spent the rest of the afternoon contacting displaced homeowners and working with them and landlords to find homes. So far, there was only one family who still needed housing, and Tessa felt confident that she'd find a suitable place.

She stood and stretched, glancing out the window at sunset colors tinting the buildings and street. She reached into her purse and clasped her fingers around Honeysuckle Hollow's skeleton key. She stared at the worn key resting in her palm. "I haven't forgotten you. Because of what you've done for others, we'll get you fixed up." She dropped the key back into her purse. "Now if I could just figure out what *I'm* going to do for permanent housing, that would be great."

After closing down and locking up the office, Tessa returned to the apartment. She changed out of her work clothes and pulled on a pair of loose soccer shorts and a T-shirt. She grabbed the listings she'd printed for herself and made notes on the positives and negatives about each house. She glanced at the copy of *Guests of Honeysuckle Hollow* on the coffee table. Tessa realized she'd been comparing all the listings to Honeysuckle Hollow. Did the listing have the same size yard? Was it located in a historic neighborhood? Would anyone refer to it as a *fairy-tale house*? Her cell phone rang, and she hesitated when she saw it was Marty again. But it might be nice to have a conversation with someone who wouldn't demand she have immediate answers about future plans or major decisions.

"Hey, Marty."

Marty launched into questions immediately. He wanted to make sure she was okay and to ask if she needed anything. He'd heard about the residences around Jordan Pond, and he'd been worried about her for days. Guilt trickled into her chest the more Marty talked. Tessa had only known Marty from the few times she'd seen him in the butcher shop, but a few weeks ago, his best friend's wife had set them up for a group date. Marty obviously thought they had bonded during that one outing, and he'd been consistently texting and calling ever since. Tessa wasn't into him, but he was so nice that she hadn't yet had the heart to tell him to buzz off.

Marty was average looking at his best—built like a grizzly bear, with hands as big as vinyl records ending in fat, meaty fingers. His brown hair thinned across the top of his pale white scalp, and his glasses were too small for his wide, pudgy face. He wore ironed khakis, creased down the center of the pants legs, and a rotation of button-down shirts in varying shades of gray and navy blue. His averageness wouldn't have been so bad if he didn't smell like a meat locker. But he was a *nice guy.* Just not Tessa's guy.

Even though Tessa hadn't wanted to talk about her plan of action for finding a home, it bothered her that after twenty minutes on the phone, Marty still hadn't broached the subject of her future. But he did want to meet for dinner at Smiley's Restaurant, Bar & Arcade in Willow Grove, and she was on the verge of agreeing but hesitated. Their conversations lacked depth and rarely ventured past anything more than discussing how their workdays had been or what movie they'd seen recently. Tessa decided to test their compatibility on a subject that was important to her.

She cleared her throat. "Honeysuckle Hollow is going up for sale soon."

Marty breathed into the phone. "That old hunk-a-junk on Dogwood? Old Dr. Hamilton's place?"

Tessa frowned. "It's not junk. It needs work, sure, but it's salvageable. A woman out West inherited it. She mentioned it being a teardown, but I think I can convince her not to."

"Why?" Marty asked. "Wouldn't it be easier to raze it so someone else can build something new and more practical?"

Tessa huffed. "It's a historical home. You don't just *raze* it."

Marty grunted. Tessa could picture the dull expression on his face.

"Would be easier, though," he said.

"If I had the money, I'd rehab it myself," she muttered, surprised at her own admission.

Marty snorted. "You? Tess, like my mama always says, 'Stick with what you know.' I know meat. You know real estate. No reason to shackle yourself to a money pit."

Tessa sagged against the couch. Maybe Marty was right. What did she know about rehabbing old homes? Close to nothing. But the idea bounced around in her head like a ball in a pinball machine. She pulled out her notebook and flipped back to her most recent list, which asked *What should I do?* Beside the number four, she wrote the question, *Rehab project?* Then she added, *Marty: No. Stick to what you know.* Beside the number five she wrote, *I could learn a new trade, couldn't I?*

"So whaddya say?" Marty asked, interrupting her thoughts.

"Huh?"

"About dinner, Tess. Meet me in an hour? We'll have a good time, and you can forget all about that dump of a house."

Tessa scowled. *But I don't want to forget about it. I promised I would help it.* "Eh, thanks, Marty, but it's been a long day. Maybe some other time. I'll talk to you later."

Tessa sighed and fluttered the pages of house listings on the coffee table. She opened the living room window to let in a breeze. Then she knelt and rested her arms on the sill. Evening clouds scattered from the darkening sky, revealing the first stars of the night. Melancholy settled around her, and she let it linger for a few minutes. She still didn't have a plan, and she would need one soon.

Her stomach growled, and she shuffled into the kitchen, grabbing her phone on the way. She texted Anna two questions: Should I sell my home? Can I learn a new trade?

Within a minute, her cell dinged. Anna texted: I think you've been offered a new opportunity to change your living arrangements. This could be an open window instead of a closed door. And it depends on the trade. You're smart and capable. But you don't want to become a chef, do you? Call me if you need to talk.

At this point, Tessa didn't even know what else to say. She grabbed her notebook. Beside number three's responses from her mama and Lily about selling her home, Tessa added Anna's answer.

Anna: Yes, it's a new opportunity. Now she had three people who were giving her the go-ahead to sell.

Tessa opened the fridge and grabbed the container of home fries. She filled the kettle, set it on the stove, and waited for the water to boil. Tessa microwaved the potatoes and walked into the living room. The mint's fat leaves were growing larger every day, stretching long tendrils across the apartment. Now its arms invaded Canada, the US's Pacific coast, and Central America. She pulled off a handful of leaves, releasing the cool scent into the air. When she inhaled, the melancholy faded.

Tessa dropped mint leaves into the porcelain teapot and doused them in hot water. Her shoulders relaxed, and she marveled at the mint's ability to relax her. Crazy Kate's voice filled her head. *Sprinkle some thyme from the garden into your potatoes, and tell me you don't know the rain is coming before everyone else.* The microwave dinged, and Tessa filled her mug with mint tea.

Whether it was because she was tired or because she was lonely without her family, friends, or a viable boyfriend around to console her, Tessa thought too long about Crazy Kate's words. She thought so long that her tea became cold, and she seriously debated whether the garden's plants might have hidden abilities. Sneaking into the garden and nipping a bit of thyme suddenly sounded like a brilliant idea.

Tessa slipped on a pair of flip-flops and grabbed a flashlight from the toolbox she found in the coat closet. She crept outside as though someone might be around to spot her, but the streets were quiet except for the evening wind rustling through the trees. Crickets chirped in the shadows. Tessa swung the light across the plants, looking for thyme. She found it halfway down the side garden and plucked off five sprigs. Already feeling completely ridiculous, she sprinted for the stairs and rushed into the apartment.

Tessa pulled off all the thyme leaves and sprinkled them on the potatoes before reheating them. Then she sat at the table, staring at the steam twirling up from the wedges, thinking maybe she'd gone round the bend this time. She ate the potatoes and drank cold mint tea until both were gone. Then she sat at the table feeling nothing but exhaustion. Before bedtime she opened the door to the apartment, stared up at the clear and starry sky, and felt nothing. No premonitions of impending rain, no thoughts of cloudy skies or sweltering heat. Nothing. A star twinkled at her, inviting her to make a wish, but Tessa wondered if wishes would make a difference.

Tessa woke the next morning to find an oppressive humidity blanketing the apartment. She glanced at the alarm clock and, upon seeing the time, wondered why the bedroom was still full of deep shadows. When she crawled out of bed and opened the blinds, she saw dark, ominous clouds hovering over Mystic Water. A sliver of dread shot through her. Mystic Water didn't need any more rain. But her anxiety snuffed out quickly, leaving Tessa feeling confused. Didn't threatening storm clouds mean rain? *No*, a voice said.

She dressed and prepared for her workday with a cup of coffee and a banana. When she stepped outside, the air clung to her skin, wet and sticky. Thunderheads loomed, and people on the streets scurried past with closed umbrellas and anxious skyward gazes. Again, Tessa felt a whisper of comfort in her mind, telling her the rain would not fall.

As she walked to the office, her cell rang. "Hello?"

"Good morning, Tessa. This is Mr. Jenkins. I got your message yesterday."

She paused in between two buildings so she could talk. "Yes, thank you for calling back. I'm looking for a contractor to help me with Honeysuckle Hollow." She informed Mr. Jenkins about the property. He was her first option because he'd restored the antebellum home on Anderson Ridge, and he'd remodeled parts of the Clarke House, another historical Victorian in Mystic Water, which was also Lily and Jakob's home.

Unfortunately, Mr. Jenkins wasn't available for three months. He told her he'd put in a call to Charlie Parker, who had apprenticed with him. Tessa told him she could meet up with Charlie that afternoon. Just as Tessa unlocked the real estate office, Mr. Jenkins called again and said Charlie could be at the house in an hour if that might work with her schedule.

Tessa did a quick email check and brewed a single cup of coffee before locking up again. A burst of wind rushed down the street and tangled her hair as she climbed into the Great Pumpkin. Thunder rumbled like an unhappy giant, vibrating the windows on Main Street. Shop owners lowered their awnings, preparing for the approaching storm, but Tessa rolled down her windows and drove to Honeysuckle Hollow, letting the outside air swirl inside the car, bringing with it the scent of crushed thyme.

Tessa parked on the curb in front of the house and called an exterminator. If Honeysuckle Hollow went on the market, it needed to be free of animals. While making the phone call, she debated rolling up the car windows but again felt as though there was no need.

She hopped through the high weeds and scattered ladybugs

hiding in the grass. Once inside Honeysuckle Hollow, she leaned one arm on the finial at the bottom of the staircase, wondering what life was like when the home sparkled with happiness and bloomed with beauty. A powerful feeling of homesickness swept over her, and she sat on the bottom stair.

"I'm lonely for a home." She looked around at the covered furniture, the lacy cobwebs hugging corners, and the dust shrouding the house. "Maybe you're lonely too," she said to the house. Tessa exhaled a shaky breath, stood, and patted the finial. "I'll convince Mrs. Steele to sell you to someone who wants to renovate rather than demolish. I know I can find someone to fix you up. You'll feel right as rain again." She wished someone would say the same to her.

Tessa wandered into the living room, seeing the trails in the dust left behind during her previous visit. She approached the bat-infested fireplace with apprehension. Reaching into her purse, she pulled out a mini bottle of face mist. If the bats attacked again, this time she would be ready. She hoped they were deterred by tangerine-scented mist.

Tessa studied the tile work surrounding the cast-iron mantel. She reached out and rubbed the edge of her fist against a tile in the top left corner. "Would you look at that. A face appears." Tessa watched as a face, one that looked like a medieval knight, peeked through the grime covering a bas-relief. She used her fingers to scrub the tile in the opposite corner. As the beautiful face of a woman appeared, she smiled. "And a princess. This *is* a fairy-tale house."

Thunder bellowed, and the chandelier in the foyer responded, throwing tinkling echoes throughout the front of the house. Tessa walked to the nearest window and peered up at the sky. Shadowy clouds billowed low and angry. "It'll pass," she whispered.

Then she noticed a shelf on the built-ins held ten similarly bound leather books. Tessa removed one and gaped at the title: *Guests of Honeysuckle Hollow.* The handwritten dates on the inside front cover dated back more than twenty-five years ago. Like the book the bats knocked from the mantel the day before, this volume was filled to the final page with guests' scribblings. Each of the ten books was crowded with the names and words of all the people who found refuge in Honeysuckle Hollow. Tessa hugged the open book to her chest. This house had touched so many, and now it was suffering. She *had* to do something.

A knock sounded at the door, and a voice called out a greeting from the foyer. Tessa returned the book to the shelf. A young woman, who looked to be Tessa's age, stepped through the front door. Her shiny black hair was pulled into a ponytail. Even though the woman was dressed in loose-fitting cargo pants and a maroon tank top, Tessa saw she had the body of a ballet dancer—lithe and willowy. An umbrella was tucked beneath her toned arm.

"Can I help you?"

"I'm here to help *you*, I believe," the woman said.

Tessa's brow furrowed. "Are you from the exterminating service? That was fast. I wasn't expecting anyone until late this afternoon. Unless . . . I mentioned to them that I would be looking for a cleaning service eventually. Surely they didn't contact a service without telling me. Did anyone explain to you the state of things here because—"

The woman held up her hand, and Tessa stopped talking. The woman's smile widened and displayed white teeth against her mocha-colored skin, making her even more attractive.

"I'm not the exterminator, and I'm definitely not the maid," she said. "I dressed as a French maid one year for Halloween—*big* mistake—but I hardly think that counts. I'm Charlie Parker."

Tessa's mouth hung agape for a few seconds. "You're a woman."

Charlie laughed. "Last I checked."

Charlie held out her hand, and Tessa shook it, feeling like an idiot. "I'm Tessa Andrews, the real estate agent for Honeysuckle Hollow."

"Oh, don't look so apologetic. It's a common source of confusion, not only that there's is a woman named Charlie but also that I'm also a contractor. I can do the job, don't worry. I grew up around houses. My dad is a mason, my uncle is a carpenter, a few cousins paint houses, and my aunt renovates kitchens and bathrooms."

"You basically have your own building company," Tessa said.

Charlie laughed. "Not much we can't do in the Parker bunch. I also have a killer red-velvet-cake recipe."

Tessa smiled. "I'd ask you for it, but I'm pretty much a disaster in the kitchen. Thanks for coming over."

"Good thing we're meeting this morning," Charlie said, tossing a thumb over her shoulder. "Looks like it's going to start raining cats and dogs any second."

"It's not going to rain," Tessa blurted. Then she furrowed her brow. "It's not," she repeated as though arguing with herself.

"Have you seen it out there?" Charlie said. She whipped out her umbrella and tapped it against her palm. "I hope you brought one of these. Is that your car? The orange one? Windows are down."

"Yeah, but it's not—" Tessa paused. *Going to rain*, a voice finished. She bit her lower lip and tucked her hair behind her ears. Her eyes darted toward the windows. Even from her vantage point, she could see the darkness hanging above the town. *How* was it not going to rain, and why did she keep thinking it wouldn't? She cleared her throat. "Let's talk about the house."

"Mr. Jenkins said you're wanting to fix up this place," Charlie said, stepping into the living room, back out into the foyer, and then into the dining room. She lifted a sheet from a dining chair before dragging a finger along the chair rail encircling the room. "Gonna take a lot of work. You thinking a total redo or touch-ups here and there? What's your end point?"

"First priority is making the house safe. Well, before that, I want to get rid of the infestation, and then I want to make sure the house is sound," Tessa said. "Right now, I need to figure out how much it will cost to get this place market ready, and I'm not sure what kind of repairs it needs. I'm hoping you'll give me an idea. Let me show you around."

While they toured the second floor, her cell phone rang. "Excuse me one minute. Hey, Mama, I'm working right now—"

"Have you seen the weather channel?" Carolyn asked.

"No, ma'am—"

"Hasn't Mystic Water suffered enough? I can't believe it's calling for a massive streak of thunderstorms. How is everyone taking it? Are they in a panic? I checked in on the renters at the house, and they're doing just fine. They aren't worried about a little rain, but I gave them your number in case they need anything local. Speaking of local, have you decided—"

"Mama, it's not gonna rain here," Tessa said, feeling more and more convinced.

"How could you possibly know that?"

"I just *know.* It'll pass right over us." Tessa exhaled. "I'll call you back, okay? I'm working." She ended the call and shoved the phone into her pocket.

When it came time to assess the exterior of the house, including the crawl space, Charlie offered to show Tessa what lay beneath Honeysuckle Hollow. But Tessa had no desire to explore the darkness hiding under the abandoned house. Armed with a headlamp and flashlight, Charlie crawled beneath the house and disappeared.

After ten minutes, Tessa stared through the crawl space opening. "You okay?"

"All's well," Charlie called, and her headlamp swung toward Tessa. "A huge black snake is hiding out in the far corner, but otherwise, it looks uninhabited."

After she emerged, Charlie wrote extensive notes and sketched in a notepad she kept tucked in her back pocket. After nearly two hours of discussion, Charlie agreed to take on the project if Mrs. Steele wanted to make repairs. Charlie was confident she and a team could start work on Honeysuckle Hollow by the end of the week. Before renovations could begin, though, Tessa needed to call Mrs. Steele concerning the budget.

As they stood on the front porch, Charlie stepped into the front yard and looked skyward. "Maybe you're right," she said. "Still ain't raining. How about I call *you* for a weather report instead of watching the news?" She strode across the yard toward her maroon F-150.

Wind, heavy with moisture, whirled across the porch, dampening every space it touched. Tessa's stomach clenched, and her palms began to sweat as she inhaled the scent of thyme. The echo of Crazy Kate's words fluttered around in her mind. Was her confidence about the rain skipping over town because of the thyme she ate from Cecilia's garden? If the garden could help Tessa predict the weather, what else could it do?

CHAPTER 8

STRAWBERRY PANCAKES

AFTER LEAVING HONEYSUCKLE HOLLOW, TESSA RETURNED TO her office, checked messages, and then looked over Charlie's notes. The house was salvageable, but extensive work was needed if it was to be returned to its former beauty. Tessa wasn't sure how much money Mrs. Steele was willing to put toward renovations, so she created a few different options. One option would focus on basic repairs—electrical, plumbing, exterior and interior supports—and get the house market ready but only as a property in need of renovation. The next option required more upgrades—flooring, windows, doors, paint, and appliances, as well as other minor aesthetics. The final option would be to restore Honeysuckle Hollow completely, to recreate what the home had been when it was first built but with modern appliances and conveniences. The more extensive the work, the higher the listing price.

Tessa called Mrs. Steele, and when she received no answer, she left a detailed message regarding possible avenues to explore. She printed a few more listings for herself and texted Lily: Wanna come over tonight?

Lily responded: Be there at 7:00.

Tessa assumed Mrs. Steele would at least want the house exterminated before listing it. Charlie hadn't mentioned the house was unsafe, so Tessa went ahead and scheduled a cleaning service. She felt comfortable paying the bill for both services until Mrs. Steele reimbursed her. Later that afternoon, she met the cleaning crew at Honeysuckle Hollow. Tessa walked them through the rooms and instructed them to do a basic cleaning—no deep cleaning until she had more information from Mrs. Steele. They scheduled to return the next day.

As the blazing red sun set, Tessa changed out of her work clothes and pulled on a pair of comfy purple joggers and her favorite LSU T-shirt. She held back her hair with a stretchy tie-dye headband and washed her face. In the kitchen, Tessa read through the recipe for strawberry chamomile tea that Cecilia had left for her. At the top of the index card, Cecilia had written, *For when you need to relax and rest.* Surely she could make a new tea recipe without causing harm to herself or anyone else. Tessa read over the ingredients. She needed strawberries, dried chamomile, honey, and lemons. She had everything, thanks to the Borellis, including dried chamomile from Cecilia's garden.

Tessa opened a cabinet and grabbed a mason jar full of the dried herb. She filled a pot with two cups of water and put it on the stove to boil. Once the water boiled, she dropped in a handful of clean strawberries. The recipe required two tablespoons of dried chamomile. Tessa figured she could eyeball it. She tried to sprinkle the chamomile over the top of the strawberries, but the herb clumped together and stuck inside the jar. Tessa tapped the glass bottom and a heaping mass of the herb dislodged and fell into the water. Tessa winced. Would too much chamomile ruin the tea? She added honey and poured the mixture through a sieve and into a pitcher. Then she squeezed two lemons into the tea and added a pinch of salt. Tessa stirred the warm liquid with a wooden spoon and ladled a bit out to taste.

She smiled. “It’s good.”

Tessa dropped in a handful of ice cubes to help cool down the tea before she found a spot for it in the refrigerator. Then she gathered the ingredients for the pancakes.

Lily called a few minutes before she was supposed to arrive at the apartment and said two-year-old Rose had decided to smash spaghetti into Lily’s hair and she needed a quick shower. Tessa’s stomach growled. She could save Lily some time if she started cooking. After the tea success, she felt brave and competent. If she could make tea, she could make pancakes, right?

Tessa found the biggest bowl in the apartment for the batter. Then she tilted the strawberries out of their carton and onto a cutting board. No matter how hard she tried to cut the berries into uniform slices, the pieces were uneven. She wouldn’t win any presentation points tonight.

She found a measuring cup in a drawer and shoved it into the flour canister. Then she dumped flour into the bowl and followed it with baking powder. She dropped in two heaping tablespoons of salt, along with a dash of sugar. She gave the mixture a quick stir, and then she whisked the egg, milk, and vanilla in another bowl. After melting butter in the microwave, she poured the wet ingredients over the dry, added the butter, and stirred. The recipe said to fold in the cut strawberries. Tessa had no idea what *folding* meant, so she dropped in a few strawberries at a time and pushed batter over top of them. When she was finished, she surveyed the batter and said, "That wasn't so bad."

Tessa warmed a cast-iron skillet on the stove. She speared a pat of butter on a fork and circled it around on the hot skillet. As the butter bubbled, it began to smoke, so Tessa turned down the heat and opened the apartment windows. A cool spring breeze eased through the apartment, ruffling book pages and tickling the hairs on the back of Tessa's neck.

Using an ice cream scoop, she dropped three uneven blobs of pancake batter onto the skillet. While popping and sizzling, the batter slid toward the middle, creating one gigantic blog. Tessa used a spatula to try and sever the batter into sections, but they kept reforming into one. When she thought the amorphous pancake was ready to be flipped, she slid the spatula beneath and tried to turn it over. The underside was too gooey, and batter flung all over the side of the skillet and splattered her shirt. She wiped the batter from her shirt and popped her fingers into her mouth. It tasted odd, but Tessa assumed that was because the batter was still raw.

She tried again to divide the pancake into thirds and was successful. Three lopsided pancakes sizzled in the skillet. She laid strips of bacon on a plate covered in paper towels and microwaved them. She poked the browned pancakes with her finger.

"See, Lily, I can cook."

By the time the bacon was cooling, a dozen misshapen pancakes sat on a serving platter. Tessa grabbed syrup, butter, and the strawberry chamomile tea from the refrigerator and set the petite table for two. At half past seven, Lily knocked. When Tessa opened the door, Lily narrowed her eyes.

"It smells like you've been cooking." Lily stepped into the apartment and dropped her purse on the couch. "Is it safe to come in here?"

"I made pancakes!" Tessa said, bouncing on her toes. "And bacon. And tea!"

Lily walked to the table and eyed the stack. "All by yourself? Should I be frightened?"

"I followed Mrs. Borelli's recipes. I couldn't possibly screw these up."

Lily smirked. "Didn't you say that about the meatloaf you made a couple of weeks ago?"

Tessa frowned. "I didn't know there was a limit to how many breadcrumbs you could add. It looked pretty when I was mixing it. But it *was* really dry."

"I almost choked on it. It lodged like a rock in my throat. And no one wants the Heimlich performed on them at a dinner party." Lily sat at the table. "This all *smells* good. Let's see how it tastes."

Tessa filled two glasses with the tea. She forked a few pancakes onto Lily's plate and then a couple onto her own. They smeared butter on the stacks and doused the pancakes in syrup. Tessa doled out bacon slices, and Lily lifted one and took a bite.

Lily nodded and smiled. "Bacon's good." Then she cut into her pancake stack and stabbed the pieces with her fork. "Ready?"

Tessa nodded, and they both shoved pancakes into their mouths. Once the taste of syrup melted away, Tessa's first instinct was to spit the food back onto the plate. Her tongue shriveled in her mouth as all the moisture was leeched. Lily's blue eyes were bugging out. They both chewed as quickly as possible and struggled to swallow. Tessa grabbed her glass of tea and gulped it down. Lily drank her tea even faster.

"Why does it taste like I made them with sea water?" Tessa whined.

"Too much salt for sure," Lily said. "You followed the recipe?"

"Yes," Tessa said defensively. She snatched the recipe from the counter. "I added the flour and baking soda and—oh . . ."

"Oh what?" Lily asked. "Should I be calling the poison-control hotline?"

"I swapped the amount of salt with the amount of sugar." Tessa slumped into her chair. "Why am I such a catastrophe?"

Lily chuckled and refilled her tea glass. "You're not a catastrophe. Well, maybe a little in the kitchen. The bacon is good, and the tea is great." Lily drank more tea. Then she yawned and covered her mouth.

Tessa exhaled. "It's been a crappy couple of days. My condo is trashed. I was attacked by vampire bats and threatened by a flea-infested cat. I smell-tasted urine and moldy carpet—" She waved her hand in the air when Lily's eyebrows rose into her blond curls. "Don't ask. I had a disheartening conversation with Marty. And now I've ruined dinner. Wow, I'm also a huge whiner right now."

Lily wiped her mouth with a napkin. "You know what will make it better?"

Tessa struggled to keep her spirits from plummeting. "What?"

Lily pointed toward the top of the refrigerator. "I see a box of Cap'n Crunch up there, and nothing makes a crappy day better than a big bowl or two of cereal." She grabbed the cereal, bowls, spoons, napkins, and milk and motioned for Tessa to follow her into the living room. "Let's watch something mindless on TV and eat cereal like we're twelve."

"Home-improvement shows?" Tessa suggested, following her and then plopping onto the couch.

Lily poured Tessa a heaping bowl of cereal, and a few Crunch Berries skittered across the coffee table. She reached out and popped them into her mouth. She passed Tessa the bowl and the milk before she prepped her own bowl. She settled onto the couch and yawned again.

"I must be sleepier than I thought."

Tessa made sure to cover each piece of cereal with a splash of milk. She spooned in a mouthful.

Lily patted her cereal into her milk, making the berries bounce like beach balls in a pool. "Tell me you weren't serious about smell-tasting urine."

Tessa tried to laugh, but she choked on her cereal and ended up coughing Cap'n Crunch all over her joggers. She stared down at her pants speckled with soggy Crunch Berries. Tessa felt an explosion of emotion, and rather than cry, she started laughing, and it was contagious. Once they both started giggling, they couldn't stop. Tessa was a mess and practically homeless, but laughing with Lily stopped anxiety and sadness from making homes in her heart.

After three bowls of Cap'n Crunch and four episodes of Tessa's favorite home-improvement show, she slouched into the couch cushions and patted her stomach. "I'm stuffed, and the roof of my mouth is completely raw. I couldn't eat another

Crunch Berry even if I wanted to."

"I haven't eaten this much cereal since that time in college when we stayed up all night trying to finish our English term papers." Lily pushed out her tongue and poked it a few times. "My tongue is definitely raw. So what's next for you? Have you given any more thought to your condo or looking at listings?"

Honeysuckle Hollow immediately came to mind, but she pushed it aside. "I've seen a few possibilities." Tessa grabbed her notebook from the coffee table and flipped to the most recent list

What should I do?

1. Don't finish waffle.

2. Move home for weeks?

3. Sell my home? Mama: Yes. Lily: Yes. Anna: Yes, it's a new opportunity.

4. Rehab project? Marty: No. Stick to what you know.

5. I could learn a new trade, couldn't I? Anna: Depends on the trade.

Three people had already told her to sell her ruined condo. She closed the notebook. "I'm going to sell my condo."

Lily whipped her head over to Tessa. "Seriously? Why are you just now mentioning this? Are you okay?"

Tessa shrugged. "Yes and no. You, Mama, and Anna all think it's a smart idea. It doesn't make sense to spend all that time and money repairing it, and if I'm honest with myself, I'm not sure it's repairable. I'm fairly certain the insurance money wouldn't even be enough to pay for new floors, much less anything else. You were right. It's not my forever home. And according to Mr. Fleming, the HOA president, it's nearly unanimous that everyone wants to sell to the developer. I don't think I'd have much choice at this point."

The evening wind blew through the open windows and pushed over the empty cereal box on the coffee table. Tessa breathed in the scent of strawberries and honeysuckle. She heaved herself off the couch and grabbed the cereal box. Then she carried their bowls to the sink and dropped the empty box into the recycling bin.

"I brought home a few listings. Do you want to look through them with me?" Tessa asked.

Lily hopped off the couch. "I'd love to. You know I love shopping."

They crawled onto the bed and sat in the center while Tessa spread out the printed listings. Tessa had already organized them by preference with her first pick on top and her least favorite on the bottom. They flipped through the papers, and Tessa explained why she'd chosen each house, while Lily approved or disapproved the choice.

Lily picked up the last listing. "Tell me you aren't considering buying Honeysuckle Hollow. It's up the street from us, but it's in awful shape."

"No," Tessa said, reaching for the paper. "The owner wants to sell, and she's asked me to list it for her. I went over there to have a look, and it definitely needs work."

"From the outside alone, it looks as though it needs *a lot* of work. I feel sorry for anyone who decides to undertake that renovation." Lily glanced at the clock on the bedside table. She yawned and stretched her arms over her head. "How did it get so late? I better get going. Rose has probably used her big brown eyes to manipulate her daddy into letting her stay up way past her bedtime. I wouldn't be surprised if she was hyped up on sugar too."

Tessa held the housing information for Honeysuckle Hollow. She hoped Mrs. Steele would invest in repairs. A flutter of excitement accompanied the thought of seeing Honeysuckle Hollow become a grand home again. She dropped the listing on her bed and walked Lily to the door.

Tessa returned to the bedroom to gather the papers from the bed, but a strong gust of wind, smelling of cloves and forest pines, blew in through the bedroom window. The papers lifted from the bed in a frenzied dance, and the picture of the Borellis on the dresser fell onto its glass face. Then the wind was gone, and the papers fluttered to the floor all over the bedroom. Tessa started gathering them when she heard the front door close again. She was sure she'd locked it behind Lily. Something heavy dropped against the living room floor.

Tessa peeked around the bedroom doorway, and her heart kicked into high gear. An intruder stood in the living room, just inside the front door, looking into the kitchen. Had he broken in using a credit card? Did that actually work? Did he own a fancy lock-picking kit? He didn't appear to be in any hurry to ransack the apartment and steal her belongings. He also didn't appear to notice her, but she couldn't take her eyes off him.

His wavy almost-black hair was disheveled, and he had at least three days' worth of stubble shadowing his handsome face. Even from a distance, she could see his eyes were icy blue. His clothes were rumpled like a man's who'd been traveling for days. An army-green duffel bag lay beside his worn thick-soled boots. He looked like the leading man in a treasure-hunting movie. He stepped into the kitchen, and Tessa looked around the bedroom for a weapon. The only thing near enough to reach was a swollen copy of her high school yearbook still drying on the dresser. She grabbed it and tiptoed through the doorway.

The man picked up a cold pancake from the stack she'd left on the table. He tore it in half and took a bite. He gagged at the same moment he became aware of her presence and looked momentarily startled to see someone in the apartment with him. Tessa lifted the yearbook over her head as though she might throw it at him. He spit the partially chewed pancake piece into his hand, and they stared at each other in a silent standoff. Then he broke eye contact, walked to the kitchen sink, and washed his hands.

He turned to look at her. "Are you going to show me nostalgic pictures or beat me with that?"

Tessa lowered the yearbook and squeezed it against her chest. There was something familiar about his smile, about the way his lips tugged up on the right, creating a dimple in his cheek.

When she didn't respond, he continued, "I've been smelling strawberry pancakes since I got off the plane. I followed the scent all the way to Mystic Water. They're one of my favorites, but those are bloody awful."

"Salt," Tessa blurted. Then she pressed her lips together and squeezed the book tighter against her.

He chuckled. "Are you using them to trap unsuspecting travelers? Tempt them with nasty treats?" He pulled a glass from the cabinet and filled it with the strawberry chamomile tea. He gulped it down and poured himself another glass.

Tessa frowned. "*Nasty* is a little harsh. They're not that bad." *Why does he seem so familiar?*

"Not bad if you're starving, and even that's debatable," he said, shoving a hand through his hair. "I hope you didn't dress up at my expense." He finished the second glass of tea.

Tessa sensed he was teasing her, but still her mood curdled. She glanced down at her worn-out clothes. She was dressed like a college student who hadn't done laundry in weeks, given the food stains on her clothes. Great first impression. *Why do I care what he thinks?* "That's rich coming from someone who looks like he's been sleeping in his clothes for days."

He looked down at himself and nodded. "Touché."

"What are you doing here? How did you get in?"

He held up a set of keys on a silver ring and jingled them. "This is my parents' place. I knew my dad hid a set of keys in a magnetic box under the outside stairs. Who are you?"

Tessa's mouth fell open. She realized why he looked familiar, why his smile reminded her of someone else. "Paul?"

It was his turn to look surprised. "Have we met? Apologies, but it's been a long day, and I'm usually good with names, but I don't recall ever meeting you. Unless you're that girl from the lift in London. The vesper martinis were dangerously strong, and I've forgotten a good portion of that evening." He sounded like he was joking.

"I've never been to London." Tessa went to tuck her hair behind her ears and realized it was still shoved back with the tie-dye headband. She groaned. An attractive man walked into her apartment, and she was wearing food-stained clothes, and her hair was a greasy mess. Not to mention, he'd eaten her awful pancakes. Not her best performance. "We've never met," Tessa said. "I know your parents."

"Why are you in the apartment?"

"Mystic Water flooded, and I lost my condo. Your parents have been letting me stay here."

Paul yawned. "Excuse me. Long day. Sorry about your condo. Nice of them to let you stay here for a while. They weren't likely expecting me." He leaned down, grabbed his bag, and walked past her and into the bedroom. He dropped his duffel on the floor next to the bed.

"They haven't seen you in five years," Tessa said, staring at him, feeling panic rise in her chest at the sight of him in the bedroom.

He sat on the bed and untied his boots. Then he pulled them off and dropped them against the floor one *thump* at a time. Tessa's stomach knotted. He gazed up at her with his pale-blue eyes. "Hope you're not planning to scold me for being the world's worst son," he said playfully, but Tessa heard the faint hint of disappointment in his voice. He yawned again.

"Should I? I'm sure they'll be surprised to see you. Especially since *I'm* staying here."

Paul laid back on the bed with his arms splayed. His eyes closed, and his head rolled toward his shoulder. "What did you put in that tea? A sleeping potion?"

Tessa's heart thudded. "Chamomile. And umm . . . you're on the bed." What was he doing on the only bed in the apartment?

"Nothing gets past you, does it?" He yawned again.

"But—but I'm a *girl*."

Paul opened his eyes and stared at her. A sleepy grin dimpled his cheek. "Very much so."

Tessa's stomach flipped upside down. The evening wind crept through the bedroom window. "I know this apartment was meant for you, but I'm staying here now. If you're planning on hanging around until the morning, you should sleep on the couch."

Paul closed his eyes. "I've been up for twenty-four hours, Ms.—" He opened his eyes long enough to look at her again. "What did you say your name was?"

"Tessa."

"Yes, well, I've been up for twenty-four hours, Ms. Tessa, maker of awful pancakes and drafter of strong sleeping potions, and I could use a nice bed to sleep in. If you're dead set on sleeping in the bed"—he patted the mattress beside him—"then have at it. I'm not sleeping on the bloody couch."

Tessa gripped the collar of her T-shirt and pulled it up higher on her neck. Was he serious? She wouldn't be caught dead sleeping in the bed with a stranger, even a handsome one. She opened her mouth to argue, but he was already snoring. Tessa exhaled a loud sigh and finished picking up the scattered papers. She left them on the dresser and turned off the bedroom light.

"This was unexpected." She dropped onto the couch and texted Lily, even though Lily would probably think it was a prank.

There's a jerk in my bed.

A few minutes later, Lily responded: Don't feed him the pancakes.

Tessa texted: Too late. She lay back on the couch and closed her eyes, wondering what she would do in the morning with Paul Borelli, the prodigal son.

CHAPTER 9

FRENCH TOAST

TESSA WOKE UP WITH A CRICK IN HER NECK AND HER LEGS dangling off the couch. Sunlight streamed through the windows, and she experienced a disorienting few seconds when she didn't know where she was. Then her mind quickly connected her fragmented thoughts. Diner apartment, strawberry pancakes, Paul. She lurched upright so quickly that black dots swam in her vision. The bedroom door was open.

Tessa combed her fingers through her messy hair, and she stood and smoothed her hands down her college T-shirt and joggers, both still dirty and wrinkled. Her mouth tasted like stale Cap'n Crunch, and when she breathed into her cupped palm, she grimaced. Maybe Paul was still asleep, and she could sneak into the bathroom, take a shower, and dress in something that didn't look like she'd found it under the bed in a college dorm.

Tessa tiptoed toward the bedroom and peeked inside. The duvet had been straightened, looking as though no one had slept in the bed. Paul's traveling bag was tucked against the wall.

Great, Tessa thought. *He's already gone and seen me looking like a disaster on the couch.*

She'd probably been drooling with her mouth hanging open wide enough to catch bullfrogs. Any decent man would have let the woman sleep in the bed. Clearly, Paul wasn't decent. Not Paul, who'd been awake for *twenty-four hours.*

She stomped her way through the bedroom, took a hot shower, and pulled on her last pair of clean slacks and a slate-blue blouse. Tessa slipped on a pair of flats and grabbed the house listings from the bedroom dresser. She'd make time to go by and see the ones she and Lily had chosen, and she hoped to receive an answer from Mrs. Steele about the Honeysuckle Hollow renovations.

When Tessa walked into the kitchen to brew a cup of coffee, she found a plate piled high with French toast made with fat rounded bread slices. A card sat tented on the table beside the plate. A small carafe of syrup and pats of butter on a small dish had been placed on the table, as well as utensils and an empty mug. Tessa reached for the card.

Dear Ms. Tessa,

Please accept my apologies for my brutish behavior last night. If it were a full moon, I would blame my werewolf-like state on it. Lack of sleep stole my manners. Thank you for allowing a weary traveler to rest in a proper bed. I hope you will enjoy one of my favorite childhood treats: French toast made with challah bread, compliments of my mom. Come downstairs and say hello before you start your day. We should be properly introduced.

Sincerely,
Paul "the Brute" Borelli

P.S. I am only somewhat loath to admit I ate the rest of your caramel creams. I'll restock.

Tessa couldn't stop her smile. Maybe Paul wasn't such a jerk after all. She glanced at the coffee table. The pink bag of caramel creams was gone. She reread his words; it was by far the politest letter she'd ever received. On paper, he sounded incredibly charming—the complete opposite of last night's rudeness.

She slid the plate of French toast into the microwave and warmed the pieces for a few seconds. He'd gotten breakfast for her. She allowed herself another smile, to relish the idea that a handsome man brought her breakfast. No one had ever cooked breakfast for her. *Okay, so his mama cooked breakfast, but the thought is there, right?* She poured syrup over a slice of toast and cut herself a bite. *Pillowy perfection*, she thought as she chewed. Tessa finished eating one whole piece and scarfed down another without a shred of guilt. Then she covered the plate with plastic wrap and put it into the refrigerator.

She rushed to the bathroom to check her hair and makeup. Then she fretted about what she was wearing until she realized she was being ridiculous. Still, she glanced one last time at her reflection, added a sweep of mascara to her lashes, and then locked up the apartment.

Scrambled's booths and tables were packed with the early-morning breakfast crowd. Tessa pushed open the door and scanned the room. Laughter barreled out from the kitchen, wrapping around Tessa and tugging her forward. She caught a glimpse of Harry. She'd never seen his grin so wide and joyful, and his eyes were brighter than Tessa had ever seen. When Cecilia floated out of the kitchen smiling, Tessa knew Paul must be in the kitchen too.

Tessa's palms felt sweaty, so she wiped them against her slacks. She licked her dry lips. Paul stepped into view from the kitchen pass-through and saw her. His crooked smile dimpled his cheek, and he leaned through the opening, resting his arms on the stainless-steel ledge. Tessa couldn't stop her return smile or the warming in her cheeks. She lifted her hand in a small wave and tucked her hair behind her ears. Paul made a motion for her to come to the back just as Cecilia stepped in front of her.

"Paul came home," Cecilia said immediately as she pulled Tessa into a surprise hug.

The air whooshed from Tessa's lungs. "I know," she said breathlessly. Cecilia smelled like rosemary, and electricity emitted from her as though she'd been plugged into a wall socket.

Cecilia pulled away, and two lines wrinkled between her dark eyebrows. "You do?"

"Yes, ma'am," she said and nodded toward the kitchen. "Looks like he's in the kitchen."

Cecilia glanced over her shoulder and shook her head at Paul. She made a shooing motion with her hands, and he pulled his head back into the kitchen. "Come on, let me introduce you."

She dragged Tessa behind her. Cecilia's smile, displaying nearly all of her white teeth, was contagious. Energy radiated from her, and as she passed the tables in the dining room, ice rattled in glasses and bacon sizzled on plates. Cecilia pushed open the swinging kitchen door, and they found Harry and Paul laughing over a grill of frying hash browns.

"Tell me you didn't *eat* the sea urchin," Harry said, flipping the hash browns and pointing to a pan on the burner. "Start that omelet, please."

Paul ladled beaten eggs into the hot pan and grabbed a spatula. "Dad, it would have been rude to say no. I didn't have a choice. It was either eat it and see the forbidden caverns or say no and be shunned by the people. And I didn't eat the whole sea urchin. Just the reproductive organs." He shuddered.

Harry burst out laughing again. "Don't tell your mother."

"Don't tell me what?" Cecilia asked.

Harry glanced over his shoulder and smiled. "Good morning, Tessa. Two surprise kitchen guests. This is turning out to be a great day already."

"Good morning, Mr. Borelli," Tessa said.

"It's Harry," he said as he reached for a mug and filled it with tea from the carafe. "Mint tea." He handed the mug to her.

"Thank you," Tessa said, bringing the tea to her lips and blowing across the steaming liquid. She welcomed a tension reliever because her insides felt unusually jittery. When she sipped, she didn't feel the usual rush of relaxation. She held the mug closer to her nose and inhaled. No calming nerves. No loosening of her tangled thoughts. Hadn't the mint tea so far caused her to feel *different*? "Is this—is this perhaps a new recipe?"

Cecilia huffed. "Not *my* mint," she said. "Paul didn't know any better. When Harry asked him to make tea, Paul grabbed the extra mint I use for backup from the cooler. He didn't even think to take it from my garden."

Tessa's heart thumped wildly. She pressed one hand against her breastbone. *That land around the diner is special. You, of all people, should know that. Tell me what happened to you tonight after you drank the tea.* Crazy Kate's voice swelled in Tessa's head like a swarm of bees. She shook her head, and the voice faded. Tessa placed the mug on a shelf beside her.

Paul sprinkled two different kinds of cheese onto the omelet, followed by mushrooms, tomatoes, and green onions. Harry slid the golden, crispy hash browns from a large spatula onto a plate. Then he reached for Paul's omelet and folded it as he shimmied it from the pan onto the plate.

"I'll take over," Harry said. "You need to meet one of our favorite customers."

Paul wiped his hands on a kitchen towel. His blue shirt matched the color of his eyes, and Tessa wondered if he'd worn it on purpose, if he knew how heart-stopping the effect was on women—on *her.* Paul stepped closer to her and reached out his hand.

Cecilia said, "This is my oldest son, Paul. He's just flown in from Germany. He's going to stay with us for a while."

Tessa slipped her hand into Paul's. It was calloused and warm, and his grip was solid and strong.

He cut his eyes at Cecilia. "For a couple of days."

Cecilia waved her hands in the air dismissively. "I haven't seen you in years. I don't think it's too much to ask to see my son for more than a day."

"Mom—"

Tessa felt the beginnings of an argument brewing, so she said, "Nice to see you again. Thank you for breakfast."

Cecilia slid two plates into the kitchen pass-through, and Laney swooped by and grabbed them. "Again?" Cecilia asked.

Tessa glanced from her to Paul, and Paul's heavy sigh ruffled

Tessa's blouse. Tessa caught the scent of cloves. Harry returned to the kitchen and grabbed two empty plates. He sat them beside the griddle.

"Here we go," Paul said. He looked at Tessa, and his blue eyes darkened. "I omitted a few facts."

Tessa's eyebrows lifted. "You mean the fact that I met you last night?"

Cecilia fisted her hands on her hips, and Harry cracked two eggs onto the griddle. "What were you doing at the hotel last night?" Harry asked, looking over at Tessa.

"What hotel?" Tessa asked.

Cecilia looked at Paul. "Didn't you stay at a hotel?"

Tessa shook her head. "He stayed with me." But when Cecilia's mouth dropped open and her brown eyes widened to the size of Oreos, Tessa blurted, "We didn't sleep together." Then she slapped a hand over her mouth and blushed so hard that the heat nearly burned the skin on her fingers.

Paul leaned his head back and laughed. "Not for a lack of trying."

Tessa's throat tightened. "What?" she squeaked. "I would *never—*"

"I'm kidding," Paul said. "Relax a bit, or you're going to overheat." He reached for a plastic menu and fanned Tessa from where he stood. Tessa snatched the menu from his hands and glared at him.

Then he looked at Cecilia. "It was late. I had no idea there was someone staying in the apartment. But Tessa was there. We had a nice chat, she gave me a sleeping potion, and I fell asleep in less than fifteen minutes. I didn't call you to tell you I was in town because it was *late*, and I was exhausted. I wanted to surprise you this morning."

Confusion filled Cecilia's expression. "A sleeping potion?"

Tessa shook her head. "I hardly think chamomile tea is a sleeping potion." *Although I did add way more chamomile than the recipe called for.*

Guilt rippled over Cecilia's features. "I never would have guessed Paul would come to town. I'm sorry if it inconvenienced you. Paul, you'll need to check into the hotel. I've already given the apartment to Tessa while she repairs her condo."

Paul frowned. "Mom, I stay in hotels everywhere I go. I don't want to come here and stay in one too. I'll stay with you and Dad."

"There's not room," Cecilia said. "You know we downsized when we moved here. We have only one bedroom. The hotel will be more comfortable."

Tessa cleared her throat. "Paul can stay at the apartment."

Paul's blue eyes found hers, and he smirked. "Made an impression on you, huh?"

Tessa huffed. "I didn't mean *stay with me* at the apartment. I'll call Lily. I can stay at her place."

"Tessa, I don't want to put you out," Cecilia said. "You've only just moved in."

Tessa saw the conflict in Cecilia's eyes. Having Paul upstairs from the diner would be the closest he'd been to them in years.

"I don't mind." Tessa forced a smile because she absolutely hated the feeling of not having a home.

"That's sweet of you, Tessa," Harry said. "It'll be nice to have Paul using the space we made for him."

"I don't mind sharing the apartment," Paul said playfully.

"It has one bedroom," Tessa argued.

"And your point?"

Tessa blushed again and tucked her hair behind her ears. Paul laughed at her unease. Even though she knew he was teasing her, part of her thrilled at the idea of spending more time with him.

"It was nice to meet you *again*. I better get going. Got a busy day," she said. "I'll stop by after work and clear out my things."

Cecilia pulled Tessa into another hug. "Thank you."

Tessa waved good-bye and weaved her way through the crowded diner. Outside, the sunshine beamed across her face, and she was finally able to inhale a full breath. She hadn't *really* settled into the apartment. It would be easy to gather her belongings and stay with Lily.

She climbed into the Great Pumpkin and pulled the papers out of her work bag. She cranked the engine and turned on the radio. While flipping through the listings and her to-do list, she sang along with Taylor Swift. A knock at her passenger-side window startled her.

Paul gazed at her through the glass. She pushed the power button for the window, and her stomach flip-flopped at the sight of him resting his tanned arms on the door and leaning inside. She had a flashback of high school, when most guys had snickered at the Great Pumpkin and she'd wanted to melt into the driver's seat.

"I've never seen a car quite this orange."

"Paul, meet the Great Pumpkin. Great Pumpkin, meet Paul. My *real* car drowned in the flood. Totaled. Kaput."

"So you stole your grandpa's car?"

Tessa snorted. "Hardly. My parents have been housing it for the past forty years. Probably for moments of desperation like this. This baby took me to high school and back." She patted the steering wheel.

"And destroyed all your possibilities of being cool?"

Tessa rolled her eyes. "Something like that." When he continued smiling at her through the window, she asked, "Did you need something?"

"What are you doing today?"

"Working."

"And what does Ms. Tessa do for work?"

"Real estate."

"Interesting," he said. "And what's on today's agenda?"

Is he serious? "Phone calls. Meeting with a couple of clients. I also have a few listings to look at for myself, and I'm working on acquiring approval to rehab a historical home."

His blue eyes widened. "Now *that* sounds interesting. I know a thing or two about architecture. Perhaps I should come along."

"With me? To *work*?"

"It's a brilliant idea. I've got time to kill while Mom and Dad work." He opened the car door and sat in the passenger seat, grinning at her while he buckled the seat belt.

"Why does this suddenly feel like Bring Your Kid to Work Day?"

Paul laughed, filling the car with his intense energy and causing the volume on the radio to rise and the engine to rev. When he started singing along with Taylor Swift, in a surprisingly pleasant baritone, Tessa wondered, *Am I dreaming? Is there really a gorgeous man sitting in my car who wants to spend time with me* and *who is shamelessly singing along with Taylor Swift?*

CHAPTER 10

HONEYSUCKLE JAM

ON HER DRIVE AROUND TOWN, TESSA TRIED SEVERAL TIMES TO drop Paul back at the diner. Each time he refused. It wasn't as though she minded his company exactly. It was the fact that he was a complete distraction, albeit a tempting one.

Paul scanned through radio songs like a man who didn't have time to waste on any one genre for more than a few minutes. The rare moments when he found a song he loved, he blasted the tune so loudly that Tessa had to roll down the windows just to release the sound waves. On the corner of Poplar and Sycamore, every windowpane within twenty yards vibrated to the Doobie Brothers' "Listen to the Music." Mr. Morris, who was standing on the sidewalk retrieving his mail, shook a walking stick at their reckless music. When Tessa attempted to turn down the volume before she died of embarrassment, Paul grabbed her hand.

He shook his head and shouted over the music. "I love this song. It reminds me of driving through Sedona."

"I don't think they need to be reminded three counties over," she shouted in response.

Paul laughed, released her hand, and turned down the volume. "Listening to music isn't illegal within city limits. I like to *feel* the bass line in my body." He thumped his fist against his chest for emphasis.

"How are you not deaf, Tarzan?"

"What?" he asked and then winked at her.

During the morning, Tessa made phone calls and stopped by a few houses to meet with clients. She wasn't used to having someone listen in on every conversation she had and then offer his opinions afterward. Paul definitely had opinions about everything. She also drove them by the properties she wanted to look at for herself. Paul scratched off every listing on her short list of choices. Each one had a fatal flaw that he couldn't overlook. She reminded him multiple times that *he* would not be living in any of them, but still, he made her feel as though his opinion should be heeded.

Tessa parked in front of the dry cleaner and searched through her purse for the ticket. Her cell phone rang. Nell had given Tessa's number to another one of her friends whose house had flooded. The family needed help finding a local place to stay, if at all possible. Tessa asked a few questions and jotted down notes on the family's needs. She promised to call around and see what she could find, while doing her best to comfort the woman and assure her they'd find something as soon as possible.

"Do you also handle rental properties?" Paul asked.

Tessa dropped her phone into her purse and shook her head. "No, but I've been helping displaced families find temporary housing."

"You're working as a go-between for a rental company?"

"No," Tessa said. "I just know a lot of the local landlords, and most of these families don't even know where to start. I'm calling around for them."

Paul's surprised expression lifted his eyebrows. "You're helping them because . . .?"

Tessa glanced at him, waiting for more. When he didn't continue, she said, "Because it's the right thing to do. And because this town helps one another in times of need."

"Hmm," he said, glancing out the window. "I thought that was only a thing in the movies."

Tessa grinned at him. "With as much as you've traveled, I know you've encountered *good people*."

"Sure," he agreed, "in other countries, but not so much here."

Tessa shrugged. "You stick around anywhere long enough, you'll find the goodness." She grabbed her dry cleaner ticket and flapped it. "I'll be right back. Don't do anything." She eyed him warily.

Paul laughed. "Like what? Use the Great Pumpkin as a getaway car? You could probably outrun this behemoth on foot. You'd catch me before I could round the corner."

Tessa frowned. "Don't disrespect the Pumpkin. It's all I have."

"I'm kidding. This car is a classic. Don't take everything I say so seriously. I promise I'll sit here like a good little boy."

Tessa doubted he'd ever been *a good little boy*. There was entirely too much mischief in his blue eyes. She paid for her plastic-wrapped clothes and loaded them into the trunk. As she slid into the front seat, her cell phone started ringing. "Hello?"

"Ms. Andrews, this is Trudy Steele."

An image of Honeysuckle Hollow bloomed in her mind. "Hey, Mrs. Steele. I'm happy you called. You obviously got my message."

"I did—"

"Great! I want to talk more in depth with you about why I think the renovations are necessary, and I have a contractor already lined up—"

"Ms. Andrews, I have absolutely no desire to renovate that house or waste a dime on minor repairs. I've been talking with another local real estate agent who understands exactly what I want, and he found an investor who wants to purchase the land. The house is worthless to me, so it will be torn down."

"What?" Tessa gasped. She never expected that Mrs. Steele actually wanted to tear down the house. She assumed it had been a figure of speech. Tessa assumed any reasonable person would see the logic in making minor repairs and then selling the house for a greater profit. But it was no surprise that the land Honeysuckle Hollow sat on, which was prime real estate, would bring in a hefty sum. "But it's a historic home—"

"That doesn't interest me. I no longer require your help," Mrs. Steele said. "The demolition crew is scheduled for this morning. You can toss the keys on the porch and let the whole thing be crushed."

Tessa's throat tightened. "Can I change your mind?"

The line disconnected, and Tessa pulled the phone away from her ear and stared at it. A black hole opened in her stomach, and she felt herself collapsing into it.

Paul touched her arm. "You okay?"

She glanced at him, wide-eyed and short of breath. "The house. She contacted another real estate agent the same time she called me. They've made a deal already, and they're going to tear down Honeysuckle Hollow because the land is worth more than the house, at least to her." Her voice hitched, and she stared straight ahead, blinking rapidly.

"It's just a house. Don't let this get you so worked up—"

"It's not just a house!" she shrieked. "It's helped hundreds of people! It needs to be saved!" She inhaled two shuddering deep breaths. "I'm sorry. I didn't mean to yell. You must think I'm a loony bird. Can we blame it on the fact that my entire life is a bit of a mess?" She pressed her forehead against the steering wheel.

"I haven't known you long enough to verify your craziness yet. And your life isn't completely unraveling. You have the Great Pumpkin and a dashing stranger in your car."

Tessa lifted her head and looked at him. "The latter probably validates my instability. What kind of intelligent woman drives a stranger around in her car?"

He smiled. "A fascinating one."

Tessa almost smiled in return. "I need to go over there . . . see it one last time. Want me to drop you off at the diner?"

"And miss seeing a place called Honeysuckle Hollow? Never. Drive on, Miss Daisy."

Tessa snorted. "If I'm Miss Daisy, shouldn't you be driving me?"

When Tessa pulled the Great Pumpkin onto Dogwood Lane, she saw a red Audi sedan and a navy-blue double-cab dually parked in front of Honeysuckle Hollow. A white Ram truck with an attached trailer hauling a small bulldozer sat across the street. Her palms sweated. She parked against the curb a few doors down.

Tessa wiped her hands on her pants. How could they bulldoze Honeysuckle Hollow? "What about the koi?"

Paul's head tilted in question. "Should I understand that reference?"

"There's a backyard river behind the house. I saw a koi still alive in it the other day. Do you think they'll just drive right over it?" A breeze blew through the open car windows, bringing with it the scent of lavender.

Paul looked at the house through the windshield, and then he glanced at the back seat. "Got a container of any kind? This sounds like a rescue mission."

"Maybe the plastic covering the dry-cleaned clothes? We could wrap it like the goldfish prize people win at the fair."

"Thinking outside the box. I like that. Let's grab the plastic and go meet these destroyers."

Tessa put up the windows and turned off the engine. She unlocked the trunk, and together they pulled off the plastic encasing her clothing. Paul tucked the wad of plastic beneath his arm. Three men stood outside the house. A man with a grizzly gray beard yelled into his cell phone while the other two stood around, kicking at weeds. The youngest of the men wore faded blue jeans with a rip in one knee. His fluorescent-yellow shirt could have been used as a beacon to guide space aliens to earth. Tessa couldn't look directly at it without feeling as though her retinas were burning. She recognized the third man because he was a real estate agent from the neighboring town, and they had been on one lousy date.

Tessa glowered at him. "Hi, Ralph."

"Tessa," he crooned in a voice that was as slippery as his slicker-than-oil black hair. "I haven't seen you in a while, too long actually. What are you doing here?"

"Mrs. Steele has been working with both of us." Tessa was somewhat mollified to see surprise flicker in his mud-brown eyes. She pulled the skeleton key for Honeysuckle Hollow from her purse. "I have the key, *all* the keys, and I've already given the house a thorough walk-through." For show she grabbed the keyring full of miscellaneous keys Mrs. Steele had sent and jingled them. Tessa had no idea what the other keys went to, but it seemed vital that she prove her standing was more important because *she* had a way to unlock the front door. But was that relevant if they were about to demolish it?

"The walk-through was a waste of time, wasn't it? She wants it torn down," Ralph said. "The prospective investor wants to put a Fat Betty's here."

Tessa inhaled like someone punched her in the stomach. Dandelion seeds burst from their pods and rushed toward her. "You can't be serious."

"They make a lot of money," Ralph said with a shrug. "It would generate hundreds of thousands for the investor."

"That's a horrible plan for this land," Tessa argued. "A Fat Betty's in a historic neighborhood? This house has been around for more than one hundred years, and it has a history that is worth preserving. Don't you have any respect for history—"

Paul interrupted Tessa's tirade. "Excuse me, but what is a Fat Betty's?"

Tessa's scowled. "It's a heart attack in a paper bag. A greasy, disgusting place where your shoes stick to the linoleum—"

"That generates a few hundred thousand dollars per store per year," Ralph said.

Tessa pointed at the house. "This home has been a haven

for longer than you've been alive, Ralph. I can't believe you're encouraging the idea to tear it down."

"Nothing's going to be torn down today," the older man growled. "Damn bulldozer won't even start, the company doesn't have a spare machine this afternoon, and this greenhorn is barely old enough to drive it."

"Hey, Greg," the younger man argued, "there's no reason to be disrespectful. The dozer was working when I left this morning."

The older man tossed his hands into the air in frustration, reminding Tessa of an angry gnome. "Take it back, and be here at eight a.m. sharp. Tomorrow you'd better not bring another piece of junk with you." Then he stalked to his dually and drove off.

The younger man shrugged and crossed the street to the Ram. The diesel engine rumbled, and he drove down Dogwood Lane, dragging the yellow monster behind him.

Ralph cleared his throat. "Listen, Tessa, I only do what my clients ask me to do."

Tessa scoffed. "Somehow I think you only do what's going to put more money in your pocket."

Ralph's back stiffened, and he smoothed a hand over his already-slick hair. "Is this about the expensive bottle of wine I wouldn't buy for dinner? I can't believe you're still mad about that. It was, what, eight months ago? You know they always try to upsell dinner, which was already putting a dent in my wallet, I'll have you know."

Tessa's mouth fell open. She flitted her eyes toward Paul before shaking her head. Paul looked held in rapt attention. "This is about Honeysuckle Hollow. I don't care about that dinner, but since you brought it up, the wine was *twenty dollars*, Ralph. I hardly think that's excessive. This is about you not caring about the people in this neighborhood and not caring about preserving the history of Mystic Water."

"That's unfair. Mrs. Steele said she had no interest in the house, and it's not even worth the time it would take to fix it up." He gestured toward the house. "Look at it, Tess—"

"Don't call me Tess."

He groaned. "Would you *look* at it? It's a derelict eyesore. Mrs. Steele asked me to search for interested investors, and I did. I only learned this morning about the investor's plans to build a Fat Betty's here. He hasn't put down the money for the land yet. Mrs. Steele has to demolish the house first, and that's not happening today." Ralph pulled out his cell phone. "I'll call the investor and let him know we've been pushed back a day. He might want to go ahead and fork over the money for the land even without the completed demo. Mrs. Steele is impatient to get this off her hands."

Ralph tried to connect the call, but he couldn't get a signal. He walked around the yard, holding his phone to the sky like a lightning rod.

"You know lifting your phone like that doesn't actually improve your chances of reception, right?" Tessa pulled her cell phone from her purse and shrugged. "I've got signal."

Paul checked his cell. "Me too."

"What is going *on*?" Ralph whined. He pressed a few buttons and groaned. "It died. My phone just died. It was fully charged this morning. Good to see you, Tessa. Sorry about the house, but you don't have to worry about it after eight a.m. tomorrow. Everything has an expiration date." He walked toward the red Audi.

Ralph revved the engine unnecessarily and drove away, leaving Tessa and Paul standing on the sidewalk. Tessa clenched her fist and the keys to Honeysuckle Hollow dug into her palm. She opened her hand. "I forgot to hand these over or *toss them on the porch* like Mrs. Steele said."

"What do they need them for if they're going to tear it down?"

"They might need them to disconnect plumbing, electrical, and gas before they can safely tear it down," Tessa said with a shrug. "But maybe they've already done that."

"Since we're here, want to show me around?"

Tessa shrugged. "Sure, why not?"

Paul nudged her with his elbow. "You've got a lot of chutzpah. Lots of passion burning inside you. You know what you believe, and you don't back down. That's admirable."

Was he serious? Tessa characterized herself as more of a self-doubter than someone trailblazing with passion. She thought of the notebook in her purse, which was full of examples of how she didn't trust her own instincts. "I just can't stand the thought of this housing being torn down." She pressed a hand to her stomach. The idea stirred nausea in her gut. "I need to call the cleaners and the exterminators. They're obviously not needed now." Tessa quickly made the calls and then walked toward the front porch.

Paul traversed the weedy front yard. "The wildness has taken over."

"It's been empty for a little more than two years. It's not as bad as it could be. At least if the bats are still here, you'll be a second option to attack."

He grinned. "I'll be the distraction while you escape, is that it?"

"Something like that."

"Queen Anne Victorian, yeah?" Paul said. "Slate roof looks good. If cared for properly, they can last more than one hundred years, unless they used soft slate. Any idea if this roof is original to the house? I'm guessing this house was built in the 1880s? This roof would still be good if the slate came from Virginia and isn't the ribbon slate from Pennsylvania. Would you look at those sash windows, wavy glass and all." Paul hopped over the broken plank and followed the wraparound porch to the side of the house, brushing his fingers against the windowpanes. "All original." A breeze kicked up dirt from the boards, creating miniature dust spirals that danced around his heavy boots. "This is a gem, Ms. Tessa. I can understand why you don't want to see it taken apart."

Tessa stumbled through the front-yard overgrowth. Two butterflies danced through the thistles. "How do you know so much about Victorian homes?"

He pressed his fingertips to one of the windows. "Received an MA in architecture in Boston."

"But . . . but aren't you a travel writer?" She'd assumed his masters was more closely connected to his writing.

Paul's expression dimmed for a few seconds. Then he walked toward her, grabbed the skeleton key from her hand, and headed for the front door. "Can't I be both?"

She followed behind him. "But *why*?"

"Why am I a travel writer, why did I receive an MA, or why am I both?" Paul slipped the key into the lock. A zipping sound like a jolt of electricity crackling down a live wire whizzed past Tessa's ears. Paul jerked his hand away from the door. "Ow!"

"What happened?"

Paul shook out his hand a few times. "It shocked me. Static electricity?" But he didn't sound convinced. He hesitated a second before reaching for the key again. This time the key turned in the antique lock without incident, and Paul pushed open the door. "As to why am I a travel writer with an MA in architecture, I counter with *why not*? As to how life led me here, that's a complicated answer," he said. "Best discussed over dinner. First, let's take a look inside." He made a sweeping motion with his hand. "After you, Ms. Tessa."

Dinner? That one word caused her emotions to quiver. For a brief moment, she imagined them dining out while Paul told her stories of his exotic travels and she gushed at him over polished silver and starched white napkins.

Paul removed the key from the lock and returned it to Tessa's outstretched hand. His boots thudded against the foyer floor as he walked toward the living room. He jumped up and down a few times. "Floors feel solid." He bent down and rubbed his hands across the wood. "There's a bit of buckling near the back corner," he said and motioned over his shoulder with his thumb. "But with sanding and polishing, these will be beautiful again."

The crystal chandelier in the foyer tinkled as though blown by a wind. "You saw the bulldozer, right?" Tessa grumbled. "It'll be back tomorrow, and it won't matter if these floors are Makassar ebony. They'll be part of a heap before noon."

Paul admired the cast-iron mantel adorning the pass-through fireplace. Tessa rushed forward, waving her hands in front of her in an attempt to warn Paul.

"No, no, no," she said, unable to form more eloquent words.

Paul stopped walking. "I feel as though you should have added *bad dog* to the end of that scolding."

Tessa blushed. "No, it's just, well, there are bats in the chimney. They attacked me yesterday."

He continued toward the fireplace and squatted in front of it. He pointed to the grate. "Guano. Definitely bats. Did you know the Incan empire assigned abundant value to guano? Though not from bats. Guano from seabirds. If anyone disturbed the birds, they were killed. Pretty intense, right?" he said. Then he stuck his head into the fireplace.

Tessa gasped. "Don't!"

"Hellooooo," he called up the chimney. Then they waited. Nothing happened. "It appears as though your bats have vacated."

Tessa's shoulders lowered from her ears. She exhaled, pressed a hand to her chest, and asked, "Do you think they're gone for good?"

"Doubtful," he said. "But you're safe for now." He reached out and smoothed his fingers over the cast-iron mantel and tile work surrounding the hearth, rubbing away years of soot, which blackened his fingers. "I haven't seen a mantel like this since I was in Cardiff doing a piece on the Llandaff Cathedral. I wouldn't be surprised if this was shipped over from the United Kingdom." He tapped one finger against a spot on the mantel. "Something is missing here. There's dust everywhere but in this spot."

"Well, Sherlock Holmes, I found a book there. The previous owner of Honeysuckle Hollow—a local doctor—kept his family home, but he didn't use this as his residence. I've only recently learned that he allowed people to stay here who were down on their luck or passing through town and stuck here for various reasons, sickness or hardship. Dr. Hamilton, that was his name, offered the house to them rent-free for as long as they needed it. The book is full of their stories and their thank-yous. There are more volumes of guest books in the family room."

Paul nodded. "So that's what you meant about this place being a haven." He wiped his fingers on his jeans. "What else do you know about Honeysuckle Hollow?"

While they walked through the house, Tessa filled Paul in on what she knew about the history of Honeysuckle Hollow. She hadn't done as much research into the historical records as she would have liked, but growing up in Mystic Water had given her some background information passed down through the years.

Paul leaned against the island in the kitchen. "The graffiti is an unfortunate addition to the home, and it's a travesty what they did to the floors and the French doors when they dragged out the appliances." He rapped the island with his knuckles. "But I wouldn't think those were cause for demolition. Don't you want to find out what the investor offered for the land?"

"Why would it matter?"

"It'll cost Mrs. Steele to tear down the house and have it hauled off to clear the land. I'd say at least $70,000. That's money out of her pocket from the overall sale. Perhaps a bid could be made that wouldn't cause the owner to part with any money for demolition."

"You think maybe the investor is offering less than what someone would pay for the house *and* the land?"

Paul shrugged. "Hard to say, but if he's shrewd, and I'd wager that he is if he's someone Ralph is working with, then he knows what it would cost to demolish the house, and he's worked that into his offer, as though he's giving her a great deal."

Tessa's eyes lit up. "When in actuality, she's going to be making less than she could be because she's going to lose a big chunk of what he's offering her. *But* if we could sell the house for even the exact amount he's offering, Mrs. Steele wouldn't lose any money and wouldn't have to do any more work with the place, so she'd be making a better deal."

Paul grinned at her. "Exactly."

"But do you think someone would want to put in the time and money to reno this place?"

Paul nodded. "I have a feeling about this house." He tapped his fist against his stomach. "My gut rarely steers me wrong. Fixing this house is going to take a lot of work, but it'll be worth it. A rehabbed house like this one would be worth a king's ransom, regardless of what Drake thinks."

Tessa scrunched her nose at him and asked, "Who's Drake?"

"*L'artiste*," he answered, pointing at the illicitly sprayed graffiti marring the kitchen wall. "That's his name there."

Tessa's cell phone rang, and she glanced at the caller's name on the screen. "Excuse me. I need to get this." She accepted the call. "Hey, Mr. Fleming."

"Hey, Tessa, I have news. I know you've been hesitant about selling your condo, but it's a unanimous vote by the other owners that the building should be sold to the developer. He'll be here in a few days to begin the arrangements. I'll be in touch."

Tessa exhaled. What had she expected? "That's it then."

"Everyone has agreed. It's a fair offer."

"I understand. Thanks for calling." Tessa ended the call and dropped the phone into her purse.

"That's a big sigh," Paul said.

"I've been having a lot of those lately." When she realized Paul wanted an explanation for the sigh, she continued. "That was the president of my HOA. An out-of-towner wants to buy the ruined condo buildings where I was living—for a good price too. And every condo owner has agreed to sell."

"You don't want to?"

Tessa shrugged. "Knowing I have to sell the place feels like accepting that I don't have a home, but it's a smart choice and not really a choice anymore. Everyone else has agreed to sell their condos."

"The decision has been made for you." Paul pushed off the island. "It feels better to make our own choices, but sometimes outside forces give us a nudge in a new direction." He walked across the broken glass from the mangled French doors and stepped through the opening into the backyard.

From the brick porch Paul surveyed the chaos. Tessa walked past him. Standing beside the narrow winding river, she looked for the koi, and before long, it pushed through the murk and popped its mouth above the water.

"There you are. I wish I could turn on the electricity and get your filter and pump running again." She glanced at Paul. "This used to be full of koi. The previous owner named them after fictional characters." The wind kicked up, tangling weeds around Tessa's ankles, and it brought the sweet scent of blooming honeysuckle vines, reminding her of the jam her grandma used to make and slather on biscuits.

"You've got a good heart, Tessa," Paul admitted. "Finding people homes, saving innocent fish, championing for historic landmarks. What else do you do on the side? Superhero at night?"

Tessa snorted a laugh. "Hardly." But Paul's words fluttered her stomach.

He walked toward the hydrangeas and batted away tall stalks of grass that brushed against his hips. "This is a mess of a different sort. Mom would love this, or at least she would love to put order back into this garden. She'll have loads of advice on what to do with it if you ask her." He turned and studied the rear of the house. Then he returned to the porch and crouched in front of one of the columns supporting the second-floor balcony. He banged the heel of his boot against the concrete footing at the bottom of the post. A hollow echo sounded. "The concrete supporting this column is crumbling. That balcony isn't safe. New concrete footings will need to be poured. Not to mention the balcony floor is rotting."

Paul's knowledge surprised Tessa. She had expected him to be the nonconventional sort, a bohemian nomad who traveled light and never stopped anywhere for long—the sort who kept his mama up at night, worrying about his lack of stability. If Tessa had questions about Timbuktu, she might have asked him, but she certainly wouldn't have thought he knew anything about crumbling concrete footings. But she didn't know what he'd retained since earning his master's degree. If he had so much knowledge of buildings and their structures, why had he chosen to travel the world and write about other places instead of using his degree? Her curiosity flared brighter.

Tessa pulled a work notepad from her purse and made a note about the balcony. "You realize that you're talking about this house as though it's going to be saved."

"Isn't it?" he asked. "Let's start with saving Huck Finn."

"Huck Finn?"

Paul pointed to the river and unwrapped the plastic from beneath his arm. "The koi. He's traveled the river. We'll take him home for now."

Paul created a watertight plastic pocket for Huck Finn and caught the koi so easily that Tessa wondered if Paul hadn't been stranded in the Alaskan Bush for months and been forced to catch his own salmon. She imagined the disaster of her trying not only to catch the fish but also to contain it without draining all the water from the thin plastic.

"Did you know that the fish we think of as koi are actually called *nishikigoi* in Japan? It means 'brocaded carp.' Koi are symbols for love and friendship in Japan. They're hardy little swimmers, which is why this guy has probably lasted so long. He's a fighter."

Tessa cut her eyes over at Paul.

Paul shrugged. "Two years ago I spent a week in Japan and wrote a story on Mt. Fuji and the cherry blossoms. I learned other random info too."

"I bet everyone wants you on their trivia team," Tessa joked.

"If they want to win, they do."

Paul cradled Huck Finn and talked to the fish in Japanese phrases while Tessa tried to call Lily but was sent to voice mail. "Lily, call me, please. I need a place to stay for a little bit. Call me. Please. Soon. Okay, call me," she said again before disconnecting.

"You think she knows you want her to call you?" he joked. "Sharing the apartment is still an offer on the table until you find a new place. I hear the couch is comfortable."

She rolled her eyes. "Tempting, but no. My mama doesn't approve of me staying with strange men."

"I'm not *that* strange," he said. "Besides, what she doesn't know won't kill her." When Tessa's mouth fell open, he laughed and added, "I'm kidding, Ms. Tessa. I wouldn't want to tarnish your reputation. Is that even a thing anymore? Can you still sully a reputation?"

Tessa opened the front door. "In the South you can," she said with a sigh. "We're still holding on to some of the most antiquated traditions, and here I am, still upholding them."

"Mob mentality. How's that working for you? I still say we don't have to tell your mom *or* mine, and if you promise not to get handsy with me, I'll let you stay."

"Is that a fear of yours? That I'll get handsy?" she asked boldly.

Paul laughed. "I'd say it's less of a fear and more wishful thinking." He winked at her, and she blushed so hard she felt like she was having a hot flash.

To alleviate the awkwardness, Tessa walked briskly out onto the porch and turned to look at him. "Coming?"

He nodded. "I almost hate to leave this place. But we'll be

back. I have a *feeling*."

Tessa snorted. "Maybe it's indigestion." As she started the car engine, she said, "Speaking of mamas, we should probably get you back to yours."

Paul let down his window. "They're fine. They'll be working all day. I'll just be in the way."

Tessa let down her window. "I think that's the point. They'd probably be happy if you were *in the way* all the time." She glanced over at him, and he gazed out the window at the wind rustling through the dogwoods lining the street.

"And you're an expert on what my parents want?" Paul asked.

An edginess coated Paul's words. It rippled over her skin like oil in a hot cast-iron skillet. His mirth rushed out the window on a gust of wind that filled the car with the scent of dying roses.

"Not an expert, no," Tessa said cautiously. "I just think they're fond of you, even though I can't imagine why." She smiled at him, hoping to lighten the somber mood that draped across his shoulders and pulled his mouth into a frown.

His cheek dimpled. "I think it's my roguish good looks and rapier wit."

"And no doubt your humility."

Paul laughed, jostling Huck Finn in his arms, as Tessa pulled away from the curb. The sound of Paul's laughter shivered across her skin, and a part of her wanted to get used to the feeling.

CHAPTER 11

SPICY SCRAMBLED EGGS

JUST BEFORE LUNCH TESSA PARKED BEHIND THE DINER AND turned off the Great Pumpkin's ignition. She heaved a sigh before unbuckling her seat belt. She kept imagining the bulldozer driving across Honeysuckle Hollow's front yard.

Paul got out and leaned back in through the open car door. "You'll let me know what you decide?"

"About what?"

"The slumber party," he said with a smile.

"Sure." She grabbed her purse and heaved herself out of the car. "Enjoy time with your parents. I'm going right now to secure my room and board for the night, which will *not* be at the apartment."

He held up Huck Finn, who looked strangely content in his plastic-bag transition home. Paul poked two of his fingers into the corners of his mouth and pulled down his lips. "This is our sad face."

Tessa snorted. "You're an odd one."

"Odd but charming?"

Tessa rolled her eyes but inwardly agreed that Paul was quite charming. She pointed at Huck Finn. "What're you gonna do with him?"

Paul held the fish up to his face and smiled. Huck Finn swam in a tiny circle. "I'm not sure, but I bet I can sneak a large plastic container from Mom and give him a larger space until I come up with a better solution."

"No koi patties being sold at the diner."

"What am I, a heartless brute? Huck Finn is part of the family now." He waved good-bye and walked toward the diner.

Lily's shop was located next door to Scrambled. She assumed Lily must be swamped at the boutique and that's why she hadn't returned her call. Tessa pushed open the door and saw Amanda, Lily's sales assistant, folding T-shirts designed with Southern sayings.

"Hey, Tessa," she said.

"Hey, is Lily in the back?" Tessa paused to admire a peach blouse hanging on the nearest rack.

Amanda shook her head. "She's gone to Wildehaven Beach with Jakob and Rose for a few days. She'll be home Saturday. They wanted to time the trip with getting their floors redone at the house since you can't walk on them for a few days."

Tessa's heart rate increased. "No," she breathed out.

Amanda nodded. "You remember that fancy boutique at the beach. They're thinking of carrying her clothes, as well as her new line of children's designs. You know how much money the tourist season brings in. I think her clothes would be perfect for a beach location."

Tessa massaged her fingers against her temples. "I'd forgotten that was this week."

"She calls in every day, though. You want me to tell her something?"

Tessa shook her head. "No, but thanks. See you later."

She stepped out onto the sidewalk, feeling the sun baking her face. Now what was she going to do? Part of her wanted to run to the Great Pumpkin, slide through the open car window like Bo Duke from *The Dukes of Hazzard* reruns her daddy loved, and drive as fast as she could to Wildehaven Beach just to be near her two best friends. They'd know what to do. Instead, she was stuck in Mystic Water with no place to live and sorrow building inside her heart because of Honeysuckle Hollow. *Why* was she so attached to that abandoned house? She kicked a stray leaf from the sidewalk.

With Paul in the diner visiting his parents, Tessa felt okay returning to the apartment for a few minutes to reorganize her cluttered thoughts and figure out what to do. She opened the fridge, pulled out the strawberry chamomile tea, and poured herself a glass. Then she sat on the couch and drank it all. Within minutes, her eyes drooped. She yawned, leaned her head against the couch cushions, and dozed.

The sound of a door closing woke Tessa. She jerked into an upright position and sucked in a breath. Paul grunted as he heaved a large plastic box into the kitchen, water sloshing with each of his steps. Huck Finn shifted back and forth in the waves with leaves of lettuce floating on the top like boats.

"You didn't get far," he said.

She blinked. Had she fallen asleep? What time was it? She glanced at the clock on the wall. "It's three in the afternoon?" She stood too quickly, and all the blood rushed from her head, giving her the sensation of vertigo. She tipped back onto the couch.

"Whoa, darling," Paul said in a phony Southern accent that would have been comical if Tessa hadn't felt woozy. "You feeling okay?"

"Yes . . . no. I mean, I just got here, and now it's three. That's impossible. It wasn't even lunch yet when I sat down." Her eyes drifted to the empty glass. A few drops of tea glistened in the bottom. Paul had called the tea *a sleeping potion* the night before. There was *way* too much chamomile in the mix. Was that the cause of it? Tessa thought of Crazy Kate. *The garden.* Paul was still watching her. She cleared her throat. "I guess . . . I was sleepy?"

"Are you asking me or informing me? Are you here because your room and board fell through?"

Tessa groaned. "I know this is awful. We don't even know each other. I should pack up and drive to a hotel, but they're all in the next town over, so now I'm quasi-stuck, with no place to go except an apartment your parents have been waiting two years *for you* to be in—"

"What do you mean, they've been waiting two years *for me*?"

Tessa looked at him. "This place. They wanted you to visit. They filled it with furniture and knickknacks that they thought you'd like. The bookshelves are full of your writings," she added, motioning toward the shelves. "And the map, well, that's all you too."

Paul walked over to the map. The tendrils of the mint plant had stretched even farther since that morning; runners twined across Canada, as far north as a pin in Maine and as far south as Brazil.

Tessa walked over to stand beside him. "It's where you've been."

"I can see that. Why? I have a brother. *They* have another son, Eddie."

"But they know where Eddie is, don't they? He's settled and checks in regularly," Tessa said, feeling the hairs on the back of her neck stand. One of the mint leaves nearest Paul bruised at the edges, causing Tessa's eyes to widen. "This is a way for them to be close to you."

Paul's eyes narrowed on the red heart-shaped pushpin stuck into Mystic Water. "What is that one?" He pulled the pin from the map.

"Where your heart is?" Tessa said, feeling stupid.

Paul's irritation intensified. "They never give up." His voice sounded petulant, and the mint shivered. He wrenched open a window in the living room and threw the red pushpin out the window.

"Umm, that's littering," she mumbled.

Paul tossed a withering, blue-eyed glance at her.

She didn't understand his annoyance. "Why are you angry with your parents for wanting to see you or wanting to map where you've been?"

His jaw tightened. "I'm not angry. What they want for my life isn't what *I* want for my life."

"A home? Or companionship, maybe marriage? You aren't married, are you?"

He studied her, and then he closed his eyes briefly before exhaling. "No, I'm not married, and contrary to conventional expectations, I can be single without a permanent home and still be happy. I like my life."

A breeze crept through the window, dispersing Paul's unhappiness as though it were fog. Tessa reached out and rubbed her fingers gently across the mint leaves.

"I brought Huck Finn home," he said, attempting to further release his discontent.

The koi nibbled on lettuce leaves. "I see that."

"It's temporary. Mom says she knows a couple who will probably take him because they have a landscaped yard with a koi pond."

Tessa nodded. She was happy to find a habitat for Huck Finn, but it didn't escape her that the fish was getting a home before she was.

Paul pointed toward the plant. "What's with that mint?"

"It's from your mama's garden. She says her plants are hardier than others—" Tessa's mouth dried like herbs in the summer sun. She swallowed. "There's something special about that garden," she mumbled, looking at the empty glass sitting on the coffee table. Was Crazy Kate right? Did the land affect everything growing in its soil?

In a daze, Tessa walked to the couch and sat. *The land.* Two and a half years before, a bakery had stood in this same spot. Tessa thought of the sparkling golden sugar contained within a hand-carved box given to Anna by her grandmother Beatrice O'Brien. Tessa remembered the way the magical sugar had singed her fingers when she grabbed handfuls and tossed it into a mixture of dough. She'd tossed in her hopes for the perfect partner too. Her heart throbbed as the memory flared to life, at all she'd lost that night. The fire. The smoke. The unsightly creation burning in the bakery, and the enchanted sugar lost to the flames, turning to ash like everything around it.

What if buried beneath the ash and soot and crumbling bricks of Cecilia's garden lay remnants of glittering golden sugar, feeding the plants like fertilizer, creating mutations more powerful than the originals?

Paul walked toward her. "Are you okay?" She glanced up at him, surprised to see sincere concern on his face. "I'm sorry I got angry."

"You said you weren't angry."

Paul shrugged. "I say a lot of things." His cell phone rang. "Hey, Dad . . . I'm upstairs . . . Sure, what time? . . . Give me half an hour." He walked past her, opened the refrigerator, and pulled out a jug of orange juice. "Dad says there's an Italian place they want to take me to for a late lunch." He removed a cup from the cabinet.

Tessa blinked away the image of twinkling sugar filling the plants with magic. "Milo's?"

"How'd you know?"

Tessa shrugged. "It's their favorite. They go there a few times a week. If you stick around, they'll probably take you more than once."

Paul pressed his lips together, creating a thin, downturned line. "I'll be leaving tomorrow. I'm trying to arrange travel for another assignment. In the Cook Islands." He tilted the glass and drank the juice.

Tessa walked to the wall map. She pointed to a cluster of islands northeast of New Zealand. "That's a long way from here."

She thought of sun-soaked, white-sand beaches; ocean breezes tangling her hair; and sipping fruity cocktails beneath a cabana with a roof made from palm fronds. "What's the story?"

"Supposedly a Spanish ship sunk in between the northern and southern islands. Local legend tells of a treasure hidden in one of the lagoons on Mauke."

She sighed. "Just the word *lagoon* makes me want to go there."

"You should."

"I don't even have a passport."

Paul nearly dropped the empty glass he held. "*How* is that possible?"

"Never got around to it."

Paul put the glass in the sink. "You've never wanted to leave this little town? I would suffocate."

Tessa narrowed her eyes. "First of all, I have left *this little town*. I went to college in Louisiana, and I've traveled to a few other states. Second, you just got here. You don't know anything about Mystic Water. It's a great place to grow up and—"

Paul held up his hands in self-defense. "I don't mean to disrespect the town. I only meant that I *have* to see the world. Aren't you curious? Don't you want to know what else is out there?"

"Sometimes . . . but I like it here. It's safe and normal and predictable." She walked to the window in the living room and peered down at the garden. *At least it used to be.* With the exception of the special gift from Anna's grandmother, the rest of life in Mystic Water was fairly ordinary. Tessa had taken one great risk so far, and that had caused devastation in the bakery. She hadn't been interested in taking risks since. Which was also why her lists were so important. She didn't make any decision without triple-checking it was the right one. But there were times when she was curious about life outside of Mystic Water. "Is that why you decided to become a travel writer?"

"One of the reasons. What are you doing tonight? You want to go to dinner with us?"

Tessa shook her head. "Spend some time with your folks. Try the lasagna at Milo's. It's amazing. I have home fries and eggs in the fridge."

What Tessa really wanted to do was test a hypothesis. Crazy Kate hinted that thyme had a connection to predicting the weather, and hadn't Tessa been able to *feel* the fact that it wouldn't rain the day everyone dressed in raincoats and carried umbrellas?

"I know a wicked recipe for spicy scrambled eggs. I'll write it down for you," Paul said. He found a notepad in one of the kitchen drawers and scribbled instructions for her. "I'm assuming you're not much of a cook based on the way you tried to poison me with pancakes, but this recipe is foolproof."

"I was *not* trying to poison you," Tessa argued. But when she saw Paul's lips twitch into a grin, she added, "But that's not a bad idea."

"I'll see you after dinner then?" Paul asked.

Tessa exhaled. "Unless I find a home in the next couple of hours, I'm afraid so."

As soon as Paul left, Tessa pulled out her notebook and found her most recent list. Beside the number six, she wrote, *Should I stay in the apartment with Paul?* Beside the question, she jotted down her own thoughts. She wrote, *Would it be so bad? He's cute, but he's leaving tomorrow.* She added a frowny face and then scratched through it. "Don't be absurd, Tessa. He's *leaving.*

It doesn't matter if you stay over tonight or not. Tomorrow the apartment will be all yours."

She texted both Anna and Lily.

Tessa: Harry and Cecilia's son Paul is in town for one more day and needs to stay in the apartment where I am staying. Should I stay with him? I need lodging. I need help. I need advice.

Anna: I stayed in the old apartment with Eli, and everything worked out just fine.

Lily: Is he cute?

Tessa: Leading-man handsome.

Lily: My vote is yes. You could use a decent fling.

Tessa snorted. Who said Paul was decent? *But he is, isn't he?*

Tessa plucked thyme leaves from the cuttings she'd taken from Cecilia's garden. She sprinkled the herb over the home fries and then microwaved them. Using a heart-shaped magnet, she stuck Paul's recipe for spicy scrambled eggs to the refrigerator. Jars of spices, along with a poorly cut onion and two diced jalapeños, littered the countertop.

Tessa wiped at her watery eyes and yelped. "It burns!" She leaned over the kitchen sink and splashed cold water onto her face. She caught her reflection in the window glass. Wet hair plastered to the side of her face, and her mascara smeared, making her look like a weeping clown. "Tessa, you're a mess." She looked over at Huck Finn blinking at her in his plastic container. "Don't judge me, Huck. It's been a rough couple of days."

Less than ten minutes later, Tessa sat curled on the couch with a bowl of spicy scrambled eggs piled on top of her thyme-covered home fries. A quick assessment of her present state had her shaking her head.

"Cons," she said aloud to herself. "I have no home, I've lost Honeysuckle Hollow to Fat Betty's, and I'm testing a hypothesis offered to me by the town nut. Oh, and I think I'm starting to believe that Cecilia's garden might be magical."

Tessa scooped eggs onto her fork and speared a potato wedge. Her eyes widened as soon as the spices hit her tongue. When she swallowed, the fiery seasoning set her throat on fire.

"Water," she croaked, reaching for her glass. She gulped half the water, but the burning didn't subside. "Not bad if I want dragon breath." She pushed the eggs to the side of the bowl and exposed the home fries. "Pros," she continued. "I have a car to drive, I have a job, and I'm sharing an apartment with a guy who's cute but mysterious." She looked over at the wall map and pointed her fork at the mint plant as though it were part of the conversation. "You're right. I should add that to the cons list. Mysterious men aren't likely a *good* thing."

By the time Tessa finished her home fries, the burning in her throat and mouth had reduced to a mild tingling sensation, and half her tongue was numb. She reached for *Guests of Honeysuckle Hollow* on the coffee table, balanced the bowl on her thighs, and opened the book. As she stared at a page, the words appeared cloudy as though a fine mist shrouded the pages. She blinked a few times, but still the words looked smeared and half concealed. Tessa put down the book and rubbed her eyes. When she opened them, the whole room was swallowed in a haze that reminded Tessa of stepping out of a hot shower into lingering steam as thick as fog. *Fog.* The word pulsed in her mind like a strobe light.

Her eyes darted to the bowl of cold, rubbery eggs. Flecks of thyme stuck to the porcelain interior. "Is this because of you?" she whispered to the leftover herb.

The front door opened. Fog rushed from the room and out the door as though sucked up by an exhaust fan. Paul stepped inside and closed the door.

"Honey, I'm home!" He dropped his keys onto the kitchen countertop.

Tessa glanced around the room. Had she imagined the fog? Were Paul's spices hallucinogenic? Was she losing it?

"Mystic Water has unusual weather," he said. "First the flood, and now there's a fog settling over everything. It's thicker than anything I've ever seen, even on the moors of England." He unlaced his boots.

"Fog," Tessa repeated. "It's going to stick around for a while. At least a day." Her own words startled her. What was she saying? The words came naturally to her, but they felt foreign on her tongue.

Paul raised an eyebrow. "What makes you say that? Mom said she'd never seen this kind of fog in town before."

Tessa glanced at the bowl. The first explanation she wanted to give—*the potatoes and thyme told me*—guaranteed Paul would think she was nuttier than a five-pound fruitcake. Instead, she shrugged and said, "Just a hunch." She walked to the window and peered out into the darkness. Almost instantly, white mist curled across the windowpanes and pressed against the glass. Within seconds, the entire view was hidden, concealing Mystic Water in a shroud of vapor. *The fog is protecting the town,* she thought, but the words felt spoken by someone else, placed into her mind. *Protecting the town from what?* Tessa wondered.

CHAPTER 12

OVER-EASY EGGS

TESSA SHUT OFF THE EARLY-MORNING ALARM RINGING ON THE bedside table. She wanted to be at Honeysuckle Hollow before they tore it down. It might not make sense to anyone else why she wanted to see the house before they bulldozed it, but maybe the house needed as much comfort as she did. Nobody wanted to be alone at the end, maybe not even a dilapidated house.

The bedroom shimmered in the filtered light. Tessa pushed herself up on her elbows and looked toward the window. She had never been lost in a snowstorm, but she imagined the view looked a lot like it did right now—opaque and white. *Fog.*

She kicked off the bedsheets and walked to the window. Morning light pushed itself through thick fog and created sparkles out of water droplets. Tessa unlocked the window and lifted the sash. Misty fog rolled through the window and spread out across the floor like vaporous glitter. She closed the window, shutting out the fog while watching the mist dissipate into the floorboards.

After a quick shower, Tessa dressed as quietly as possible and then tiptoed through the living room. She glanced at Paul's sleeping form and paused. He'd taken off his shirt and lay sprawled out on the couch in nothing but his boxers, having thrown off the light summer quilt during the night. Fog pressed against the windows and cast a pearly glow onto every surface. Paul resembled a tan Italian statue carved from marble, and Tessa's mouth twitched. It wasn't proper to stare at his half-naked form, but she took in one more long look anyway before she headed toward the door.

"I feel so used," Paul said in a husky morning voice. "Leaving without a good-bye?"

Tessa flinched with her hand on the doorknob. She glanced over her shoulder. "I didn't want to wake you."

He yawned and sat up. His lack of clothing caused her cheeks to burn. She glanced at a spot on the wall above his head. Paul reached for his watch on the coffee table. "Where are you off to so early?"

"Honeysuckle Hollow. They're going to tear it down by eight."

"And you're going to assist them?"

Tessa frowned. "Of course not. I'm going . . . Well, I don't know why I'm going exactly, but I want to be there."

"You're not going to chain yourself to the front porch, are you?"

Tessa laughed.

"Because I don't think that angry old guy would hesitate to bulldoze right over you."

She sighed, and the mint plant wiggled in its pot. "I want to see it one last time. Before it's gone."

Paul reached for his T-shirt and tugged it over his head. "Did you make us coffee or breakfast?"

Tessa snorted. "Why would I make anything when I have your folks downstairs?"

"Fair point." Paul stood and stretched his arms over his head.

Tessa tried not to stare and failed. Her fingers itched to text Lily and Anna and tell them she had stayed in the same apartment with Paul without a third person confirming it was a good choice. But it was worth counting her own opinion this time because she couldn't remember the last time she'd had an attractive, likeable man in her living room—or *temporary* living room.

"Why does it look like we're in a cloudy snow globe?" he asked.

"Dense fog."

Watery sparkles twinkled across the dark wood floors. Paul toed a few with his bare foot.

Tessa cleared her throat. "You're leaving today?"

"This afternoon."

Tessa stepped toward him and held out her hand, feeling a twinge of disappointment. "It was nice to meet you. I hope you have a safe trip to the Cook Islands. I look forward to reading your story in print."

Paul's cheek dimpled. He stepped around the coffee table, grabbed her hand, and pulled her into a hug. Tessa stumbled against his chest and made a noise that sounded like *oomph* as her breath squeezed out. On the next inhale, she breathed in the scent of cloves. She couldn't control herself from relishing the feel of his arms around her, and she sighed. He let go and righted her.

A goofy grin deepened his dimples. "Did you just sigh?"

Tessa's stomach clenched. "No. I was *breathing*. You nearly squeezed me to death."

"This was an unexpected rooming situation, Ms. Tessa, but I thank you for your hospitality."

"Safe travels," she said. "I'll put a pin on the islands after you're gone." Disappointment expanded inside her, but she forced a smile. All good things must end, but she'd hoped this good thing might last longer than a few days.

"Interested in keeping tabs on me? I like it," he said. "Maybe we could keep in touch."

Was he serious? "Like pen pals?"

He chuckled. "Calling each other 'pen pals' went out of fashion with teased hair and Aqua Net. Give me your number, and I'll text you mine."

Tessa called out her number, and in a few seconds, her phone dinged, alerting her that Paul's number was waiting for her. She would add him into her contacts later, but she promised herself she wouldn't hold on to the hope that their communication would stretch much further than today. She lifted her hand in a small wave, shouldered her bag, and walked out into the whiteness. A wall of fog rolled into the apartment, and Paul stood in the doorway. Tessa tried to navigate the stairs without missing one, but the haze was nearly blinding.

"You're disappearing," Paul called from the landing. "You sure it's safe to drive in this?"

Tessa hesitated halfway down the staircase. Hope flared in her; she gripped the handrail tighter. If the fog was this heavy everywhere, would it stop the bulldozer? *And then what, Tessa?* she asked herself. She glanced up at Paul's ghostly silhouette at the top of the stairs.

"I'm hoping no one will be out in this weather."

"Does that include the bulldozing bullies?"

Tessa smiled. "It's like you read my mind."

Tessa could have arrived at Honeysuckle Hollow faster if she had walked rather than driven. Navigating the cloudy streets made her feel as though at each corner she just might fall off the edge of the world. Every now and then the lights of an approaching car peeked out of the fog like the glowing eyes of a dragon. By the time Tessa reached Dogwood Lane, her fingers were sore from the knuckle-white grip she had on the steering wheel.

She parked the Great Pumpkin along the street. "Let's get this over with."

Tessa walked up the sidewalk, parting the fog like a boat rowing through a swamp. As she neared Honeysuckle Hollow, she saw that the bulldozer had already arrived, and it sat waiting across the street. Two men argued in the front yard, looking like two ghosts rising from mist. Fog encircled their legs and crept around their waists. The older man's temper had not improved since the day before, and the fluorescent shirt on the young man made him look like a human glow stick.

"Listen, Greg," the young man said, "I can't control the weather. It's not safe to run this machine in this kind of visibility. You can't even see the front door from across the street."

"You young people and your excuses," Greg snarled. "I'll do it myself."

"You know you're not allowed to drive the dozer. It's company policy."

Greg shoved the young man out of the way and stormed

across the street. The young man chased after him, yelling at Greg to get off the trailer and then to get out of the bulldozer and then not to dare turn it on. The bulldozer rumbled as the engine started. The trailer shuddered. While Tessa watched, Greg backed the bulldozer off the trailer and into the street. The yellow monster lurched across Dogwood Lane with grinding gears. Tessa felt the irrational desire to jump in front of the machine and beg Greg to stop, but even through the mist, she could see him glowering in the cab.

The young man hopped up and down beside the bulldozer, waving his arms like an inflatable windsock. His yells were lost to the noisy roar of the diesel engine. The bulldozer's blade dropped onto the sidewalk, cracking the concrete, and pushed forward. Tessa backed away, clutching her purse to her chest and feeling the sting of tears. She thought of Dr. Matthias Hamilton and the beautiful damask roses he used to share with everyone in the neighborhood. She thought of the hundreds of guests who'd ended up on Honeysuckle Hollow's doorstep in need and how the house had always opened its doors. Could they have ever imagined the house would be flattened for a Fat Betty's?

The bulldozer rolled through the yard, ripping and tearing the earth, and when Tessa heard the splinter of wood as the stairs were crushed into the front porch, she plugged her fingers into her ears and clenched her eyes shut. But before she could inhale another breath, the noise stopped. Everything stopped. Tessa lowered her hands and opened her eyes. The bulldozer sat in the front yard, and the fog hovered around the tires. The young man stood gaping at the machine while Greg swung open the cab's door.

"What in the hell is wrong with this thing?" he barked. "It

drives like it's drunk, and the engine is failing. I can't even get the damn keys out of the ignition."

Without provocation the engine turned over, and the bulldozer reversed. Greg worked the gears as it jerked backward across the street. In the middle of Dogwood Lane, the bulldozer's engine died, blocking any traffic from being able to pass on either side. The young man ran to the machine.

"Greg, get out of the dozer. You know I have to report this."

Greg climbed down and glared at the machine. The two men continued to argue in the street, and Tessa inched forward to survey the gaping hole created by the bulldozer's blade. A front section of the porch was demolished, and two of the columns cracked, causing the roofline to sag.

A gust of wind blew across the yard. Fog swirled in the hole like a whirlpool before emptying, revealing a long slender shaft of wood partially covered with earth. Tessa knelt and reached for the object. She tugged, but the ground wouldn't release it. She eased down into the hole and dug around with her hands in the wet soil until she freed an arrowhead-tipped spear.

Tessa climbed out of the hole with the object. She rubbed her fingers over the staff, which removed clotted dirt clinging to the spear and revealed a carved design. Tessa's fingers tingled, and the hairs on the back of her neck lifted. Her breath exhaled in short puffs.

"Ma'am?" a voice called.

Tessa lowered the staff to her side and slowly eased it behind her back. The young man stood on the ruined sidewalk.

"Whatcha got there?" he asked.

"Oh, just some junk from the hole."

"Did Ralph send you over this morning?"

"No," Tessa answered. "But I'm working with the owner of this house too." *Sort of.*

"I don't know where Ralph is, but I've got to call a tow to get this dozer out of the street—" He stopped talking because his cell phone rang. Based on the conversation, Tessa knew the caller was Ralph. After he ended the call, the young man said, "Ralph's car died about two miles away. We'll reschedule. Doesn't seem like this house wants to be torn down. Sorry for the inconvenience."

Tessa's hands trembled, and she smiled at Honeysuckle Hollow. "We gained another day," she said to the house as the young man walked away.

Greg yelled into his cell phone as he climbed into his truck, and Tessa's eyebrows rose at his creative use of swear words combined with new ways to describe a broken-down bulldozer. Once Greg's truck disappeared into the fog and the young man was preoccupied with his phone, Tessa waded through the haze down the sidewalk and climbed into the Great Pumpkin.

She laid the spear on the passenger seat. Tessa wasn't sure how old it was, but she assumed the arrowhead spear was a Native American relic, which meant it had the potential to be more than a hundred years old. Or it could be an elaborate stage prop. She snapped a few pictures using her cell phone and emailed them to a friend, an anthropology professor at the University of Georgia. She'd set up Wenton McDougal with his prom date senior year, and Wenton and Lila were now happily married. Wenton owed her a favor or two. She texted: Found this beneath a historic home that's been standing for more than one hundred years. She paused and then added: I didn't steal it. But she erased the last sentence because a voice in her head asked, *Oh yeah? Then what's it doing in the car?*

"I can return it later," she said, trying to placate the accusatory voice in her head.

Tessa dropped her phone into her purse, turned on the engine, and did a U-turn on Dogwood Lane since the bulldozer blocked the street. She drove toward her office because she needed to make calls and check her email. The damage assessment on her car was supposed to happen today too. She didn't need to be present for the inspection, but she wanted to stay on top of the insurance company to prevent delays.

The Red River wound through town, and around the water, the fog was especially dense. Tessa slowed the car to less than fifteen miles per hour. As she passed the road that led out of town, the Great Pumpkin made an awful wheezing noise followed by a shudder that made her teeth clatter. She steered the car toward the side of the road, and it rolled to a stop. Tessa turned off the engine and then turned the key again. Nothing happened. She tried the ignition again. Nothing. She dropped her head against the wheel.

"You've got to be kidding me," she groaned. She glanced toward the spear. "Is this because I stole? Because I was *going* to take you back."

After several minutes Tessa figured out how to release the hood, but when she propped it open, she had no idea what she was looking for. Smoke and fog mingled together and made it nearly impossible for her to even see the engine parts. And even if she *could* see a problem, it wasn't as though she could fix it.

She grabbed her phone to call a local mechanic, and car lights knifed through the fog. A black sedan pulled up beside her, and the passenger-side window lowered. The man behind the wheel leaned into the passenger seat, and Tessa bent over to see his face.

She shook her head in disbelief. "Of course it's you."

Paul grinned at her. "Don't tell me the Great Pumpkin has given you his last."

"I'm not giving up on him yet. I was just about to call the mechanic."

"Get in," Paul said. "I'll give you a lift."

"You look like you're on your way out of town. I don't want to inconvenience you."

Paul tossed his bag into the back seat, making room for Tessa beside him. "I like this whole damsel-in-distress moment. Makes me feel chivalrous. I can't remember the last time I picked up a woman from the side of the road."

Tessa snorted. "I hope never."

Paul's laugh carried out the window and dispersed the fog around the car. Tessa grabbed her purse and the spear. Then she locked the Great Pumpkin, lowered its hood, and climbed into Paul's car.

He reached for the spear. "What have you got there?"

"Careful. The arrowhead is still sharp. I found it at the house."

"Looks like you found it in a mud pile." He rubbed his fingers over the carvings.

"Close enough."

Paul's questioning expression demanded she explain.

"Oh, okay, the bulldozer dug up the porch and died. I climbed into the hole it made and found this."

Paul's blue eyes shone with amusement. "You pilfered this from the house site?"

She frowned. "You make me sound like a thief."

"I'm just assessing the facts. But the bulldozer died? Again?"

"At present, it's stuck in the middle of Dogwood Lane."

"Maybe you're Honeysuckle Hollow's good-luck charm, Ms. Tessa."

She smiled at the thought.

Paul studied the spear. "This is old. Really old. It's highly unusual to find a wooden artifact in such good shape. You'd think the wood would show signs of rot, but I don't see any."

"You think it's a fake?"

"If it is, it's a damn good one, and I'd ask why someone would go to the trouble of burying it. I've never seen this type of carving on a spear before. It's definitely Native American."

"I snapped a few photos and sent them to a friend who works at UGA," she said. "He's a professor of anthropology."

"I think you might have found something special here," Paul said. "I'm interested in what he thinks."

Tessa glanced toward the back seat at Paul's bag. "Aren't you leaving?"

"Soon enough," he said. "Now where should I take you? Home?"

Home. The word crept into Tessa's chest and pushed out her breath. "Which would mean you're taking me nowhere," she said, aware of how sullen she sounded.

Paul shifted the car into gear. "The apartment it is." He pulled away from the curb and drove back toward town.

Tessa rolled the spear round and round between her palms, dirtying her hands and fingers.

"Hey," he said, reaching over to pat her leg, "it could be worse."

"A swarm of locusts could descend on us?" Tessa said, unable to stop her smirk.

Paul laughed. "Let's stop by and grab a dozen balloons for that pity party, shall we?"

She met his teasing gaze. "Only if we can toss confetti." They both laughed.

CHAPTER 13

THIEVES ON THE RUN

Tessa marveled at Paul's ability to adapt and live without the need for a permanent home. As though reading her mind, he interrupted the silence. "A temporary home is better than no home."

Tessa stared out the window at the walls of fog surrounding them. "You'd know," she said before she realized how rude the truth of it sounded.

Paul parked in front of the diner. "Better than anyone." He got out and shut the door without saying another word.

Guilt forced her out of the car in a hurry. She clutched the spear and slung her purse over her arm. "Paul," she called. He stopped on the sidewalk and turned to look at her. "Thank you for the ride, and . . . I'm sorry. What I said was rude."

Paul lifted one shoulder in a slight shrug. "You think the truth is always kind?"

"But you like your life. All the traveling and not having a permanent place, right?"

"I've had a lot of great experiences."

The swirling mist intensified the paleness of his eyes. Sunlight created sparkles in the air around them. Not having a place to call her own was slowly breaking apart Tessa's feelings of security and comfort. She didn't understand how anyone could live so carefree, never knowing where he might land, but if anyone could enjoy it, she imagined Paul was the perfect fit for that lifestyle. But now his eyes looked full of uncertainty.

He broke the tension. "Since I'm still here, I'm going to eat. Mom will likely stuff me full of food, and I'll need a nap before I attempt to leave again. My schedule is flexible. If you hear from your professor friend, let me know what he says about your thievery."

"I'm not a thief. I *borrowed* this," she explained. "I was going to take it back."

"To the hole?"

"Yes."

"I bet."

She narrowed her eyes. She knew he was being playful, but her composure felt fractured and her emotions unwieldy. "I'm going to work." She marched up the sidewalk in the opposite direction.

"Hey, Ms. Tessa, should I *borrow* food from the diner for you? Will you want something later?"

"I kind of loathe you right now," she said without looking at him. "But I never turn down carbs."

Paul's laughter echoed down the sidewalk, rippled over her skin like a wave of heat, and shoved the fog ten feet away from them in every direction. She looked at him over her shoulder and saw him still smiling at her, and she wasn't the least bit sorry he'd been the one to rescue her from the side of the road.

Tessa called the local mechanic, Norman Benson, and he promised he would tow the Great Pumpkin before nightfall. Their shop was backed up with calls from people who'd tried to brave the unusual weather and ended up in ditches all over town. Mr. Benson also told her he had received a call to tow a bulldozer for the first time ever. Tessa didn't mention she had been there on Dogwood Lane when the bulldozer refused to cooperate.

At the office, she went through emails and returned phone calls. She had a few showings scheduled for late afternoon and early evening, but those clients wanted to reschedule because of the weather. Her entire schedule had been rearranged before noon, leaving her with a relatively open afternoon.

The insurance company had evaluated her car and, as expected, totaled it. They informed her paperwork and an insurance check should arrive within two weeks. Tessa pulled out her notebook and started a new list. *What kind of car should I buy?* She numbered down the side of the page and paused. Wasn't it more important to focus on what kind of car *she* wanted rather than ask other people what she should buy? Apprehension slinked into her mind. Trusting her gut was unfamiliar, and what if her gut *was wrong*?

A new email dinged its arrival and interrupted her thoughts. Professor Wenton McDougal wrote: Looks old. I forwarded the pictures (I hope you don't mind) to one of my colleagues in the department, Austenaco (Austen) Blackstone, whose focus is Native American societies. He asked for your number, and I gave it to him (I hope you don't mind). He said he would like to speak with you once his classes are done this morning. Hope all is well, Tessa.

Tessa's cell phone rang, displaying a number she didn't recognize. "Hello?"

Austenaco "Austen" Blackstone introduced himself and explained how he'd come by her number. His interest in her findings was obvious within the first minute because he asked a lot of questions in quick succession. How heavy was the spear? Did it look old? Had the wood splintered? Was the arrowhead sharp? How deep were the carvings? What type of wood was it? Tessa could barely process one question before he asked another, and she had few answers to offer. Before she could object, Austen invited himself to Mystic Water to see the artifact in person and announced he would be there by late afternoon. Tessa ended the call and cut her eyes over to the spear leaning against the wall in her office. *Now, why would anyone drive three hours on the spur of the moment to see a stick with an arrowhead point?*

Tessa called Scrambled and asked Cecilia whether Paul was still there. Cecilia told her Paul had gone up to the apartment to take a nap more than an hour ago, and Cecilia slipped in the fact that she was hoping Paul would sleep so long that he wouldn't leave town. Tessa imagined Paul as Rip Van Winkle, sleeping for twenty years on the couch in the apartment above the diner.

Cecilia asked Tessa to convince Paul to stick around for dinner, but Tessa wasn't sure anyone could convince Paul to do anything he wasn't interested in. Tessa dialed Paul's cell number, and when he answered, his voice sounded delayed and sleepy, making her realize she'd woken him. She explained that Austen would be in town later in the day, and Paul said he wanted to hear what the anthropologist had to say. Relief swelled in her chest. As soon as she realized she was grinning like a love-struck teenager, she stopped herself. Why was she relieved that Paul wanted to wait around and hear about a stick?

Tessa worked a few more hours into the afternoon until Austen called her from the city limits sign. She gave him directions to the apartment and then closed down her computer for the day. She locked up the office, grabbed the dirty relic, and walked to the apartment.

Tessa couldn't believe the sun hadn't burned off the fog. It rippled across the streets, clung to the lampposts and street signs, and covered cars like misty blankets. People appeared out of the fog like ghosts, and Tessa paused at the diner's garden. She pinched a bit of thyme between her fingers and let her imagination create the possibility of a world with magical herbs.

When she opened the apartment door, Paul was sitting on the couch, reading one of her paperback romance novels. He marked his place and put the book on the coffee table beside *Guests of Honeysuckle Hollow* and a pink bag from the candy shop.

He pointed at the romance novel. "I'm all for reading a variety of genres, but seriously, how can you read that?"

Tessa shrugged. "It's better than real life."

He tapped his finger against the cover. "So you want Greywolf to rescue you from a fort on the frontier and take you home to his teepee?"

Tessa snorted. "If that guy shows up at my door, he can take me anywhere."

Paul picked up the pink bag and shook it. "I bought you more caramel creams, and I haven't even eaten one for myself yet. I was waiting."

"How gentlemanly of you." Tessa dropped her purse onto the kitchen table and propped the spear against the bookshelf.

"I'm glad you appreciate my willpower. It wasn't easy," he said. "But now that you're here . . ." Paul unrolled the bag and stuck his hand inside. "Ouch!" He yanked out his hand. He upended the bag onto the coffee table, spilling caramel creams across the surface. Tessa noticed one red object that did not belong. "What in the hell?" Paul lifted a heart-shaped pushpin from the table.

Tessa's eyes widened. "That was in the bag?" Her eyes darted toward the wall map and then back to Paul.

Paul stared at the pushpin in his palm. "Did you do this?"

Tessa laughed even though her heart jackhammered against her ribcage. "How would I have done that? It probably fell into the bin at the candy shop."

"The same pin I threw out the window?"

Tessa wrinkled her forehead and shook her head. "That's not the same pushpin."

But Paul had voiced the same question she'd been thinking. Was it the same pushpin? She wanted to run down the stairs and dig through the garden until she found the heart-shaped pin he'd thrown out, but what if she couldn't find it? *What if . . .*

A knock sounded at the door, startling Tessa. She opened the door to a tall, imposing figure with broad shoulders and hair blacker than licorice. Tessa stared at the man with tanned skin, intense chestnut brown eyes, and high cheekbones. He smiled at her, and her brain thought, *Wow*. Thankfully, her mouth said, "Hi."

Fog rolled over the threshold and curled into the room

around Tessa's feet.

"Ms. Andrews? I'm Austenaco Blackstone," he said, holding out his panther-size paw of a hand. "But, unless you're my mother, I'd rather you call me Austen."

Tessa's hand disappeared into his, and she smiled. "Austen it is. Although Austenaco is unique."

"Too unusual for most people. It was my grandfather's name, from the Cherokee language."

"Nice to meet you. I'm Tessa. Come on in."

Austen's smile widened, and Tessa tried not to stare at how it changed his face, softening the angular lines of his face and jaw.

"I've never seen fog this dense. Is it usual for this area?" Austen asked as he stepped into the apartment, filling the space with his presence.

"Not at all," Tessa said. She motioned over toward Paul. "This is Paul Borelli . . . a friend. His parents own this building and run the diner downstairs."

Paul crossed the room and dropped the heart-shaped pin into the trash can. Then he introduced himself with a handshake.

"I appreciate you letting me see the artifact myself," Austen said. His dark eyes found the spear propped against the bookcase. "Is this it?"

Tessa nodded and motioned with her hand for Austen to have a look. "I'm curious. What made you come all this way based on a picture? I've gathered the spear must be old, but being an anthropologist who studies Native American societies, you've probably seen hundreds of spears, right? What's special about this one?"

Austen pulled a pair of latex gloves out of his pocket and slipped them on. Then he knelt in front of the spear and lifted it carefully in his hands. Paul squatted beside Austen.

"The carvings?" Paul asked. "They're tribal writings, aren't they?"

Austen nodded. "Cherokee language. Spears don't normally have writings on them because they were tools. They had a specific purpose—to hunt. Tribe members wouldn't have taken the time to write elaborate messages on them. It would be the equivalent of writing messages on a shotgun. Why bother?"

He rotated the spear in his hands, touching the wood gently as though it might crumble if he handled it too roughly.

Tessa stood behind them. "Can you translate it?"

"Only a few words. I brought a cleaning tool kit," Austen said, looking up at Tessa. "Would you mind if I cleaned it?"

Tessa shook her head. After Austen walked out, Paul turned to her with an unreadable expression on his face.

"What?" she asked, sensing he had something on his mind.

"This isn't exactly legal."

"What isn't?"

"This find doesn't belong to you. It belongs to the lady who owns Honeysuckle Hollow. You know that, right? She owns the land. Therefore, she owns the spear."

It didn't seem right that Trudy Steele, who didn't even want the house, should have any sort of claim to what lay beneath the ruins, but Tessa knew he was right. It still didn't make her want to hand over the artifact to Mrs. Steele or the potential investor, who wanted to destroy the integrity of the neighborhood by dropping Fat Betty's onto the street. The investor wouldn't likely see the value in the spear, unless it meant monetary gain for him.

As though reading her mind, Paul said, "I'm not going to call her and tell her you *borrowed* anything from her land, because I don't think she would care about the importance of the find.

But a professor of Native American studies drove three hours to Mystic Water because he saw a few blurry photographs, which leads me to believe this spear is more than a random tool found in the dirt. If it *is* unique, then people will find out soon enough, including the owner. It won't be something you can hide for long."

Tessa nodded. Austenaco Blackstone wouldn't have insisted he see the artifact right away if it weren't a fascinating find. "What should we do?"

"What do *you* want to do?"

"I want to know what the spear says," Tessa said.

Paul nodded. "Me too. Let's hear what Greywolf has to say, and then you can make a decision."

Tessa's brow winkled. "Greywolf?"

"He looks like the ridiculously handsome Native American on the front cover of the novel you're reading. You were giving him dreamy eyes."

Tessa snorted. "I was not."

"Weren't you?" Paul eyed her. "He might take you home if you ask him nicely."

"Stop it," she whispered as the front door opened again.

Austen held a rolled-up piece of brown leather tied with a thin leather band. He placed the spear on the kitchen floor and unrolled a rectangular tool kit full of pockets that held brushes of differing sizes and a couple of items that looked like tiny picks meant for loosening rocks or debris.

While she and Paul watched, Austen worked on the spear in silence, brushing away the caked mud. Eventually the carvings were completely revealed. "I had my suspicions," he said, "but I wouldn't have believed it if I hadn't uncovered the entire carving." He stood and stretched his legs.

Tessa had been rereading parts of the romance novel on the couch, but she closed it and walked over. Austen towered over her in the kitchen.

"This spear has a Cherokee prayer for protection engraved on it," Austen explained. "I've never seen one before. I know the prayer, and I've heard talk of this type of engraving having been done before. These objects were usually passed down through families and kept for generations. It's unusual that it wouldn't have been kept with the family."

"Maybe it was lost. Or left behind," Tessa said, her skin prickling with goose bumps.

"Maybe," Austen said. "Where did you find this?"

Tessa glanced toward Paul before answering. "Beneath a historic home in town."

"Interesting. And you are remodeling and found it?"

"Eh, not exactly remodeling, but working on the porch. It was buried beneath the front of the house." Tessa avoided Paul's gaze, but she felt him staring at her.

"The piece of wood is in remarkable condition. On one hand, I know it's old. On the other hand, it shows no sign of being affected by the elements. It's as though it's been perfectly preserved in the ground and kept protected from animals and time."

Tessa's stomach knotted, and the tingling spread to her fingers. She tucked her hair behind her ears. "Maybe the protection prayer worked," she said with a small laugh.

Austen looked at her with his dark eyes and tilted his head before one corner of his mouth lifted into a smile. "And you believe in Cherokee protection prayers, do you?"

"Do you?"

Austen's expression was noncommittal. "I'm a researcher, Ms. Andrews. I believe in proof. I appreciate you taking time out of your day to allow me to study the spear. I assume you know that what you have here is unique, and the probability that it's valuable is quite high. As a researcher, I'd like a day or two to see if there have been any other similar findings that I'm not aware of before you inform anyone about the spear."

Tessa's brow wrinkled. She looked at Paul, wondering if he understood Austen's meaning. *Who am* I *going to tell? Who even cares about a wooden spear?*

Paul stepped up beside Tessa. "He's saying that the owner of this spear could probably sell it for a good chunk of money based on its rareness alone. But he'd like for you to wait and see what he discovers." He looked at Austen. "If there are others to compare it to, you might be able to guesstimate an age for the spear?"

"I know it's at last two hundred years old because that's about the time the Cherokee language began being written down. But the physical spear could be much older."

Paul nodded. "You'll most likely try and convince the owner to put it in a museum. Am I right?"

"I don't support the sale of antiquities, especially not to people who hide them from the world," Austen said. He focused on Tessa, and the kitchen lights flickered. "I prefer it be returned to the Cherokee Nation."

She nodded. "I'll wait to hear from you."

Austen's gaze softened. He removed the latex gloves and dropped them into the trash can. "I'll be in touch. While I'm in town, I'm going to visit a family friend. She'd like to know about this, and if anyone knows why a prayer was carved on a spear, she will. Her family has lived around here for years. There's a good chance she knows which families used to live on this land. Her records date back hundreds of years. She lives at the end of Juniper Lane, near the river."

Tessa's eyes widened. "That's where Crazy Kate lives."

"Excuse me?" Austen asked. His thick, black eyebrows disappeared behind the hair brushing across his forehead.

Paul chuckled, and Tessa cleared her throat. "Kate Muir?"

Austen nodded. "That's her."

In a desperate attempt to make up for her disrespect, Tessa said, "She has a lot of beautiful suncatchers. Just don't let any of them fall into your hands, because she'll never forget it." *Tessa, stop talking.*

Austen and Paul exchanged puzzled looks. "Thanks," Austen said, reaching out to shake Tessa's hand.

His grip was firm, and Tessa winced. She rubbed her fingers as Paul and Austen said good-bye. Paul closed the door and walked across the room to pluck a caramel cream off the coffee table.

"Seems a shame that something so rare is owned by someone who won't care except for its salability," Paul said. "You sure you can't market that house in the next couple of days to someone who might actually want to rehab it? It shouldn't be demolished."

His words caused her heart to race. She wiped her sweaty palms on her pants. Honeysuckle Hollow could be someone's home again, and *she* needed a place to live. Tessa stared at the wall map. Her eyes traced the silver pushpins, following Paul's travels. She was amazed by his ability to go and go and go and never yearn for that *one* place to return to every evening, that *one* place that was his.

Tessa thought about her condo. This time the idea of letting go didn't twinge as bad. There was nothing else left there that she could salvage. She'd saved everything she could, and her few possessions crowded the apartment, waiting to be taken to a new home. A voice in her head asked, *Would the money from the condo sale be enough to buy and rehab Honeysuckle Hollow?* She had a savings account that had been growing for years—although she'd never decided what she was saving the money for. A house for a family one day? A European vacation? Retirement? Maybe for all of those or none. She just might be able to afford to buy the house, but would there be enough money for renovations? "I can't buy Honeysuckle Hollow."

Paul's laugh swelled against the living room walls and wrapped around Tessa's shoulders. She looked at him. "I'm not implying that *you* buy it. Someone with rehab experience. Someone who wants a challenge."

Tessa huffed. "I have experience with properties." Thoughts of Honeysuckle Hollow in ruins ballooned in her head until her left eye twitched. Her pulse throbbed in her neck and then at her temples.

"You're a real estate agent."

Tessa fisted her hands on her hips. "And you're a travel writer with a master's in architecture. I can't have other skills?"

"Do you?" he asked. Then he held up his hands in defense. "Do you have *rehabbing* skills?"

"Some." She picked up *Guests of Honeysuckle Hollow* and waved it at Paul. "This house *saved* people. It was there for hundreds of them. I can't let it go."

Paul's expression shifted from serious to gentle. "I appreciate your spunk, and I've got a soft spot for that house now too. I can't quit thinking about it, but that's a massive undertaking, and maybe it's best suited for professionals."

Tessa's shoulders slumped. He was right, of course. She could call in help for the construction and labor, but would she have enough money to complete a project of that size? The house wasn't even livable at present. She dropped the book onto a couch cushion.

Paul held out a caramel cream in his palm. "Talk about taking the wind out of someone's sails. With your enthusiasm, I bet you can do anything you set your mind to, but I'm trying to be a voice of reason."

"I hear you, Jiminy Cricket, but that doesn't mean I like what I hear."

Paul grinned. "How about I fix dinner?"

Tessa reached for the candy. "Aren't you leaving?"

"Are you pushing me out of town? Ready to have this place all to yourself?"

Tessa unwrapped the candy and sighed. "Not really." Technically, she didn't really know Paul, but, like kudzu covering a house, in the past two days he'd become tangled around nearly every aspect of her life. Tessa was currently homeless, without a car of her own, and possibly trying to make a ridiculous life-altering decision, and Paul seemed to be the only stable part.

His blue eyes crinkled around the edges when he smiled. "I have the perfect dinner idea." He walked into the kitchen and opened the refrigerator. "But I'm not sure we have all the ingredients. It's a dish I ate in Australia."

"We can go to the grocery store," Tessa said. "What's the dish?"

Paul closed the refrigerator. "It's perfect for the occasion. It has polenta-crusted poached eggs and Spanish chorizo served on top of crispy corn tortillas with a sprinkle of roasted mushrooms and queso fresco. It's called Thieves on the Run. Perfect for us, yeah?"

Tessa groaned, and Paul laughed.

"I'm rethinking my decision on whether I want you to stay a little longer. And for the last time, I didn't *steal* the spear."

"Yeah, yeah, so, we'll call it Borrowers on the Run. Better?"

She grabbed her purse from her bedroom and saw the stack of house listings on the dresser. She eased Honeysuckle Hollow's information page from the bottom of the pile. When she inhaled, she smelled honeysuckle growing on the vine mixed with the earthy scent of cloves. The smell of sage and rosemary lingered too. Her fingers trembled, causing the paper to flutter in her hands. She couldn't deny the emotion bubbling up through her. She *wanted* Honeysuckle Hollow for herself. Spear, bats, and all.

CHAPTER 14

COURAGE QUICHE

Tessa woke up with two words bouncing around in her brain: *Honeysuckle Hollow.* It was probably a harebrained idea to buy a run-down property and attempt to rehab it. She'd seen people get in over their heads with a financial disaster, and she'd always sworn she would never purchase a home more than ten years old. She preferred new, shiny, and efficient. It was no secret that older homes were high-maintenance and came with *expensive* problems, but she'd always been drawn to their handcrafted character and their rich histories.

Her condo had been a great fit for her. Less than three years old, clean, and just the right size. In contrast, Honeysuckle Hollow was more than one hundred years old, falling apart, and too much square footage for what she needed. What would she do with four thousand square feet? Listen to her echo bounce around the empty rooms? Still, the house called to her. Honeysuckle Hollow had never turned its back on anyone. Could she turn her back on it?

Tessa grabbed her notebook, and at the top of a clean page—because this question deserved its own page—she wrote, *Should I buy Honeysuckle Hollow?* She numbered down the side of the page, and beside the number one, she wrote, *I want to.* Even though in the past she'd decided not to count her own opinions, it felt necessary to start the list with what her heart was telling her.

She crawled out of bed and shuffled to the bathroom. After taking a quick shower and brushing her teeth, she pulled on a pair of capris and a sleeveless button-up blouse. She tiptoed through the living room. Paul's deep breaths fluttered the pages of a notepad on the coffee table. She peered down at the lined paper. The words *Mystic Water* and *Cherokee* were legible even upside down. Was he outlining an article about the spear?

Tessa closed the apartment door as quietly as possible and headed for the diner. She wasn't surprised to see a flurry of activity already happening inside Scrambled. She waved to Laney, walked toward the kitchen's swinging door, and pushed it open.

"Good morning," Tessa said to Harry's back.

Harry turned from the griddle and lifted his spatula in the form of a wave. "Morning, Tessa. I don't see you much behind the scenes." He flipped over a pile of hash browns and revealed their crispy, browned underside. "Perfection. How are you?"

Tessa lifted her shoulders. "Full of thoughts. Sorry to bother you while you're working, and I know this is cutting in line ahead of your waiting customers, but do you have any quick dishes I could get to go?"

Cecilia walked out of the back room that housed the coolers and freezer. Her smile widened. "There's the charmer who's convinced my boy to stay a while longer."

Tessa glanced behind her, and Cecilia's laugh caused Harry to pause in his work and smile at his wife.

Cecilia pulled Tessa into a hug, squeezing her tight. "I don't know how you've done it, but knowing that Paul is staying another day is more than I could have hoped. You've worked some sort of magic on him."

"Not *me*," Tessa said, making a scoffing noise in her throat. Why would Cecilia think Tessa had anything to do with Paul's extended stay? Sure, she *borrowed* the spear, and he was interested in learning more about it, but he wasn't staying because of *her*. Based on what she'd seen on his notepad, Paul was working on a story about the artifact. He could probably find a story anywhere, even in Mystic Water. "I think he's been enjoying spending time with y'all."

Cecilia's cheek dimpled just like Paul's did when he smiled. "I think he's spent more time with you than with us, but he couldn't have picked a sweeter girl to be with. He's lucky to know someone as accomplished and pretty as you."

Tessa stared at Cecilia as warm fuzzies tickled through her. "Me?"

Cecilia laughed again. "Yes, *you*. If you could see yourself the way we do. The way *Paul* does. He was telling us about how you're helping the townsfolk, which we're not surprised by, and how funny you are, not to mention how pretty he thinks you are—"

"Cece, that's enough," Harry said.

"Oh, hush, Harry," Cecilia said.

Paul thought she was funny *and* pretty? Tessa's heart did a rapid thump in her chest.

Cecilia huffed at her husband. "Don't stand there and act as though you haven't been wondering the same thing."

"Wondering what?" Tessa asked.

"About you and Paul," Cecilia answered.

"Me and Paul what?"

Cecilia pointed at Tessa with a manicured fingernail. "About you and Paul. *Together.* You two seem to get on well. Finally, Paul has found someone who makes him pause."

Tessa's breath caught in her throat. A tiny twinkle of hope glowed in her chest before she released it on her next breath. "It's not like that. We're not *together.*"

Cecilia narrowed her eyes at Tessa as though she didn't believe her answer. Based on the way Tessa's heart thumped against her ribs, she wasn't sure if *she* should believe her answer either. *But we're* not *together. We're not anything. Okay, maybe we're quasi friends who've exchanged numbers and possibly agreed to being pen pals, but that's it.*

"Word around here is that you're involved in Honeysuckle Hollow," Cecilia said. "Paul mentioned he'd been out to see the house with you."

Tessa nodded. Nothing ever stayed hidden in small towns, not for long. "I've been working with an out-of-town owner. I'd like someone to rehab it."

Cecilia nodded. "That'll be a lot of work. After Matthias died, I think they pretty much let the place go, though I don't know why. It was such a beautiful house. Matthias was one of our very first customers. Such a nice man. He used to come in here every Wednesday morning, and we shared gardening tips. Did you know he transplanted sage and rosemary from my garden into the garden there?"

Tessa's eyes widened. Plants grown in the diner's special soil were now growing at Honeysuckle Hollow. *The magic spreads.*

"Paul had quite a lot to say about the house and what you hoped would happen with it." Cecilia's eyes were full of optimism. "He couldn't stop smiling when he was talking about the architecture. It's been a long time since I've seen that."

Tessa cleared her throat and tried to avoid Cecilia's searching eyes. "I was asking Harry, is there anything quick I could take off your hands this morning for breakfast?"

Cecilia eyed Tessa a moment longer before nodding. She pointed to a warm, buttery quiche sitting on one of the countertops. "It's a Courage Quiche. If you can believe this, I went out to the garden this morning to grab rosemary, and I noticed a few dozen crocuses popping up through the dirt. They're all in bloom, and it's not crocus season. Not only that, they are . . . what are they called again, Harry?"

"*Crocus sativus.*"

"That's right. The kind of crocus that yields saffron."

Tessa had a feeling she knew the answer, but she asked anyway. "Does that mean they're special?"

"Of course they are. Saffron is rare and expensive, and I certainly didn't plant them in the garden." She shrugged. "Who knows who dropped them there."

Tessa glanced over her shoulder as though she might be able to see the garden from the closed-in kitchen. Now the garden was pushing up not only out-of-season plants but saffron-producing crocuses?

"I brought the saffron threads inside and put them in a small jar. Then I accidentally tipped the entire jar into the eggs. It wasn't worth fishing them out. I wanted to throw out the quiche, but Harry told me that someone might want it. I guess that someone is you."

Tessa walked over to the quiche. It wasn't as yellow as a crayon, but it was brighter and sunnier than other quiches she'd seen. "Why is it called Courage Quiche?"

Cecilia lifted her hands. "Old tales say that saffron gives strength and courage to those who ingest it. My *nonna* used to add threads to her risotto—"

"The best I've ever eaten, may she rest in peace," Harry interjected, causing Cecilia to glance his way and smile.

"This was one of her recipes too. She always called it Courage Quiche," Cecilia said, sliding the quiche into a brown paper bag. "Bring back the pan when you're done. With the amount of saffron in it, I'd say you'll be courageous enough to take on the world. Perhaps even to take a chance on love with a wayward young man—"

"Cece," Harry warned.

Cecilia shoved the bag into Tessa's hands. "Take it." She shook her head at Harry. "Can you blame me, Harry? Tell me you don't love having Paul around."

Tessa cleared her throat again. "Thank you for the quiche. How much do I owe you?"

Cecilia waved her hands in the air. "Nothing. Share it with Paul if he's around. He'll only raid the kitchen for free anyway."

Tessa scooted out of the kitchen before the conversation became any more awkward. She slipped out of the dining room and stared at the garden as she walked past. Purple crocus blooms huddled together, waving to her in the breeze.

At the top of the apartment stairs, she paused. Why *was* Paul still staying? Even during dinner the night before, he hadn't mentioned when his second attempt at leaving town would happen. *It's not because of me*, a voice whispered in her head. For a moment, long enough for her to inhale and exhale a heavy breath, she imagined what it would be like for a man like Paul to stick around because of her.

Tessa opened the door and crept into the kitchen without disturbing Paul. She grabbed a fork and carried the quiche into the bedroom, where she pulled the fluffy duvet off the bed and dragged it into the bathroom. The bathroom contained an oversize garden tub, a tiled walk-in shower, and a double vanity with a mirror spanning the wall behind the two sinks.

Tessa checked to make sure the bathtub was clean and dry. Then she dropped the duvet into the tub, causing it to look like a giant oval filled with marshmallow fluff. It was a strange place to want to sit, she knew, but as a child, when she truly wanted to be alone, she'd always retreated to the bathroom. And if she was going to "hide out" in the bathroom, why not be comfortable? She grabbed her cell phone and notebook. Then she removed the quiche from the bag, closed the bathroom door, and crawled into the tub, careful not to drop the quiche.

The first bite of Courage Quiche tasted earthy, and the flaky, buttery crust melted on her tongue. She ate bite after bite, watching the sunbeams stretch across the bathroom tiles and fill the room with pink and gold light. Before she realized it, she'd eaten the equivalent of two entire slices of quiche. She hadn't bothered cutting the quiche into equal segments, so it looked as though someone had eaten willy-nilly from the pan.

Words crept into Tessa's mind, blowing through her thoughts like a spring breeze. *Buy Honeysuckle Hollow.* This time, she didn't hesitate. She didn't worry that it was the most absurd and irresponsible idea she'd ever had. She didn't need three people to give her life advice. She *needed* to save Honeysuckle Hollow, and there was no way to do that without purchasing it herself.

Tessa called Ralph. "Huh?" He rasped his greeting into the phone.

She heard rustling around and muffled groans. "Did I wake you?"

"It's not even nine, Tessa. No one gets out of bed before nine."

Tessa frowned. "Seriously, Ralph? No one? How much is the investor giving Mrs. Steele for the land?"

Whether it was because she'd woken him and he hadn't thought to shield his answers or because he felt no reason to protect his client, Ralph gave her an honest answer. He seemed surprised when she thanked him and ended the call immediately.

Tessa dialed Mrs. Steele's number. She doubted she would receive an answer because of the time difference between the east and west coasts, but Tessa left a detailed message, including the price she was willing to pay for Honeysuckle Hollow.

She continued to get ready for her workday, drying her hair and putting on makeup. All the while she felt the excitement about her decision to buy Honeysuckle Hollow growing inside her like a seed, sprouting and spreading. The words *Honeysuckle Hollow* and *home* tangled around each other until they felt synonymous. *I can do this.*

Within half an hour, Tessa was lounging in the duvet-filled tub again when the condo developer called. She set up a time to meet with him in the afternoon. His offer was generous given the state of the building. Since her condo was paid off, she'd be able to include the money from the buyer into the purchase of Honeysuckle Hollow and its rehab. She brainstormed ways she would allocate the money for Honeysuckle Hollow repairs. She felt confident Mrs. Steele would not reject her offer, and she needed to call the bank and make arrangements for transferring money from her savings account to Mrs. Steele. She sank deeper into the tub, letting the duvet wrap around her, and grabbed her cell phone.

As if on cue, her cell phone rang. “Hello?”

“Ms. Andrews? This is Trudy Steele. I can’t imagine why you want to buy anything so worthless, but your offer is above what I was hoping to get from another investor. I’m prepared to accept your offer.”

Tessa bolted upright in the tub. “You are?” A rush of energy zinged through her. She blurted, “Of course you are.”

“Excuse me?”

Tessa’s insides felt jolted with electricity. “Email the paperwork to my office. I have a contact at the bank who can probably expedite this process. I’d say that within two weeks, you’ll have the money in your account, and I’ll have the deed.” The call went so silent that Tessa heard her own heart pounding in her ears. Her confidence wavered. “Mrs. Steele?”

“Are you sure you want to do this?” Mrs. Steele asked, her voice more brittle than ever. “That’s a lot of money for a house that has brought nothing but misery and heartache.”

“What kind of misery and heartache?” Tessa asked, frowning into the phone.

Then, as though she’d never paused in the business transaction to show concern, Mrs. Steele said, “I’ll email these papers to you, and although I’ve never heard of a bank working quickly on anything, I’ll take your word for it. I require earnest money so that I know you’re serious. I won’t have you saying you’ll buy it only to change your mind when you realize what a mistake it is. I’ll have my lawyer draft up a new contract.”

“Earnest money, of course. How much?”

Mrs. Steele said she wanted half of the offered

price—thousands of dollars—and Tessa's stomach fluttered. She sat in silence.

"Changing your mind already?"

"No—no, ma'am. I'm thinking. I can go to the bank today and wire the money, but I'll need the contract first. Can your lawyer pull it together quickly?"

Mrs. Steele assured Tessa her lawyer would work at whatever speed she requested, and Tessa promised to go to the bank as soon as she received the contract. Mrs. Steele ended the call, and Tessa stared at her cell phone. *I'm really doing this!* Her mind created a to-do list. She would need the cleaners and the exterminator over there as soon as possible. She called both companies, and to her surprise, they could be at the house after lunch. Tessa's pulse raced.

Then she called Charlie Parker and asked if she would be able to board up the broken windows until they could start renovations. Charlie said someone could drop off the supplies today, but she wouldn't be able to nail up the boards immediately. Tessa asked Charlie to keep her updated about when she could work the reno into her schedule.

A knock at the bathroom door startled her, and Tessa dropped the phone into the feathery clouds of the duvet. "Yeah?"

The door opened, and Paul popped his head into the bathroom.

"Hey!" Tessa shouted. "I didn't say *come in*. I might not have been decent."

"Are you ever decent?" He smirked. When he spotted her in the bathtub, his brow furrowed. "Should I even ask why you're in the tub with the blanket?"

"I just bought Honeysuckle Hollow."

His smile dimmed. "What do you mean?"

"Just what I said. There's paperwork to be completed and money to be shifted around, but it *will* be mine." She covered her mouth with her fingertips and released a girly squeal.

"Whoa," Paul said, sitting down on the edge of the tub. "Are you serious? When did this happen?"

"Less than five minutes ago."

"And you're sitting in the tub because?"

Tessa hunted through the fluffy folds for her cell phone. "For extra privacy. I didn't want to wake you while I ate breakfast and made phone calls." She pointed toward the vanity. "Your mama gave me a Courage Quiche."

Paul crossed the bathroom while Tessa tried to crawl out of the tub as gracefully as possible. The duvet slipped on the smooth ceramic surface, and she tumbled out of the bath, landing with a loud *thump*, sprawled on the bathmat. Paul looked at her over his shoulder.

"Don't you dare say a word."

He pointed to the quiche. "May I *say a word* about this quiche? I have never in my life seen anyone eat a quiche like this."

"I wasn't paying attention. I've been a little distracted this morning."

Paul sat on the edge of the bathroom counter and crossed his arms over his chest. "I think finding a new place is a great idea. I know you've been eager to have a home."

She saw doubt in his eyes. "But . . ."

"Are you sure about buying Honeysuckle Hollow? It needs serious work."

Tessa walked out of the bathroom shaking her head, and Paul followed her into the living room, balancing the quiche on one hand. "Weren't you the one championing me to save it? I'm aware of how much work it's going to take. I can handle it."

"Have you ever done this sort of work before?"

"I have people I can call. It's not as though *I'm* going to make the repairs myself."

Paul put the quiche on the kitchen table. "If I can pry for a moment . . . what about the money? Expenses can escalate rapidly when rehabbing homes, and I think this particular home could be an expensive project."

Tessa knew Paul was only saying out loud what she'd already been thinking, but she wasn't deterred. "I have savings, and I plan on using the money from the condo sale to buy and repair the house."

Paul's frown deepened. "Have I mentioned this is a massive reno?"

Tessa pressed her lips together. She could tell by his expression that he didn't have confidence in her decision. "Listen, Jiminy, I can do this." Her cell phone rang, giving her a momentary reprieve from Paul. "Hello?"

"Ms. Andrews? This is Austen Blackstone. How are you this morning?"

Paul opened the silverware drawer and removed a fork. Then he opened the refrigerator, pulled a few leaves from the head of lettuce, and closed the door. He sat at the table and worked on the quiche from the opposite side of Tessa's destruction.

"Busy. How are you?" She walked to the wall map. The mint stretched across the Atlantic and wrapped around silver pins in Ireland, Spain, and Morocco.

"Surprised, actually," Austen said. "After searching for similar finds or tools with Cherokee language inscribed on them, there are a spare few, less than five across the country. Their research included radiocarbon dating the wood, which we didn't do, but the others are dated to be at least a thousand years old.

Not the inscription, of course, but the wood."

Tessa's knees buckled. She stared at the spear leaning against the bookshelf. "That's impossible. *Look* at it."

"I have to agree it's in immaculate shape—"

"Impossible shape. What does that *mean*?" she asked.

Paul looked up from his breakfast and tilted his head at her, asking her questions with his blue eyes. He tore lettuce leaves into small pieces and dropped them into Huck Finn's plastic container. The fish swam circles in the water as if saying thank you.

"It means you have a priceless artifact in your possession," Austen explained. "I'd like to discuss options with you on how to proceed from here. The university would welcome an opportunity to study it further, and I know a few people in Washington, DC, and in Chicago who would be more than happy to take it off your hands and display it for the world."

"Email me some information, and I'll get back with you." Tessa gave Austen her email address and ended the call. She explained Austen's findings, and then she and Paul were silent for a few heartbeats.

Paul grabbed his notepad from the coffee table. "This is quite the find for a small town like Mystic Water. I'll call a few magazines today, let them know what's been found here, and see who will want to print the story."

"What story?"

"The story that I'm going to write about Mystic Water being home to a one-thousand-year-old Native American spear with a Cherokee prayer carved into its shaft," Paul said, jotting notes into his notebook.

Lines of concentration wrinkled his forehead. She thought of Cecilia downstairs and what she'd said to Tessa this morning. *There's the charmer who's convinced my boy to stay a while longer.*

"So you're not leaving?"

He nodded without looking up. "Not until I finish the story. I'll need to go eventually, but my trip to the Cook Islands is on hold." He paused and glanced up at her. "Is that okay? I didn't even ask if you wanted a story written about the spear, but it's a rare piece of history. It wouldn't seem fair to keep it all to yourself. Others can benefit from this finding, from knowing something like this exists. And its connection with the house is remarkable. A house that's been a refuge for hundreds and with a spear of protection buried beneath it. Coincidental?"

"It's a strange connection, I agree. I don't mind if you write about it, as long as we leave the actual location of the spear a secret. I've watched episodes on treasure hunters, and some of those seekers are intense. Intense enough to show up here."

A knock sounded at the door, and Tessa glanced at Paul, who looked as surprised as she was. Tessa opened the door, and a gust of wind smelling like lavender and green pine needles rushed into the room. Tessa's mouth dropped open when she saw Crazy Kate standing on the landing.

Crazy Kate's face was pinched and angry. "Where is it?"

"Where is what?"

Crazy Kate pushed her way into the living room.

Paul stood quickly from the couch. "Morning, ma'am."

Crazy Kate frowned at Tessa. "What have you done with the spear? It's mine."

CHAPTER 15

Hot Cross Buns

Crazy Kate was dressed in her usual colorful attire, wearing an ankle-length turquoise skirt, a purple blouse overlaid with a patchwork vest stitched together in a rainbow pattern, and a black scarf tied over her silver-streaked hair, which laid in a long braid down her back. Wisps of hair fell around her sharp cheekbones.

"Please, come in," Tessa said, not bothering to hide her sarcasm. "You must be confused about the spear."

"I'm not confused about anything," Crazy Kate said, rounding on Tessa. "You shouldn't have taken it from the house."

Tessa's skin tingled. "Why?"

"Why do you think?" Crazy Kate said. "It was protecting the house. It has been for a lot longer than you've been alive."

Tessa couldn't stop the laugh bubbling up her throat. Crazy Kate narrowed her eyes, and the sun shifted behind the clouds outside, throwing the room into shadows.

"You haven't wondered why those men were unable to tear

down the house? Not a second thought as to why their machines failed?"

Tessa inhaled sharply. She met Paul's gaze. His blue eyes were as wide as hers. "What do you know about that?"

Crazy Kate stepped toward her. "I know that the reason they failed is because of the one thing you stole from the house. Still haven't outgrown your thieving ways, I see."

A flush crept across Tessa's cheeks, and she felt as though her mama had scolded her. "That's not fair. I was a *kid*—"

"A thieving kid."

"I *borrowed* the spear. I only wanted to learn more about it."

"So you have. What you need to do right now is give it back to me," Crazy Kate said. "It belongs to my family and to the house. It's not yours any more than my suncatcher was yours."

Crazy Kate's eyes filled with tears. Tessa felt an overwhelming desire to console the strange woman. Sunlight eased back into the room and lightened the dark walnut floors.

"Actually," Paul said, "the spear belongs to Tessa because Honeysuckle Hollow belongs to her. That means she's the rightful owner of anything *in* the land as well."

Crazy Kate's mouth dropped open, and she pressed a hand to her chest. "*You*? You bought the house? When?"

"This morning," Tessa said. "It's not official yet, but I have a verbal agreement with the current owner. Honeysuckle Hollow *will* be mine."

"Trudy." Crazy Kate hissed the name as though it burned her tongue.

"How do you know Mrs. Steele?" Tessa asked.

Crazy Kate's thin fingers rolled into her palms, and she clenched her fists. "I won't let you tear down that house."

"I have no plans to tear down Honeysuckle Hollow, but why is the house so important to you?"

"For reasons you would never care about," Crazy Kate said.

Tessa shook her head. "It's just an old spear with carvings. It's ludicrous for me to believe it's the reason they couldn't tear down Honeysuckle Hollow. The bulldozer wasn't working the first day, and the second day was because of the foggy weather."

Crazy Kate tossed an exasperated expression at Tessa. "And what caused the weather? You don't think the weather protected the house?"

Tessa made a scoffing noise in her throat. "You think the spear *caused* the fog?" But she remembered the feeling she'd had the night the fog arrived, the feeling that the fog was concealing Mystic Water, protecting it. "That's absurd." Tessa's fingers itched to grab her notebook and write the question, *It's absurd to think the spear caused the fog, right?*

Crazy Kate hummed in her throat. "Is it, Tessa? You don't believe in the garden either? I didn't think you were a thief *and* a liar."

"Excuse me?" Tessa asked, bristling. "I am *not* a liar."

Crazy Kate stepped close to Tessa, and Tessa tried to step away but ended up with her back pressed against the living room wall. Crazy Kate spoke in a hushed tone, "You've experienced how the garden changes you, yet you continue to deny it? Maybe you need to ask yourself why you're denying the truth."

Paul stepped toward them, asking Tessa with his eyes if he should manhandle the wild woman out of the apartment. Tessa shook her head.

"What's this about the garden?" Paul asked.

Tessa groaned. There was enough insanity going on in the

room right now without telling Paul that his mama's garden was quite possibly magical. Crazy Kate looked at Paul and smiled, her expression softening. There was no denying the mischief in Crazy Kate's gaze.

"It's what brought you here," Crazy Kate said to Paul.

"My parents brought me here. I came to see them."

Crazy Kate looked at Paul and then at Tessa. "Does it give you comfort to deny the obvious?" She reached into her pocket and pulled out a small object. Then she stretched out her closed palm to Paul, offering him whatever was hidden in her hand. He held out his open hand, and she dropped a red heart-shaped pushpin into his palm. She nodded her head toward the wall map. "You cannot escape the truth forever. It will keep turning up until you accept it."

Tessa's heart slammed in her chest. Frantic, desperate beats that caused her vision to blur as she tried to focus on the red pushpin in Paul's hand. His lips parted, but he said nothing. He stared at the pushpin until his fingers closed around it. Neither one of them tried to stop Crazy Kate as she snatched the spear from the living room and rushed out of the apartment.

Without a word, Paul walked into the bathroom. A few seconds later, Tessa heard the rush of water through the pipes as the toilet flushed. When he returned to the living room, his hands were empty. He grabbed his notepad, cell phone, and pen from the coffee table and barely glanced at Tessa.

"I'm going for a walk," he said as he left the apartment.

Tessa stood alone in the living room before sitting on the couch and staring at the wall map. She exhaled a deep breath, and the mint shivered, filling the room with its calming scent. Tessa looked at Huck Finn swimming in his plastic home. "What have we gotten ourselves into, Huck?" The fish had no answer.

With no idea how to react to Crazy Kate's appearance and what had been said, Tessa grabbed her laptop and purse. She bagged what remained of the Courage Quiche and slid it into a canvas grocery bag. Then she walked up the street to work.

Tessa sat at her desk, staring out the window. Was owning Honeysuckle Hollow really within her grasp? Her computer dinged, alerting her that a new email had arrived in her inbox. The email was sent from a lawyer's office in California. She clicked open the email while holding her breath. *The contract for the earnest money.* She opened the attached email file and read through it. Another email containing the full real estate purchase agreement arrived. Tessa's heart performed a pirouette in her chest. She called her contact, Mr. Wagner, at the local bank branch. He was a close friend of her daddy's, and she knew he had ways to quickly push through the necessary paperwork and approvals.

Tessa informed Mr. Wagner that she wanted money wired from her savings account for the earnest money. Even through the phone line, Tessa heard the skepticism and questioning tone in Mr. Wagner's voice. "Are you one hundred percent sure about this?" he asked.

Is anyone ever 100 percent sure about anything? she thought. "Yes, sir, I am."

"That's a lot of money, Tessa," he said. "Have you talked to your dad about this?"

Am I a kid? "My parents respect my choices," she said, but it was likely only half true. She opened her notebook and turned to the most recent list asking, *Should I buy Honeysuckle Hollow?* Beside the number one, she'd written, *I want to.* Without anyone else's opinion or advice, she'd proceeded with an offer for Honeysuckle Hollow. Beside the question at the top, she squeezed in another question: *Should I drain my savings for Honeysuckle Hollow?* Beside the number two she wrote, *Do I have a choice?* There's always a choice, and Tessa's choice was to buy Honeysuckle Hollow. She asked Mr. Wagner to initiate the necessary paperwork and told him she would be at the bank in fifteen minutes to wire the money.

After the wire transfer, Tessa sat in her car and stared at the receipt. She'd never spent so much money at once, not even to put a down payment on her condo. She electronically signed both the earnest money contract and the real estate agreement, alongside Mrs. Steele's signature, and emailed them to the lawyer. Now all she had to do was wait for the fully executed contract to return to her. The house was as good as hers.

Tessa should probably feel sick to her stomach for making such an impulsive decision without conferring with her friends and family, but instead, excitement bubbled through her veins. The sun shined through the windshield and warmed her cheeks. She opened her notebook and flipped to the question: *Should I drain my savings for Honeysuckle Hollow?* In the past two and a half years, she'd never made any decisions without making sure she asked three people for their opinions, and now she'd made two life-altering choices without so much as her mama's input. What *was* her mama going to say?

Tessa returned to her office. Sitting at her desk, she cut into the cold quiche and forked it into her mouth. She chewed slowly, thinking about the house, and then her thoughts drifted to Crazy Kate. She recalled her first real run-in with Crazy Kate at Sweet Stop when she hinted at the magical properties of the garden. Tessa forked another piece of flaky pastry into her mouth, then she gaped at the quiche—Courage Quiche. Had the quiche given Tessa courage to buy Honeysuckle Hollow? Was it false courage? Would she snap out of it in a few hours and realize she'd made an impulsive mistake?

At this point, Crazy Kate was the only person who might have the answer, and Tessa had questions for her too. Why would she have buried a spear of protection beneath Honeysuckle Hollow? Crazy Kate told Tessa when the rosemary in the garden was mature, she wanted brewed tea. *Are you really thinking of having tea with Crazy Kate?*

"Why stop there?" she asked out loud. "Why not stay for dinner?"

Her cell phone rang, and the local mechanic, Mr. Benson, informed her that the Great Pumpkin had not died. They'd tinkered with the inner workings and brought it back to life. One of the shop guys needed to go downtown, so he was going to drop off the car for her. Mr. Benson said he'd send her an electronic invoice, and she could pay it online. Tessa thanked him. Now with a car, there was still time for a visit with Crazy Kate before her afternoon meetings.

At the diner, Tessa found Cecilia in the back room, and she asked if they'd brewed any rosemary tea for the day. Tessa explained she needed it for a friend and asked if she could have some to go. She also asked for a tin of dried lavender from the garden. Fifteen minutes later Tessa walked out of the diner with a tin of lavender and a bottle of rosemary tea that smelled like wildness and green pine needles. She found the car keys to the Great Pumpkin on the right front tire, and she drove toward Juniper Lane before she could change her mind.

The dirt driveway leading down toward Crazy Kate's cottage had potholes the size of kiddie pools. Trying to navigate the Great Pumpkin around the craters was about as easy as cuddling a beehive without being stung. Colored glass bottles had been placed onto branches, turning the trees into kaleidoscopes. Tessa parked and climbed out of the car. Wind chimes whispered in the trees, mesmerizing her with their tinkling, music-box notes. Suncatchers shimmered in the sunlight, and Tessa stared, completely charmed by the magic of the forest.

"Come to steal a new prize?" Crazy Kate asked.

Crazy Kate's voice pulled Tessa from her daydream, and she lifted the glass bottle of tea and the tin. "I come bearing gifts."

Crazy Kate's eyebrows rose. "This is unexpected." She walked back into her house, leaving Tessa standing in the side yard.

After a moment Tessa crossed the front yard toward the front door. Standing on the threshold, she said, "Umm, Cra— Ms. Muir?"

"Mrs.," Crazy Kate yelled from inside the cottage.

Tessa stood on the front stoop and peered through the door. "Excuse me?"

Crazy Kate appeared in front of her, startling Tessa. "It's *Mrs.*, not *Miss.*"

"Oh." *She was married?*

Crazy Kate reached for the bottle and the tin, and Tessa handed them over. "Thank you." She disappeared into the depths of the cottage. "Either come in or stay out, but don't stand there with the door open. The blue jays like to come inside, and it's the devil trying to get them out."

The wind rustled through the trees, filling the air with the tinny sounds of music. Tessa stepped inside and closed the door. The interior of the cottage was nothing like she expected. She had imagined a hoarder, an old lady squirreling away magazines or newspapers from the past one hundred years. She wouldn't have been surprised to be overwhelmed with the scents of rot and decay, of a life that had stopped moving years ago.

Instead, Crazy Kate's cottage was clean and *cozy*, and it smelled like freshly cut lavender and roses. Overstuffed leather armchairs and a chocolate-brown couch gathered around a stone fireplace. A suncatcher hung in one window and beamed rainbows across the small living room. The open kitchen connected to the living room, and Crazy Kate stood at the stove, pouring rosemary tea into a widemouthed kettle. The gas stove ignited, and Crazy Kate grabbed a wooden spoon. She stirred the tea in slow, deliberate circles.

Tessa cleared her throat. "I didn't know you were married."

Crazy Kate huffed. "I don't suppose you know much about me at all."

Tessa felt the sting of her words. She had never bothered to know much about Crazy Kate, other than accepting what people had told her. "Your husband—"

"Gone." Crazy Kate's shoulders tensed and then stooped forward. She exhaled. "Two years now. I miss him every day."

Tessa couldn't even imagine what kind of man Crazy Kate would have been married to. Was he as odd as she was? Did he wear rainbow colors and bury spears in the ground? She glanced around the living room and noticed a grouping of photographs on an end table. Tessa stepped over to it and leaned down to get a closer look. She was shocked to see a young woman, who had to be Crazy Kate in her twenties, standing with a young man. They smiled at the camera, looking as though nothing could have ruined their moment together. Not only was Crazy Kate stunning, but the man who had his arm wrapped around her waist was gorgeous. *Her husband?*

In another photograph, Crazy Kate and the man stood with two dark-haired children, one boy and one girl. *She has kids?* And still in another photograph, the children were teenagers caught laughing with Crazy Kate and the tall man, who looked vaguely familiar to Tessa.

With her back turned to Tessa, Crazy Kate said, "You didn't come to bring the tea and lavender."

Tessa frowned. "Actually, I did."

"Actually," Crazy Kate said, "you came to ask about Honeysuckle Hollow."

Crazy Kate poured the warmed tea into delicate blue porcelain teacups and placed them on a modest kitchen table made of reclaimed wood. She sat and motioned for Tessa to do the same. Crazy Kate brought her cup to her nose and inhaled deeply. Her eyes closed, and she sipped her tea. Tessa wrapped her hands around the teacup and allowed the porcelain to warm her fingers. After Crazy Kate took a second sip, her eyes popped open. She stared at Tessa and lowered her cup immediately. Her fingers trembled, and the cup danced in its saucer.

"Are you okay?" Tessa asked. *Oh, please don't die while I'm here. How will I ever explain this to anyone?*

"I remember," Crazy Kate whispered, her eyes brimming with tears. "Too much. The rosemary is too strong."

"I'm sorry," Tessa said as though she had something to do

with it. "I didn't brew it. Mrs. Borelli did. Do you want her to make you a milder batch? I can throw this one out."

Seeing Crazy Kate's tears caused Tessa's throat to tighten. Knowing she had had a husband and children out there somewhere forced Tessa to rethink who Crazy Kate really was. And why was she alone as an old woman? Tessa pushed her chair back from the table and tried to stand, but Crazy Kate gripped her wrist, pinning Tessa's arm to the table.

"It's not your fault. It's the garden," Crazy Kate said. Her eyes closed, and her fingers loosened on Tessa's arm. "I loved him. I loved them *both*, but him first."

When she didn't say anything more, Tessa asked, "Who?"

"Geoffrey Hamilton."

She spoke the name with such reverence she could have been speaking a prayer. Her cheeks pinked, and a slow sigh escaped through her lips. Tessa had never imagined Crazy Kate other than being called the town nut, so she couldn't picture Crazy Kate being in love with anyone.

For a moment Crazy Kate had the expression of a young woman with eyes full of hope and wonder. She reached her thin fingers up to her face and touched her cheek. The longing in her dark eyes made Tessa's chest ache.

"Youngest son of Alfred Hamilton, long-ago resident of Honeysuckle Hollow. The house . . . it belonged to the Hamiltons for more than a hundred years until Matthias, my husband, died a couple of years ago."

Tessa's forehead wrinkled. "You were married to Dr. Hamilton? The same Dr. Hamilton who took care of Honeysuckle Hollow? No one ever said anything to me about that . . . and you . . . were in love with his *brother*?"

Tessa didn't know much about the Hamiltons other than that they were one of the founding families in Mystic Water, and they had been exceedingly wealthy.

"Before Matthias," Crazy Kate said. She brought the cup to her lips and drank. "Geoffrey was a boy then, barely eighteen and just out of high school. I was sixteen, and he was the first boy who ever noticed me."

There was definitely a story here, and Tessa's curiosity overcame her. "What happened?"

Crazy Kate released a shuddering breath and lowered the cup, sloshing tea over the lip. "What am I?"

Tessa shifted in her chair. "I'm not sure what you're asking."

"When you look at me, what do you see?"

An incredibly unusual person seemed like an inappropriate response. "A woman."

"And sixty years ago, do you know what you would have said?"

Tessa shrugged. "A girl?"

"An outsider," Crazy Kate said. "My mama was a full-blooded Cherokee, and my daddy was a Scottish man madly in love with her. In the fifties, being different or foreign brought on a lot of discrimination. My daddy was a successful architect—brilliant, charming, and imposing—and my mama worked as a midwife. Because of that, Mystic Water mostly accepted them. They lived out here in this cottage, and they never paid much attention to what people thought about us, but people had their opinions. I had an older brother, Evan. He was handsome and popular, and I was his opposite. A little girl who belonged entirely to no one's world. I was *different*, and not just because of my dark skin."

Tessa nodded to encourage Crazy Kate to continue.

"Geoffrey didn't care that I was different, not at first." She turned and stared at a spot in the living room as though seeing the young man's face before her. "But that didn't last. Once he found out about my gift, he couldn't handle it. I was heartbroken. Young hearts are so fragile." She blinked away the tears in her eyes. Then she smiled. "But Matthias was there. Good, strong, dependable Matthias. He was so handsome, and he loved *me*, no matter what. He respected my gift."

"Wait," Tessa said, feeling indignant for Crazy Kate. "Geoffrey broke up with you because of a gift? What *kind* of gift?"

Crazy Kate's eyes shone like black pearls in the moonlight. She stood, grabbed her teacup, and poured out the rest of her tea into the sink. Sadness rippled off her. Dishes trembled in the cabinets, and wind wailed around the cottage like a lament. Tessa heard the frantic, high-pitched tones of the wind chimes clanging together. Crazy Kate exhaled and the wind quieted.

"A gift I couldn't control. I'm not talking about having a talent for singing or building houses. I'm talking about a gift too difficult for most to accept. But it's also why I buried the spear beneath Honeysuckle Hollow."

Tessa stared at her cup of tea. What memories would surface if she drank it? Would she splinter inside like Crazy Kate seemed to be doing? Would a long-buried yearning surface? "What kind of gift?" she repeated.

Crazy Kate's serious expression didn't waver as she said, "I can see the future."

Tessa eyebrows rose on her forehead. She thought of fortune-tellers at carnivals, hidden behind heavy drapes and burning incense. "Like with a crystal ball?"

Crazy Kate scoffed and tapped her finger to her temple. "In here. All sorts of futures tangled together like yarn. I know things before they happen."

"Like premonitions? Is that why people call—"

"Call me *Crazy* Kate?" A small smile tugged her lips. "People are generally afraid of what they don't understand. The name doesn't bother me anymore. It helps remind me that I'm special."

Crazy Kate sees the future? Why not? There is already the possibility of a magically potent garden and a house-protecting spear.

"My mama once described it as being able to see the future in broken pieces. But making sense of the visions would be the same as trying to make complete pictures out of the shattered glass in a suncatcher." Crazy Kate stared out the window. "But not all of my visions are so broken. Sometimes they are clear. Mama warned me never to change what I saw, never to act on my visions. I was meant to be a bystander."

The tone of her voice caused Tessa to ask, "But you didn't obey her, did you?"

Crazy Kate's eyes darkened. "Would you?"

Tessa hummed in her throat. "Depends, I guess. I might ask for advice first."

Crazy Kate shook her head. "You don't trust your heart."

Tessa rolled her eyes. "I've been impulsive one too many times, and it has brought me nothing but misery."

"Allowing others to navigate your life will bring you the same."

Tessa huffed. Now she was receiving advice from Crazy Kate? "Back to the spear. Why did you bury it at the house? Because of a vision?"

Crazy Kate nodded. "Fifty years ago, I saw that a terrible sickness would come through Mystic Water just before Christmas. I saw . . ." She paused as though recalling the memory resurrected the grief along with it. "I saw that many people would become sick, and some would die."

"The Hamiltons?" Tessa asked, sliding to the edge of her chair and staring at Crazy Kate.

"I saw Dr. Hamilton—their father—would bury his wife and all four sons."

"*All* of them?" Tessa's hand knocked into her teacup, and amber liquid sloshed onto the saucer.

"It was tradition for the sons and their wives and children to come to Mystic Water and spend Christmas at Honeysuckle Hollow. There was nothing I could do to deter them. Mrs. Hamilton wouldn't listen to my warnings. She never accepted that Matthias chose me as a wife." Crazy Kate's smile was slow. "Can you blame her?"

"But you tried to save her *and* the whole family with the spear?"

Crazy Kate walked toward the suncatcher in the living room. She touched it with her fingertips. Pale, fractured light skittered across the wood floor. Tessa turned in her chair to follow Crazy Kate's movements.

Crazy Kate sighed. "I tried, but the future is not so easily changed. The spear had been in Mama's family for hundreds of years, and it hung in my childhood bedroom my whole life. When I married, Matthias and I moved into our own house in town, and I left the spear behind. But I snuck back in here when it was still my parents' home one evening and took it. I couldn't let the Hamiltons die. I *couldn't*. Not Matthias. Not Geoffrey, but . . ." Crazy Kate turned to look at Tessa, and tears streaked her weathered cheeks. "It wasn't enough. I couldn't save them all. We lost Benjamin and Geoffrey. They faded in the night like snuffed candles inside Honeysuckle Hollow. Lost to their fevers and fitful dreams."

Tessa gasped. "No." Chills rushed up her arms. "I'm so sorry. But you tried. You saved Matthias and another brother and their mom, right? They should have thanked you for that. You did all you could."

Crazy Kate returned to the kitchen and grabbed the bottle of rosemary tea and held it up into a shaft of sunlight. The tea sparkled like sea glass. Her shadow trembled on the floor, and Crazy Kate crossed the small space and placed the bottle on the table in front of Tessa.

"Take this away. Those memories are too strong."

Tessa grabbed the bottle. "I'm sorry. I didn't know—"

"Don't apologize for what you could *never* have known. I'm going to rebury the spear, and no one should ever touch it again," she said. "Do you understand? You may have bought the house, but this spear is mine, and it belongs there. Trudy Steele wants to see the house torn down because she's still angry and blames Mystic Water for taking her husband, but I won't let that happen. Matthias and I didn't live in the house, but he still loved it and his family. He spent his life making that house a place of goodness and hope."

Tessa paused, trying to connect pieces of the past with the present. "You didn't take Matthias's last name?"

"I wanted to keep my daddy's name," Crazy Kate admitted with a shrug. "It's not so unusual these days, but back then it was practically a social faux pas. I never was one to follow the crowd."

Tessa said, "How rebellious of you. I don't understand why Trudy Steele owned the house and not you."

Crazy Kate shook her head. "I never wanted Honeysuckle Hollow. It belonged to the Hamiltons in a way I never did. When Matthias died, he left the house to another relative, Trudy Steele."

"But who is she?"

"Geoffrey's widow."

Tessa let that truth resonate in her brain before she spoke again. Crazy Kate's first love had married someone else, and that *someone* now wanted to tear down Honeysuckle Hollow because Geoffrey had died there. No wonder the old lady was so bitter about it. "But her last name is Steele. Did she remarry?"

Kate nodded. "Briefly, but it didn't last long. Why she kept his name, I'll never know."

"You don't have to bury the spear. Since I own the house—or practically own it—you could keep the spear inside. I wouldn't let anyone mess with it."

"I'm to trust that you won't sell it or give it back to the Cherokee Nation like Austenaco Blackstone suggested?"

"Aren't you technically part of the Cherokee Nation? Besides, it's yours, and you can decide whether to trust me or not," Tessa said. "Nothing in the world would make me want to sell the spear or give it away now."

Crazy Kate narrowed her eyes. "Why? It's worth a lot of money. I doubt anyone alive has ever seen a spear like it."

Tessa shrugged. "I don't know how to explain it, but I've been drawn to Honeysuckle Hollow since I first stepped foot in it a few days ago. If it weren't for you, your protection prayer, and your love, I would never have been given the chance to own it."

"And this chance to own Honeysuckle Hollow is the right decision for you?"

Tessa chuckled. "It's probably the most impulsive, stupidest decision I've made in a couple of years. It'll probably bankrupt me, but *my heart* is telling me yes."

Crazy Kate smiled. "Finally, you are learning. You're a slow one."

Tessa wasn't sure if Crazy Kate was insulting her or teasing her. "Who am I to stop protecting Honeysuckle Hollow? Bury the spear, or we can display it inside the house. Should we do it immediately? For protection?"

"The right time with present itself."

Tessa stood from the table and grabbed the bottle of tea. "You know better than I do." She studied the bottle in her hand. "Do you think the garden causes you to do things or *say* things that you wouldn't do otherwise? Like this tea and your memories?"

"That's not how it works," Crazy Kate said. "It only enhances what's already there inside you. The tea didn't *create* those memories. It drew them out of me in a way that was stronger than I wanted, almost like reliving them in the present."

Tessa thought of the Courage Quiche. Had it only heightened her bravery, not manufactured it? "But the thyme . . . I can't predict the weather normally. That's *not* a skill I have."

Crazy Kate smiled slowly at Tessa. "You'd be surprised by what you're capable of once you open your mind to the possibilities."

Tessa let those words sink in. "I should get going."

"And what about Paul?"

A breeze tickled Tessa's skin. "What about him?"

"He's tangled up in all this too. What does he want with the house?"

Tessa shook her head. "He's not part of this. I don't think he wants anything." Tessa walked toward the door. She remembered the heart-shaped pushpin Crazy Kate had given to Paul. "Where *did* you find that pushpin? Paul threw one just like it out the window."

Mischief flashed in Crazy Kate's dark brown eyes. "In my morning coffee. Sometimes we find the truth in the most unlikely places. And you're wrong about him. There is something he wants—a place to pin that heart."

CHAPTER 16

LADY AND THE TRAMP

After leaving Crazy Kate's, Tessa stopped by a gas station and bought a bag of chips and a Pepsi. She finished both while sitting in the Great Pumpkin and replaying the conversation with Crazy Kate over again in her mind. Afterward she met with a client at a new build that hadn't been affected by the flood, and then she drove to her wrecked condo to meet with the interested buyer. They spent less than half an hour talking, because what was there to discuss other than next steps? He assured Tessa she would have the closing paperwork by the beginning of next week. Then she would officially be condo-free and on her way to living in a dilapidated mansion. As soon as she had the money from the sale of her condo in the bank, she'd pay off the rest of the house and start the renovations. So far, all the pieces were coming together easier than she could have predicted.

By the time Tessa returned to the diner apartment late that

afternoon, Paul was lounging on the couch, typing on his laptop. A large map was spread out on the coffee table, and a pink bag of caramel creams sat on the west side of the map. She dropped her purse on a kitchen chair and glanced around the kitchen.

"Where's Huck Finn?" she asked.

Without looking up at her, Paul answered, "In Mr. Fletcher's pond with approximately thirty other koi. His family just expanded exponentially. I dropped the plastic tote back off at the diner, and Mom told me to bring you Belgian waffles. They're in the fridge."

Tessa smiled even though Paul still hadn't made eye contact with her. His laptop was balanced on top of a pillow that sat on his thighs. She could get used to seeing a good-looking man stretched out on her couch. That thought caused her pulse to thump against her throat. She walked into the living room. "Whatcha working on?"

He paused his typing. "An article about Mystic Water. I pitched the idea to *Southern Living.* They're interested in running an online article on must-sees and what to do in this quaint south Georgia town. When I shared the information about a century-old Native American spear, their interest skyrocketed." He resumed typing. "If they accept the online piece, they said they'd consider a longer feature in the next issue of the printed magazine, including photographs."

Tessa realized the unfolded map was of Mystic Water. He'd circled the location of Honeysuckle Hollow. She reached for a caramel cream and unwrapped the candy. "I learned more about the house today."

"Library research?" He scrolled through his document and then resumed typing.

"No," she answered, "I went to see Crazy Kate—or *Mrs.*

Muir, I guess, would be more appropriate. She's not actually as kooky as people say."

Paul stopped typing. He saved his article and closed the laptop. Then he sat up on the couch and slid the computer from his lap. "You went to see the lady who stole your spear?"

Tessa nodded and popped the candy into her mouth. "Mm-hmm."

"Did you get it back?"

"That's an interesting story."

"A long one?" He stood and stretched before grabbing his boots and pulling them on.

Tessa's disappointment flared. "Going somewhere?"

He looked up from tying his boots. "No, I just thought if it was a long one, you might want to go walking with me. You could tell me the story on our walk."

"Oh," she said, glancing at her work attire. "Yeah, sure, I'd love that. Let me get changed." She disappeared into the bedroom. Why was she so excited about a walk? Because the idea of spending more time with Paul thrilled her. She pulled on a T-shirt the only pair of shorts that had survived the flood. She smiled down at her gray "good luck" tennis shoes. When she entered the living room, Paul held the map of Mystic Water in his hands. "Did you want to walk through town?"

Paul turned the map around so she could see it. "Nope. I want to go here." He poked at a large green area with his finger. "Why would we walk through town when you have a state park?" He refolded the map and dropped it on the coffee table.

Tessa bit her bottom lip. "I'm not much of an outdoorsy girl."

Paul grinned. "Where's your sense of adventure?"

Tessa frowned. "I just bought a run-down house. I think that qualifies as adventurous."

He chuckled. "I guess I should have asked, 'Where's your sense?'" Then he nudged her lightly in the arm as though they were teammates. "Tess, I'm kidding. You look like you want to knock me out."

She couldn't be annoyed with him, not when he was grinning at her and calling her *Tess*. "Okay, Borelli," she said in mock irritation, "take me on an adventure."

Tessa tried not to sound like Darth Vader as she hiked up another hill, but she failed. Breath wheezed in and out of her burning lungs while she retold Crazy Kate's story about Honeysuckle Hollow, the Hamiltons, and the spear. Tessa felt sure that one more hill would have her bent double, sucking air like a bagpipe player. Thankfully, Paul stopped at the top of the next rise.

"That's quite a story. I need to rethink my article. Kate's story will be an excellent addition to the town's history and the history of the house. I can revise the article to focus on preserving history, which would include maintaining Southern historic homes, especially a home that has served as a refuge for people who needed help and hope." He looked out over the evergreens thriving in the valley at the bottom of the ridge. "That's the greenest valley I've seen in a long time. Feel like hiking down to the river?"

"Feel like calling the EMTs?"

Paul laughed and pulled a bottle of water out of his backpack. "Here. Hydrate. I can't have you passing out on me in the middle of nowhere. What would the town say?"

Tessa gulped the water and wiped her mouth with the back

of her hand. "If I had known you wanted to hike all over this place, I would have suggested we drive to the top of the park and leave the car there instead of at the lower entrance. When you said *walk*, I thought you meant the kiddie trail."

Paul poked out his chest. "Do I look like the kind of man who hikes the kiddie trail?"

Definitely not.

He pointed off to the west. "What's up that way?"

Tessa opened the trail map. "Lovers Pointe."

Paul smirked. "We definitely need to check that out."

Tessa looked at him. "We do?"

"Again, do I look like the kind of man who would pass up an opportunity to see Lover's Pointe?"

Tessa's skin flushed. "It used to be called Look-Off Pointe, but so many kids kept parking up there and—well, after a while, a new name stuck."

Paul's grin widened. "I bet it did." He pointed toward a hill that rose toward the east. "And over there?"

Tessa hummed in her throat as she scanned the map. "Oh," she said and looked up. "That's Red River Hill. No one spends much time over there."

"Why?"

Tessa hesitated, feeling silly for what she was about to admit. "It's haunted . . . or so they say. I mean, I can't verify that it is, but I haven't ever ventured over there. A Civil War battle was fought in that part of the forest, and a lot of Confederates died. So many that they say the river ran red, which is why they renamed the river that runs through town and why that place is called Red River Hill."

Paul shielded his eyes from the sun and stared at the hill. "This town is full of mysteries, giving me even more ideas for the article on Mystic Water. Red River Hill is cursed, huh?"

"Being haunted and being cursed aren't the same."

"Slip of the tongue. And speaking of tongue, let's go check out Lover's Pointe."

Tessa gaped at Paul, and the heat returned to her face. His laugh echoed through the valley, and the sound wrapped happiness around Tessa.

While Paul took a shower, Tessa towel-dried her hair in the kitchen. She scrolled through her email on her phone, and a new one popped up. The fully executed real estate contract from Mrs. Steele's lawyer had arrived. Tessa was now officially the owner of Honeysuckle Hollow, and the rest of the money was due to Mrs. Steele within thirty days. She stared at her cell phone, knowing she should call Anna and Lily—and especially her mama—about Honeysuckle Hollow, but she was afraid they'd tell her it was a rotten idea. *But what if they don't? What if they're excited for me?* Still, she hesitated. *I'll call them later.*

A breeze blew through the open living room window and disrupted papers on the coffee table. Shimmery pink light from the setting sun pooled on the floor. The mint rustled in the wind, and even from across the room, Tessa smelled the scent of its leaves and sighed. She looked at the wall map. The mint's long tendrils had not stopped their pursuit of the globe. They now reached as far as Japan, curling around the silver pushpin there, and they looped around the pins in Sweden, Romania, and Egypt.

Paul walked out of the bedroom, fresh-faced and clean-shaven. He grabbed his laptop from the coffee table. "Mind if I go ahead and finish this article? I'd like to send it off before dinner."

As soon as Paul completed the story, he could leave. That's what he'd said, after all. He was only there until his research was done. The idea of him leaving deflated her. She'd known Paul *three* days, and already she'd become attached. Lily, Anna, and Tessa had joked that Tessa could fall in love faster than lightning. But she wasn't *in love* with Paul. Could she be falling in love with him? That was a possibility.

Even after he's gone, I'll still have the house, and that's something to be happy about. "Are you eating dinner with your folks before you leave tonight?"

Paul frowned. "I'm not leaving tonight." Then he narrowed his eyes. "Are you kicking me out? Is this because I drank the orange juice out of the carton?"

"You've been drinking out of the carton?" Tessa shook her head, refocusing her thoughts. "You said you'd like to send off the article before dinner." Paul nodded. When he didn't elaborate, Tessa added, "And you said as soon as you were done with the article, you were leaving."

He leaned back against the couch cushions. "I did, but it's Friday. I might as well see the weekend out. You should have seen Mom's face this morning when I mentioned that I might stay until Sunday." He shrugged. "I figured it wouldn't hurt to spend a few more days in Mystic Water."

Tessa opened the refrigerator just so she could hide the surprised smile on her face. She scanned the contents and then peered around the door. "Are you eating dinner with your parents?" she asked again.

Paul shook his head but continued to type. "Mom has some ladies function at the church. It's Dad's turn to help with Meals on Wheels, and his team is meeting"—Paul glanced at his watch—"right now in the diner. I assumed you and I would be having dinner together." He finally looked at her.

Tessa closed the refrigerator door. "What if I have plans?"

"Do you?"

She averted his gaze. "Well, not *tonight*, but sometimes I have dinner plans."

Paul grinned. "I'm sure you do, but tonight you have plans with me. Give me an hour to finish up with the article and email it, and then I say we cook up Lady and the Tramp."

Tessa tucked her hair behind her ears. "You don't mean we're eating dog, do you?"

Paul choked on a laugh. "Tess, you must really think I *am* a brute. First, you believe I'd eat Huck Finn, and now you think I'd serve up cocker spaniel and mutt." He made a fist and mimicked a stabbing motion, hitting it against his chest. "You wound me."

Tessa snorted a laugh. "You've been all over the world. How am I to know that you don't eat dog?"

"First of all, it tastes like chicken—"

Tessa poked her fingers into her ears. "Don't say any more."

Paul mouthed. "I'm kidding." Then he made the motion for her to unplug her ears.

"Is it safe?"

He winked. "It's never safe with me."

Now, that I believe.

"Lady and the Tramp is an old Borelli family recipe. It's a fancy name for spaghetti and meatballs."

"The meal from the cartoon movie."

"Sound good?"

Tessa nodded. "Sounds great."

He returned to his laptop, and Tessa grabbed her cell and slipped it into her back pocket. She watched Paul type for a few seconds. "I need to run over to Honeysuckle Hollow and make sure the cleaners finished. Charlie was going to drop off supplies to board up the windows. While you work, I might try to put those up myself. I'd feel better knowing the house was more secure. I'll be back by dinner."

Paul stopped typing. "That's not an easy job to do alone. Give me an hour to finish this, and then I'll whip up dinner. We can board up the house together."

Tessa smiled. "I'd appreciate that. Can I do anything to help you prepare for dinner? I can make a grocery-store run."

Paul stretched for his notepad and a pencil. Then he scribbled a list of ingredients onto the paper. He tore the page off the pad and handed it to Tessa. "Can you grab those last few herbs from Mom's garden? I'll probably be finished by the time you get back. Thanks, Tess."

Her chest expanded, and she smiled at him, even though his eyes were already locked back onto his computer screen. "See you soon." She was amazed at how those three words buoyed her spirits and caused her heartbeat to quicken. *I could get used to this.*

Tessa and Paul had talked nonstop all through dinner and not just about his travels, which fascinated her. Paul was curious about Tessa's life, which she argued was much less interesting than his, but he didn't agree. He said Tessa's life in Mystic Water was charming, and she made him tempted to slow down and rethink having a life that offered comfort in more ways than just having a home. In the moment, she hadn't been brave enough to ask him if he was considering staying in Mystic Water on a more permanent basis, but the dream fluttered around in her heart.

Now Tessa rubbed her belly and slumped against the passenger seat as Paul parked alongside the curb in front of Honeysuckle Hollow. "Lady and the Tramp has done me in. I can't believe I ate two helpings."

Paul unbuckled his seat belt. "I counted three. The fifth piece of bread was especially risky, but you finished it like a champ."

Tessa moaned. "I may not be able to move. Think I can hammer in nails from here?"

"Not unless you have extendable arms."

Tessa unhooked her seat belt and opened her door. She held her arms straight out in front of her. "Arms extend!"

Paul's laughter billowed over the hood and slipped into her heart. Tessa closed her eyes and smiled. He walked around to her side of the car. "I sense a malfunction." Then he grabbed her hands and pulled her out. "Next time, should I limit how many times you fill your plate?"

Tessa narrowed her eyes. "Don't you dare."

Because the front porch had been destroyed by the bulldozer, Charlie had created a ramp from the yard to the front door using a large sheet of plywood. The difference the cleaners made was immediately noticeable. Tessa's shoes no longer left dust tracks on the floor. Gone were the lacy cobwebs from the corners and the stairwell. The dank smell of mildew had faded, leaving behind a faint scent of lemon cleaner. Tessa also smelled the blooming honeysuckle in the backyard.

Paul stepped up beside her and nodded. "Definitely an improvement. One step closer to seeing how great this house is going to shine when we're all done here."

Tessa startled beside him; her eyes widened. *We're? He just lumped us together. In a sentence.*

Paul walked toward the stack of plywood left behind by

Charlie. He opened a box of screws and tested the weight of the power drill in his hand. "I say we get started, or we're going to lose the light."

We're, Tessa thought again. *Twice. Me and him. Together.*

"Hey, Tess, am I losing you to a food coma?"

Tessa blinked. "Huh?"

"You look dazed."

She tucked her hair behind her ears and felt a flutter in her stomach. "No, I'm good." *I'm just thinking about you and me being a we.* "Let's get started."

Paul and Tessa walked through the house, taking inventory of which windows needed to be boarded up, but it was clear when they finished that Charlie had already done most of the work. She had measured the windows and cut the plywood panels to fit.

"Charlie is your contractor, right?" Paul asked as he squeezed the trigger on the drill and it whirred.

Tessa nodded. "She apprenticed under a local contractor who does great work. He says she's good people, and I trust his judgment."

"Charlie's a girl?" Paul said.

Tessa huffed. "You say that like girls can't be contractors."

Paul whirred the drill. "I'm surprised, that's all."

"I'm only giving you a hard time because when I first met her, I thought she was the maid service."

Paul chuckled. "She knows what's she's doing. She's given us corrosion-resistant screws that are longer than two inches, which means they'll hold fast into the framing, and they'll be easier to remove than nails. She also picked galvanized panhead screws because of their flat-bottomed heads that won't sink into the plywood and weaken it."

"I have no idea what any of that means."

Paul held out the drill. "Do you know how to use this?"

"Sure." It couldn't be that difficult, could it? She squeezed the trigger and winced.

"I'm going to regret this, aren't I?"

Tessa huffed. "Borelli, just tell me what to do."

Paul lifted a sheet of plywood and carried it to the first window. "Drill pilot holes through the plywood at least one inch from the edge of the panel. We'll probably want holes every sixteen inches. Once we get the pilot holes done, we'll drive in the screws. And don't stab me. I doubt you're offering worker's comp."

They boarded up the broken windows, and by the time they were done, the sun had nearly set for the day, turning the interior of the house moody blue. Tessa stood in front of the broken French doors. She stared into the darkening backyard. "What should we do about this opening?"

Paul walked up the hallway and joined her. "There's a tarp in the living room. We could hang that up and tape it around the edges. It'll be a temporary fix. Not a great one, but it'll work until we get these doors replaced." Paul left to gather the supplies.

Lights blinked in the backyard and darted through the weeds and the branches of the oak. Tessa stepped closer to the doors. *Lightning bugs.* Hundreds of them swarmed and gathered within the span of a breath. Wind weaved through the yard, bringing laughter that stirred the grass.

Paul put the supplies on the kitchen island. "Is that laughing? Are there kids in the yard?"

Tessa stepped through the broken doors and onto the backyard brick patio. The lightning bugs twirled and danced, leaving trails of light behind them like comet tails. Their lights twined together, and laughter seemed to rise from the honeysuckle, from the river, from the unruly sage. While Tessa watched, the fireflies joined together in two large, whirling groups until they looked like the twinkling bodies of two children playing in the backyard. Tessa stared, slack-jawed, in awe. The next strong breeze dispersed the lights, and the laughter faded. She pointed. "Did you . . ."

"Did I what?"

Tessa shivered. *Did you see the glowing kids?* "Never mind."

Paul slipped his arm around her shoulders. He smiled down at her and gave her a squeeze before dropping his arm. "We're almost done. Help me put up this tarp before we're swallowed by the darkness."

After they'd hung the tarp, Tessa glanced one last time out one of the kitchen windows. The lightning bugs blinked and flitted around, but there were no children, no echoing laughter. Had she imagined it?

The evening stretched into the house and shadowed everything. Paul's silhouette lingered in the hallway, his expression hidden. "Ready to for us go home?"

She might have imagined the glowing kids laughing in Honeysuckle Hollow's garden, but she hadn't imagined Paul using the words *us* and *home* in the same sentence, as though they were connected. But for how long?

CHAPTER 17

Strawberry Pop-Tarts

Tessa dreamed of laughing children and a delicate wedding dress worn when roses were in bloom and the spring rain left dewdrops on the bright-green leaves and drenched the grass. When she opened her eyes the next morning, butter-yellow sunbeams reached across the foot of the bed. She kicked off the covers and stretched. Then she padded out into the living room.

Paul slept quietly on the couch. One arm stretched over his head and rested on his forehead. Tessa leaned her head against the doorframe and sighed. After she showered and dressed, she found Paul sitting up on the couch with his laptop open. His unruly dark hair stuck up on the side he'd been sleeping on, and the sleepy expression on his face made her stomach twitter. A crooked smile lifted his cheek.

"Should I even ask what you're smiling about?"

"Who just published an online article with *Southern Living*, the magazine with approximately fifteen million devoted readers? And whose feature will also be in print form next month? And *who*, might I ask, will most likely be writing for them on a consistent basis?"

Tessa's eyes widened. "They published your article?"

"The first one, yes, that focuses on what travelers will find in Mystic Water and what they should do and see. For example, Scrambled is a local gem of a diner and can't be missed. The longer printed article will feature more about Mystic Water's history, its Cherokee heritage, its historic homes, and one adventurous Southern lady who bought Honeysuckle Hollow just so she could save it."

"Congratulations! I'll have to tell Mr. Wallach at the library and Tracey at the bookshop. They'll want to order copies. This town loves reading about themselves." She paused. "Did you say you wrote about *me*?"

"I *will* be including you in the print edition. How could I leave you out? You're at the heart of all this, in more ways than one."

Tessa looked at her bare feet before glancing at the mint plant, which had wrapped new tendrils around pins in Australia, New Zealand, and an island north of Antarctica. "Can you write for them and work for your other outlets—like the one who hired you to write about the Cook Islands?"

Paul rubbed the back of his neck. "Freelance work is flexible. Short answer, yes, I can work for multiple outlets. Obviously, the travel articles require that I visit locations, and usually that work demands more travel abroad. Writing for *Southern Living* would still require some travel, but a much smaller area. Being a regular writer would mean steady work and income."

Her expression softened. "You might consider not having a willy-nilly life?" She waved her hands around in the air. "No more bouncing all over the place, never knowing where you're going to land? You're considering having something steady?"

Paul locked eyes with her and then shrugged. "I like willy-nilly, as you say, but I like landing here too."

Hope pressed its needy hands against Tessa's heart, expanding her ribcage with an inhale. "You like it here?"

"For multiple reasons." Paul moved his laptop to the coffee table. "Mom said that you go to the diner on the weekends for a lumberjack-size breakfast. I'd hate to disrupt your routine. Can I join you?"

Tessa nodded. Paul's cell phone rang, and the mint twitched in its pot. Paul glanced down at the blinking face of his phone, and his eyebrows drew together. He stared at the screen while the phone vibrated in his hand, flashing colored lights against his cheeks.

"Something wrong?" Tessa asked.

His expression was blank, and his unfocused gaze stared at a spot over her shoulder. "It's Monica. My ex-fiancée." He accepted the call. "Hello?"

Air whooshed from Tessa's lungs. *He had been engaged?*

Paul stood. "No, I'm in Mystic Water with Mom and Dad." He glanced at Tessa and jerked his head toward the bedroom. Then he walked into the room and closed the door, officially shutting out Tessa.

Tessa's throat tightened, and she stared at the closed door. She was surprised at how strongly this was affecting her. It's not as though she didn't have a past littered with exes too. Of course Paul had a life before she'd met him. He was exactly the kind of person women wanted to marry: charming, handsome, intelligent, independent, and humorous. Monica was his ex-fiancée, but why would his ex be calling him? Maybe she wasn't over him. Maybe she wanted him back. Maybe she was gorgeous and talented and witty and perfect for Paul. The walls of the apartment pressed in. Tessa had to get out of there. She grabbed her purse and left the apartment, leaving Paul and Monica alone to reminisce about willy-nilly lives and wedding planning that might need to be kickstarted again.

Tessa skipped Scrambled and opted to buy a pack of strawberry Pop-Tarts and a Pepsi from the pharmacy, which had the most random assortment of snacks tucked among medications and ointments. The carbonated bubbles burned her throat on the first swallow. If only she could swallow down the disappointment too. Gone was the feeling of being buoyed by Paul's attention and interest. Now she slumped on a bench outside of the hardware store eating her breakfast.

A few minutes later, a whirl of wind whipped around the street corner and blew Tessa's hair into her eyes. She pushed out her bottom lip and puffed the hairs from her face just in time to see a curly-haired redhead plop down beside her on the bench.

"Tessa!" Nell Foster said with a smile as wide as the crack in Tessa's heart.

"Hey, Nell. How's the rental?"

Nell's green eyes sparkled with a joy that had been missing in their last meeting. "Great. Just great. I can't thank you enough. Liam is happy. The kids are happy. *I'm* happy. You're the bee's knees, Tessa. I've been telling everybody what you did for us. For *all* of us."

"It's the least I could do. I'm glad it's working out."

Nell's smile was infectious, and Tessa's lips tried to mimic her joyful expression.

"Now, you didn't mention this to me, but you know how people talk, and I heard that your condo on Jordan Pond flooded. And there you were helping me, and you didn't have a place either. I felt awful when I heard that." Nell leaned closer to Tessa and lowered her voice. "But then someone said that the Borellis were letting you stay in the apartment above the diner. I also heard they're oldest son came for a visit, and *he's* staying there."

Tessa stared at the branches of a dogwood bending in the wind across the street. Thinking of Paul made her feel as though she burned from the inside with a slow, deliberate smolder. The Pop-Tarts squirmed in her stomach. Nell's questioning expression and wide green eyes confused Tessa. "Was there more to that story?"

Nell's mischievous grin scrunched the freckles scattered across her nose. "Is he staying there?"

"Yes."

"With *you*?" Nell giggled like a girl. "I know it's none of my business, but, Tessa, he's a real looker, isn't he? A regular Italian movie star. And those gorgeous blue eyes. I wouldn't blame you a bit if you were *getting to know him*."

The back of Tessa's neck burned with embarrassment. "It's a one-bedroom apartment."

Nell's eyes twinkled, and she whispered, "Even better."

Tessa shook her head. "No, no that's not what I mean. I'm in the bedroom. He's on the couch. We're not doing anything, and I'm not . . . well, I'm not staying there now." Even though she was lying, the words felt like the truth. "I bought Honeysuckle Hollow yesterday."

Nell gasped. "Dr. Hamilton's old place? Gosh, last I heard it was a real wreck."

Tessa sighed. "That pretty much sums it up, but I'm going to rehab it. I'm going to stay there."

Nell gaped. "You mean *now*? Before it's rehabbed?"

Tessa shrugged. The idea crept into her heart and beat steady and strong. "Yes."

"Aren't you a brave one!" Nell said. "Braver than me. I nearly died staying with my mother-in-law. I can't imagine having the kids in a run-down house."

"Well, that's the thing, isn't it? I don't have anybody. It's just me. Just me and Honeysuckle Hollow." Tessa wasn't sure if this new idea was brave or stupid.

Liam Foster walked out of the hardware store and nodded hello at Tessa before looking at his wife. "Ready, honey?"

Nell patted Tessa's hand. "You be careful over there. Don't . . . I dunno, fall through the floor or anything."

"It's not *that* bad," Tessa said, but Nell looked unconvinced. She waved good-bye and climbed into an SUV with her husband. Did Tessa even believe her *own* words?

She dialed Charlie's number. When Charlie answered, Tessa explained how she'd boarded up the windows the night before, and she asked when Charlie's workers could get started on the rehab. Once the money from the sale of her condo was in her bank, and after she'd paid off Mrs. Steele, she planned to pay the workers for as much work as possible.

"I hoped I could have a group out there on Monday, but it

might be the following week or even longer," Charlie said. "I'm sorry. I didn't realize how far behind my guys are because of the flood."

Tessa chewed her bottom lip. "Nothing sooner?" Could she live in a house for weeks without electricity? She hadn't thought to check the plumbing. Did it still work?

"I don't wanna make you any promises about an exact date. But . . ."

"But what?" Tessa asked when Charlie didn't continue.

"A lot of guys are out of work *because* of the flood. They're scrambling around for money because their job sites are out of commission, especially the guys in the basin areas."

Tessa smelled the lingering sweet scent of honeysuckle blooms being carried on the breeze. She thought of how Honeysuckle Hollow had come to the rescue of so many in need. "Do you think any of them would be willing to work on a run-down Victorian?"

"I think they'd jump at the opportunity for work. They have families to feed."

Tessa thought of the weeds that were fighting for dominance of Honeysuckle Hollow's garden. "Do you know a good landscaper? Someone who's not afraid to tackle a yard that's grown out of control?"

"I'll call around. If anyone—landscaper or worker—is free today, I can talk them through the basics. If I find interested people, could you meet us at the house?"

"The sooner the better."

Tessa stood on the cracked sidewalk in front of Honeysuckle Hollow while husband-and-wife landscaping team Porter and Sylvia Potts worked on the weedy front yard. They'd already removed the knee-high weeds and brambles, which were now piled in the back of their landscaping truck. The herringbone-patterned brick path leading up to the front door had been revealed. It needed leveling, and a few bricks poked vertically out of the ground as though they'd been slammed upward from beneath the earth.

Dr. Hamilton's prize damask rose bushes, now pruned and no longer choked by weeds, would once again flourish and bloom. The heat-tolerant Bermuda grass had been overtaken by crabgrass, ragweed, and what looked like dry hay, but the Potts had cleared the whole yard. The bright-green spiky blades covering the lawn proved Bermuda was difficult to kill, and the yard looked less and less like a wasteland. In a couple of hours, the curb appeal of Honeysuckle Hollow would closer resemble the manicured yards on Dogwood Lane.

Charlie was easy to spot among the workers milling around inside. She wore a simple white tank top and a pair of worn jeans with her thick-soled work boots. Her shiny black hair, pulled back into a smooth ponytail, highlighted her slender neck. She could have easily been mistaken for a performer about to execute a knockout dance routine to "She Works Hard for the Money." What impressed Tessa the most was that even though Charlie was unquestionably attractive, the others respected her and listened to her guidance and directions, rather than acting like a beautiful woman couldn't be a competent leader and contractor.

Charlie and the workers walked through the different rooms while she explained what needed to be addressed first. Tessa followed behind them, nodding and tossing in her opinions where relevant. Her cell phone rang, and she walked out of the kitchen to answer it so Charlie could continue the tour without disturbance. But when Tessa saw that Paul was calling, she silenced the call. A minute later, the voice mail alert dinged. An irritating combination of hope and angst tangled in her stomach. Distant thunder rumbled. A gust of wind buffeted the tarp covering the French doors, rippling the fabric like a sail.

Tessa wanted to play the voice mail, and her ears grew hot. Another burst of wind slammed against the tarp and ripped the tape away from the doorframe, snapping the thick fabric against Tessa's legs. She flinched and backed away, leaning over to rub her calves. A slam reverberated upstairs, and something banged against a wall over and over again like a screen door butting against a house during strong winds. Tessa grabbed the tarp and tried to adhere the tape to the doorframe again. Charlie and the crew reentered the kitchen.

"We'll get it," Charlie said, motioning for one of the men to help her. "What's that banging?"

Tessa glanced at the ceiling. "I'll check it out."

The stairs creaked as Tessa ascended them. The repeated thumping grew louder, and Tessa slowed. A door in the hallway had swung open, and the doorknob bounced against the wall. Tessa stood in the open doorway that revealed a set of stairs leading to the attic. A steady rush of air billowed down the staircase, and Tessa stood rooted at the bottom. Charlie had inspected the attic days ago, but Tessa hadn't gone with her.

"I don't like creepy attics," she said to no one. "It goes beyond my better judgment to go up these stairs." But curiosity pushed one foot in front of the other, and she grabbed the handrail.

"Please don't be creepy. Please don't be creepy."

Tessa exhaled in relief once she reached the top. Other than the musty scent of dust and aging keepsakes and a few dangling cobwebs, the attic was ordinary and emptier than she'd expected. Air circled around the space and whipped dust around Tessa's feet.

One round window against the far wall allowed in a circle of light that shone a muted sunbeam onto an antique steamer trunk. The window wasn't damaged, so where was the breeze coming from? Thunder rumbled again, and gray clouds lumbered across the faded denim-blue sky.

She unlatched the trunk. Stacked inside were hardback novels and photo albums. She grabbed one of the albums and sat on the floor. Written in calligraphy on the inside cover were the words *Wedding Day, 1957.* After looking at the first few photographs, Tessa realized the wedding had taken place in Honeysuckle Hollow's backyard garden.

Tessa flipped through the pages and smiled at the happiness that radiated from the fading pictures and warmed her fingertips, traveling up her arms to her heart. A photograph adhered to the bottom of the next page captured two young men, who had to be brothers, and one young girl, standing with her hands clasped together in front of her, smiling shyly at the camera and staring at Tessa with her dark almond-shaped eyes. Tessa lifted the book closer to her face. *Crazy Kate.*

Rain slapped against the round window. The sounds of laughter erupted from the backyard. Tessa stood and peered out the window. Rain fell from the sky, and she squinted down at the yard. Were people outside? Tessa didn't see anyone, but what she did see trapped her breath halfway up her throat.

Watery outlines of people gathered in the cloudy light of the backyard, and their muffled faraway voices rose up to meet her. Three misty people stood near the oak tree. Two of them held hands and looked at each other while the third person held an open book in his hands. A group of guests sat facing the couple. *A wedding?* Thunder disturbed the silence. The ghostly group looked up, and then they scattered, holding their hands over their heads and running for the house. Most of the guests disappeared, leaving only a few standing in the yard, staring up at the rain. Tessa heard their joyous laughter.

The storm clouds split apart, and thick beams of sunlight filled the yard. The watery gathering was gone. Tessa closed her eyes. When she opened them, the rain had stopped, and the backyard was empty. She returned the photo album to the trunk, allowing her hand to linger on the cover for a few moments. "Am I totally losing it? Or . . ." She glanced around the attic. "Honeysuckle Hollow, are you trying to tell me something?"

CHAPTER 18

Blackberry Cobbler

Tessa flinched when her cell phone rang in her pocket. *Paul.* She squeezed the phone in her hand, desperately wanting to answer it, but she was afraid of what he might say. Her mind instantly made up elaborate possibilities, such as Paul saying, *That was Monica, my perfect not-for-long-ex-fiancée. She loves willy-nilly living, and I'm leaving immediately so that we can get on with our perfect lives. Good luck in the run-down house.*

Tessa wanted to tell Paul what she'd just seen out the attic window, imagined or not, and about the photo album showing Crazy Kate attending a backyard wedding. But maybe what she needed more was distance—distance between Paul and her growing attachment to him, especially since he planned to leave at the end of the weekend. She silenced the phone.

Tessa pulled out her notebook and tapped it against her palm. "I need a plan. I need a place to stay. I can stay here, but I'll need . . . a bed." She flipped through the pages of questions. Most of them had three numbers filled in with advice offered to her by friends and family, until she reached the newest pages. She'd been impulsive and what her mama would call *reckless.* She'd bought a house, and not just *any* house. A massive fixer-upper that might financially bankrupt her.

Tessa closed the notebook and slipped it back into her pocket. Looking around the dimly lit attic, she said, "Maybe staying here won't be so bad. It'll be like camping. Even though I hate camping and bugs and killer bats and no toilets . . . but this is camping *indoors.*" *Is it?* "I'd better check the plumbing."

Tessa found Charlie downstairs finishing up with the workers. She pulled Charlie aside. "How about the pipes?"

Charlie stared at her with her deep-brown eyes. "Could you be more specific?"

"The plumbing. Can I use the water? Or the toilets? Or just *a* toilet would be nice because I just *can't* stay here without a working toilet, and I *have* to stay here. I mean, what would I do without a toilet? I could *never* use the backyard as a bathroom—"

Charlie waved her hands around. "Whoa, whoa. Hold on a minute, will ya? I feel as though you're about to get an eye twitch."

Tessa lifted her fingers to her left eye and pressed. "I almost unraveled. Sorry."

"Almost?" Charlie asked. "The pipes are good. They were updated a few years ago, so there are no problems with the plumbing that we know about. The water was never shut off, for whatever reason. I have a contact down at the water works, and she told me that it's still on. Here, I'll show you." Charlie led Tessa into the downstairs bathroom where Tessa had found the cat. Charlie flushed the toilet, and Tessa watched the vortex of water swirl in the dirty bowl and disappear.

"That's a relief."

Charlie nodded. "No backyard bathrooms for you. Are you planning on moving in here? I mean, before it's finished?"

Tessa felt her confidence wobble, and she wished for more of Cecilia's Courage Quiche. "Tonight."

Charlie's lips pulled into a grimace. "I'm not sure that's a great idea."

"Oh, it's not, but it's the only plan I've come up with so far."

Charlie jabbed her thumb over her shoulder. "There aren't doors in the kitchen. There's a tarp keeping the outside from creeping in."

Tessa walked out of the bathroom, up the short hallway, and into the kitchen. She stared at the thick canvas material covering the busted-up French doors. "It'll be like camping."

"Don't you have somewhere else you could stay?"

Tessa shook her head. "Nope. This is it. This is my home." The word *home* tingled her lips. "My only other option is to stay in a one-bedroom apartment with a handsome Italian traveler who cooks like a chef."

Charlie's eyes widened, and she smirked. "And you're choosing *this* over him? Should I even ask why?"

Tessa's heart expanded and forced a sigh from her lips. "Best not to." She glanced around the kitchen, her gaze lingering on the graffiti. "When can they start?"

"A few are heading out to gather supplies, and they'll be back in a couple of hours. Now that I know you're planning on staying here, we might want to check this framing and get a new pair of doors installed." Charlie lifted the tarp and studied the walls around the French doors.

An older man shaped like a wine barrel with a frizzy halo of graying hair, stepped into the kitchen. "You the one fixing this place up?"

Tessa nodded. "That's my hope."

He scratched the coarse stubble on his cheek. "When my mama's house burned twenty years ago, Dr. Hamilton let my parents and me stay here for a few months. I remember walking around this place, thinking it was a castle. He was a good man, and I'd hate to see this place fall apart." He stepped closer to the tarp. "Looks like you need a pair of doors."

"French doors," Charlie confirmed.

"I got a pair in my garage," he said. "The lady at the last build decided against them, and I was gonna return them next week, but if you're needing a pair . . ."

"Seriously?" Tessa said. A guy who had been spontaneously called to help rebuild Honeysuckle Hollow had just what the house needed. Some of the tension in Tessa's shoulders released.

Charlie asked, "You think they'll work?"

He nodded. "I measured the opening earlier. They're a perfect fit. I can probably get them installed today if the walls around it are sound."

Charlie rapped her knuckles against the wood framing the opening. "They're solid and undamaged by the break in."

The man smiled. "Be back in an hour."

"Thanks, Leon," Charlie said, shoving her hands into her pockets.

Tessa's heart pounded as Leon walked away. Everything in the house seemed to be aligning so that she *could* start making it her home.

Charlie raised her eyebrows at Tessa. "You know there's no

electricity, right?"

Tessa shrugged. "I'll get it sorted on Monday. I can rough it until then."

Charlie's lips quirked. "You don't strike me as the roughing-it type."

"Oh, I'm not, but I'm going to think of this as an adventure. That's going to be what keeps me from completely falling into a blubbering mess and eating the grocery store's summer supply of ice cream and cookie dough."

Charlie chuckled. "Where are you gonna sleep? The bedrooms aren't in great shape, and I don't imagine the dining room table is ideal. Maybe a sleeping bag?"

Tessa pulled her notebook out of her back pocket and flipped through the pages. "I hadn't gotten that far in my plan. I know I need a bed, but I won't find one today. Think I can get a sleeping bag at the hardware store?"

Charlie's gaze turned serious. "I was kidding."

"I'm not," Tessa said.

Charlie yelled to one of the workers. "Thad, does your dad sell sleeping bags at his store?"

A lanky young man with legs like a praying mantis loped into the room. His jeans were ripped at the knees, and his white T-shirt had colorful splotches of paint from dozens of projects. His ball cap sported an Auburn logo. "Sure. Tents too. All the basic gear you'd need. You going hiking?"

Charlie nodded her head toward Tessa, and Thad's eyes widened. He smirked and adjusted his ball cap.

Tessa huffed. "You think I don't camp, right?"

Thad shrugged, still grinning. "I'm not one to judge, ma'am, but I should warn you that the woods are full of wild animals, and when someone isn't used to camping, it can be an unsettling experience."

Charlie laughed. "She's camping *in here.*"

Thad made a show of wiping the back of his hand across his brow. "That's good to hear. I certainly didn't want to learn about you getting lost in the woods or eaten by a cougar. Then where would we work?" He lifted his cap and scratched his messy blond hair before situating the hat back on his head and walking off.

Tessa didn't bother to tell him that she was more of a danger to herself than any cougar could have been.

When Tessa cranked the engine on the Great Pumpkin, her cell phone vibrated in her back pocket. *Paul.* Tessa blew out a puff of air and answered. "Are you stalking me?"

"That depends," Paul said. "Are you ignoring me?"

Not exactly. "You're not easy to ignore. I'm at the house. Some of the workers started today."

"Really?" Paul asked. "I didn't think they could start until next week."

"Charlie found another crew. Some of them are here now. They're installing a new pair of French doors in the kitchen. That way I can stay here tonight. I'm on my way to the hardware store to pick up a few things." *For my camping adventure.* The phone call fell so silent that Tessa thought she'd lost service. She pulled the phone away from her face and stared at it. "You still there?"

"You're staying in the house tonight? Why?"

Tessa's throat tightened, but she tried to force happiness into her tone. "I'm just so excited to move in. It's rustic for now, but the plumbing works. You'll finally have the apartment all to yourself. I appreciate how accommodating you've been, but now I have a place to go. No more couch surfing for you. You can have the bedroom, at least for your last night in town."

Paul paused again. "I don't mind having you here."

Tessa held her breath. His words trembled against her heart. She wanted to ask, "What about Monica?" Instead, she said, "I appreciate it, but I'll come over this afternoon and pack up my stuff."

"I won't be at the apartment this afternoon. I'm going out with my parents."

Why did he sound disappointed? "Have fun! I should go, work to do . . . and stuff."

Paul made a noise of objection in his throat, but Tessa ended the call. She dropped her phone in her purse and drove to the library before going to the hardware store. She wanted to see if they had any Mystic Water history books with photographs of historical homes. Outside the library Tessa sat in her car and made a quick list of the items she thought she'd need to survive in the house. Near the bottom of the list she wrote, *Sanity.*

Tessa unlocked the apartment. "Hello?" No one responded. She shuffled into the living room and hefted the flattened boxes and heavy-duty tape onto the couch. The living room smelled like cloves and mint, and a pink bag of caramel creams sat opened on the coffee table along with Paul's laptop.

Tessa taped the boxes together and packed quickly. The idea of still being in the apartment when Paul came home made her heart race. His easy smile would lure her back in again, tempting her to give in to his charm, but in less than a day, he would be gone. She had to stay resolute in her decision to put space between them.

Within an hour, the Great Pumpkin was packed with boxes. She returned one last time to the apartment and stood in front of the mint plant. The mint had used the pushpins the way honeysuckle used lattice; it climbed and stretched and curled around itself into impossible knots. “How am I going to get you home? I can’t leave you here. Paul will be gone, and then you’ll be all by yourself.”

A spring-scented wind rushed up the stairs and banged the front door against its stopper. The air swooped around the living room, and the mint leaves flapped against the map like green butterflies. Then in a breath, all the tendrils dropped from the pushpins and dangled down the edges of the pot, carpeting the floor. Tessa gaped at the plant.

“Well, if that’s not the weirdest, coolest thing I’ve seen in a while. I guess you’re ready to go too.”

Tessa gathered up the mint and piled the longer vines on top of the pot. Then she hoisted the heavy pot up to her hip and carried it down the stairs, placing it into the passenger seat. By the time she was done, the Great Pumpkin smelled like Christmas.

Tessa rolled down the windows and cranked the engine. Her cell phone rang, and she smiled at the caller’s name and picture blinking at her. “Lily!”

“Hey, stranger! I am so sorry I haven’t called sooner. I know you’ve probably been knee-deep in work and water and mud, and I had totally forgotten about my Wildehaven Beach trip when I was with you last weekend. Are you okay? How’s the condo? Did you decide to sell it? Who’s this Paul guy you’re talking about?

Did you end up staying together? Tell me everything."

Tessa leaned back against the seat and laughed. "I will when you stop talking. I can't believe you said all of that without breathing."

"It's a skill. So, how are you? Oh, and Anna's here. Let me put you on speaker."

Tessa heard Anna's voice in the background. "Hey, Anna! I have something to tell both of you."

"Oh, the suspense," Lily said. "Should we be sitting down? Are you having Paul's baby?"

Tessa choked on a laugh. "Lily—"

"I'm kidding."

Anna laughed. "Go on, Tessa. Spill the beans. I'll tape Lily's mouth shut."

Tessa cast a sideways glance at the mint plant. "I decided to sell my condo, although I didn't have much choice since all the owners wanted to. And . . . well, I . . . I bought a house."

Lily squealed. "Tessa! You've been holding out! When did this happen? I've only been gone for a long weekend. What did you buy?"

"Let her talk," Anna scolded.

Tessa smiled. "I bought a house on your street, Lily. On Dogwood Lane."

"You did?" Lily asked. "I didn't know there was a house for sale."

"Honeysuckle Hollow was," Tessa said.

Tessa heard waves crashing in the background. A lone seagull called. Her friends remained silent. "Hello?" Tessa tried to imagine the faces of her two best friends. Were their eyes bulging? Were their mouths hanging agape like cartoon characters?

"I could be wrong," Lily said with hesitation in her voice.

"You're talking about the place Dr. Hamilton used to own, right?"

"Yes."

"Didn't he pass away?" Anna asked.

"Two years ago," Tessa said.

"And the house hasn't been touched in just as long," Lily said. "Tessa, is this a joke?"

Tessa's throat tightened. She squeezed the steering wheel. "It has great bones."

"Tell me you're not serious," Lily said. "It's a disaster. I mean, it was great years ago, but now it could pass for a haunted house."

"Lily," Anna argued, "Tessa knows houses. She wouldn't buy something if she thought it was a terrible idea. Right, Tessa?"

"It needs work," Tessa admitted.

Lily scoffed. "It needs more than work. How can you afford it? How are you going to pay for all the renovations? It's going to cost a fortune."

"I have my savings," Tessa explained. "And I'm going to use the money from the sale of the condo to pay for some of the rehab."

"You know I love you, Tess," Lily said, "but I think this is one of the worst ideas you've ever had. Anna hasn't seen the place, so she can't vouch for its dilapidation, but you should know better. What in the world were you thinking? Why would you use your savings on a money pit? Why not buy a new build like your condo was? Something that doesn't look like nature is reclaiming it? Where's your notebook? Did you get three people to tell you this was a great idea? I can't believe your mama agreed to this."

Tessa clenched her jaw and felt a spark of fury flare inside her. "You don't know what you're talking about. You don't know anything about Honeysuckle Hollow. It's a house worth preserving, and I don't need a stupid notebook to tell me what I should and shouldn't do—"

"Tessa," Anna interrupted in a tone meant to calm her, "you have been impulsive before—"

"This is different," Tessa argued. "This house needs me, and I need it. We *need* each other." Tessa's voice pitched high and desperate. She was one tick away from sounding irrational, but she kept on. "I'm going to live there—starting tonight."

The phone fell silent again. Tessa's heart thumped in her ears.

Anna spoke quietly. "Have you talked to your parents?"

Tessa pressed her forehead against the steering wheel. "No."

"Don't you think you should at least call them?"

"No. Yes. I dunno." Tessa lifted her head. "Why can't you both just support my decision?"

Lily huffed. "Because it sounds half-cocked, that's why."

Tears prickled in Tessa's eyes.

"Lily," Anna scolded. She cleared her throat. "What she means is that we're not trying to sound unsupportive. But we're concerned, and we want what's best for you. Buying an expensive fixer-upper sounds a little out of your comfort zone, and we don't want you to get in over your head."

"Too late," Tessa said. She squared her shoulders. "But I'm not changing my mind. I need to go. I have to get back to the house. Thanks for . . ." *For making me feel worse? For making me feel as though I've made another stupid harebrained decision?*

"For calling. I'll talk with y'all later."

Anna said, "Tess—"

But Tessa ended the call. Then she covered her face and cried. If no one else on the planet agreed with her decision, Tessa had held on to the hope that her best friends would be on her side. If they thought buying the house was a reckless, ridiculous idea, what would they say about her possibly falling for a man who was leaving town before they ever had a first date? Why did her friends' lack of support make her doubt her own gut feelings about the house? Were they right? Was she?

Tessa gave herself exactly five minutes to feel sorry for herself, and then she wiped her eyes and blew her nose. She looked over at the mint plant. "Should I call my parents?" The mint plant wiggled in the breeze. "You're right. Best to get this over with." Tessa grabbed her phone.

"Tessa, how are you, honey?" her mama asked. "Hang on. Clayton, it's Tessa, will you please turn that down. I can't even hear myself think. Nobody on this street gives two licks about what we're watching, but at that volume, they can surely hear it. Okay, now, let's try this again."

"Hey, Mama."

"Don't just '*hey, Mama*' me. You haven't called me back for days. Are you avoiding me? You're not sitting around moping, are you?"

"Only for the past five minutes," Tessa said, sniffling.

"Is that sarcasm?" Carolyn asked. "Tell me about the condo. What's happening? I feel out of the loop."

"You're on vacation. You're supposed to be out of the loop. How're you and Daddy?" she asked, stalling and trying to inhale courage into her lungs.

"Your dad is as happy as a clam at high tide. Did you know they have all-you-can-eat apple pie out here? I think he's going to eat himself sick every night, but every day he starts all over again. The weather is gorgeous. No humidity, of course, which means we can take a walk without needing a shower afterward. The house we're in is a real class act. A turn-of-the-century Victorian with all original hardwood, moldings, two-inch thick pocket doors, you name it. You should see the staircase, especially when the sunrise hits it."

Tessa sighed, picturing Honeysuckle Hollow in her mind. "Wow, Mama, that sounds nice. I'm glad y'all are having a good time. Everything here is . . . fine."

"*Fine* is a loaded word."

Tessa's eye twitched. She pressed her fingertips against it. "I'll sign the final paperwork to sell the condo next week. And if you can believe it, a new listing popped up. I think it's a good fit for me, so I put in an offer."

Carolyn inhaled sharply. "You did? Well, honey, that was fast. I'm proud of you for making a plan and following through with it. Clayton, Tessa found a house." Tessa heard her daddy's grumbly voice in the background.

"It's a historic home, and it needs a bit of work, but it's nothing I can't handle."

Her mama made a noise in her throat. "How much work? Where's the house?"

"Dogwood Lane."

"Are you being vague on purpose?"

Tessa puffed out air, and the mint quivered beside her. *Rip it off like a Band-Aid.* "I bought Honeysuckle Hollow, and I've already put down my earnest money and signed the final contract, and I can't turn back now, and I'm moving in tonight," she said in one breath.

Carolyn made a choking noise. "I'm sorry, what? Dr. Hamilton's place? Tessa, the last time I saw that house, it was hiding behind a forest of weeds. I don't think *a bit of work* is an honest description. No one has lived in that house in years as far as I know."

"It's a great house, Mama."

"It was a great house twenty years ago. Now it's a tragedy.

Here's what you should do. You should call back the seller and tell him that you suffered from temporary insanity because you lost your condo in the flood and you would like your earnest money back. There is no reason on this earth that you should purchase a fixer-upper, especially a mansion that's falling apart. You can't even change a flat tire. What in the world makes you think you can rehab a home or even have the money for it?"

Tessa's body trembled with an emotion akin to outrage. Why was everyone so determined to destroy Honeysuckle Hollow or leave it to decay? "I used my savings to purchase the home. I'm not asking for my money back because I can't. And even if I could, I don't want to. This is what's best for me."

Her mama laughed. "Now I know you're joking. You'd never use your savings on such an impulsive decision."

Tessa wiped at the tears on her cheek. "You don't have to support me or believe that I can do this, but I'd hoped you would."

"Tessa," Carolyn said in a gentler voice, "I *do* believe in you, but I know you've had a habit of rash behavior that has led to unfortunate consequences. I only want to help you and guide you. I love you and know where your gifts lie, and, honey, you've never rehabbed anything in your life. It's best if you choose a different project. Maybe start small and work your way up."

Tessa shook her head, even though her mama couldn't see her. "This is what I want, Mama. Tell Daddy I said hey and that I love him."

"Tessa—"

"Mama, I need to get going. Y'all have fun, and we'll talk soon."

"I'm worried about you," Carolyn said.

Tessa's throat tightened. "Don't be. I'll be fine. I'll call you soon, okay?" Tessa said good-bye, and although she knew her mama wanted to talk more, she allowed Tessa to go.

Tessa sat in the Great Pumpkin with her bottom lip quivering. Everyone in her life thought she'd made an awful decision, and nausea swelled inside her body. Sweat beaded across her forehead. She looked at the mint. "My best friends and my mama don't think I can fix the house. Paul . . . I'm not sure his opinion matters, but he was doubtful too." She rubbed her temples. "What do you think? Do you agree with everyone else?" she asked the plant.

A breeze blew through the open car windows, and runners of mint unfurled and stretched across Tessa's thigh. Another tendril curled around her wrist, and Tessa stared at the spear-shaped leaves pressing against her skin. "Is that a no?" She glanced out the windshield, blinked away her tears, and nodded her head. "I have a mint plant on my side, and let's not forget about the protection spear. Oh, and the town clairvoyant agrees with my decision. What a team."

CHAPTER 19

HONEYSUCKLE WINE

IN THE EARLY EVENING, TESSA PARKED THE GREAT PUMPKIN against the curb in front of Honeysuckle Hollow as the burnt-orange sun descended toward the horizon. Lightning bugs performed a coordinated dance in the front yard, flicking on and off, signaling one another in a light show of wonder. An ache pulsed against Tessa's temples, and her stomach growled, a sign that her discouragement was waning and her appetite returning. "Focus on the positive. Focus on the positive," she repeated like a mantra.

The Potts had re-laid all the bricks in the herringbone pathway, and without the unruly overgrowth, Tessa saw the distinct outlines of flowerbeds. Dr. Hamilton's damask roses displayed thorny branches punctuated with buds of green.

Pressure-treated wood, acting as temporary columns, structurally supported the front porch roofline, hindering any further collapse. Someone had spray-painted a smiley face on the plywood ramp leading to the front door.

Tessa popped open the Great Pumpkin's trunk and grabbed a few bags of supplies for her overnight stay. Crickets chirped as she wobbled up the trembling ramp. Once inside the foyer, Tessa exhaled and thought, *Mine.* The boards on the living windows had been removed. Tessa could see some repair work had been done to them, and someone had washed the glass, allowing falling sunlight to stream through.

She continued to unload the car until all of her belongings and her hardware store purchases crowded the living room. Tessa did a quick walk-through to see what the workers had completed in her absence. The French doors had been replaced. The upstairs carpet had been removed, thankfully along with the acrid scent of urine. Stacks of supplies were shoved against a wall in the kitchen. A note written in black marker was pinned to the kitchen island with a hammer. It read, *We'll be back at 7:00 a.m. on Monday.*

Tessa moved all the covered furniture in the front living room against one wall. Then she upended the bags from the hardware store. The electricity couldn't be turned on in the house until an inspector checked the wiring and circuitry, which wouldn't happen until Monday. So Tessa unpacked two LED lanterns and hand cranked both until they illuminated the front room in a soft, white glow. Lightning bugs flashed near the front windows as if watching her.

She unrolled the sleeping bag that smelled of newness and plastic and spread it on the hardwood floor. She lay down on it and shrugged. It wasn't the most comfortable thing she'd ever slept on, but it wasn't the worst either. Tessa looked at the tent box. She didn't need a tent since she was inside the house, but she'd convinced herself she was camping. And once she told the store employee she needed camping gear, Tessa hadn't wanted to explain it was for an indoor excursion. Now she was committed to setting up everything, but she hesitated before tackling the tent. Tessa vaguely recalled Anna earning a Girl Scout camping badge and learning how to properly set up a campsite, but Tessa had avoided that badge. She had only been talked into Girl Scouts for the cookies anyway.

After reading through the instructions on how to properly erect a tent, Tessa attempted to set it up. If ten-year-old Anna could set up a tent, then adult Tessa could. However, half an hour later, Tessa cursed when one of the poles separated in the middle and the entire tent folded over on her head. She sat on the floor, shrouded in the forest-green canvas, and her bottom lip trembled.

She thought of Anna and Lily and their shocked, worried responses about her purchase of Honeysuckle Hollow. She heard her mama's voice: *I know you've had a habit of rash behavior that has led to unfortunate consequences. Had* she been too impulsive? Was it a mistake so gargantuan she could never recover from it? Tears blurred her vision and dripped down her cheeks. She swiped them away with her fingertips. Pity swooped in like a vulture and attacked her self-assurance.

A rapping sounded against one of the living room windows. Tessa peeked her head out of the collapsed tent and saw Paul's hands and face pressed to the window. When he saw her, a silly grin stretched across his face, and he lifted what looked like a paper sack.

"I brought dinner," he shouted through the glass, pointing

toward the bag.

She crawled out of the tent and raked her fingers through her hair. “Hi,” she said, opening the door. She could barely make out his facial features in the dim orange glow from the streetlights, but even his silhouette was a welcome sight.

“I come bearing gifts,” he said, handing the bag to her.

The brown sack felt warm in her hands. She inhaled the scents of gooey cinnamon rolls, crisp bacon, and melted cheese. Tears filled her eyes again. “This is a surprise.” Tessa stepped out of the doorway and motioned for him to come inside. In the shadow of the door, she wiped her eyes. “Enter if you dare.”

Paul walked inside and stood in the archway leading to the living room. They both stared at the green blob of fabric that should have been a cozy, two-person tent. “You know I was an Eagle Scout, right? I can probably whip that into shape in about five minutes.”

“Have at it,” she said with a wave of her hand. “I had already accepted that it would be used as a blanket for the evening.”

Paul chuckled. “Mom and Dad wanted to come upstairs to say hello tonight, but they didn’t know you’d moved out. I told Mom that you’d decided to push the limits of your outdoorsy nature. She thought I was kidding. Once I convinced her you had, in fact, abandoned me, she insisted I bring you food since you’d decided to live in a—a new place.”

“A dilapidated mansion?” Tessa asked, able to smile for the first time in hours. As much as she had tried avoiding Paul, she didn’t want to anymore. Just being in the room with him caused her shoulders to lower from her ears and her breathing to deepen.

“‘Dilapidated mansion’ were not her exact words, but the meaning is similar.” Paul removed his backpack and knelt in front of the tent.

Tessa picked up the stapled booklet she'd removed from the tent box. "You want the instructions?"

"Don't need them," he said. "I brought silverware, plates, and cups." He pointed over his shoulder toward his backpack.

Tessa sat on the floor and opened Paul's pack. "It'll almost be like a picnic." Her eyes widened when she removed a bottle of honeysuckle wine and a corkscrew.

He slid one metal pole through a loop of fabric. "From Mom," he said when he saw her holding the wine bottle. "One of her customers makes it locally. She said it would be perfect for the house and would dull your senses after you realize what you've done."

Tessa would have been offended if Paul hadn't winked at her in the lamplight. "Thank you," she said. "For the food and the wine and the Eagle Scout assistance."

He slid another pole into place. "It gives me something to do. The apartment is too quiet. There's no one there to argue with or to make me poisonous food."

"Aww, you missed me?" she asked before she could stop herself.

"Who wouldn't?"

Tessa stopped unpacking the food. She wanted to remember that one second when her heart quivered because someone missed having her around. And not just anyone, but Paul.

Paul lifted a pole and paused, stopping to look at Tessa. "I mean it. It's too quiet without you, and not just the lack of having someone to talk to. Not having *you* around feels all wrong." His brow furrowed. "Which is odd, admitting that, because I haven't spent much time with any one person in years. Until you." He focused back on the tent.

Tessa was at a loss for words, so she finished pulling food from the paper sack, marveling at all the choices Cecilia had given. There were cinnamon rolls, waffles, bacon, sausage, a container of blackberry cobbler, and breakfast turnovers filled with eggs, cheese, and spinach. She placed two bottles of Coke and two of water beside the food. Even with Tessa's ravenous appetite, it was enough food for a family. "This is too much."

"You've seen me eat, and I've seen *you* eat." With a swift pop, the tent spread and locked into place. Tessa clapped. Paul bowed. "It would have been embarrassing if that hadn't worked." He sat beside her on the floor and studied her face.

Tessa busied her hands unwrapping the silverware and napkins. When she glanced up, he was still looking at her. "What?"

His pale-blue eyes filled with gentleness, almost enough to unravel her. "You're upset."

Her hands stilled. "Not at the moment."

"But you were."

She passed Paul a plate. "I've had one of those days."

"Care to elaborate?"

Tessa sighed. "Not really."

"I'd like for you to. Over a picnic dinner? You tell me your story, and I'll tell you mine."

"As long as this isn't *show*-and-tell," she mumbled.

Paul laughed. "If you want to take it in that direction, I'm not going to object."

Tessa's mouth went dry, and she wanted to tell Paul that she wouldn't mind a little show-and-tell. Instead, she arranged the food in a semicircle around them. "I hope buffet-style works for you."

He uncorked the wine. Then he poured a small amount into

two plastic cups. He passed Tessa one. "Cheers to new beginnings in Honeysuckle Hollow!" He raised his cup.

Tessa stared at the cup. When she looked at Paul, he smiled at her and moved his cup closer to hers.

"Are you going to leave me hanging here?"

She lowered her cup. "No, it's just . . . are you happy for me?"

Paul stopped smiling. "What do you mean?"

"About the house. Do you think I'm a reckless imbecile who made the worst decision of her life?"

Paul lowered his cup. "I sense the need to answer that question carefully. Do I think you're reckless? Not since I've known you. You definitely don't strike me as an imbecile. Worst decision? I flipped through your high school yearbook, and it's possible that your senior-year hairstyle was a greater misstep."

Tessa snorted a laugh. "It was the *style*," she said, but then the annoying tears returned. "I'm sorry. I'm not trying to fall apart on you, but everyone in my life thinks me buying this house is a ridiculous idea. They think I'm in over my head."

"Are you?"

Tessa shrugged. "Possibly, but it doesn't feel like the wrong decision. It's a lot of work, I know. But I can do it. I *want* to do this. And I just want *one* person to believe in me enough to trust that I'm doing what is best *for me*."

"Do you believe in you?"

Tessa nodded. "I do," she said, and then her heart thumped hard against her ribs because the words resonated so deeply within her. She repeated them with more gusto. "I *do*."

Paul lifted his cup again. "That's what matters. Following your heart takes a lot of courage. It's easy to go along with what other people are doing. It's easy to do the safe thing, believe me.

The others will come around. Until they do, you have me, and I believe you can do this."

A flood of gratefulness washed through Tessa. She tapped her cup against Paul's. "Thank you."

"Cheers to the second-worst decision you've ever made and to new hairstyles," Paul said, grinning at her.

Tessa snorted into her cup before she sipped the wine. "Don't pretend you never had a bad hairstyle."

"Hairstyle? No. Bad fashion? Yes. Ask Mom. There are a few doozies still framed in their house. There's shot of me and Eddie wearing high-waisted jeans with T-shirts tucked in."

Tessa grabbed a plate and laughed. She unwrapped a breakfast turnover. "Story time?"

"Ladies first," Paul said just before he bit into a cinnamon roll.

Tessa talked about her day, starting that morning at the house, leaving out his phone call from Monica. She explained how Charlie had rounded up a crew of displaced workers and how Leon offered to bring over a pair of French doors that were the perfect size. She pointed toward the ceiling and told him about the trunk of pictures in the attic. Then she repeated her conversations with both Lily and Anna and with her mama. When she was finished, Tessa split a cold waffle into quarters. "Discouraging, right? No way your story can top mine."

Paul smiled at her and leaned his arm against hers. "If this is a contest, I should at least get a turn to see how my story ranks."

Tessa made a sweeping motion with her hand. "Please proceed." She couldn't imagine how Paul's story would be depressing. He was a globe-trotter who took adventures every week, had just signed on to be a frequent writer for *Southern Living*, and had at least two women vying for his attention.

"You know why I came to Mystic Water?" he asked.

"To see your parents?"

Paul shook his head. "I could have visited anytime, but I always used the excuse that I was busy. Because I *was* busy, but people make time for what they want to make time for. And because I was playing the role of the unfortunate son, I didn't make time for my parents the way I should have. But I finally found some free time to spend with them."

Tessa nodded. "That's good."

"Do you know why I have the free time? I lost my job. It was freelance, in a way, because it wasn't a desk job, but the outlet offered me consistent work, and the pay was great. It was too consistent, though, because their legal team decided with the amount of work I was getting, I should have been a salaried employee with benefits, and in case I would ever get the idea to sue for either, they cut me loose. I am currently unemployed, with no paycheck, no home, no place to go. Lousy reason to finally make time to visit my parents."

Tessa put down her plate. "You—you don't have a job? But what about the Cook Islands and the article you were writing? Did you make that up?"

"No," Paul said. "The Cook Islands article was the last one being funded. I'm still required to write the article as part of the deal since they already paid me for it. And the article on Mystic Water is legit. *Southern Living* has already published it online, and the feature will be in their next publication. The article will help get my name back out there. I haven't had to pitch myself for jobs in a long time, so it's like starting over."

"But you have a portfolio, so that should help, right?" Paul nodded. “Did you tell your parents?”

“Of course not. Mom would worry, and Dad would try to get me to work at the diner. Settle down here.”

“And that would be awful,” Tessa said with an eyeroll.

Paul poked his finger into her knee. “I never said that, but settling down is difficult for me. I’ve been on the run for years.”

Tessa furrowed her brow. “What are you running from?”

Paul locked eyes with Tessa, and she couldn’t look away. A mockingbird sang outside. “Monica.”

How swiftly that one name caused her stomach to clench. She put down her half-eaten waffle. “The fiancée.” The word burned on her tongue like a jalapeño seed.

“Ex,” Paul said and clenched his jaw.

Tessa reached for a bottle of Coke and unscrewed the top. “But she called this morning.”

“So?”

“Does that make her less *ex*?”

“Hell no,” Paul said.

Anger rippled off him like bubbles of boiling water spilling over the sides of a pot. The mint shivered beside Tessa. She petted the leaves, releasing its sweet fragrance. “Careful,” she said. “You’re upsetting the mint.” She tried to smile at him.

Paul rolled his head on his neck. “Five years ago I lived in Boston. I took a job as an architect at a local firm when I was just out of college. I worked my way up. Good clients. Good pay. Monica worked there too, and she was also the owner’s daughter. We dated for a couple of years. I proposed. She said yes. We started planning a wedding, but she decided married life wasn’t for her.” He popped a piece of bacon into his mouth.

Tessa waited. Paul reached for the blackberry cobbler and a spoon.

"And?" Tessa asked.

"And that's it." He shoved his spoon into the dark fruit and crumbly topping.

"No way. You can't end the story there. What kind of girl decides married life isn't for her? What did she want instead of you? Was she out of her mind? How did she even *say* that? 'Oh, by the way, I've decided married life isn't for me,' and you, what? Just said, 'Okay, have a nice life'?"

Paul chuckled. "Thank you for thinking that a girl must be out of her mind to turn me down." He slid a spoonful of cobbler into his mouth.

Tessa shrugged. "If the shoe fits."

His grin widened. "This is really good," he said pointing at the cobbler with his spoon.

Tessa nodded. "Your mama makes the best."

Paul continued, "Monica probably decided marrying me wasn't what she wanted when she went on a weekend getaway with Jerry from the Cooper build."

Tessa's mouth fell open. "She was running around with someone else?"

Paul nodded. "I shouldn't have been surprised. Women threw themselves at Jerry, and who could blame them? He's rich, charismatic, and successful. He's probably a great guy if you forgive the fact that he was my coworker and knew we were engaged. She begged me to forgive her and to understand that she and Jerry were soulmates. She blubbered all over the office, like she was the victim. I said I'd forgive her in about five years, but until then, they needed to stay out of my face.

"I couldn't stand seeing them together, so I quit. I needed a change. I had taken a trip to Paris during college, so I wrote a travel article about finding your way around the city if you don't speak French. An online magazine ran it. I wrote another one and another one, and one day, I had a steady job. I left Boston and never went back. I figured Monica and Jerry deserved each other. They'd get married and have perfect kids. Except he's now rekindled his romance with his high school sweetheart and hung Monica out to dry."

Tessa couldn't hide her surprise. "Is that why she called this morning?"

Paul nodded. "She wanted to know if I'd forgiven her yet." He refilled Tessa's plastic cup with honeysuckle wine.

"Have you?"

"Mostly," he said with a shrug. "It still gets under my skin sometimes." Paul looked at Tessa. "She wants to try and work it out. She said she wants to be *us* again."

Tessa's breath caught, and then she tried to release it in the calmest way possible. She didn't want Paul to know how much his answer mattered to her. "What did you say?"

Paul looked at Tessa like he couldn't believe she didn't already know. "I said hell no. What did you think I said? I don't want any part of that. I already tried it, and it didn't work."

Tessa's lips twitched. "If you don't have a job, do you have to leave tomorrow?"

Paul shook his head. "Not if you need me for something."

Oh, I need you for a lot *of things*, she thought. But she said, "You know what I really need? An architect who can redesign this place the way it was when it was first built. Someone who can walk me through everything that needs to be done here to ensure it's rehabbed correctly."

Paul stared expressionless at Tessa until he smiled so widely that she chuckled.

"Why are you grinning like that? Should I be frightened?"

Paul laughed. "Are you offering me a job, Ms. Tessa?"

"Are you thinking of taking it?"

Paul gently tapped his cup of wine against Tessa's. "I'm the best man for this undertaking."

"Your humility astounds me." She paused long enough to imagine seeing Paul every day and working on the house together. "Do you really want to help?"

"Without a doubt. But I have to know . . . what kind of benefits package do you offer?"

"Free camping whenever you need to leave the comforts of home," she said, motioning to the space around them. "Free food and lodging, courtesy of your parents. Free use of the Great Pumpkin."

"Until you threw in the Great Pumpkin, I wasn't sure this was the right job for me, but who could turn down that classic ride? Do you have paper and a pen? I have some thoughts already."

"I went by the library today. Emma, the librarian's assistant, helped me find an old book of pictures of historical homes in Mystic Water. I photocopied all the ones of Honeysuckle Hollow. It hasn't changed a lot, but the photographs might help with the interiors." Tessa dug through her bags and found the papers. When she turned around, Paul was inside the tent, unzipping the sleeping bag. "What are you doing?"

"Making a pallet for us so we can stretch out."

Tessa's pulse thumped against her throat. The tent seemed to shrink in size so that she and Paul wouldn't be able to *stretch out* without their arms touching. Paul opened the sleeping bag and placed two pillows near the tent opening. Then he patted one side of the sleeping bag. "Come on in," he said.

Tessa hesitated, wondering what her mama would say. *Tessa, you're a grown woman. It doesn't matter what your mama would say. She's not here, is she? Should I ask Anna or Lily if this is okay? No! Just get in the tent. When is the last time a handsome man invited you into his tent? Did Greywolf's sweetheart hesitate before crawling into his teepee?*

"No," she mumbled aloud.

Paul wrinkled his brow. "What?"

She shook her head and then crawled into the tent. The lack of usable space inside became obvious. What had seemed like a roomy area when she was alone now felt as though she and Paul had climbed into a potato sack together. Paul seemed unaffected. He flopped onto his stomach, propped his elbows on a pillow, and spread out the papers on the floor in front of him.

Tessa inhaled and then exhaled. *You can do this.* Then she laid down next to him, praying her heart didn't beat right out of her chest and into the tent.

Paul tapped his drawings with the pen. During the past hour, Tessa's head inched closer and closer to his shoulder. A sheet of paper wouldn't have fit between their bodies.

"That's all the ideas for the house," he said as he slid the top sheet to the bottom of the stack. "And the backyard should be cleaned up to look like this, don't you think?"

Tessa slid a couple of the black-and-white photographs toward Paul's drawing. She pointed to the winding river and traced her finger along the curving lines. "Looks like the only thing Dr. Hamilton changed was the addition of the river, and we should keep that."

Paul nodded. "We can restock the pond and tell Huck Finn

to visit anytime." When Paul turned to look at her, their faces were so close she could have bopped him on the nose with hers. "When I visit the Cook Islands for the article, you should come with me."

The cogs in Tessa's mind locked up like a bicycle chain in need of grease. "Huh?"

"You could lie around on the beach all morning while I work, and then we could spend the rest of the day exploring the islands together."

Tessa struggled to connect Paul's words to reality. "I don't have a passport," she blurted.

Paul shrugged. "We can have one expedited. Is that a yes?"

Tessa felt like a kid bouncing on a trampoline, unable to find solid footing yet wanting to laugh. "What about the house?"

"It'll still be here when we get back." He reached out and tucked her hair behind her ear, his fingers gently grazing her cheek.

Tessa stilled. "When *we* get back?"

His warm hand rested against her cheek. "Is that a yes?" he asked, leaning toward her.

Tessa had been daydreaming about this moment, and now that it was here, all she could do was stare at Paul. When her lips parted, she said, "Uhh."

Paul chuckled long enough for Tessa to think, *Great, now you've completely ruined the moment.* But Paul leaned in again and kissed her. In that moment with Paul's lips against hers, Tessa believed she would follow him into an active volcano. When he kissed along the edge of her jaw, her bottom lip went numb, but she still managed to ask, "Do they serve piña coladas on the islands?"

Paul laughed against her neck. "With little umbrellas."

"Perfect," she said and shivered as Paul kissed her neck and returned to her lips. *Perfect.*

Tessa blinked in the feeble green morning light filtering through the tent fabric. When she rolled her head to the side, she stared at Paul's back. A slow smile, accompanied by a sigh, stretched across her face. A rattling noise came from somewhere nearby. Tessa parted a tent flap and zeroed in on the front door. The doorknob jiggled. Her body tensed.

Paul grunted beside her. "Are the bats back?"

"Someone's trying to get in."

Paul flipped over with another grunt and opened the other flap. A click sounded like a dead bolt turning, and the front door swung open. Tessa sucked air into her lungs. She heard *shuffle, shuffle, clunk. Shuffle, shuffle, clunk.* An elderly woman with snow-white hair swept on top of her head in a cotton-candy coif stepped into view. She gripped a curved silver-topped cane in her right hand and looked around with a pinched expression of disgust. A second shadow stretched across the hardwood, but Tessa couldn't see the other person.

The old woman's burning gaze found Tessa and Paul peering out of the tent. Her hazel eyes narrowed. "What are you doing in my house?"

Tessa's stomach lurched. She recognized the brittle, angry voice. "Mrs. Steele?"

CHAPTER 20

EGGS BENEDICT

Mrs. Steele moved toward the archway leading into the living room. She lifted her cane and pointed it at the tent. "I won't have squatters in my house. Get out!"

Her anger seethed across the floor and curled the edges of the papers in front of the tent. Paul dropped the tent flap and looked at Tessa, offering them flimsy privacy. "Is that the lady who sold you the house?"

Panic rose so violently in Tessa that when she opened her mouth, a squeaky noise squeezed out of her throat.

Paul touched her arm. "You look like you're going to either pass out or throw up. I can deal with a lot of things, but I'd prefer it not be vomit. Can you choke it down?"

Paul's words joggled Tessa's mind free from the claw-like panic gripping her. She glanced down at her bare legs. Her pants were in a pile at the bottom of the tent with her socks and shoes. "I'm not wearing pants. I can't go out there like this."

Paul grinned at her. "You *could*."

"I can hear you!" Mrs. Steele barked.

An object hit the top of a tent pole, and Tessa flinched. Paul made a move to crawl out of the tent, but Tessa latched onto his arm. "You're not dressed."

Paul glanced down at his boxers and smiled at her. "I doubt it's anything she hasn't seen before."

"Not in at least fifty years."

"Get out of there!" Mrs. Steele demanded, whacking the tent pole again.

"Grandma, hold on a minute. Give the people a few minutes. We obviously *surprised* them."

"This is *my* house, and I don't have tolerance for people who break into houses and think they can sleep wherever they want and *do* whatever they want. This is private property."

Paul snatched his jeans from the bottom of the tent, yanked them on, and crawled out before Tessa could stop him. The old woman gasped, and for a moment, Tessa knew the two women shared common ground. The sight of a bare-chested Paul also made Tessa lose her breath. Tessa scrambled down to the bottom of the tent and tugged on her pants.

"Excuse me, ma'am, but I think there's been a misunderstanding," Paul said.

Tessa grabbed Paul's shirt, lurched out of the tent, tripped over a pillow, and stumbled to her feet. She combed her fingers through her messy hair. Mrs. Steele's baseball-size eyes stared at Paul's bare chest, as did the woman with Mrs. Steele, whom Tessa assumed was her granddaughter. Tessa tossed Paul's shirt to him.

Tessa stepped toward the older woman and held out her hand. "Um, hi, I'm Tessa Andrews. We've spoken on the phone." Mrs. Steele turned her hazel eyes toward Tessa, and Tessa wilted beneath her glare. Tessa lowered her hand and pressed her sweaty palm against her thigh.

The bejeweled brooch pinned at Mrs. Steele's neck sparkled like stars in the light. "Making yourself comfortable, I see." Mrs. Steele voice warbled like an antique phonograph. "And what have you done to the front porch? That sad excuse for a ramp is a hazard. I could have fallen off." Mrs. Steele toed the empty bottle of honeysuckle wine with her shiny low-heeled shoe and curled her lip.

Tessa tucked her hair behind her ears. She glanced at Paul and then took notice of the younger woman accompanying Mrs. Steele. Tessa guessed the woman was closer to her age, probably a little older, in her midthirties. Her thick chestnut hair framed a heart-shaped face with wide-set eyes, a thin nose, and cupid's bow lips. Her expression was more welcoming compared to Mrs. Steele's shriveled features.

Tessa stepped toward the younger woman. "I wasn't expecting anyone from the family to come all the way here, but it's nice to meet you. I'm Tessa Andrews. I'm the woman who bought the house. The bulldozer destroyed the front porch before it stalled out. That's why there's a makeshift ramp for now, but there are plans to rebuild the porch and stairs."

The woman shook Tessa's hand. "Nice to meet you, Tessa. I'm Dorothy. I'm here as Grandma's traveling companion. It's a long way to come on her own. She told me about you buying Honeysuckle Hollow."

Mrs. Steele shuddered and pointed her cane at Tessa. "You're the one who *tried* to buy the house. But I'm not selling."

"Grandma—" Dorothy gasped.

"Hush, Dorothy. I've had enough with this place. Just being inside here makes my stomach turn. I won't rest easy until this place is a pile of dust."

Tessa felt as though she were tumbling down a flight of stairs. "Excuse me?"

Paul pulled his shirt over his head and stepped toward Mrs. Steele. "You agreed to sell the house to Tessa. It's my understanding you've both signed the real estate agreement. There's no reason for the house to be torn down."

Tessa's heart slapped against her chest, followed by a wave of dizziness. "That's not how you treat something just because it's busted up and needs a little work. You don't crush it. You work on it. You *help* it."

Mrs. Steele smacked the bottom of her cane against the floor. "It's *my* house, and I can do whatever I want with it."

Tessa's throat tightened. "I sent you earnest money. *A lot* of earnest money, and you accepted it."

"And now I'm backing out." Mrs. Steele dug through her purse and pulled out a cashier's check. "Here's your money. Take it. There's nothing in the world that would make me want to see this house restored."

"What? Why?" Tessa babbled.

"Not that it's any of your business, but I've enough days to stew about this, and this house doesn't deserve to see another sunrise."

A strong gust of wind smelling of lavender blew through the open front door, and the tent shivered and collapsed. Tessa pressed her hand against her chest and stared at the check but didn't reach for it. "Can I change your mind?"

Mrs. Steele flapped the cashier's check at Tessa. "What you

can do is leave."

Dorothy touched her grandmother's arm, but Mrs. Steele shook her off and banged her cane against the floor again, shooting vibrations across the room.

Paul hooked his fingers around Tessa's. "Let's get our stuff together."

"But the house," she whimpered.

Paul grabbed the check from Mrs. Steele and gave it to Tessa. Then he pulled the pillows and sleeping bag out of the fallen tent. She tucked the check into her pocket and knelt beside him. "We'll figure something out." When Tessa's eyes filled with tears, he squeezed her hand. "I promise."

Tessa nodded but didn't say anything more until they were outside loading her belongings into the back of the Great Pumpkin. Mrs. Steele's actions were traitorous—a Benedict Arnold–style betrayal. Tessa closed the trunk and stared at the house. From outside, she could hear the *clomp, clomp, clomp* of Mrs. Steele's cane against the hardwood. "Sorry for getting so emotional in there, but I'm shocked. *How* are we going to fix this?"

"I need to think," Paul said, pulling his keys out of his pocket. "First off, is this legal? Can she back out?"

Tessa nodded. "There are always exceptions. She could claim emotional attachment."

"So emotional she wants to tear it down? Let's go to the apartment. I'll drive. But let's grab breakfast from the diner first. I can't think on an empty stomach."

Tessa glanced at the fresh layer of dirt where the gardeners had filled the hole created by the bulldozer. "No," she said. "Crazy Kate. She *knows* her." Tessa pointed toward the house.

"They were related, she and Mrs. Steele."

"By marriage, right? It doesn't seem like it's a close relationship."

"It's worth a shot. Maybe Crazy Kate can talk sense into Mrs. Steele. She doesn't want the house torn down either."

Paul shrugged. He opened the driver's door on the black sedan rental. "Sounds like breakfast will have to wait. Let's go see Crazy Kate."

As Paul turned the car onto the driveway leading to Crazy Kate's cottage, Tessa pressed her hands against the dashboard and leaned forward. Paul placed his hand on her thigh. "We'll figure this out."

Tessa unclenched her jaw. "I feel sick to my stomach. Maybe everyone was right about me and the house. Maybe it isn't meant to be."

Paul parked the car. "I think you're wrong."

Tessa unhooked her seat belt and glanced over at him. "Why do you say that?"

He pointed toward the cottage. "Because she knew we were coming, and she's ready to go with us."

Crazy Kate hurried across the yard in a streak of color. She opened a rear door of Paul's rental car as though she'd called for a ride share. "Took y'all long enough," she said. "I've been waiting for an hour."

Tessa turned around in her seat to look at Crazy Kate. The older woman's deep-brown eyes were wild, and the tan skin on her face was pulled tight into an expression of anger and determination. "Waiting for what?"

Crazy Kate slapped the back of the driver's seat. "Drive!"

Paul shifted the car into gear, reversed into a smooth turn, and bounced them back up the driveway.

Tessa buckled her seat belt before looking back at Crazy Kate again. "Mrs. Steele is at the house. She doesn't want to sell it anymore. She says she's going to tear it down." Tessa pulled the wrinkled cashier's check out of her pocket and displayed it for Crazy Kate. "She gave me back my money."

Crazy Kate gazed out the window and gripped the door handle with her thin fingers. "I knew she was coming. When I woke up this morning, I knew today was the day." Her other hand rested on her chest. "I've felt a storm cloud inside me ever since she arrived in town."

Paul glanced at Tessa with raised eyebrows. He looked at Crazy Kate in the rearview mirror. "You *knew* she was coming? Did she call you?"

Crazy Kate scoffed. "Don't be dense. She hasn't talked to me in nearly fifty years."

"This is going to be a fun reunion," Paul said.

Tessa bit her lower lip and shoved the check back into her pocket. "Do you think you can change her mind?"

Crazy Kate's expression softened. "I don't know the ending to this story."

"That's not reassuring," Tessa said, turning around in her seat and strangling the seat belt with her hands.

Minutes later Paul parked on the curb in front of Honeysuckle Hollow. A tan crossover SUV was parked nearby, a sign that Mrs. Steele and her granddaughter, Dorothy, must still be in the house. Tessa didn't feel mentally prepared enough to face Mrs. Steele again, but she was relieved they were still in the house. That meant a negotiation might be possible.

Crazy Kate opened her car door and stared at the front of the house. "Oh, Matthias," she said, "I'm glad you can't see what they've done." She shook her head and closed the door. Then she marched across the yard and up the makeshift ramp.

Tessa hurried after her. "Shouldn't we make a plan or something? Talk about how we're going to approach her?"

Crazy Kate twisted the doorknob and shoved open the front door. "I'll approach her the way I always have. Intentionally." Then the old woman disappeared into the house.

"Oh," Tessa said, lingering in the doorway.

Paul stepped up beside her. "I've never seen two old ladies in a brawl. This could be newsworthy."

"I feel like I'm going to throw up."

Paul slipped his arm around Tessa's shoulders and squeezed her against him. "If given a choice, I'd rather have crazy on my side than bitterness. I have a feeling we're going to win this fight, Tess." He kissed her temple. "But let's not miss the show." He tugged her forward into the house.

The crystals in the chandelier clinked together, sending frantic chimes throughout the front of the house. The floorboards vibrated beneath Tessa's feet. She followed the sounds of voices and found Crazy Kate standing at the open French doors. Mrs. Steele and Dorothy were outside on the brick patio, looking at the freshly groomed back garden.

"Trudy," Crazy Kate said, not bothering to hide the anger in her voice.

Mrs. Steele's back stiffened. Sweat formed on Tessa's forehead, and Paul squeezed her hand. Dorothy turned and looked at Crazy Kate framed in the doorway. The young woman's expression was not one of recognition. She glanced between her grandma and Crazy Kate. Clouds crept across the vibrant blue sky and smothered the sun's light, muting the colors around them.

Mrs. Steele turned and leaned heavily on her cane. With her curled lip and her narrowed gray eyes, she transformed into an exemplification of an evil queen. "Kate." She said the name like it was toxic in her mouth. "I had hoped I'd never see you again."

Crazy Kate's unyielding gaze locked on Mrs. Steele. "Then you shouldn't have tried to ruin our family's home."

Mrs. Steele laughed, but the sound of it raised the hairs on the back of Tessa's neck. "Family? We're not *family*, Kate. We haven't been a *family* in fifty years."

Crazy Kate stepped onto the patio, and her navy-blue skirt swirled around her ankles. "Geoffrey's death didn't stop us from being part of the same family, Trudy. That was your choice for being unwilling to accept or see truth."

Mrs. Steele's hand trembled on the cane, and then she slammed it against the bricks. "The truth that you tried to steal my husband's love from me? The truth that you were a no-good woman doing whatever you wanted with whomever you wanted?" She lifted her cane and pointed it toward Tessa. "Just like that one. Thinking she can come into someone's home and do inappropriate things with men. I'm not surprised you two know each other."

Tessa's mouth fell open. She stepped through the French doors behind Crazy Kate. "Excuse me? You know *nothing* about me."

Mrs. Steele's glared at Tessa. "Kate can offer you plenty of ways to trick a man into loving you."

Dorothy grabbed onto her grandma's arm. "Grandma, how about we calm down a little. This doesn't have to be so offensive."

Mrs. Steele snatched her arm away. "Don't you act as though I'm overreacting. You have no idea what that woman did to me. What she did to my family!" she yelled in her brittle, broken voice.

A chilly wind swirled around Crazy Kate's feet and rushed up Tessa's legs. Leaves tumbled across the yard, and a blackbird landed on the fence, singing a tune that caused goosebumps to rise on Tessa's arms.

When Crazy Kate spoke again, her voice was calm, gentle even. "Trudy, I loved Geoffrey, but that was years before he met you. We were kids. Stupid, silly kids. After he left for college, there was nothing ever between us again. Nothing. I've told you that. Matthias was the only man I wanted to be with. I tried to save them." Crazy Kate closed her eyes and pressed one hand against her heart. "You know I *tried*."

Mrs. Steele's face scrunched as though she'd eaten rotten fruit. Her gray eyes watered as she inhaled a shuddering breath. "You didn't try hard enough, did you?" Her shoulders slumped. "You got to keep Matthias, but what about me? What did I get? I got to be a widow with two small kids and a husband who called out for *you* when he was dying."

Crazy Kate's sharp inhale startled the blackbird, and it took flight, cawing into the sky. "What?" She crossed the patio in deliberate, slow steps.

Mrs. Steele's jaw clenched. "In his fever, minutes before he finally succumbed, I sat at his bedside, praying he wouldn't leave me, telling him how much I needed him, and he looked over at me and said, 'Take care of Kate. I loved her. Promise me you'll give her what she wants.'" Mrs. Steele's frail body quivered with rage. "*You.* That's who he was thinking about as he was dying. Not me, not his kids. You, this house, this town, this whole family *ruined* me. It took everything from me, and I hate you for it."

Tessa crossed the patio, feeling a rush of boldness. Her heart hammered erratically in her chest. "You don't know what you're talking about, Mrs. Steele. She tried to *save* your family, the *whole* family, even though Geoffrey mistreated her when they were together. Did you know that? Did he ever tell you what he did? I doubt it. You have no right to show up here with your bitterness and blame the whole town and this house just because you're angry that your husband wanted you to *take care* of Kate.

"There's not a quota on how many people you can love. So what if he loved Kate? He loved you too. He married you and had children with you because he wanted to. Him mentioning Kate must have hurt you, because obviously that's what you've been focusing on all these years. I'm sorry you were hurting, but rather than let it go, you've let that pain make you angry and bitter. I want you to know what went on here after you left. Matthias didn't want to live in the house either, not after what happened. So he made this house a haven for those who were in need, for those who were sad or lost or sick or broken. For the past fifty years, *this house* has helped people, and you're going to destroy that because a man you loved wanted you to take care of someone who was important to him? Do you even realize what you're doing with his last request? You're ignoring it."

Mrs. Steele and Dorothy stared at Tessa, and no one spoke.

Sunlight escaped through the clouds and warmed Tessa's cheeks. She glanced up at the attic window. Faint laughter, accompanied by the sound of rainfall, drifted down, featherlight, around her.

Tessa thought about the photo album in the trunk. A swiftly moving chill swept down Tessa's body, racing from her head down to her toes. She looked at Mrs. Steele. "You were married in this garden, weren't you? And it rained on your wedding day, but you didn't care because you were so happy to be with Geoffrey. And your kids used to play in this backyard. They'd run around laughing, chasing lightning bugs."

Mrs. Steele blinked in the sunlight. Tears caught in the creases of her cheeks.

"It's not too late to do what Geoffrey asked. You can still help Kate. You can help *all* of us by letting us repair a home that has made a significant difference in so many lives."

Mrs. Steele reached out and clamped her weathered hand onto Dorothy's arm. "We're leaving." Without making eye contact with Kate or Tessa, Mrs. Steele pushed past them, dragging Dorothy beside her and banging her cane with each step. "And get out of my house."

CHAPTER 21

SINGIN' THE BLUES GRILLED CHEESE

TESSA DIDN'T HAVE A CHOICE BUT TO RETURN TO THE APARTment with Paul. She spent most of the day distracting her mind with work and halfheartedly online searching for a new car. Paul ordered pizza for dinner, and they sat mostly in silence while watching a history series about ancient civilizations. Tessa slept fitfully when she slept at all. Losing Honeysuckle Hollow to a nasty old crone—which was the shameful name she'd taken to calling Mrs. Steele during the wee hours of the morning—felt worse than losing her condo to the flood. At least the flood was a natural disaster and not caused by hatred or resentment.

"I'd probably be sour too if I'd had my knickers in a knot for fifty years because of jealousy," Tessa said as she tossed back the covers and sat up in bed.

"Am I interrupting?" Paul asked from the bedroom doorway.

"Please interrupt. That chat with myself was going nowhere

fast."

Paul sat on the edge of the bed. "How'd you sleep?"

Tessa grunted. "I've been going through everything in my mind over and over again. I keep trying to come up with a way to convince Mrs. Steele that she's making a mistake. But I'm coming up empty. No ideas, no fixes, nothing."

"Let's talk to someone who knows her better than we do."

"Crazy Kate? She was there yesterday, and she didn't offer any suggestions. She didn't even speak to us the entire way back to her house." Tessa sighed. "I'm not sure there's anything she can do either."

Paul tapped his finger to his chest. "I have a feeling this morning."

"Is it indigestion?"

Paul's grin made Tessa want to believe everything would be okay. "Get out of bed, Tess, and get a shower. I'll make coffee."

An hour later, Tessa and Paul were caffeinated and on their way back to Crazy Kate's house. When they arrived at the cottage, Crazy Kate wore a floppy large-brimmed sun hat and was bent over a flowerbed in the front yard, pulling weeds. She stood and tossed the weeds into a woven basket as Paul parked the car.

"Come inside," she said. "No wonder I bought extra cheese from the store. I'm having guests for brunch." Crazy Kate grabbed the basket and carried it around the side of the house.

Tessa and Paul followed her around to the backyard, and Tessa paused at the sight of the garden. Crazy Kate's garden was a stunning display of colorful, vibrant, and organized chaos. Flowers, herbs, vegetables, and greenery spanned across at least half an acre. Tessa saw signs of the river waters having risen and stretched into the yard during the flood, but if there had been any major damage, it had been repaired already.

Crazy Kate left the woven basket by the back stoop, opened the door, and walked inside. She motioned for them to follow. She pointed toward the round kitchen table. "Have a seat. I'll make tea first."

"Not rosemary tea," Tessa blurted out.

Crazy Kate looked over her shoulder at Tessa. "Something tamer, I agree. Honey and lavender." She filled a kettle with water and then placed it on the stove. The gas burner clicked a few times before igniting. "I know you're looking for answers, but I don't have any."

"There must be *something* you know that could help," Tessa said. "*Anything.* You know Mrs. Steele—"

"*Knew.* I don't know the woman she is now. She's had a good half a century of discontentment boiling in her veins." Crazy Kate opened the refrigerator and pulled out a half-moon of blue cheese, a package of bacon, and a stick of butter. "For some questions, it's best to have patience, and the answers will come to you."

Tessa frowned. "But we don't have *time* to wait for the answers. Mrs. Steele is going to have Honeysuckle Hollow demolished."

Crazy Kate grabbed a cast-iron skillet from a lower cabinet and placed it on a burner. "What makes you so certain?" The teakettle whistled, and she removed it from the stove and placed a tea infuser full of loose tea leaves into the kettle.

Paul shifted in his chair. "You heard what she said yesterday."

Crazy Kate nodded. She dropped a few slices of bacon into the skillet. "I'm curious about what she didn't say."

Tessa's brow furrowed. "What does that mean?" She wanted

Crazy Kate to help, not discuss vagaries. She kept thinking about Honeysuckle Hollow being razed. When she closed her eyes, she could already picture a line of people ordering greasy burgers and fries from Fat Betty's. Clueless people would shuffle across a linoleum floor that was built on top of a priceless historical home.

Crazy Kate filled three cups with the steaming tea and brought two to the table. She placed a cup in front of Tessa. "It means you should drink your tea and wait and see what the day brings."

Crazy Kate sandwiched soft blue cheese and cooked bacon between two pieces of butter-soaked bread and smashed it against the hot cast-iron skillet. Once the sandwiches were browned, she flipped them onto paper plates. Then she carried the grilled cheese sandwiches to the kitchen table.

"Thank you," Paul said, taking the offered plate. "Smells great. Aren't you going to eat?" he asked Crazy Kate.

"You two go down to the river and eat. There's a bench where you can sit." Tessa glanced at Paul in question, but Crazy Kate made a shooing motion with her hands. "Out. You two need to be outside where you can breathe and wait."

Paul shrugged, and Tessa followed him outside and down to the river's edge, where they found the wooden bench.

"That was weird," Tessa said.

"Did you just call the town weirdo weird?" Paul joked.

She nudged him with her elbow. "I'm serious. We come to see her and talk about what to do, and she makes us sandwiches. And who, by the way, eats grilled cheese for brunch? Anyway, we're here to see her, and she sends us outside to play like children."

"Though this be madness, yet there is a method in it."

Tessa rolled her eyes. "Thanks, Hamlet."

Paul pointed his sandwich at her. "Actually, Polonius said that."

She lifted her sandwich and bit into the crusty bread. It probably tasted amazing, because that's how it smelled. But Tessa's senses felt dulled, and she chewed mechanically. The river bubbled over its rock-strewn bed. A cardinal chirped in a nearby tree, and a car engine traveled closer. Tessa turned around on the bench seat and watched a car traverse Crazy Kate's driveway. The car parked beside Paul's rental, and Tessa gasped when the driver stepped out.

"Mrs. Steele is here," she whispered, sliding down on the bench in an attempt to slip out of view.

Paul turned around and watched. "No need to hide. She's not even looking this way. I wonder what she's doing."

"You don't think she's coming over to yell more, do you?"

Paul grabbed Tessa's hand and tugged her off the bench. "Let's go find out."

They crept toward the back of the house and squatted in front of an open window. Mrs. Steele stood in the living room as though she didn't know what to do now that she was there.

"Tea?" Crazy Kate asked.

"I didn't come for tea," Mrs. Steele said.

"Why did you come, Trudy?"

Mrs. Steele leaned on her cane but did not turn her gaze to meet Crazy Kate's. When she spoke, her fragile voice was barely a whisper. "I ignored his request. All these years. Geoffrey would have been—" Her voice faltered, and her hand trembled on her cane. "He would have been so upset with me. I was angry and had no one to blame, so I picked you. I don't know what to do with this anger. I've carried it for so long that it *is* me." She bowed her head.

Crazy Kate closed the space between them. "It doesn't have to be you. You can let it go now, Trudy." She placed her hand on top of Trudy's where it rested on the cane. "It's been more than long enough."

Mrs. Steele nodded and wiped at her eyes. "I don't want the house, but after all that Matthias did, helping all those people, it would be wrong of me to tear it down. Matthias was always good to me, and he checked on me and the kids all the time up until he—until recently. He never forgot about us, and I guess you didn't either. I can't imagine why a young woman would want to rehab Honeysuckle Hollow and live in that stuffy old house, but if she wants it, she can have it. I won't have it destroyed."

Crazy Kate walked into the kitchen and refilled the kettle with hot water. "Chamomile was one of the first herbs my mama planted in the garden, and after all these years, it still flourishes. I believe it makes the best chamomile tea around. It soothes the soul."

Mrs. Steele took a seat at the kitchen table and propped her cane against the wall. "I'll be the judge of that."

Crazy Kate pulled two porcelain cups from the cabinet. "I assure you, this tea can turn a skeptic into a believer. You want honey?"

Mrs. Steele relaxed against the back of the chair. "I could use some sweetening."

"I second that."

The sound of Crazy Kate's and Mrs. Steele's laughter filled the small cottage. It dispersed out through the open windows.

Tessa exhaled and looked at Paul. She lowered herself down

onto the soft grass. "Did we just win?" she whispered.

Paul grinned. "Thanks to you and Crazy Kate." He sat beside her, cupped her face with his hands, and kissed her.

CHAPTER 22

Settle My Heart Hot Tea

Tessa and Paul returned to the bench and finished eating their grilled cheese sandwiches. After tea with Mrs. Steele, Crazy Kate came outside and retrieved them. Mrs. Steele assured Tessa that Honeysuckle Hollow was hers, so Tessa returned the cashier's check so she could issue a stop payment. Crazy Kate mentioned the photo albums in Honeysuckle Hollow's attic, saying Mrs. Steele might want to see them. Paul offered to drive them to the house, but Mrs. Steele declined because she wanted to stop by the hotel and pick up Dorothy, and Crazy Kate offered to ride with her.

Paul and Tessa waited in the car outside Honeysuckle Hollow while their conversation jumped all over the place with ideas about renovations and the future. Once Mrs. Steele arrived with Crazy Kate and Dorothy, Tessa unlocked the front door with the skeleton key. Crazy Kate led Mrs. Steele and Dorothy up the staircase, and Tessa stared at the key in her palm before wrapping her fingers around it. She could never have guessed that this one key arriving at her office would change her life so quickly and so profoundly.

Paul stood in the front yard, gazing at the pruned rose bushes. Tessa stepped toward the railing. "You coming inside?"

"It's lunchtime. We haven't had much to eat. The sandwich was good, but not enough to fill me until dinner. Think the ladies are hungry too? I could run to the diner and grab food."

Tessa smiled at him. "That's really thoughtful. I bet they'd appreciate it. You don't mind?"

He shook his head. "It can be a celebration meal. I'll be back with an assortment. Don't start the party without me."

"Wouldn't dare."

Tessa closed the front door and hurried up the staircase, causing every other stair to moan and pop. Voices flowed down from the attic. Mrs. Steele sat in a dusty wooden chair with a faded embroidered cushion. Crazy Kate sat in a rocker that creaked with every movement, and swirling dust motes danced around the floorboards. Dorothy had pulled over a stepladder beside her grandmother's chair. Mrs. Steele flipped through a photo album and pointed out the people on the pages. Crazy Kate used her toes to rock herself in a slow, steady rhythm that fell into sync with Tessa's heartbeat.

Four portraits were lined up near the window, two leaning on the trunk and two on either side. Moth-eaten sheets lay puddled on the floor. Four dark-haired young men stared at Tessa. Curiosity pulled her to them. "Where did these come from?"

"They've been stored up here for years," Crazy Kate said.

"Matthias didn't want them hung in the house. I think he worried something would happen to them, but now they've grown old and worn."

"Like us," Mrs. Steele said.

Tessa touched one of the hand-carved wooden frames. "Who are they?"

Crazy Kate's voice filled with warmth when she answered, "The Hamilton brothers."

Tessa felt the answer before she'd been given it. The young men looked too much alike to not be related. With the same dark hair and strong jawlines. The *clomp, clomp, clomp* of Trudy's cane sounded against the floor.

"That's Benjamin," Mrs. Steele said, pointing with her cane. "The oldest and wildest. Then Richard, the follower. He did anything Benjamin asked him to." She looked over at Crazy Kate. "Do you remember when Benjamin dared Richard to spend the night on Red River Hill?"

"But it's haunted!" Tessa blurted out.

Mrs. Steele laughed a brittle, raspy sound that shook her frail body. Laughter changed the old woman's face, and Tessa saw how she once had been lovely before the years of resentment had withered her features.

"Richard jumped at shadows for weeks," Crazy Kate said, shaking her head. "He swore there were ghosts living in those woods."

Mrs. Steele's smile pushed wrinkles across her cheeks. "Those last two are Matthias and Geoffrey."

Tessa exhaled a breath of admiration. *Without a doubt, the two most handsome brothers.* "I can have these restored and then rehang them in the house."

Mrs. Steele leaned on her cane. "I hope you know what you're doing, trying to rehab this whole place." She shuffled across the floor toward the chair.

"I don't, but knowing the house is saved gives me hope that the good guy can win sometimes."

Mrs. Steele sat, and one thin eyebrow rose on her forehead. "Should I assume that I'm the bad guy?"

"Well, no, I mean, not *now*, but maybe for a few minutes. Well, that's rude, isn't it? Have mercy, my mama would be—" Mrs. Steele's laugh cut off the rest of Tessa's words, and she glanced at her feet before clearing her throat. "Paul went to get lunch, if anyone's hungry. We could eat downstairs in the dining room. Maybe you both could tell us how the house used to look, back when it was taken care of. Share a few stories."

Mrs. Steele leaned forward and cut her eyes over at Crazy Kate. "We have more than a few stories about this place and about the Hamiltons. Never a dull moment with those boys."

Crazy Kate leaned her head back against the rocker, closed her eyes, and shook her head. "Never."

By the time Paul returned with bags of warm food, drink carriers with coffee and lemon-balm tea, disposable plates, napkins, and utensils, Tessa had the dining room cleaned and ready for lunch. After hearing about the rocky reunion, Cecilia had taken lemon balm from her garden and brewed a batch of tea. She'd said her *nonna* always swore that the herb could bring peace to even the most unsettled heart, and Tessa believed her. She no longer doubted the power of the garden nor the mystical possibilities all around them.

The atmosphere in the dining room was one of happiness and renewal. It was almost as if Mrs. Steele and Crazy Kate had been friends for all the years they'd spent disliking one another.

Paul jotted notes and stacked sketches around him as he listened to the women. Mrs. Steele and Crazy Kate had given them so much detail about the house, and Paul had pages' worth of ledger-lined notes. Tessa pulled apart a cinnamon roll and pushed one half toward Paul. He reached out for it without lifting his pencil from the pad.

"When we're all finished, you'll have to come back," Paul said to Mrs. Steele. "Bring your family so they can see where the magic happened."

Tessa flinched, thinking Mrs. Steele's experience with losing Geoffrey in the house outweighed the fact that she'd fallen in love with him in the same house, that her children had played there every summer, and that the whole Hamilton family had celebrated holidays there for years. But Mrs. Steele nodded her head.

"I'll expect a formal invitation and not to be disappointed by the renovations. I can't have my family thinking their father and his family lived in a dump," she said.

"I hardly think this could ever be called a dump," Paul said. Then he tapped his fingers on the table. "Except for the graffiti in the kitchen and the boarded-up windows."

Tessa grinned. "Don't forget the bats and the mangy cat."

"Since when have you cared so much about a home?" Crazy Kate asked him, but her words were gentle.

Paul looped his finger around one of Tessa's. "Since I showed up in Mystic Water, ate Tessa's poison pancakes, had her question my ideas about always being on the move."

Tessa snorted, but her chest felt warm, and her stomach turned to marshmallow fluff. She squeezed his finger, thinking that everything—the house, her life, Paul—was falling into place, and she didn't see how anything could go wrong.

The next morning Tessa rolled over and sighed at the sunlight trickling into the apartment bedroom. Warm, pale-yellow sunbeams illuminated the bed. Paul stepped into the doorway as though sensing she was awake.

He sat on the edge of the bed. "I came up with more ideas about the house last night, and I woke up early thinking about them. Let's go downstairs, have breakfast, and get over to the house. Aren't the workers going to be there at seven? I want to talk to Charlie."

"Whoa there, cowboy," Tessa said. "I need a shower first."

"Yes, you do."

Tessa reached behind her, grabbed a pillow, and threw it at Paul. He caught it, laughed, and tossed it back at her faster than she could lift her hands in defense. The pillow smacked her in the face and dropped into her lap. She narrowed her eyes at him, and he jumped off the bed.

As he backed out of the bedroom door, he said, "You have fifteen minutes to make yourself lovely, but you don't need that much time. Even with that hair." He winked.

After Tessa brushed her teeth, showered, and dressed, she and Paul popped into Scrambled. The Monday morning crowd was already nestled into their usual spots, and Tessa sat in a booth while Paul slipped into the kitchen to speak to his parents.

On her next pass through the dining room, Laney filled two cups with coffee and raised her eyebrows at Tessa. "Interesting development," she said as she dropped a handful of creamers onto the table.

Tessa reached for two creamers. She knew exactly what Lanie was referencing. "For me too. I didn't like Paul at first, but he's so *charming*. He could charm the pants off anyone—not that he charmed the pants off *me*. I was being figurative. Oh man, that sounded racy, didn't it? Pretend I didn't say that. But yeah, I wasn't expecting it." She smiled up at Laney. "But it's nice."

Laney propped her fisted hand on her hip. "I was talking about the rumor I heard about you buying Honeysuckle Hollow."

Tessa's eyes widened. "Oh."

Laney laughed. "I didn't know you'd put the moves on the Borellis' son. Good for you. He's handsome."

Paul exited the kitchen, causing Laney to scurry off. He slid in across from Tessa. "Mom's going to make us buttermilk pancakes with bacon maple syrup. She said it's one of your favorites."

"Everything here is one of my favorites," Tessa said, pouring creamer into her coffee. Her cell rang inside her purse. "Excuse me for a minute. Let me see who that is because it might be the condo buyer. He said he'd call early this week." Tessa pulled out her phone and hesitated. "It's Anna. The last chat we had was dismal."

"One of the naysaying friends?" Paul asked. Tessa nodded, and he shrugged. "They probably meant well, but sometimes our friends are wrong. Give her an opportunity to admit it."

Tessa accepted the call. "Anna, hey, how are you?"

"Hey, Tess! I'm so glad you answered," Anna said. "I'm in town. In Mystic Water. Eli and I got home late last night. One of our workers, Natalie, is covering for us at the bakery for a couple of days. She's great. Anyway, we stayed at Mama and Daddy's. We want to see the house and see you, so tell me when you're free. I promised Lily we'd call her too. She wants to come over."

Tessa frowned. "Y'all said that me buying Honeysuckle Hollow was a terrible idea."

Anna sighed. "We could have handled it differently. I'm sorry. We were surprised is all. It's such a big undertaking, but we don't want you to think we don't believe you can do it. You're smart and resourceful, and we're excited for you. You'll be down the street from Lily, almost neighbors. We want to support you."

Tessa looked across the table at Paul. He lifted his eyebrows in question. "Paul and I are having breakfast right now, but afterward, maybe in an hour or so, we'll be at the house. Y'all can meet us over there."

"Paul?" Anna said, and Tessa heard the smile in her best friend's voice. "Can't wait to meet him. We'll see you soon. I'll call Lily."

Tessa disconnected and dropped her phone into her purse. "My two best friends want to meet us at the house this morning."

Paul lowered the coffee cup to its saucer. "That's unexpected pressure."

Tessa tilted her head in question. "What do you mean?"

"Meeting your two best friends is more challenging than meeting your parents. They're going to judge me."

Tessa snorted. "You've got nothing to worry about. They're gonna love you. I was just telling Laney that you can charm the pants off anyone."

Paul smirked. "That's a hypothesis I'd like to test. Are you available at," he glanced down at his watch, "eight a.m.?"

Tessa's cheeks warmed, and she pressed her lips together as she stared at her coffee cup. "You're a scoundrel," she said, lifting the cup to her lips.

"Can you blame me? You're beautiful and passionate and adorable . . . should I go on?"

Heat flamed in her stomach. "Is there more?"

"I could go on for days," he teased, but she saw sincerity in his eyes. "But first I need to know, has anyone used the word *scoundrel* in the last fifty years?"

She grinned against the rim of the cup. "I'm bringing it back just for you."

Paul chuckled. "You like me *because* I'm a scoundrel. You don't have enough scoundrels in your life. The question is whether or not I'm an irresistible one."

Yes! Absolutely, 100 percent, yes. "As the Magic 8 Ball would say, 'outlook good,'" she said, matching his smirk with her own.

By the time Tessa and Paul finished breakfast and arrived at Honeysuckle Hollow, the crew had already started working. Much of the plywood had been removed from the antique windows in the front rooms, and workers strengthened the window frames and added new molding where the original had rotted. One man used a professional wallpaper steamer to remove the peeling paper on the wall leading up the staircase. A paint-splattered drop cloth covered the entire staircase, and chunks of sticky, goopy wallpaper fell away in patches as he pulled. Charlie stood at the dining room table with paperwork spread across the top. She looked up when Tessa and Paul entered.

"Good morning, Charlie," Tessa said. "This is Paul Borelli. He's in town for a while, and he'll be the architect on this job."

Charlie's cheek twitched as she smirked. She slid a pencil stub behind her ear. "Is this the handsome Italian traveler who cooks like a chef?"

Paul passed a glance at Tessa. "Is that how I've been

described?"

Charlie chuckled. "I can see why the one-bedroom offer was dangerous."

Tessa cleared her throat. "Paul, this is Charlie Parker."

Paul reached out his hand to Charlie and grinned wider. "Hello there, Yardbird. Nice to meet you."

Tessa gaped at him. "Paul, why would you say that?" To Charlie, she said, "His manners are sometimes lacking."

Paul looked affronted. "Charlie Parker was a famous jazz musician nicknamed 'Yardbird.' It wasn't meant to be offensive."

Charlie leaned her hip against the table and crossed her arms casually over her chest, which accentuated her toned arms. "No one, and I mean, *no one* ever knows that. My parents were huge fans of his. Supposedly I was created during one of his more famous tunes."

"They have good taste," Paul said. "When I was in Paris, I visited a nightclub called Le Caméléon. I knew there was someone special playing in the vaulted, downstairs room because at least a hundred people were trying to squeeze through the door. We were packed in so tightly that we could hardly breathe, which wasn't so horrible because the club reeked of stale sweat and cigarettes. But in that cramped, damp space, a group of musicians transported the crowd to the 1930s with Charlie Parker's greatest tunes, and we lit the space with our luminous cocktails and the fiery glow of cigarettes."

Charlie smoothed her hand down her ponytail, and her expression softened. "Wish I could have been there." Her voice sounded much too dreamy for Tessa's liking.

"You would have loved it," Paul agreed. "I could have shown you—"

"Paul," Tessa interrupted, shaking off the enchantment he

had cast. She felt surprised by the pricks of jealousy in her stomach. She didn't want to think of Paul showing Charlie *anything*. "Can we focus on the house for a minute?"

Even though Charlie looked mildly disappointed that the conversation was shifting, she refocused her gaze on the drawings Paul added to the papers on the table.

"Here's what I've been thinking," Paul said. He explained each drawing in detail before unrolling the blueprints. He gathered a few tools and weighted down the corners of the curling paper.

Tessa turned her attention to the front door when she heard someone knocking. The door opened, and Lily, Anna, and Eli stepped into the foyer. Tessa squealed, startling both Paul and Charlie, and she hurried over to her friends.

"You're here!" She hugged Lily and Anna and then gave Eli a side hug.

Eli gave her a quick squeeze in return. "Long time no see. This is some place you got here, Tess."

"Wow," Anna said as she drifted toward the staircase railing. "Look at the craftsmanship. It has all the original woodwork and molding? Look at the millwork. The running trim spandrels."

Tessa raised her eyebrows in question.

Anna shrugged. "What? I've listened to you talk about them enough through the years. I *was* listening. Most of the time."

Lily looped her arm through Tessa's. "You forgive us for raining on your parade when you told us about the house? We weren't trying to make you feel bad, but I know we did. We were surprised by you making such a big decision without talking to anyone. That's not like you, not these days. This house needs a lot of work, but I can see you've already gotten off to a good start. Cleaning up the front yard makes a ton of difference already, and, whoa, is that Paul? Ain't he all easy on the eyes!"

Anna stepped away from the staircase and peered into the dining room. Paul leaned against the dining room table with one hand shoved into his front pocket. He lifted the other hand and waved. Just looking at him almost made Tessa swoon.

"Holy smokes," Anna whispered.

Eli cleared his throat. "I'm standing right here."

Anna grinned at Eli over her shoulder. "You're my number one, but Tessa picked a solid ten."

Tessa's stomach fluttered. "Come meet him, and then I'll give y'all a tour." She led them into the dining room and introduced Paul.

"We've heard *so* much about you," Lily said, making it sound like Tessa had blabbered about Paul to the extreme, which she hadn't, but she knew Lily liked to stir up intrigue.

"Yeah?" Paul asked, grinning at Tessa. "Like what?"

Lily continued before Tessa could stop her. "Tess mentioned you might be leading-man handsome."

Paul laughed. "Like Cary Grant or like Ryan Reynolds?"

Lily said. "Why not both? But other than that, she's been pretty tight-lipped about her new *friend*, other than your sleeping arrangements. So, if you'd care to enlighten us—"

"Why don't I show y'all around?" Tessa interrupted before Lily could create a more embarrassing situation. She put her hands on Lily's lower back and shoved her out of the room.

In the kitchen, workers chipped the tiles from the island while one man lay on his back, his body half hidden in the cabinetry below the kitchen sink. The French doors were open so another worker could carry in a stack of two-by-fours.

"The kitchen has good bones and lots of usable space," Anna said. She pointed at the graffiti marring the kitchen wall and cabinets. "Can they sand down the cabinets and restain them?"

Tessa nodded. She led them around the ground floor and told them about the guest books she'd found and how the house had helped so many people. Neither one of her friends had known how much Dr. Hamilton used Honeysuckle Hollow as temporary housing.

"This house *is* special, Tess," Anna said. "You're doing something meaningful here, saving a historic haven."

Tessa felt uplifted by her friends' compliments and support. Before they toured the upstairs, Tessa led them out into the backyard. Eli stepped off the brick patio and walked into the garden, following the winding river and the pathways.

Tessa shielded her eyes from the sunlight. "The Potts, a local landscaping and gardening team, will be back tomorrow, and they've already cleaned out so much. You should have seen how wild it was back here. Once they're all done, we'll replenish the river with koi."

"We'll?" Lily asked. "Who's the 'we' in that sentence?"

Tessa tucked her hair behind her ears. "Just a general statement."

Lily looked skeptical. "Uh-huh." She glanced sideways at Anna. "You believe that?"

Anna smiled. "Not really."

Tessa sighed. "Paul is the acting architect. He has a lot of great ideas and has experience with historic homes. It's a team effort. Sometimes I automatically say *we* when referencing what *the team* is doing with the house."

"I thought he wasn't sticking around," Lily said. "You mentioned he was leaving. Days ago, right?"

Tessa toed a dandelion fluff, scattering white seeds into the air around her feet. "He changed his mind."

Lily grinned like a best friend who had mischief on her mind. “He changed it, or *you* did?”

“Lily, we’re not here to interrogate Tessa about her love life,” Anna said. Then she nudged Tessa. “Unless there’s more you *want* to tell us.”

“You two are like good cop, bad cop. But okay,” she said, glancing over her shoulder at the house and then lowering her voice, “I think he’s sticking around for me. I mean, I *hope* he is. He’s great, isn’t he? Lord have mercy, he’s so handsome, and he kisses like I imagine movie stars kiss in rom-coms. It’s like he fell straight out of one my romance novels, but not a hokey one. I don’t know what he sees in me, but he’s . . .” She sighed. “Perfect. Or close to perfect. Or perfect *for me*.”

“Isn’t it obvious what he sees in you?” Lily asked, looking at Anna for backup.

“Of course it is,” Anna agreed. “Tessa, you’re a five-star catch. Don’t look at me like that, you *are*! You’ve never given yourself enough credit. Why do you think you’re the one who was always going on dates and fielding a gazillion calls from potential dates?”

Tessa paused and then rolled her eyes. “Because I was desperately looking for a partner?”

Lily snort laughed. “That’s only about ten percent of the reason. The other ninety is because you’re funny, smart, beautiful, quirky, and completely loveable. *That’s* why Paul is smitten.”

All three girls giggled, not noticing Eli had returned to the group. He groaned. “I think I need to go inside and talk about nails or hammers or plumbing.”

“Sorry, not sorry,” Tessa joked. “What do y’all think about the garden? It’s a little further along than the house, of course, but it’ll be lovely out here when they’re all done.”

Eli pointed toward the oak tree. "It'll be a great place for a small wedding."

Tessa agreed. "They used to host weddings here. People were married in the garden, and then they used the house as the reception area."

Eli cleared his throat. "I meant for *our* wedding. Anna, are you gonna tell them, or should I?"

"Guess the cat's out of the bag," Anna said. "Eli proposed, and I said maybe. I'm kidding. I said yes!"

Eli pulled a ring out of his pocket and passed it over to Anna. She slipped it on her finger and held out her hand toward Tessa and Lily. The diamond sparkled like magic in the sunlight, casting shimmery rainbows on Anna's cheeks.

Tessa oohed and aahed over it. "It's beautiful."

Lily reached for Anna's hand and shook her head. "How could you not have told me?"

"I wanted to tell you both at the same time. We came back home for a few days so we could tell my folks. They already knew because Eli asked them for permission, but they didn't know when he was gonna ask." She looked around at the garden. "But I agree. This would be a great place to be married. If Tessa will let us."

Tessa's broad smile made her cheeks ache with joy. "I'm honored, but, wow, do I have time to fix it up? Have you set a date? It'll probably take me three or four more months at least."

Anna touched Tessa's arm. "Breathe. You have plenty of time. We were thinking six months or so. When the weather is cooler."

Tessa hugged Anna. "I'm so excited for you." Then she hugged Eli. "You're one lucky guy. You got the best girl from Mystic Water."

"Hey," Lily pouted, "what about me?"

"You're already taken," Tessa said, poking Lily in the ribs. "Come on inside and let me show you the upstairs. We can brainstorm ideas about how we should decorate for the wedding."

Once inside, Paul joined them, and they toured the upstairs. From the second-floor balcony, Anna and Lily gazed out into the garden. Lily lifted her arm and pointed. "Imagine everyone down there, and you up here in your wedding dress looking like Juliet. Gorgeous pictures."

Anna glanced at Eli over her shoulder. "Will you recite Shakespearean poetry to me from the garden?"

"Do I have to?" Eli asked, causing Paul to laugh.

"Best to keep the woman happy," Paul teased.

Tessa's cell phone rang, and she slipped it out of her back pocket. "It's Mr. Fleming. He must have news about the condo buyer. Excuse me one second while I take this." Tessa answered the call and stepped into the nearest bedroom. "Hey, Mr. Fleming."

"Tessa, I'm glad I caught you," Mr. Fleming said. "I have great news. Mr. Kincaid has finalized his offer to buy the buildings. He has all the necessary funds, the paperwork has come through just as promised, and everyone will receive what they were offered according to the individual agreements. We'll just need your signature. I've emailed an electronic agreement to you."

"What a relief. Is there anything more I need to do?"

"Not other than signing the contract and returning it to me as soon as you can. I'll keep you updated if anything changes, but I think it's all smooth sailing from here."

Tessa ended the call and sighed. There were workers downstairs who expected to be paid for the work they'd done so far.

She'd already spent a chunk of her savings on the earnest money, and with the remaining amount of her savings plus the condo money, she planned to pay off Mrs. Steele, and the rest would go toward the beginning stages of rehab. Would it be enough to finish everything that needed to be done? She didn't know, but it was at least a start.

Paul stepped into the room. "Everything okay?"

Tessa slipped her phone back into her pocket. "The condo sold. I should see the money soon. At least we have more funds coming in so we can continue with the rehab without delays."

Lily walked in behind Paul, followed by Anna and Eli. "That's great, Tess," Lily said. "One less thing to worry about. Do you—do you think you'll have enough to repair everything, even with the condo money?"

Tessa shrugged. "I don't know. Paul and I can sit down and go over the costs. We've made a couple of lists. We based the needs on priority and necessity versus wants. I'm hopeful."

Paul nodded and slipped his arm around Tessa's shoulders. "Buying this house wasn't a mistake."

Someone cleared their throat in the doorway, and Tessa noticed Charlie with a look of concern on her face. "I have a question about the balcony. Do you have a minute?"

Tessa nodded. "Be right there." She looked at her friends. "Y'all free for dinner?"

Anna walked over and hugged Tessa. "I agree with Paul. I'll call you this afternoon, and we'll make dinner plans."

Lily hugged Tessa and voiced the same thoughts. Then the three of them walked out, leaving Tessa and Paul in the bedroom. Tessa lowered her voice when she said, "You do think we'll have the money for the basics, don't you? Is it possible my impulsive actions are going to work out this time?"

Paul entwined his fingers with hers. "Impulsive or trusting your gut? But don't worry. The condo money is going to give us enough for all the basics. Let's see what Charlie needs, and then we'll go to the apartment and sort through financials."

In the hallway, Charlie walked them toward the balcony doors, talking about structural support and concrete footings. When Paul went downstairs to grab his notepad, leaving Charlie and Tessa alone, Charlie asked, "Are you having money troubles? Be honest. I have a lot of men depending on this job."

Tessa's stomach clinched, but only for a moment. Charlie was only voicing a fear Tessa had already been fretting over. "Paul and I are going to crunch the numbers just to be sure, but we both feel confident that everything will work out." She smiled, and it felt genuine. "I want to help the workers. I don't want those guys out of a job. We definitely have the money for a lot of the repairs that we'll need to make this house livable."

The crease between Charlie's brows lessened. "I know you want to help, but you have to make sure you take care of yourself too. Don't make decisions that will harm you."

Tessa snorted. "I should have had that tattooed on my forehead years ago. I won't keep the men working if I can't pay them. I promise. But I think we're going to be okay. Honest."

Charlie nodded her head. "I believe you."

Paul bounded up the stairs, and then he and Charlie continued their discussion about the balcony. She hadn't realized she'd been carrying around the worry about whether the condo would sell and whether they'd have more money to help with repairs. Now that the deal was made, there was a good chance she could save Honeysuckle Hollow and herself.

CHAPTER 23

WHITE-LIGHTNING GRITS AND THUNDER EGGS

LATER THAT AFTERNOON, TESSA AND PAUL RETURNED TO THE apartment. She tossed a folder full of her financial paperwork on the coffee table while Paul sat on the couch with his open laptop. She filled a glass with ice and water for Paul. Then she opened her twenty-ounce Pepsi, took a large gulp, and plopped down on the opposite end of the couch so she could stretch out her legs. As soon as she was comfortable, her cell phone rang.

"Charlie, hey, what's up?"

"Do you have a minute?"

Tessa sat up straighter on the couch. "Of course."

"The electrician and a friend of mine who's a master mason just left. You know we already discussed the fact that you have knob and tube wiring all throughout the house, and, well, it's not up to code. There's no way we'd be allowed to professionally renovate this house and not update it. We wouldn't even be able to get permits. Plus, you'd never be able to resell the house or be properly insured. It would be a mess. Anyway, the electrical will have to be replaced."

"I figured as much," Tessa said. "Any idea what that'll cost?"

Charlie paused long enough for the acidic Pepsi in Tessa's stomach to bubble and push burning liquid up her esophagus. "They'll need to disconnect the old system, run new wiring, install modern junction boxes, replace fuses and breakers, and update any outlets, receptacles, and fixtures connected directly to the wiring. It'll be time-consuming, and they'll need full access to the house, which I don't think will be a problem. You'll need somewhere to stay while they're working. The job will be easier since you have an attic and a crawlspace, but due to the size of the house and the fact that the garage will need rewiring too, it'll be a big job. Plus, you'll have to patch holes in the walls when they're all finished. Not a problem to do that, but I just want you to know what'll be going on—"

"Charlie," Tessa interrupted, "what kind of cost are we looking at?"

Charlie hesitated, then answered, "Around twelve thousand dollars."

Tessa's eyes widened, and she pressed her hand against her collarbone because the Pepsi burn had turned into full-blown indigestion. Paul's expression turned inquisitive.

"There's more," Charlie continued. "The master mason looked at the chimney and the brickwork surrounding the foundation as well as the actual foundation, since it's brick too. The mortar is more than one hundred years old, and due to natural wear, it's deteriorating. Unfortunately, it will continue to worsen. His suggestion is not to replace the foundation, which should ease your mind a little, but he suggests repointing the bricks."

"Meaning what?"

"In layman's terms, he'll fill in and repair the joints in the brickwork. It's kind of a dying art. I wouldn't be comfortable with you using anyone else. He's the best."

Tessa sagged against a couch cushion and exhaled. "And how much does *the best* cost?"

"This is a guesstimate, but I'd say you're looking at twenty-five thousand dollars."

Tessa pitched forward. "Twenty-five thousand! Are you serious?"

"Think it over tonight. I'll call you in the morning. But, Tessa, I wouldn't suggest it if I didn't think it was important to be done. I know you're in . . . in a tighter position financially. Think it over, and we'll talk tomorrow."

Tessa still had the phone pressed to her ear when she heard the disconnection beeps. Paul hadn't taken his eyes off of her.

"What's twenty-five thousand dollars?" he asked.

"Only part of two new additional costs," Tessa said. "I *knew* all of this was a possibility because I've seen houses like this before, but I kept hoping this time it would be different."

"Tell me."

Tessa shared Charlie's explanations concerning the knob and tube wiring and the brickwork that needed to be updated and repaired. When she finished, he typed the information into the spreadsheet he created for keeping track of repair costs. He moved his laptop to the coffee table and faced Tessa.

She wrung her hands together in her lap. "Let's hear it."

Paul tapped his finger against the coffee table. "With the addition of the electrical needs and the masonry repairs, you're looking at a cost of"—he highlighted the grand total in red on the spreadsheet—"and I'm leaving room for error, so maybe it could end up costing less, but I don't want to play it that way. The house will be livable. You'll have plumbing and electrical, and the foundation will be solid. You'll be able to repair either the kitchen or the bathrooms, but not both. You can update the kitchen with cheaper appliances or used ones until you can afford top-of-the-line appliances. You can refinish the flooring downstairs in the most important rooms—foyer, kitchen, dining room, and living room—but not the upstairs. We can probably hook up laundry in the garage for now. The balcony will have to wait, but we can fix the front porch. And as for aesthetics, there won't be any money for that."

"So no painting or repairing plaster or landscaping," Tessa said. "No bathroom updates because I'll need to have a kitchen. Cheap appliances, okay, I can handle that. I'm not that great of a cook anyway. Laundry room in the garage, got it. No flooring upstairs, so I'll be walking on unfinished hardwoods. I won't be able to afford furniture—I have my sleeping bag and tent." She rubbed her fingers against her temples.

"At least the dining room and living room still have a few pieces of furniture." He slid closer to her on the couch and grabbed her hand. "You can stay in the apartment for as long as you need."

Her throat tightened. "I wanted to be able to do this."

"You *are* doing this," he argued.

"Anna and Eli want to be married in the backyard in October."

"A lot can happen in a few months."

Tessa sighed. "I wish your optimism were contagious."

Paul pulled Tessa against him, and she rested her head on his shoulder. "Why don't you relax for a while? Take a bath or whatever it is you like to do when you need to unwind. I'm going for a walk."

"Are you coming back?" She winced at the pathetic tone in her voice.

Paul chuckled. "You think I'm bailing on you?"

"I wouldn't blame you for hightailing it out of here. This could be a snowball effect, leading straight to a black hole. You might not want to taint your name with this project."

"I assure you I have tainted my name sufficiently on my own," he said. "Now go relax. Why don't we make plans with your friends tomorrow?"

Tessa nodded and glanced at the wall map. After Mrs. Steele had kicked them out of the house on Sunday morning, she'd brought the mint plant back to the apartment. It had stretched its long tendrils around the silver pushpins again. Tessa's eyes trailed to Mystic Water on the map. "If you stick around, won't you miss your adventures?"

Paul followed her gaze. "Who said this isn't one?" He leaned down and kissed her. Then he pulled her to her feet. "I'll be back." He grabbed his laptop, slid it into his bag, and walked out the door.

In the bathroom, Tessa turned on the faucets and filled the claw-foot tub. She could handle living without the nicest furnishings and proper paint on the walls. Possessions could be acquired over time. But Tessa wondered whether she could adjust to living without Paul. Would she have to? Or would this new adventure be enough to keep him in Mystic Water?

Tessa dangled her romance novel over the side of the tub and dropped it onto the bathmat. Paul had been right. The bath *had* relaxed her initially, but now an uneasy feeling crept into her chest. She sat up, shimmery bath bubbles sliding off her arms, and a bolt of lightning zigzagged across the sky outside the bathroom window. A cannon blast of thunder ripped through the silence, and Tessa flinched. She quickly stumbled out of the tub and drained the water.

After she'd toweled off and put on pajamas, she walked into the living room at the same time Paul hurried through the door. Rain splatters covered his clothes, and he'd shoved his laptop bag beneath his shirt as best as he could, giving him a square belly. Water had soaked through the top half of a brown paper grocery bag he held.

"Storm's a'brewing," Paul said in a British accent, leaning against the door to close it. "Winds from the east, bringing in gray mist and cold rain. 'Good old Watson! You are the one fixed point in a changing age. There's an east wind coming all the same, such a wind as never blew on England yet. It will be cold and bitter, Watson, and a good many of us may wither before its blast. But it's God's own wind none the less, and a cleaner, better, stronger land will lie in the sunshine when the storm has cleared.'"

"Watson?" Tessa asked, walking over and taking the grocery bag from him so he could remove the laptop from its captivity.

Paul placed his laptop bag on the couch and pulled out the

computer so he could inspect it. Satisfied, he plugged in the computer and left it on the couch. Then he scrubbed his hand through his hair, shaking rainwater into the air. "From Sir Arthur Conan Doyle's 'His Last Bow.' I was channeling Sherlock Holmes," he said, pointing to himself. "That makes you Watson—"

"Who was *a guy*," Tessa said. She started unpacking the grocery bag.

"Not in my story. In my story, Watson is a beautiful woman who buys historic homes."

Tessa grinned, but a twist of unease spiraled through her chest, and she paused from unpacking the groceries long enough to rub her fingers across her collarbone. "Is it bad out there?"

Paul nodded. "It's wild. The wind nearly blew me off the sidewalk."

Disquiet bubbled inside her. "You think the house will be okay?"

Paul sorted through the groceries. "Barring any natural catastrophe, yes. She's a sturdy broad." He nudged her with his elbow. "Hey, it'll be okay. It's just a storm."

"*Just a storm* is probably what everyone said right before half the town nearly floated away or drowned in the flood." She lifted a mason jar full of clear liquid. "This doesn't look like something you bought at the store."

Paul smirked and grabbed the jar. "White lightning."

"*Moonshine*?" Tessa gaped at him. "Where did you—"

He pressed his finger against her lips. "Don't ask."

Tessa jabbed her finger against the jar. "There is no way I'm drinking that."

A streak of lightning lit the darkness outside, and Tessa stared at the windows as thunder vibrated the panes. The mint plant shivered and released a sweet, fresh scent into the air.

"It's the perfect night for white-lightning grits and thunder eggs," Paul said.

Tessa raised an eyebrow. "There's no way that's a real thing."

Paul grinned. "An old family recipe. Not *my* family, but someone's."

Tessa shrugged. "There's always plan B if dinner doesn't turn out."

"What's plan B?"

She pointed to the cereal box on top of the refrigerator.

"It'll turn out." He moved around the kitchen, pulling out the necessary pots and pans.

Tessa walked over to the window and stared out into the darkness. Rain splattered against the glass, and strong winds swirled around the building, whining in the night. She pressed her fingertips against a pane. "You sure she'll be all right?" Tessa asked as she rubbed the back of her neck.

Paul turned on the stovetop. "It's just a rainstorm, Tess. She's withstood much more."

Tessa nodded, but she couldn't shake the feeling that the east wind would leave more than scattered leaves and mud puddles behind. The word *destruction* slithered around in her mind like an uneasy serpent.

CHAPTER 24

A Wicked Broken Egg

The next morning Tessa's cell phone rang and vibrated off the bedside table. She grumbled as she dangled off the side of the bed and stretched her fingertips out for it. She answered just before her voice mail picked up. "Hello?" Her dry mouth caused her voice to come out as a croak.

"Tessa?"

She heaved herself back onto the bed and glanced at the alarm clock. It was five minutes past seven in the morning. "Charlie, hey."

"You need to get to the house."

Tessa's shoulders tensed at the tone of her contractor's voice. "Is everything okay?"

"You need to get here. Like five minutes ago. Can you leave now?"

Tessa swung her legs off the bed and stood. "What's wrong?"

"Just get here."

Charlie disconnected, and Tessa stared at the phone, giving her own anxieties a full minute to quadruple inside her chest. She ran to her closet and pulled on yesterday's pair of already-worn jeans and a T-shirt. She yanked a comb through her hair and brushed her teeth. Then she hurried into the living room. She leaned over Paul's sleeping form on the couch and touched his shoulder. "Paul."

His eyes fluttered open. "Hmm?"

"Charlie called. She sounded freaked out. I'm going to the house."

Paul pushed himself up onto his elbows. "Now?"

Tessa nodded and grabbed her purse from a kitchen chair. "I'll call you when I find out what's going on." She dug her car keys out of the depths of her bag.

Paul kicked off the quilt covering his lower half. "I'm going with you. Give me five minutes."

On their way to Honeysuckle Hollow, Tessa gripped the steering wheel as though she intended to choke the life out of it. Downed tree branches and overturned garbage cans littered the sidewalks and yards. A million green leaves—ripped from their trees—coated the streets, making it look as though they drove along a forest path. The wind blew the car around as though it were made of paper. Tessa navigated the streets like a drunken driver. When she parked behind a work truck in front of Honeysuckle Hollow, she exhaled and released her grip on the steering wheel.

Paul leaned forward and peered out of the windshield. "Looks okay to me."

When they climbed out of the car, the wind rushed at them,

yanking at their clothing and tangling Tessa's hair. It was the kind of intense wind that could steal hearts, breaths, and hopes.

Charlie flung open the front door and met them halfway across the yard. She held her hands out like someone offering surrender. "Now, don't freak out."

"That *makes* me feel like freaking out," Tessa said. "What's going on?" Another gust of wind whipped her hair into her eyes.

"It's the backyard. The oak," Charlie said. "It looks like lightning struck it. There's a huge scar running straight down the entire trunk."

Tessa wrinkled her brow. "And it's dead?"

Charlie shook her head. "No, but one of the largest branches was blasted off the tree, ripped from the trunk. There are wood shards everywhere."

Tessa glanced over at Paul and then back at Charlie. "That's it? You thought I would freak out that we lost a tree branch?"

Charlie hooked her thumbs into her front pockets. "That *branch* flew into the side of the house and crushed the roof, ripped off the second-floor balcony, and landed in the kitchen."

A buzzing—like the sounds of a thousand swarming bees—filled Tessa's head. Her vision narrowed until only a pinprick of light could be seen. Then her knees buckled, and Paul caught her before she dropped into a full faint. She gripped his arms, and he steadied her. "I need to see it."

Charlie puffed out her cheeks before she exhaled a sigh that was lost in the wind. Tessa and Paul followed Charlie through the foyer. Halfway down the hallway that led to the kitchen and living room, Tessa saw the mangled oak branch that had smashed through the house like an angry giant with a club. Gray sunlight streamed through the gaping hole in the back of the house, shining against puddles of water and dampness. She pressed both hands against her mouth and gasped. Paul kept walking, but Tessa's shoes were glued to the hardwood.

Workers on Charlie's team milled around the kitchen, scratching their heads and shuffling their feet as though they felt as discouraged as Tessa did. One man swept water out through the back of the house with a broom. Another man gathered pieces of the splintered branch like someone collecting firewood. Leon, the man who'd given Tessa the French doors, stepped into her line of vision. Without asking, he slid one arm around her shoulders and gave her a squeeze. She crumpled against his barrel chest.

"Damn shame," he said with a voice that rumbled like thunder.

"I—I don't—This is too much," Tessa stuttered.

Leon moved to stand in front of her and grabbed her shoulders in his large hands. "We can fix this."

Tessa's bottom lip trembled. "It's—it's a three-sided house. The money. It'll take a miracle to fix this."

Leon nodded. "Miracles happen every day."

After spending three hours at Honeysuckle Hollow talking with a constant stream of people, including her insurance company again, Tessa felt like she'd spoken with nearly every person in Mystic Water, even without her brain engaged. She clutched a stack of documents—estimates and repair designs scribbled on paper—to her chest like a favorite stuffed animal. Paul opened the passenger-side door of the Great Pumpkin and held out his hand for the car keys. She dug around in her purse and pulled out the car keys and her notebook. After handing him the keys, she sagged into the seat like a wet blanket.

Tessa opened her notebook to the most recent list, which was the reason she'd taken this leap of faith that was now turning into a leap of catastrophe. She'd written, *Should I buy Honeysuckle Hollow?* Instead of asking anyone else's advice, like she'd been doing for the past two and a half years, she'd eaten Cecilia's Courage Quiche and drained her savings account to afford the down payment, just because she'd wanted to. Just because it *seemed* like the right choice.

"You don't know this about me, but I've made a string of lousy, impulsive decisions," she said. "Everything from poor dating choices to accidentally setting off a chain of events that burned down a bakery—don't ask. But after that, I made a promise to myself that I would ask at least three people about what to do before I made any decisions." She showed Paul the notebook. "I've been true to that until recently. While eating your mama's Courage Quiche, I got the wild idea to purchase Honeysuckle Hollow, and I didn't ask anyone if I should. I bought it because I wanted to. Because it sounded like the best idea I'd ever had. Maybe because of the Courage Quiche. Maybe because I decided to believe I was brave and didn't need anyone's advice to follow my heart. But look where that got me. This is awful."

Paul was quiet for a few seconds before responding. "I've never heard of quiche infusing someone with courage *or* with lousy ideas, but people believe in stranger things. Tess, I still stand by you going with your gut and buying Honeysuckle Hollow. So you've made bad decisions in the past. Who hasn't?" He tapped his finger against her notebook. "You don't need a list of other people's opinions on how to live your life, and I think you know that. I admit this current situation isn't ideal, but that doesn't mean you aren't brave or capable of making your own decisions. And this isn't a total disaster."

Her cell rang and rather than answer it herself, assuming it was Charlie or another worker, she handed it to Paul. She lacked the energy to deal with anything else.

Paul looked at the blinking phone. "It's Anna. Don't *you* want to answer?"

Tessa shook her head. "Send it to voice mail."

"Hey, Anna," Paul said, ignoring Tessa's command. "She's right here, but we've had a long morning. Lunch? Today?" When Paul glanced over at her, Tessa shook her head. "She'd love to. Fred's Diner at 12:30. See you then."

Tessa slapped her hands against the papers in her lap, completely aware that she was on the verge of a meltdown. "Why did you agree to that? Didn't you see me shaking my head?"

Paul started the engine and pulled away from the curb. "The last thing you need to do is sit at the apartment. You need to get out and surround yourself with people who care about you."

Tessa's bottom lip trembled. "But I *want* to sit around and feel sorry for myself."

Paul reached over and patted her paper-covered leg. "You have at least an hour and a half to wallow, and then we're going out." He glanced over at her. "They'll want to know what's happened."

Tessa sighed and stared out the window. As much as she wanted to lock herself away in the bedroom with a bag of caramel creams and a romance novel, she felt her spirits lift, if only slightly, at the thought of being with her best friends.

Paul opened the door to Fred's Diner and motioned for Tessa to enter. The scents of greasy comfort foods—salty french fries, hamburger patties sizzling on the griddle, and buttery sandwich bread—beckoned Tessa inside. The noon crowd was busy eating and wiping their fingers on too-thin brown napkins pulled from dispensers on the tables. Conversations hummed around the room like a few dozen radio stations all broadcasting at once.

Tessa glanced around until she saw Anna raise her hand from a back corner booth. Tessa weaved her way through the tables. Lily, Jakob, Anna, and Eli sat at a rounded booth, and Tessa slid in beside Anna so Paul could sit on the outside seat.

Tessa struggled to make eye contact while she said hello to everyone. Paul held his hand out across the table toward Jakob. "I'm Paul Borelli."

Jakob shook his hand and introduced himself. "Heard you were helping Tessa with the house. We live down the street from Honeysuckle Hollow. That was some storm last night, wasn't it? Our street looks like every tree in the neighborhood dropped their branches. Good thing you haven't moved in yet. I'm not sure anyone slept well."

Tessa made a strangled noise in her throat. Then, because she was worried she might start crying, she cleared her throat a few times before reaching for her glass of water and drinking half of it.

Anna focused in on Tessa. "What is it? You were beaming like a sunburst yesterday, and today you look like you did that time we lost the three-legged race at field day."

Tessa pressed her lips together in an attempt to control her emotions. "Let's order. It's been a long morning. We can talk while we eat."

Anna looked only momentarily satisfied with Tessa's

answer, and Tessa knew she wouldn't be able to withhold much longer. No one but Paul needed to look over the menu to make a selection, so Tessa pointed out the local favorites on the laminated pages.

After the waitress took their order, Lily clasped her hands together on the tabletop. "Spill it. You ordered a salad from Fred's Diner. You're not well."

Tessa felt Paul's hand slide over hers on the vinyl seat, and he squeezed her fingers. She cleared her throat one last time and went into detail about the destruction of the house and how she had no choice but to forfeit the majority—if not nearly all—of the rehab projects she'd planned. Most of her money would have to be used to repair the roof and the exterior wall of the house, including all the damage in between. When she was finished talking, everyone sat in a silence so heavy it felt as though a sopping wet sleeping bag had been dropped over Tessa's head.

"I was this close." Tessa separated her forefinger and her thumb an inch apart. "I really thought it would all work out. Now—now I don't know what I'm going to do."

Anna's compassionate expression caused Tessa's eyes to water. "Will the house be livable once the major repairs are made? Can you still move in?"

Tessa shrugged. "I'll have to. I won't have finished floors or a working kitchen. The electrical and the plumbing will work because those are necessary for all the permits." She folded a napkin in half and then in half again, pressing firmly along the creases. "But in college we survived with only a microwave." She glanced across the table at Lily. "Remember? We did okay then."

Lily scoffed. "We lived off macaroni and cheese and ramen noodles. I hardly think that constitutes as ideal."

"Lily," Anna scolded, "positive thoughts."

"I love macaroni and cheese as much as anyone," Lily said. "Upside, it's not as though you're an avid cook." When Anna glared at Lily, she added, "Hey, what about a scratch-and-dent appliance store? Couldn't you check one out for deals? I bet you could find a good enough cooktop and refrigerator until you find what you really want."

Tessa propped her elbows on the table and rubbed her temples. "I'm not sure I'll be able to afford much more than a low-wattage microwave. Maybe in a year or two I could save up enough."

"Will the house be safe to live in?" Anna asked.

Paul nodded. "Safe, yes. Comfortable? Depends on your definition of comfort."

"You have indoor plumbing," Eli said. "That's something."

"Yeah," Tessa mumbled.

The group quieted again, and the waitress delivered their food. The silences were punctuated by idle chitchat about the weather, what funny thing Rose—Jakob and Lily's daughter—had said recently, or the new baked goods Anna had created at her bakery in Wildehaven Beach.

"I'm sorry I'm bringing down the lunch atmosphere," Tessa said. "It's just—does anyone mind if I—if Paul and I go? That way you can enjoy the rest of the meal. I don't have much of an appetite anyway."

Anna put her hand over Tessa's hand on the table. "Tess, we want to help you, but I'm not sure what we can do. You're not in this alone, though." She glanced over at Lily. "We'll call a few people we know, see if anyone has items they want to give away. Appliances, furniture, spare *anything*."

Lily nodded. "Jakob's mama knows everyone in this town. She'll call around too."

Jakob agreed. "Who knows what can happen in a day, right?"

Numbness had swept into Tessa's body, and she nodded her thanks. Paul dropped enough cash on the table to pay for his and Tessa's lunches. "Let's get home." He looked around the table. "I'll be in touch later this afternoon. I have a few ideas to go with yours."

They said good-bye, and Tessa apologized again for being out of sorts. During the car ride to the apartment, she couldn't pull her thoughts out of the doldrums. She hadn't lost the house, and she reminded herself of that over and over again. It just wouldn't be rehabbed the way she had hoped, and it definitely wouldn't be ready for Anna's wedding.

Paul parked on the street in front of the diner. "Do you mind if I run to the library for a bit of research?" Tessa shook her head. "I'll be back soon."

Tessa nodded and closed the door. When she rounded the corner of the building toward the exterior steps that led to her apartment, she halted. Crazy Kate sat on metal stairs, holding a pink bag from the candy shop.

"Right on time," Crazy Kate said as she used the railing to pull herself onto her feet. She held out the bag toward Tessa.

Tessa's shoulders sagged. "The house—"

"I know," Crazy Kate said. "Inside." She tossed her thumb over her shoulder, indicating the apartment. "I'm too old to sit on metal stairs all day."

Tessa grabbed the offered bag. "What's this?"

"Comfort. Now come on," she said, turning around and walking up the stairs.

Tessa followed her. Crazy Kate stepped out of the way long enough for Tessa to unlock the apartment, and then they both entered. Tessa dropped her purse onto the kitchen table.

"Want something to drink?" Tessa asked.

Crazy Kate pointed to the couch. "You sit. I'll make tea." She pulled a metal tin from a fabric bag hanging on her shoulder.

Tessa obeyed and opened the pink candy bag, finding it full of caramel creams. Her bottom lip quivered. Crazy Kate bustled around the kitchen, putting a kettle of hot water onto the stove and grabbing two mugs from the cabinets. While the water heated, Crazy Kate sat at the kitchen table.

"Lavender," Crazy Kate said. "It helps bring peace to the mind. I've brought a mix of dried lavender from home—what my mama planted—and Cecilia's from downstairs. The combination should be what you need."

Maybe a mix of dried herbs would give her exactly what she needed, even if she couldn't even pinpoint what that was. "You know what happened to the house?"

Crazy Kate nodded. "Yesterday I knew—"

"Yesterday? Why didn't you tell me? Or anyone? We could have done something." Tessa's throat tightened, and she clenched her fists in her lap.

Crazy Kate chuckled. "Done what? Cut down branches in a storm? Be sensible."

"What about the spear?" Tessa said. "Should we have returned it sooner? Did this happen because I took the spear?"

Crazy Kate shook her head. "You can't stop what has already been set in motion. This was necessary."

"Necessary for what?" Tessa's voice squeaked as she stood with her chest constricting. Tears blurred her vision. "The house is destroyed! Now I can't fix it!"

Crazy Kate stood from the table as the kettle whistled. She dropped a mesh bag of dried tea into the kettle and set it on the counter to steep.

Anger and frustration rose so violently in Tessa that she stomped into the kitchen. "How can you act as though you don't care? The house—the one you've been protecting for years—has been torn apart, and you *knew* it would happen? All of my plans are ruined!"

Crazy Kate looked at Tessa as though she were a child throwing a tantrum. "Robert Burns said, 'The best-laid plans of mice and men often go awry.' Sit." She pointed to a kitchen chair.

Tessa glared at her but dropped into the chair. She swiped her fingers across her wet cheeks. Crazy Kate poured tea into two mugs and then brought them to the table.

"Drink."

Tessa lifted the cup. The steaming liquid warmed her throat and then her chest as it flowed into her body. Her shoulders lowered from her ears.

Crazy Kate cupped her hands around a mug. "We can't plan for everything, Tessa. Misfortune can sometimes be a blessing in disguise. It can become an opportunity."

Even as Tessa's heart rate slowed, she still struggled to control her emotions. A sob hiccuped its way up her throat. "An opportunity for what?"

"To see what happens. To allow a new path to unfold. This is not the end of Honeysuckle Hollow."

Tessa pushed her tea aside. Then she folded her arms on the table and dropped her head onto her arms. "It's the end of having it rehabbed properly." Her voice echoed in the cavity created by her arms. "A giant tree branch crushed the entire backside of the house."

"It was necessary," Crazy Kate said.

Tessa popped up her head. Before she could argue with Crazy Kate for her complete lack of empathy and compassion, the older woman pointed to Tessa's cup of tea. "Drink that before you say something you'll regret. You're upset. I understand, but bricks and mortar can be repaired. Walls can be rebuilt. Nothing has happened that is irreparable."

Tessa swallowed more tea and sighed. "Sure they can, but it costs money. *A lot* of money. More money than I have."

Crazy Kate shrugged. "Your money did not build that house, nor did it keep it standing all these years. Perhaps *your* money won't be what repairs it completely. You've started the process of bringing Honeysuckle Hollow back to life. Perhaps others will finish it with you."

Tessa's forehead wrinkled. "What does that mean? Am I supposed to be comforted by that?"

Crazy Kate gave Tessa a scathing look. "You're *supposed* to be comforted by that tea." She lifted her mug to her lips and sipped. "You'd rather sit around here and mope? Or you'd rather I tell you that everything will work out according to *your* plans?"

Feeling admonished, Tessa shrugged. Crazy Kate reached across the table and placed her hand on Tessa's arm. Tessa looked into the woman's dark eyes.

"Our plans are not always the best plans," she said. "Right now, you don't see how this one unfortunate event will connect together to form a part of the greater story. This is not what you *want*, but perhaps it is what you *need*. What this town needs." Crazy Kate stood. Tessa watched her open the apartment door. "You're not cast adrift on your own in this. That should give you comfort. Get some rest, because tomorrow is a new day, and I have a feeling it will be interesting." She smiled, stepped outside, and closed the door.

Tessa finished her mug of tea. The desire to stay home and wallow faded, and she decided to walk up the street to her office.

Paperwork kept her busy for an hour, and emails and phone calls kept her busy throughout the rest of the afternoon. When her cell phone rang, she was startled to see it was nearly five in the afternoon.

"Where are you?" Paul asked.

"At the office. Find everything you needed at the library?"

"It was productive. Mom and Dad want to go out to dinner tonight. You up for it?" When Tessa hesitated a couple of seconds, Paul continued, "I thought you'd feel that way. I told them it would be just me. But I'm making dinner for you, one of my specialties called a Wicked Broken Egg."

The sound of the smile in his voice relaxed her. "I'll be there in ten minutes. And, hey, you know you don't have to make me dinner. I can fend for myself."

"I want to," Paul said.

Tessa ended the call and gathered her belongings. A dump truck with a bed full of broken limbs rumbled past, and Tessa wondered if the workers had been able to clear all the debris from the backyard and from inside the house. She should call Charlie, but she didn't want to face more discouragement, so she ignored it as best as she could for the moment.

The apartment smelled like a sweet and salty affair, and Tessa's stomach growled for the first time all day. "You're going to spoil me. I'll be ruined. Never able to return to my cereal dinners."

Paul wore an oven mitt on one hand while he flipped a piece of ham over in a cast-iron skillet. "Somehow I don't think you'll ever give up your cereal, no matter what I cook."

"You're probably right," she said as she walked into the kitchen and peered over his shoulder at the browning ham and two yellow yolks frying in the pan.

He bumped her out of the way with his hip and opened the oven. He pulled out what looked like a sliced bagel with cheddar cheese melted on both halves. As the aroma of the bagel wafted through the air, she wrinkled her nose.

"That smells sugary."

"It should," Paul said, sliding the bread halves onto a plate. "It's a glazed donut."

"With cheese?"

"Don't look at me like that. You haven't tried it yet. After one bite, I guarantee you won't ever be the same again."

"Because I'll be scarred for life? Who eats donuts like that?"

Paul stacked crisp bacon, browned ham, potato sticks, and two over-easy eggs on the sliced, cheesy donut. Then he mashed the two halves together. He set the plate on the table with a flourish of his hand.

"Dinner is served, madam." He folded a paper towel in half and slid it beneath the edge of the plate.

Tessa sat and stared at the donut breakfast sandwich. "This might be the weirdest thing I've ever eaten."

"That's doubtful. Someone mentioned a mayonnaise-and-barbecue-Fritos sandwich phase."

Tessa snorted. "I was a kid, but they are good."

"And so is this," Paul said. "Try it. I'm going downstairs to help Mom and Dad finish up, and then we're going to dinner."

Tessa picked up the sandwich with two hands, closed her eyes, and took a bite. As she chewed, her eyebrows lifted. "Mmm. Deceptively delicious, and not nearly as weird as I thought." She wiped her mouth on the paper towel. "For such a strange combination of foods, it *is* palatable. Thank you."

Paul grinned. "You're welcome. I might swing by the library again after dinner if there's time. I didn't finish one of my projects."

For as much as she wanted to be alone earlier, she didn't want that so much now. Paul was obviously working on his freelance writing, which he loved. Now that the house was a destruction zone and she wouldn't need him as an architect to help with the rehab, would he want to stay in town? Or would the call of adventure yank him from her?

Paul leaned over and kissed the top of her head. "Relax in the silence. I have a feeling tomorrow won't be nearly as quiet."

Tessa chewed and swallowed. "You're the second person to say something cryptic about tomorrow."

Paul shrugged. "Best be prepared for it then. It'll be here before you know it."

Paul left, and Tessa finished her dinner. Afterward she called Charlie to check in on the day's progress at the house, but she had to leave a message on Charlie's voice mail. Then she called her parents to let them know that catastrophe had struck yet again in her life, but they, too, weren't answering. She mindlessly flipped through streaming services, but when she couldn't find anything interesting to watch, she texted Lily and Anna. Neither one of them answered. *So much for not being cast adrift on my own*, she thought.

She walked over to the mint plant and ruffled its leaves. "What do you think about tomorrow? Do you think we'll be ready for it? Will I be able to handle it? Will I be on my own? Is Paul going to stay in Mystic Water with me?" Then she rolled her eyes. "Seriously, Tessa? The mint is not a Magic 8 Ball."

With no one to talk to and nothing to watch on TV, Tessa decided to read a book in bed. She started toward the bedroom when she heard something bouncing across the hardwood. Tessa turned and glanced around, seeing nothing at first, but then her eyes focused on a small object on the floor. She walked over to it, and her fingers closed around a red heart-shaped pushpin, which had a mint leaf stuck on its metal point. She gaped at the mint plant.

"Where did you get this?" she asked, as though it wasn't incredibly weird to believe a mint plant had been hiding the pushpin.

Paul had been the last person to have the pushpin after Crazy Kate gave it to him. Tessa left the pushpin on the coffee table and walked backward into the bedroom, pointing two fingers at her eyes and then at the plant. If her mint plant could respond to her, it was anybody's guess what strangeness tomorrow would bring.

CHAPTER 25

SHAMROCK EGGS

TESSA AWOKE THE NEXT MORNING WITH A PULSING HEADACHE. She'd fallen asleep before Paul came home, and the novel she'd been reading was still on the bed beside her. Her mind kicked into gear before she could stop it from creating scenario after scenario of what might happen with Honeysuckle Hollow. She dragged herself to the shower. When she reemerged from the bathroom, clean and more awake but still anxious, she opened the bedroom door to the scents of bold coffee and warm donuts.

Paul sat on the couch drinking from a cardinal-red mug. "Morning. How'd you sleep?"

"Skip," Tessa said as she walked toward a ceramic mug on the table. Steam coiled into the air above the dark brew.

"Did you just swipe my question away?" he asked in a teasing voice.

She lifted the mug, and Paul nodded that it was hers. She took a tentative sip, and the hot liquid slid down her throat. On an exhale, Tessa said, "If only I could swipe away the last two days."

"Should I be offended that swiping out those days removes me too?" He stood and joined her in the kitchen.

"Nah, I'm only figuratively removing the unfortunate events. Believe me, if I could have swiped you into my life years ago, I would have."

Paul leaned over and kissed her cheek. "Mom and Dad are downstairs, and they asked to see you as soon as you were dressed and ready."

"I don't normally drink coffee black, but I probably need this extra jolt to make it through today." Tessa glanced around the kitchen. "I smell donuts. Did you pick up some?"

Paul's eyebrows lifted. "Must be coming from downstairs."

"The diner doesn't normally serve donuts. What did y'all do last night?"

Paul cleared his throat. "We had dinner at Milo's. Again. You were right about the lasagna."

Tessa finished her coffee. "And afterward? I didn't hear you come home."

"I doubt you could hear anything over your snoring." Paul put his mug into the dishwasher.

Tessa huffed. "I don't snore. Do I?"

Paul winked. "After dinner I ran a few errands and plotted."

"As in land or as in crimes?"

"*Crimes* is a bit too aggressive. Let's call it a secret mission. Let's go downstairs, and you'll see."

Tessa's wary gaze caused Paul to continue smiling at her. Her stomach flip-flopped. "I sense mischief."

"The best kind."

Before Tessa and Paul reached the front door of Scrambled, she heard a multitude of voices. As they came around the side of the building, people were crossing the street toward the diner, and a large crowd huddled together on the front patio, talking and sipping coffee from to-go cups. Tessa noticed hand-painted signs shoved into the garden with thin metal stakes. Tessa read, "Save Honeysuckle Hollow! Eat at Scrambled! A portion of the proceeds will be donated to restoring this historic home!" Blue block letters had been painted across the spanning front window of Scrambled: "Keep Mystic Water's History Alive!"

A repurposed wooden lemonade stand had been set up on the front patio of the diner. "Fresh Baked Goods" was painted in pink letters across the wooden banner section of the stand, and a plastic gallon milk jug, with its top portion cut off, sat on the narrow top. "Money for Honeysuckle Hollow" had been written in black marker across the jug. Pastries, donuts, cookies, brownies, and cakes covered an accompanying rectangular folding table.

Tessa stopped beside the low stone fence in front of the diner. "What is going on?"

Paul grabbed her hand. "Mom and Dad want to help. The best way they can show their support is to encourage people to eat at the diner and donate fifty percent of the profit to the restoration of Honeysuckle Hollow. They don't want you to be unable to rehab the house the way we'd intended. And it's also a historical landmark. Dozens and dozens of people have already seen the signs and come in for breakfast. We've raised a few hundred dollars in only a couple of hours.

"Anna and Eli asked if they could set up a bake sale to help you as well. They were up all night using the kitchen. They're probably inside refilling on juice and coffee. Once word spread that Anna O'Brien was baking homemade goods in Mystic Water again, people flocked here like blackbirds." He squeezed her hand. "I requested to post an addition to the original article I wrote for *Southern Living.* And I found a dozen other websites that let me post articles about the house and about the unexpected damage. I mentioned that due to a storm, the town was seeking financial support to restore the house. People have been posting on social media too. You wouldn't believe the amount of people interested in sending money. All for you, Tess."

Tessa's tears came easily. "For me?" She lifted their joined hands and pressed them against her cheek. "I—I can't believe it. I'm speechless."

Paul smiled. "You inspired me to do this. All this talk about the town always helping each other, you finding people places to stay after the flood, and Dr. Hamilton helping people with Honeysuckle Hollow. I wouldn't have believed this kind of love and support was real, but in Mystic Water it is. Come inside. You can say hello to everyone who wants to help Honeysuckle Hollow *and* you."

Tessa felt so overwhelmed by the gesture that she had to remind herself to breathe. Scrambled was full of well-wishers and encouraging words. People by the dozens drifted over to her table in the hour and a half she and Paul sat there eating Shamrock eggs—a special recipe Cecilia served just for the occasion. Green bell peppers were sliced into rings to resemble four leaf clovers, and a sunny-side up egg was cooked in the center of each ring. A side of breakfast sausage and hash browns finished off the meal.

While Tessa and Paul ate, people shared stories about how Honeysuckle Hollow had played some part in their lives. "Happy to help" was the most common phrase she heard, and Tessa's heart swelled every time they spoke it. She couldn't say thank you enough, and after a while, she wondered if the people *really* knew how grateful she was, that she wasn't only saying the words but that she felt them deeply.

Nell Foster pushed open the diner door with her kids and two women in tow. Her eyes found Tessa's, and she waved. She hurried over with her group on her heels. They crowded around the booth.

"Anna said you were in here," Nell said. She shoved a folded envelope into Tessa's hands. "It's nothing big, but we scrounged up some money for you and Honeysuckle Hollow. I admit I thought you were off your rocker when you said you were going to rehab it and live in it at the same time, but after knowing how much you helped all of us"—she motioned to the two women beside her—"when we were in desperate need of a place to live, we knew we had to help you. If you need another good mason, Liam's your man, and he'll volunteer his services, as long as it's on the weekends."

Tessa stared at the envelope and then looked up at Nell. She slid out of the booth and hugged Nell. "Thank you." She thanked the two women with her as well. "When it's all fixed up, I'll have y'all over for dinner. We'll throw a big party."

Nell smiled. "We'll be there. You let me know if you need Liam's help."

As the women and children walked off to find a table big enough to hold them, Tessa slid back into the booth. Paul cut through a cinnamon roll that had gone cold at least half an hour earlier. He forked the piece into his mouth and eyed her.

"Do you—do you think this will actually raise enough money for all the repairs and restoration?" Tessa asked.

Paul slid the other half of the treat toward Tessa. "It'll take a lot of money to repair the whole house, but this . . ." He looked over his shoulder toward the patio where Anna and Eli were surrounded by people wanting baked goods. "All of this is going to help a lot."

Tessa ripped off a piece of cinnamon roll, even though she was full, and popped it into her mouth. "This town has always been so supportive, but still I'm surprised by the overflow of help."

"They *want* to help."

A hefty man with a head full of wild sandy-brown hair and a bushy beard pushed open the diner's door. His gaze met Tessa's, and he walked toward her.

"Ms. Andrews?" the man asked in a gruff voice.

"Yes, sir."

He held out his hand. "I'm Donald Tripper from the community college. I teach a busload of students about civil engineering. Most of them are majoring in construction management. My brother lives here in town, and he called me this morning about a rehab project you're working on. He thought it might be a good hands-on experience for the kids. It would give them experience with a different sort of build, and it'd give you free labor from a good many talented workers. I wouldn't offer this if I didn't think they'd do a stand-up job."

Tessa looked at Paul, and he nodded his head. Then he held out his hand toward Mr. Tripper. "I'm Paul Borelli, the architect on the Honeysuckle Hollow rehab. I'd be glad to talk you through the plans and let you decide if the students would benefit from assisting with renovations. I know we could use the help, and we appreciate your offer. If you have a few minutes, we could step outside and talk."

"Sure, sure," Mr. Tripper said. "Nice to meet you, Ms. Andrews."

Tessa stacked their empty plates and walked into the kitchen to hug Cecilia and Harry. She thanked them for their extravagant generosity. Then she slipped outside to talk with Anna and Eli. "I can't thank you both enough."

Eli grabbed a chocolate cake and traded it for a twenty-dollar bill. "This was all Anna's idea, but as usual, it was a good one."

Anna slipped her arm over Tessa's shoulders. "It's been a long time since I've seen you so passionate about a decision. We're here to support you and help you in any way we can. Every little bit will help, right?"

Tessa leaned her head against Anna's shoulder. "I really appreciate it."

"It's nice to be back in Mystic Water, baking for the town. I've seen folks I haven't seen in two years. We're going to run out of treats soon, and at least half the people want to know if I'm going to be here again tomorrow."

Tessa shook her head. "No, you and Eli enjoy yourselves while you're here. I don't want you working yourself ragged on your days off. You've done enough."

"Are you kidding?" Eli laughed. "This is Anna's *thing.* Put her in a kitchen with the essentials, and she's as happy as a pig in the mud."

Anna poked Eli in the ribs. "You just compared me to a pig."

"At least subtract from the profit to pay for supplies," Tessa said.

Anna shrugged. "I'll think about it. Besides, we have ulterior motives. We want to be married at Honeysuckle Hollow, and we figure you'll rent it to us for free, so we're just paying our dues now."

Tessa grinned. "Clever."

Anna handed Tessa a chocolate-covered Oreo. "Lily has been accepting gently used clothing all morning at her shop," Anna said. "The town has donated clothes in carloads, and Lily's putting the sales of the merchandise into a special Honeysuckle Hollow fund. You should see the spot she's set up near the front to display the donations. You wouldn't believe how many people have flocked there already. It's a win-win because it's pulling people into Lily's shop who might not have been in there yet, and she's making crazy sales on her merchandise too."

Tessa bit into the Oreo and smiled around the cracking chocolate coating. "This is too much."

"The food or the assistance?" Anna teased. She squeezed Tessa's hand. "This is just what you needed, what everyone needed. Look how happy the town is. Honeysuckle Hollow is bringing them together. I had no idea the house had helped so many people, and now they're able to help it *and* you."

"This is not following my plan at all," Tessa said, smiling as she remembered Crazy Kate's words from the day before. "It's a much better one." She grabbed another chocolate-covered Oreo for sustenance later. "I'm going to go see Lily. Thank you again."

Anna made a shooing motion with her hand. "I'll get you back during the wedding. Take Lily a box of peanut butter truffles. She'll pout otherwise."

Tessa took the short walk to Lily's downtown boutique. Inside, at least two dozen people crowded around racks and shelves of clothing. Tessa found Lily dancing around the clothing racks, passing clothes to shoppers and pointing them toward items she knew they'd love. Lily had a way of knowing exactly what would fit and flatter each body. She barely had time to chat with Tessa, and she waved off Tessa's thanks, saying she loved helping out in a way that was in her element. Lily did pause long enough to take the truffles and hug Tessa.

"I'll call you tonight," Lily said as she gave Tessa a loving shove toward the door.

Tessa stepped out onto the sidewalk and noticed a handwritten poster board taped to the front window of Cavelli's Deli across the street. The sign read, "Today's Proceeds Support Honeysuckle Hollow's Rebuild!"

Sunlight streamed down, and the milky globes on the streetlights glowed like miniature moons. People flittered up and down Main Street, and Tessa felt overwhelming gratitude expanding in her chest like a bubble. She crossed the street toward the deli just as the town veterinarian, Dr. Jenni Ingles, rounded the corner, walking five dogs at once. One thick leash sprouted five leashes halfway down, and the dogs—all varying sizes—bumped into one another as they jostled down the sidewalk like a sled dog team.

The door to the deli opened, and Emma Chase, the town's assistant librarian, stepped out with an armful of to-go bags. The dogs wagged their tails and headed straight for her. She smiled at the veterinarian. "Looks like a furry Hydra."

Jenni smiled and struggled to slow the dogs' forward motion. "Grabbed food at the deli to support the house, Tessa. I look forward to seeing it rehabbed. Good to see you both."

"Hey, Tessa," Emma said as she shifted the lunch bags in her arms. "Morty and I just supported the rebuild too. I love old houses. Does yours have a library?"

"The house does have somewhat of a library, in the living room. Lots of built-ins. Thanks for the support. I can't believe how much aid the house is receiving. I'm stunned."

Emma smiled. "A house with books is a house that can be trusted. Morty probably hasn't seen you to tell you yet, but he heard about Honeysuckle Hollow this morning at breakfast. His parents stayed there for a couple of weeks when he was a baby. They'd bought a house, and the contract fell through for some reason or another, but Dr. Hamilton took them right in until they could find another one. Anyway, Morty started a book drive at the library. He's put out the word that people can drop off books, and then we'll price them and resell them for deals until they're gone. All the money is going to Honeysuckle Hollow. You wouldn't believe all the people showing up with boxes of books. It's been so busy that we haven't even been able to stop for lunch, hence the mandatory food run."

Tessa's mouth dropped open. "Thank you, Emma. Tell Morty thanks too. The whole town—I just—wow, all this support for a house."

"It's more than just a house. It's been a *home* for a lot of people. Good luck with everything. Morty will be in touch." Emma hurried down the sidewalk toward the library a few blocks away.

"It's so much," Tessa said to no one. "The diner, the deli, the boutique, the library, the college kids, the town . . ."

"Better not be caught talking to yourself. You might replace me as the town crazy."

Tessa turned to see Crazy Kate standing behind her, grinning, and carrying a canvas bag on her shoulder. "Can you believe all of this? Have you seen what everyone is doing?"

Crazy Kate nodded. "Matthias was a good man—the best. I wish he were here to see how the house has brought everyone together. Like ripples that start from a tiny pebble dropped into water, Honeysuckle Hollow has touched so many for decades. More people than we ever imagined. See what one act of kindness can do." She spread her arms wide. "It can change an entire town." The sunlight glistened on her tan skin and reflected in her eyes.

"How can I ever pay back the town for all the money?" Tessa asked.

"It's not about the money to them. The house loves this town as much as they love it." Crazy Kate adjusted the bag on her shoulder. "Give it to them."

"Give what to them?"

"Honeysuckle Hollow. Give Honeysuckle Hollow to the town by letting it help them when they are in need. Let them continue to love it, like Matthias did."

Give the town Honeysuckle Hollow? Tessa leaned against a streetlight. Pearl light highlighted the sidewalk at their feet. She nodded slowly as the realization of what she needed to do sunk in. "Let the doors be open to others. Not exactly a B&B, but a house for people who need an in-between place."

One corner of Crazy Kate's mouth rose, causing an expression of mischief to fill her face. "As long as you're not cooking for them." Crazy Kate and Tessa both laughed. Then Crazy Kate glanced behind her at a fifty-something couple talking with a tall young man. A young woman, raven-haired and with caramel-colored skin, stood off from them, staring toward the park at the end of the street. When she turned her face toward them, Tessa was struck by how much she looked like Crazy Kate but fifty years younger, with her dark, mysterious eyes and a solemn gaze. "My family would like to see the house when it's all done."

"That's your family?"

"My son and his wife," Crazy Kate answered. "And my grandchildren, Erik and Leilah."

Tessa smiled and embraced Crazy Kate before she could stop herself. Crazy Kate stiffened in Tessa's arms before she relaxed and laughed. "Of course," Tessa said when she let go. "I wouldn't have this house if it weren't for you."

Crazy Kate made a scoffing noise in her throat. "This was your path, even when you tried to refuse."

Paul crossed the street and slipped his arm around Tessa's waist. He nodded at Crazy Kate. "Mrs. Muir, can I steal Tessa away for a minute?"

Crazy Kate nodded and shifted the bag to her other shoulder. "We're going to the library for the sale. I have a bag full of books to give away." She walked down the sidewalk toward her family.

"She's here with her son and grandkids," Tessa said to Paul. "She's not alone."

"Neither are you."

Paul led Tessa across the street to meet with people who were offering their services for the reconstruction. In between meeting people and discussing the house, Tessa told Paul about her plan to keep the doors to Honeysuckle Hollow open to the town while also living in it herself, and he'd hugged her so tightly that her laughter released as gasps of air. They spent the rest of the day wandering around town talking with people, thanking nearly everyone they saw, and making plans for how they would begin anew on Honeysuckle Hollow.

After the sun set and stretched deep-orange sunbeams across the apartment's floor, Tessa dropped onto the couch beside Paul. She leaned her head back against the cushion and massaged her jaw. "So much smiling. I'm so exhausted that I'm not sure I can move again even if I need to."

Paul dug folded papers and receipts out of his pockets and dropped them on the coffee table. "A lot of money was donated today. More than I could have hoped for."

Tessa opened her eyes and looked at him. "Do you think we'll have enough money to rehab the whole house?"

"There's a lot to do," he said. "And it'll be a long haul for the rehab. The money will stretch far but not all the way. Don't worry, though. We'll get it completed eventually." He leaned over and kissed her gently. "Just don't quit your day job, and I won't sell the hammer."

His fingers wrapped around an object on the coffee table, and when he sagged against the couch cushions again, a red heart-shaped pushpin sat on his palm. He stared at it and pulled the speared mint leaf off the metal point. Then he rolled the pushpin between his fingers.

Tessa held out her hand. "Give it to me, and I'll toss it in a drawer somewhere so you don't have to throw it away again."

"Not this time." Paul stood and walked over to the wall map. "This time I know exactly where it goes." He stared at the expanse of oceans and continents and patted the mint plant, causing its leaves to dance. Then he pushed the heart-shaped pin into the map and turned, showing Tessa where he'd pinned his heart. *In Mystic Water.*

EPILOGUE

A soft-pink and pale-orange October sunrise painted the sky as Tessa drove toward Honeysuckle Hollow. The changing leaves on the dogwoods, maples, and sycamores were afire with color, framing Dogwood Lane with honey yellows, Braeburn-apple reds, and marmalade oranges.

Tessa parked in the garage and unpacked the few bags she'd brought with her. She slung the canvas bags over her shoulder and closed the car door with her hip.

"Good morning."

Tessa jumped and spun around. Crazy Kate stood behind her on the driveway.

With her hand pressed to her heart, Tessa said, "You scared me half to death. What are you doing here so early? The wedding doesn't start for hours."

Crazy Kate gripped a long wooden stick. "I need to bury my wedding gift before everyone else arrives."

Tessa eyed the spear. "You don't hear that very often. 'Hey, I got you a gift for your wedding, but I buried it.'"

Crazy Kate hummed in her throat. "You prefer I buy them a

place setting of froufrou china instead?"

"I'm kidding," Tessa said with a grateful smile. "The spear is the best gift anyone has ever given Honeysuckle Hollow, and knowing it'll be here to add more magic to what I know will be a gorgeous wedding is even better."

Kate nodded her agreement. "It's time I put the spear back where it belongs."

"Austen Blackstone called again for the umpteenth time. He still wants me to reconsider my decision about the spear and consider displaying it in a Cherokee museum, locked in a glass case with one of those fancy nameplates. He's promised to list my name as the generous donor."

Crazy Kate harrumphed. "What did you say?"

Tessa rolled her eyes. "As if I can be seduced by having my name on museum signage. No one reads those anyway. I told him the spear is right where it belongs."

Crazy Kate looked toward the front yard. "I'll get to work."

"Let me put down these bags, and I'll help you."

Crazy Kate entered the garage and grabbed a shovel. "You go about your business. I'll come inside when I'm finished."

Tessa frowned. "It would be better if I dug the hole for you because—"

"Because I'm too old?" Crazy Kate chuckled and walked out of the garage. She spoke to Tessa over her shoulder. "There's still some pep left in these old bones. You should focus on your own to-do list."

"No arguments from me." Tessa unlocked the house and stepped inside. The scent of honeysuckle and roses filled the air. Tessa dropped her bags on the kitchen counter and wandered through the house in amazement.

The florists and the decorators had finished adorning Honeysuckle Hollow with pastel-hued ribbons, delicate lace, and crystals that would catch the light like dewdrops. Floral arrangements of ivy, magnolia blooms, and white lilies with pink centers draped around open doorways. Twists of twine, greenery, white hydrangea blooms, and ivory roses wrapped up the staircase banister and pooled around the bottom of the newel base.

She opened the French doors to the garden. Porter and Sylvia Potts, along with Crazy Kate, added fall-blooming plants specifically for this event, and now the garden was in full bloom with asters, mums, joe-pye weed, Heliopsis, and coneflowers. An intimate gazebo had been erected beneath the scarred oak tree, and a garland of soft-pink roses, greenery, and more crystals caught the early-morning sunlight. White wooden folding chairs were arranged in rows on both sides of an aisle.

An arching bridge had been built over the lazy river, and Paul had carefully restocked and renamed every koi added to the Honeysuckle Hollow family. Huck Finn had been brought back home, and now he was joined by an array of characters—Sherlock, Anne Shirley, Indiana Jones, Bilbo, Aslan, Pippi Longstocking, Harry Potter, and Hermione. They swam the river, streaks of flaming orange and white, periodically lifting their mouths to the surface in the hopes of fresh food.

Tessa sighed happily and then unpacked her bags, laying out the lists she'd created to keep track of every part of the wedding—the caterers, the wedding planner, the guests, the attendants, the musicians, and the drivers who would shuttle people from a local church parking lot to Honeysuckle Hollow.

Within hours of the sunrise, the house filled with a flurry of people. The wedding planner, Jessi Reed, had lists of her own, and she kept all parts of the ceremony moving with the efficiency of a pro. One of Anna's college friends, Ali Kendrick, who was a master baker, brought in the wedding cake and assembled the four-tiered ivory creation with sugar-paste daisies flowing down the sides. As Ali and her catering team unpacked dozens of sweets and filled pewter platters with their creations, the air smelled like a sugarcoated dream. The cellist, violinist, and harpist set up in the backyard and tuned their instruments. The wind carried the string instruments' music down the street and into town, drawing people to them like fairy magic.

When the time came for Tessa to rush upstairs and get dressed with Lily, Anna, and the other bridesmaids, Paul arrived wearing a tux and tennis shoes. He spotted Tessa on the staircase and waved an envelope in the air. "Mail call."

Tessa was speechless for a few seconds, taking in his blue eyes that looked nearly transparent because of his lingering summer tan. His usually disheveled dark-brown hair had been cut and combed. He looked like a man ready for a film premiere, except for his shoe choice. "Wow."

A small smile tugged his dimples into view. "You like?"

"Minus the shoes, yeah." Tessa looked up the stairs at Lily. "I'll be right up."

Lily grabbed Tessa's hanging bag and glanced at Paul. "You have one minute. This girl needs to get dressed. Is my husband dressed?"

Paul nodded. "Last I checked, all the groomsmen were heading to the pub." Lily's mouth fell open, but before she could respond, Paul said, "I'm kidding. They're at your house, trying to tie bow ties and failing miserably. I'll return and help out, but first"—he handed the envelope to Tessa—"you need to open this. I swung by the apartment to grab my dress shoes, which is why I'm still wearing these, and the mail had already arrived. Open it."

Tessa raised one eyebrow. "Now?" She glanced at the envelope and said, "We're in a hurry. Can you keep it for me?"

Paul's stern expression caused her to shove her finger beneath the flap on the back and tear open the envelope in jagged pieces. A navy-blue booklet was tucked inside. "My passport?"

He reached out his hand for her, and Tessa came down the stairs to stand with him. He hugged her. "Just in time."

"Time for what?"

Paul grinned. "For when we decide to take a trip."

Tessa slipped her arms around his neck. "It's official. We'll have our first adventure."

"Our *next* adventure," he corrected.

Lily shouted from upstairs. "Tessa!"

Tessa handed Paul the passport and the torn envelope. "Keep these for me? I have to go before I'm in serious trouble. Make sure you and the guys are back here in half an hour."

Paul saluted her. "Yes, ma'am. Can't wait to see you in that dress."

Tessa kissed him quickly and then hurried up the staircase.

A couple of hours later the ceremony was finished, and the live musicians had been replaced with a DJ. Tessa's and Anna's parents gathered around a high-boy table situated along the fence line. Tessa's mama had been a combination of aghast and amazed to learn Tessa hadn't backed down from her Honeysuckle Hollow challenge, but when Carolyn learned about Mystic Water's support and love for her daughter, she couldn't help but join the others in their cheering. Now Carolyn barely skipped a day without telling Tessa how proud she was of her sticking with her decision. No one could deny that Honeysuckle

Hollow's restoration was glorious to see.

Beneath the twinkling backyard lights, Tessa danced with Paul. Anna looked like a fairy princess in her elegant V-neck dress made of white chiffon. The A-line skirt flowed gracefully as Eli twirled her across the tiled dance floor. Lily and Jakob bounced to their own rhythm while their daughter, Rose, weaved in and out of their legs. Paul spun Tessa away from him, lifting their arms into an arch. When he spun her back toward him, she stumbled into his chest and laughed. She pressed her hand against his suit jacket and said, "You're vibrating."

"That's your phone," he said, reaching his hand into his inside coat pocket.

She didn't recognize the number, but she excused herself and walked off the dance floor. "Hello?"

"This is Kate," Crazy Kate said. "Meet me in the foyer."

"You have a cell phone?" Tessa asked in shock, already walking across the patio and weaving through the wedding guests.

"Don't be ridiculous. I borrowed it from my daughter."

Tessa found Crazy Kate beneath the chandelier in the foyer with Trudy Steele, who stood in the open front doorway. "Mrs. Steele! I had no idea you were in town. Come in, come in." Tessa motioned for Mrs. Steele to come inside, but the old woman didn't budge. Tessa continued, "We're right in the middle of a wedding reception. Paul and I were going to call you next week to ask when you and your family could visit. But I'm glad you're here now." Tessa spread her arms wide. "Come inside and look around. What do you think of the renovations? Does it look like you remember?"

Mrs. Steele didn't move or speak. Tessa glanced at Crazy Kate with a searching expression.

Crazy Kate placed her hand on Mrs. Steele's arm. "Trudy,

come inside."

Mrs. Steele's eyes filled with tears as she placed her hand over Crazy Kate's. "It—it was easier to hate this place when it was falling apart. But now—it looks—it looks just like it did when we were married, doesn't it?"

"Remember when you walked down those stairs?" Crazy Kate asked, leading Mrs. Steele toward the staircase. "And Geoffrey wasn't supposed to see you beforehand, but he rounded the corner, and there you were, and he was speechless. You were so beautiful that day. Like an angel."

Mrs. Steele blinked at her tears and rested both hands on her cane. "It was the perfect day. Even with the rain. I was so happy—*we* were so happy. I still miss him," she said as her voice broke. She looked at Tessa. "You've done something I didn't think was possible. You've brought Honeysuckle Hollow back to life."

"I had a lot of help," Tessa said. "Months of it, from the whole town actually."

"Unbelievable," Mrs. Steele said, not seeming to care about the tears on her cheeks. "It looks just like it did, back when we were all still here. When we were young and beautiful and happy and the house was full of laughter." She looked at Crazy Kate. "It's like being transported back through time."

Tessa smiled. "I'm glad you approve."

Mrs. Steele walked toward the dining room. "It's an awful big home for one young woman."

Tessa shook her head. "I won't be living here alone."

"Oh," Mrs. Steele asked with raised eyebrows. "That man convinced you to marry him?"

Tessa hesitated. "No, not exactly. Not *yet*."

Mrs. Steele pursed her lips. "You *do* know that a proper

Southern woman would *never* live with a man before she's married, don't you?"

Tessa snorted a laugh. "As if I've ever been proper."

Mrs. Steele looked affronted, and then her face broke into a laugh. Crazy Kate joined her.

Tessa said, "What I meant was that I'm going to use Honeysuckle Hollow the same way Matthias did—to help those in need or to host beautiful weddings just like yours. I'll live here, but I expect the house will always be full of guests."

"Matthias would be proud of you," Mrs. Steele said.

Crazy Kate looped her arm through Mrs. Steele's. "Let me show you around, Trudy. Wait till you see the gardens."

They left Tessa standing in the foyer. Paul walked up the hallway with a look of concern. "You okay?"

Tessa clasped her hands together in front of her chest. "It's been the perfect day. My cheeks ache from smiling. Anna and Eli's wedding was beautiful, and they're so happy with how everything turned out. The reception is the best kind of party for the town to enjoy, and Mrs. Steele made a surprise visit. She loves the house. I don't see how this day could get any better."

Paul reached into his coat pocket and pulled out his cell phone. He opened an airline app and handed the phone to Tessa. "What if I told you that we need to leave early tomorrow morning if we're going to make the flight?"

The app displayed two tickets, one with Paul's name and one with hers. "What flight?"

Paul grinned. "The flight for our next adventure." He tugged her body closer to his. "You know the travel outlet put this article on hold for months, but they're finally ready for me to finish it, so I'm taking you to the Cook Islands. You've been working nonstop on this house for the past six months, not to mention you *didn't* quit your day job. You deserve a vacation in a place where they have those little paper umbrellas garnishing your tropical drinks."

Tessa swiped through the digital tickets again. "This flight leaves tomorrow night from Atlanta. I'm not packed. I have work—"

"Lily started packing for you. She said she knew exactly what you needed to take," Paul said. "And your mom agreed to handle all your clients while you're gone. It's all been arranged. All you have to do is say yes."

Tessa's mouth dropped open. "Everyone *knew*?"

Paul pressed a kiss to her lips. "We've been plotting behind your back for weeks. What do you say, Tess?"

A laugh of surprise and pleasure widened her smile. She threw her arms around Paul's neck. "I was wrong. The perfect day just got better. Take me on an adventure, Borelli."

AUTHOR'S NOTE

I've always had a love for historic homes. When I was younger, I'd buy house-plan magazines and tear out my favorite floor plans (always Victorians) and save them for one day when I'd live in my own magic house. I've yet to live in a Victorian home, but what's the next best thing? Creating a story where one of my characters gets the chance!

The original edition of this story was titled *Honeysuckle Hollow*, named after the house we first heard about in *The Necessity of Lavender Tea* (book 2 in the Mystic Water series) when Kate visits the Hamiltons. While refreshing the series, I wanted to draw you in with the magical element that bolsters Tessa's bravery, Cecilia's Courage Quiche. I've had times in my life when I could have used a slice or two myself! And not only did the title change, but so did the cover, as Julianne St. Clair once again designed a gorgeous sparkly cover to emphasize the whimsical, sometimes mysterious, happenings in Mystic Water.

When I was drafting this story more than ten years ago, a four-thousand-square-foot historic Victorian mansion went on the market in my city. Just shy of begging, I asked a realtor to pretty please show me the house. Could I afford its multimillion-dollar price tag? Not at the time! But anything is possible, right? Fortunately, the realtor understood my burning desire. We toured every room at a slow, mesmerizing pace. I wish I could take you on a trip through my memory so you could see the sweeping handcrafted staircase, the antique crystal chandeliers, the soaring ceilings, the library with floor-to-ceiling bookshelves, the ornate dining room with its coffered ceiling, the turret tower room tucked away like a secret, and the ballroom with its polished marble floor. Let's not forget the half-acre rose gardens with winding brick pathways, a gazebo, and water features. This house became the inspiration for Honeysuckle Hollow in Mystic Water.

Maybe your dream isn't to own a historic home like Tessa, but whatever your dream is, I hope you'll follow the call of your heart, no matter what anyone says or thinks. Only you truly know what's best for your life. Need a bit more courage to take the leap? Take a road trip to Mystic Water, swing by Scrambled, and grab yourself a slice of Courage Quiche. It works every time!

ACKNOWLEDGMENTS

RETURNING TO MYSTIC WATER IS LIKE COMING HOME TO A place where I know life is good and kind, where my dreams come to life and the birds sing songs just to see me smile. I wouldn't be here, returning to this magical place, without you, my dearest reader. Without all of you. Even if I said thank you on repeat from morning until night for decades, it would never be enough to show you how much your support, kindness, encouragement, and joy have carried me along throughout this writing journey. Thank you for loving Mystic Water, thank you for wanting to pack a suitcase and take a road trip with me, and thank you for returning again and again. You are essential.

Karissa Taylor—Call me a broken record or a parrot, but seriously, you are the most epic editor an author could ever have. You gave Tessa a home, you challenged me to show you why our handsome Paul loves our beloved Tessa, and you ask all the right questions, even if they make me say, "I dunno!" But you help me find the answers, and because of that, this story expanded and grew stronger. Also your sense of humor cannot be matched when it comes to a combination of kindness, sarcasm, and delight. I am so incredibly thankful to you, your guidance, and your love of our sweet Mystic Water.

Julianne St. Clair—you are a magician. You create masterpieces out of sparkles and ideas, and your talent continues to amaze me. Our friendship is one of the most precious gifts I've ever been given. Here's to a billion more years of it! Thank you for adding your stunning designs to this book cover and for adding so much love to my life.

Marisa Gothie—every author would be blessed to have you as a friend, supporter, and cheerleader. I'm so grateful we found each other through our love of books and authors. Thank you for writing such thoughtful discussion questions for this edition. I hope we have many more collaborations and years together. Readers and authors: Find Marissa on Instagram @ Marisagbooks at Bookends and Friends.

Jacqueline Hritz—superstar editor, proofreader, and knower of all things grammatical and life! Your attention to detail and eye for what "sounds" right is incredible, and your awareness of what makes a story fantastic is unmatched. I am so grateful for your kind nudges in a more thoughtful direction for my characters, my storyline, and my writing. You are a true treasure to have on my team!

Author buddies are vital to my writing. I often find myself in need of a brainstorming partner, someone to tell me what's working and what's not with loving-kindness and honesty, and people who will read the earliest, roughest stages of my drafts. Natalie Banks and Jeanne Arnold, y'all are steadfast, ever-present writing friends and amazing authors who consistently show up and both challenge and encourage me to elevate my craft. This road would be far lonelier without you. Thank you on repeat!

RECIPES

Courage Quiche

This magical quiche recipe is baked in a super flaky homemade pie crust and filled with a variety of mood-boosting ingredients, including saffron. One slice and you're guaranteed to feel braver. Eat willy-nilly from the dish, and prepare yourself to be amazed at what happens next.

Prep Time: 2 hours, 40 minutes

Baking Time: 1 hour, 20 minutes

Total: 4 hours

Yield: 8 slices

Ingredients

1 10-inch piecrust, homemade or store-bought

4 large eggs

½ cup whole milk

½ cup heavy cream

2 teaspoons salt

1 teaspoon ground black pepper

1 pinch saffron = 20 threads

2 teaspoons lemon zest

1 cup shredded or crumbled cheese such as feta, cheddar, goat cheese, or gruyere

2 cups of add-ins: diced white potato, mushrooms, asparagus (any ratios you like equaling 2 cups total; all vegetable add-ins should be precooked before adding to quiche)

Thinly sliced tomatoes for top, optional

Instructions

1. Prepare pie crust: To save time the day of baking, make pie dough the night before because it needs to chill in the refrigerator for at least 2 hours before rolling out and blind baking (next step).
2. Roll out the chilled pie dough: On a floured work surface, roll out the chilled dough. Turn the dough about a quarter turn after every few rolls until you have a 10-inch circle. Place the dough into a 9-inch pie dish. Don't trim the overhang; instead tuck it in with your fingers, making sure it is completely smooth. Chill the pie crust in the refrigerator for at least 30 minutes and up to 5 days. Cover the pie crust with plastic wrap if chilling for longer than 30 minutes.
3. While the crust is chilling, preheat oven to 375°F (190°C).
4. Partially blind bake: Line the chilled pie crust with parchment paper. Fill with pie weights or dried beans. Make sure the weights are evenly distributed around the pie dish. Bake until the edges of the crust are starting to brown, about 15-16 minutes. Remove pie from the oven and carefully lift the parchment paper (with the weights) out of the pie. Prick holes all around the bottom crust with a fork. Return the pie crust to the oven. Bake until the bottom crust is just beginning to brown, about 7-8 minutes. Remove from

the oven and set aside. (Crust can still be warm when you pour in the filling.)

5. Reduce oven temperature to 350°F (177°C).
6. In the bowl of a stand mixer fitted with a whisk attachment or using a handheld mixer, beat the eggs, whole milk, heavy cream, lemon zest, saffron, salt, and pepper together on high speed until completely combined, about 1 minute. Whisk in add-ins (cheese and precooked veggies) and then pour into crust. If desired, decorate the top of the filling with thinly sliced tomatoes.
7. Bake the quiche until the center is just about set, about 45-55 minutes. Don't overbake. Use a pie crust shield or tinfoil to prevent the pie crust edges from over-browning.
8. Allow to cool for 15 minutes.

Strawberry Pancakes

These strawberry pancakes are light, fluffy, and packed with flavor. This is Cecilia Borelli's special recipe to bring you comfort and to stir the hearts of loved ones.

Prep Time: 10 minutes

Cooling Time: 10 minutes

Total: 20 minutes

Yield: 6 medium pancakes

Ingredients

1 cup all-purpose flour

1 tablespoon brown sugar

1 tablespoon baking powder

1 teaspoon salt, or to taste

1 cup milk

1 large egg

2 tablespoons melted unsalted butter

1 tablespoon vanilla extract

1 cup chopped fresh strawberries

Instructions

1. In a medium bowl, whisk flour, brown sugar, baking powder, and salt together.
2. Whisk together melted butter, egg, vanilla, and milk.
3. Add the wet ingredients to the dry ingredients, and whisk until well combined. There may be a few lumps, but don't worry about these.
4. Let the batter rest for 10 minutes.
5. While the batter is resting, chop the strawberries into small cubes,

discarding the leaves on top.

6. Fold the diced strawberries into the pancake batter.
7. Heat a flat-bottom pan over medium-high heat, and add a pat of butter or a tablespoon of oil to the surface of the pan. Scoop one-quarter cup of the batter, and pour it onto the heated pan.
8. When small bubbles appear on the surface of the pancake and burst, flip the pancake. Cook the other side for 2-3 minutes, until edges are slightly brown and set.

DISCUSSION QUESTIONS

1. Tessa has a difficult time trusting her instincts because of choices she made earlier in her life. She makes lists and consults her friends before making decisions. Do you reach out to others for opinions when making decisions or do you trust your gut?
2. In this story, Tessa sees herself as someone who has made poor life choices. But in meeting Paul, helping out others in the town, and trusting herself, she realizes that some people see her as strong and brave. How did having someone believe in her lead to Tessa finally believing in herself? When in your life have you experienced someone believing in you giving you the courage to believe in yourself?
3. At the start of the novel, there is a flood and Tessa and many others are displaced. Even though facing the prospect of having nowhere to live, Tessa helps others find rentals. For someone who doubts her own ability to make life choices, what do you think of Tessa's actions?
4. Tessa doesn't initially want to sell her condo, even

though it's obvious "salvaging" what's left is unrealistic. Why do you think she struggles with letting go of the condo? If your house flooded and someone offered to buy it, would you be happy or distraught to sell your home?

5. Honeysuckle Hollow is more than a house. When Tessa first enters it, the disrepair is hard to miss, but she still feels that it deserves to remain standing. The house has a greater purpose. How do you think Tessa's purpose and the house's purpose align?
6. Even though Tessa doesn't immediately believe in the garden's powers, she soon sees that Kate and also Mrs. Borelli are speaking truth. Do you believe that the garden's herbs are magical or do you believe it is the power of suggestion?
7. Paul is surprised when he learns that his parents have followed his adventures and decorated the upstairs apartment for him. Why do you think he stayed away so long? Do you believe that he will be satisfied living in Mystic Water? Why or why not?
8. Trudy Steele is a force in the book and someone who has been hanging onto the past for far too long. She states that it's been easier to hate the house than to remember the good times. However, when she finally relents and allows Tessa to own the house, Trudy says she wants to come back and see the rehab results. Have you ever felt strongly attached to a house? For instance, your childhood home? When you moved from this home, did you have regrets? Would you ever go back to visit?
9. Kate's family spear has been protecting the house for

years. When Tessa digs it up, she has no idea what she's found. Austenaco Blackstone encourages Tessa to return the spear to the Cherokee or at least offer it to a museum. Ultimately Tessa decides to return the spear to Honeysuckle Hollow where it belongs. Would you have given the spear to the Cherokee or a museum, or would you have agreed with Tessa and allowed Kate to rebury the spear?

10. Are you interested in home rehab or improvement shows? If an HGTV show was based on Honeysuckle Hollow, would you watch it? If it were possible for you, would you consider buying a historic home and rehabbing it? Why or why not?
11. If the Mystic Water series were adapted for film and this story in particular, who would be your dream cast? What songs would you choose for the soundtrack?
12. If you stopped by Scrambled for a real diner meal, what would you choose from the menu? Which character from this book would you invite to eat with you?
13. If given the opportunity, would you eat a slice of Courage Quiche? Why or why not? In what part of your life would you hope the quiche instilled bravery?

About the Author

Photo by Matt Andrews

Born and raised in southern Georgia, where honeysuckle grows wild and the whippoorwills sing, Jennifer Moorman is the bestselling author of the magical realism Mystic Water series. Jennifer started writing in elementary school, crafting epic tales of adventure and love and magic. She wrote stories in Mead notebooks, on printer paper, on napkins, on the soles of her shoes. Her blog is full of dishes inspired by fiction, and she hosts baking classes showcasing these recipes. Jennifer considers herself a traveler, a baker, and a dreamer. She can always be won over with chocolate, unicorns, or rainbows. She believes in love—everlasting and forever.

Connect with Jennifer at jennifermoorman.com
Instagram: @jenniferrmoorman
Facebook: @jennifermoormanbooks
BookBub: @JenniferMoorman

LOOKING FOR MORE MYSTIC WATER ADVENTURES? LOOK NO FURTHER!

Mystic Water Series

Delight in a town where anything can happen—and usually does.

The Baker's Man
The Necessity of Lavender Tea
A Slice of Courage Quiche

Visit online to learn more:
jennifermoorman.com

From the Publisher

Sharing Is Caring!

Loved this book?
Help other readers find it:

- Post a review at your favorite online bookseller
- Post a picture on a social media account and share why you enjoyed it
- Send a note to a friend who would also love it—or better yet, give them a copy

Thank you for reading!

Milton Keynes UK
Ingram Content Group UK Ltd.
UKHW010727130923
428592UK00004B/198